# August's Treasure

A Novel by
## CARROLL C. JONES

*Carroll C. Jones* (signature)

Jan-Carol
Publishing, Inc

## AUGUST'S TREASURE
### CARROLL C. JONES

Published May 2017
Little Creek Books
Imprint of Jan-Carol Publishing, Inc.
All rights reserved
Copyright © Jan-Carol Publishing

This is a work of fiction. Any resemblance to actual persons, either living or dead is entirely coincidental. All names, characters and events are the product of the author's imagination.

This book may not be reproduced in whole or part, in any manner whatsoever without written permission, with the exception of brief quotations within book reviews or articles.

ISBN: 978-1-945619-25-0
Library of Congress Control Number: 2017942380

You may contact the publisher:
Jan-Carol Publishing, Inc.
PO Box 701
Johnson City, TN 37605
publisher@jancarolpublishing.com
jancarolpublishing.com

*This book is dedicated to my daughters, Kelly and Amanda.
They are smart and beautiful and kind, and represent a treasure far richer and
more meaningful than any I could have hoped for in this life.*

# Letter to the Reader

The memory of sitting in my Aunt Nannie's farmhouse kitchen and holding a glass jar filled with a golden-grained substance is as plain as day. Being just a boy, I reckoned it was gold since Nannie's late father—my grandfather—spent twenty years or so out West, while taken with the gold fever. It was never clear to me why he actually left the western North Carolina mountains and ended up in Skidoo, California, where he pursued his hard rock mining passion. So left with no reasonable explanations, I have invented this fanciful story that could explain such a hasty exodus from the Carolina highlands to the wild West.

In *August's Treasure*, the third novel of my *East Fork Trilogy*, the young character named August Hargrove is at once subjected to a life-altering experience. A horrible accident along the railroad he is building forces him to flee to the West to save his neck. August is given opportunities to ply the icy waters of the Mississippi River in a steamboat, ride the rails to California on a speeding transcontinental train, mine for gold in a boom town named Skidaddle, and build a steam-powered sawmill and logging operation high up on the Pigeon River's East Fork. As you might expect, all of these so-called opportunities are fraught with danger, drama, suspense, and even romance.

It is a rich legacy that August leaves behind for later Hargrove generations to contemplate. When an old treasure map falls into great-grandson Clint Hargrove's lap, so to speak, he sets out with his friend, Claire Shook, to unravel some of the Hargrove family secrets. Along the way they explore the depths of their own relationship and Clint struggles to excise a personal demon.

If you thought *Master of the East Fork* and *Rebel Rousers* were good reads, get ready for another taste of historical fiction that is also flavored with the dialect and wild settings of the western North Carolina highlands. No doubt, *August's Treasure* will leave you surprised and content, as the third novel in a trilogy should.

Best regards,
Carroll C. Jones

# Author's Note

The scenic lands along the upper Pigeon River and its tributaries have a rich and intriguing history. Although these had been Native Indian hunting grounds for millennia, by the end of the eighteenth century the Cherokee had been pushed out and white settlers were beginning to penetrate the wilderness setting.

Reliable historical resources have allowed me to create fictional characters and to imagine fanciful stories based on some of the actual pioneering families who tamed the wilds surrounding the settlements at Forks of Pigeon and Pigeon River (present-day Bethel and Canton, North Carolina.) The specific names of individual characters portrayed in the book, although common to the area, have been made up for the most part.

And no representations made or tales told within these pages should be construed as anything other than historical fiction.

# Acknowledgments

The historical setting and fabric of *August's Treasure*, and the two preceding novels that comprise the *East Fork Trilogy*, are based on extensive study and research supporting the publications of my previous works of historical non-fiction: *The 25th North Carolina Troops in the Civil War, Rooted Deep in the Pigeon Valley,* and *Captain Lenoir's Diary*. The source materials cited in those publications are applicable in this one as well.

I remain very grateful to the descendants of Captain Thomas Isaac Lenoir—especially to Dr. Mary Michal, her brother Joe Michal, and the late Emily Terrell and her husband Hugh K.—who were so supportive of my initial work on the Lenoir family, including the loan and use of the Captain's treasured Civil War diary. It was, after all, Thomas Isaac Lenoir whose personage and circumstances offered the inspiration for Basil Edmunston, the principal character in *Master of the East Fork*, the patriarch in the sequel *Rebel Rousers*, and the grandfather of one of the principal characters in *August's Treasure*.

Larry Griffin, current Vice-President of the North Carolina Society of Historians and acclaimed author in his own right, was kind enough to take time from his busy schedule and read the manuscript for *August's Treasure*. It is my honor to include in this book the very insightful and colorful foreword that he penned.

The enticing artwork that graces the cover of *August's Treasure* was provided by my double second cousin, Edie Burnette. She offers readers a glimpse of the main characters fording the river in a buggy, just above the railroad bridge at Pigeon River. Edie's artistic and literary talents are simply unbounded, and I am extremely grateful for her contribution to this work and the close friendship that we enjoy.

Last but not least, I would like to thank my wonderful wife Maria for her unfailing devotion and support. Without her I would have neither the inspiration nor the courage to take on these writing projects that consume so much energy and time. Thank you, Maria!

# The East Fork Trilogy

Following *Master of the East Fork* and *Rebel Rousers*, *August's Treasure* is the third novel in the *East Fork Trilogy*. The original story, *Master of the East Fork*, was set more than a decade before the American Civil War and begins the tale of Basil Edmunston, who is exiled to oversee his family's immense farm in the remote East Fork River Valley of western North Carolina. His father told him "it's your familial duty," and the son could not rightly refuse. Lonely and unsure he is up to the task, the young man immediately falls victim to slave vexations and the allure of two mountain belles. As he resolves the romantic triangle, sorts out myriad tenant and slave problems, and suffers a prolonged and savage feud with a despicable antagonist, the young Master of the East Fork is forced to grow up in a hurry.

*Rebel Rousers* is the sequel and continues the saga of Basil Edmunston and his family just as the Civil War erupts in all of its horrible fury. A youthful Rebel soldier named Edmunston and his best buddy, Hack Hartgrove, almost immediately become immersed in the wartime drama. This story's historical and dramatic fabric is woven with military clashes, personal conflict, romance, tragedy, and an interminable battle of wits and brawn with the unforgettable antagonist named Bugg.

*August's Treasure* alternates between a late nineteenth-century setting and modern day. The story begins to unravel in 1883 when young August Hargrove is forced to flee from the Carolina highlands to save his neck. Unbelievable fortune and misfortune follow him westward all the way to California and continue to bless and curse him after he returns home to western North Carolina.

August's adventures aboard a steaming Mississippi riverboat and speeding transcontinental trains, mining for gold in California, and logging the wild wilderness of the East Fork River Valley leave a baffling legacy for later Hargroves to comprehend. Great-Grandson Clint Hargrove, a man with troubles of his own, stumbles upon an old treasure map and uses it to try and sort out this Hargrove legacy.

# Foreword

### By Larry Griffin

    I became acquainted with Carroll Jones through mutual involvement in the *North Carolina Society of Historians (NCSH)*. During the 75th Anniversary Celebration of NCSH, held in North Wilkesboro, North Carolina, Mr. Jones received two awards for his book, *Rebel Rousers*—inclusive of the prestigious President's Award for Excellence. He has, however, a concatenation of four award-winning books to his credit, written prior to this last award-winner. Now, he has added a sixth title to his collection, and I had the opportunity to read it in advance of its publication.

    *August's Treasure* is the third in a book series that Carroll refers to as the *East Fork Trilogy*. The author takes the reader inside the life and times of young August Hargrove, the son of former Rebel soldier, Hack, and his Yankee wife, Harriet. The story unfolds in the year 1883—August is working as an assistant surveyor for a railroad enterprise that is furiously attempting to forge a line across the rugged, oft-unfriendly terrain of the western mountains of North Carolina. While out surveying, August witnesses the senseless, unprovoked murder of his friend, perpetrated by the Cherokee County Sheriff's son, Lester Posey. As he kneels next to the lifeless body of his friend, attempting to ascertain any life-signs, August succumbs to a retributive impulse born of grief—he picks up a rock and smashes it against Posey's face, crushing part of his skull and killing him instantaneously.

    Sheriff Buford Posey, angered by his son's death and convinced that he was murdered, subsequently arrests the Hargrove boy who had killed him. When August, abetted by a friend, escapes the local lock-up and an inauspicious appointment with the hangman, the enraged sheriff doggedly pursues him. And the game is afoot—a chase that takes the reader from one coastline to the other, through one adventure after another, replete with danger, life and death struggles, the exhilaration of love won and the heartbreak of love lost, abject defeat and ultimate victory.

Running parallel to this 19th-century escapade is a 21st-century grandson's quest to discover the legacy of a great-grandfather—a quest buried beneath bergs of the bones of both men and beasts of burden, near a valley known by the name of "Death" and eclipsed by the highest precipice in the Panamint Range. Clint Hargrove, on a forced sabbatical from his teaching position and attempting to exorcise the " demon of excess," stumbles across an 1899 missive containing a mysterious map depicting the location of a mine—The Southern Jackass—staked by the dual-ownership of R. A. Rosehl and August Hargrove—the latter being Clint's great-grandfather. Both story threads eventually weave into a common strand in southeastern California, where the lives of two Hargroves intersect—the first 106 years ahead of the second.

It is through the alchemy of science and art that historic novels are written. To be believable, the author has to breathe life into characters whose fiction has a factual underpinning. To write that combination can be a daunting task; however, it is one at which Carroll Jones excels. His ably-crafted opening scenes capture the reader's imagination and quickly insinuate him into the lives of two men and their quests—one who is laboring to rebuild a life from the unfortunate shambles wrought by a life-altering impulsive action; the other attempting to repair his by extricating himself from the seductive, sedative solace that he could find only at the bottom of a bottle of Jack Daniels. Similar struggles separated by a century.

If it is adventure laced with intrigue that you crave—though vicarious in variety—then *August's Treasure* is your ticket to escape the mundane for the mysterious. All that is required is to turn to the first page and fasten your seatbelt.

*Larry J. Griffin, International Education Consultant and founder of The Griffin Education Institute for Study and Teaching (T-GEIST), has trained thousands of teachers, administrators, and parents across this country, in Canada, and in Europe. Over the last three years, he has received six awards from the North Carolina Society of Historians—including the distinguished Paul Jehu Barringer Jr. & Sr. Award of Excellence and the prestigious President's Award of Excellence for chronicling the history of Wilkes County, North Carolina.*

# Introduction

In the year 1883, almost two decades after the South's surrender to Union forces, the brutal hardships and sufferings of Reconstruction were mostly at an end. Certainly, the rebellious fires that once burned in the hearts and minds of many western North Carolina highlanders were well-nigh extinguished. That was true for the Edmunstons, of the East Fork River Valley, and the Hargroves, who lived below Forks of Pigeon. They were decent folk who had tried to put the terrible memories of the Civil War behind them, and were working to forge better lives for themselves and promising futures for their children.

The railroad had reached the tiny settlement of Pigeon River in the previous year. Located approximately five miles below Forks of Pigeon, astride the Pigeon River, the village had immediately gained an importance beyond all anticipation of the locals. Instantly, the community became a rail hub where stock, timber, and produce could be shipped to markets outside of the surrounding mountains. And it was not long before wealthy outlanders began to converge there to experience the grandeur and refreshing climate of the Carolina highlands. To serve the needs of the railroad at its temporary terminus in Pigeon River, a depot station was constructed, and Hack Hargrove was hired as the station agent.

Ever since Hack's rousing days as a Rebel soldier, he had found many ways to keep busy. He and wife Harriet—a Yankee, of all things—were raising a daughter and son—Beth and August. Certainly, supporting their children and providing them comfortable circumstances were foremost in their minds. Hack farmed and worked as a teacher and county surveyor to provide for his family. But he did not limit himself to these pursuits. By serving the public as an elected commissioner and school-board member, he was able to give back to the community and further prove his worth. One might be inclined to say he was a useful citizen, with the new job as the Pigeon River station agent being another manifestation of his usefulness.

At this particular time, August Hargrove was seventeen years old and beginning to feel his oats. Not at all content with his lowly status on the Hargrove farm and the demand of endless chores involving crops and stock, August aimed to broaden his horizons. As luck would have it, the rail line was being extended beyond Pigeon River to the extreme western region of North Carolina. The W.N.C. Railroad was in need of a surveyor's assistant, and young August Hargrove figured he fit the bill. With the backing of the new Pigeon River station agent, he landed the job.

# Contents

| | | |
|---|---|---|
| Chapter 1 | What a Mess | 1 |
| Chapter 2 | Busting Out | 10 |
| Chapter 3 | WANTED! | 20 |
| Chapter 4 | Alias Mr. Hipps and Mr. Woody | 29 |
| Chapter 5 | Keeping On Getting It | 38 |
| Chapter 6 | A Swedish Beauty | 47 |
| Chapter 7 | Full Steam Ahead | 57 |
| Chapter 8 | Riding the Rails | 66 |
| Chapter 9 | Opportunities and Possibilities | 77 |
| Chapter 10 | Birthing Skidaddle | 86 |
| Chapter 11 | Last Sheriff Standing | 96 |
| Chapter 12 | Free at Last | 105 |
| Chapter 13 | Return of the Prodigal | 114 |
| Chapter 14 | A Christmas Token | 122 |
| Chapter 15 | Scouting the Big East Fork | 131 |
| Chapter 16 | Molly | 140 |
| Chapter 17 | Futile Warning | 148 |
| Chapter 18 | A Killer on the Loose | 157 |
| Chapter 19 | Conflicted | 167 |
| Chapter 20 | August's Choice | 178 |
| Chapter 21 | Taking A Stock to Things | 187 |
| Chapter 22 | Seeds of Doubt | 198 |
| Chapter 23 | The Damned Splash Dam | 207 |
| Chapter 24 | East Fork Treasure | 219 |
| Chapter 25 | Lost Burro | 230 |
| Chapter 26 | A Dark Family Secret | 239 |
| Conclusion | | 250 |

# Chapter 1

## WHAT A MESS

(In the year 2005)

*What in hell am I doing up here anyhow,* Clint Hargrove fretted as he carefully made his way across the barn loft to an old wooden trunk in the corner. The flooring was not only rotten, but it was pocked with gaping holes concealed under the decomposing hay strewn everywhere. The lighting wasn't good either. *Sure wouldn't be a good thing to fall through this floor and get hurt–can't afford to do that right now,* he mulled. Finding some firm floor boards, he crept closer and kneeled next to the old steamer trunk. It was literally covered with spider webs and dried splatters of chicken shit, which he hesitantly tried to brush away. "Shoo—what a mess!" he muttered, sniffing and almost tasting the pungent air. Then he set about unbuckling the stiff leather straps fastening the top.

Very carefully Clint opened the filthy chest and peered into its dark interior, straining to make out its contents. He was sorely disappointed. It was almost empty, with the exception of a pile of old newspapers and magazines. Reaching inside, he took up an antiquated 1929 issue of *Look* but quickly tossed it aside. Then he started rummaging through the rest of the periodicals. Most of them were from the same time period he determined—1920s and 1930s. *What in the hell am I doing? I'm not going to find anything up here,* he began to realize. Surely his Hargrove kinfolk would already have discovered anything of historical value amidst the barn plunder. Besides, his head was hurting, and he had done about as much sleuthing as he wanted to do on this cool spring day. But just when Clint had worked out in his mind it was time to escape the barn loft and head back to Asheville, he felt something else buried underneath the layer of vintage journals. It had a hard metallic feel about it.

Hurriedly he fished out a rusty tin container about the size of a cigar box. It was so dark up there in the loft, Clint could hardly see it. He puffed blasts of air from his puckered mouth, blowing away most of the heavy layer of dust covering the container. Then he held it closer to his squinting eyes for examination. Three faint words were barely legible on the tarnished lid—*Penn's Spells Quality*. Puzzled, he tilted the box a bit so that he could see its side. More discernible script could then be made out—*Penn's Natural Leaf Thin*. "Hmm," he mumbled, surmising it must be an old tobacco tin that he was holding. *Let's see what's inside this thing.*

One thing was for sure, Clint had felt better. A nasty headache and hangover were remnants of the previous night's bender. Drinking alone at a tavern near his Asheville condo, one Jack Daniels and water had led to another and then another until—well, until it didn't matter how many drinks he had downed. The last thing he remembered was watching a recorded telecast of Tiger Woods vanquishing an impressive field of professional golfers and claiming yet another PGA Tour victory. How and when Clint had gotten home was beyond him.

The year was 2005, and last week Clint had received a call from his uncle, who resided on the old Hargrove homeplace in Haywood County, twenty-some miles west of Asheville, North Carolina. Come to find out, the barn that had stood on the property for a century or more was about to be torn down. It would be Clint's last gander before a backhoe ravaged the structure. His father's ancestors had lived there in the Pigeon Valley since the early 1820s, and Clint had always harbored prideful feelings of his Hargrove heritage. Even in his post-intoxicated state, he was motivated somehow to get out of bed and drive over to Haywood for one last look. And that is how he came to be plundering in the barn loft.

The lid of the reddish-colored tobacco tin was hinged, so Clint scratched around to find a crevice wide enough to insert a fingernail and pry it open.

Finally, he popped the tight-fitting top loose and delicately lifted it back on its rusty hinges, while anxiously studying the contents.

"Whoa!" It was chock full of fusty items that were being exposed to the light of day for the first time in ages! Immediately, Clint spotted a pair of flimsy wire-rimmed glasses with odd orange-tinted lenses. Then he gingerly picked out a narrow, red cardboard box, sliding the top off to reveal a folding razor. *Now whose could this have been?* he pondered, as he fingered the ornately-carved ivory handle and sharp blade. Carefully storing the razor back in its box and putting it aside, he next came upon a whetstone. Heavy wear patterns on both sides revealed it had surely been put to good use, honing sharp edges on knives and—undoubtedly—this razor.

In the next minute or two, Clint lifted a leather coin purse out of the tin container, an empty pill box, a hand-wrought iron nail, and a tiny pony horseshoe. He also found a wooden-handled pipe cleaner, a small screwdriver-like tool, one vial of a gravelly ore-like substance, two tiny arrowheads with broken points, and a tattered newspaper clipping. Lying at the very bottom of the tin, he noticed a small yellowish envelope with the faded name "Mr. August Hargrove" written on it. Removing it for closer perusal, he instantly detected an address scrawled under the name—"Canton, N. Carolina."

*It must be a letter to my great-grandfather,* Clint deduced. Noticing that the posting was from Los Angeles, California, he pulled out the aged contents—two flimsy, folded pages—and hastily began reading.

*Los Angeles City*

*Feb. 3rd, 1899*
*Dear Mr. Hargrove,*

*I am Dick Rosehl's daughter and I send you this letter with deepest regrets to inform you that my Father has been killed in a hard rock mine accident near Skidaddle, California. When I received the notice of his death from the Inyo County Sheriff we went over to the mining territory to retrieve his personal effects and settle some matters of estate. As we understand the circumstances, he was working alone at one of his claims, the Southern*

Jackass I believe, when a slide buried the mine's entrance before he could get out. The sheriff informed us of this unfortunate incident and said there was no feasible way that Father could ever be dug out of the mountainside.

When going through his things I found several of your letters from Canton, North Carolina and the enclosed crude map. I remember how highly Father spoke of you. Since your name is on the map I decided to send it. It may be of no value to you but I enclose it anyway with a feeling that Father would have wished it.

I sold Father's rock house near the Hargrove Spring. Or might I better say I gave it away because it brought so little money as to hardly pay for the travel expenses to those remote Panamint Mountains.

Again, thank you, Mr. Hargrove, for being a friend to my Father and I hope that good fortune has shone on you in the Carolina mountains, where I understand Canton is.

I am sincerely yours,
Martha Rosehl Pattison

*Well I'll be,* Clint mused as he shuffled the other page into the dim light to have a look at it. *Wonder what this is.* "August Hargrove, R. A. Rosehl, the Southern Jackass Mine—ha, what a hoot!" he read aloud and laughed, with his eyes remaining fixed to the tattered diagram. *It's a damn treasure map, that's what it is!* he figured. Then his eyes locked on an ominous place name shown on the map—Death Valley.

Clint could easily make out the geographic details. After all, the sciences were his profession—he had earned a master's in geology from North Carolina State University, after playing football for the Wolfpack for four years. But recently, his backsliding from prudent, temperate behavior had landed him a one-term, unpaid suspension from cushy teaching duties at the Asheville School for Boys. The Headmaster had not minced words when he informed Clint that this was it—his last chance. If he did not get himself into a program and sober up before the fall term, then he could look elsewhere for a job. Clint's current throbbing headache showed how well he was heeding the dean's well-intended warning.

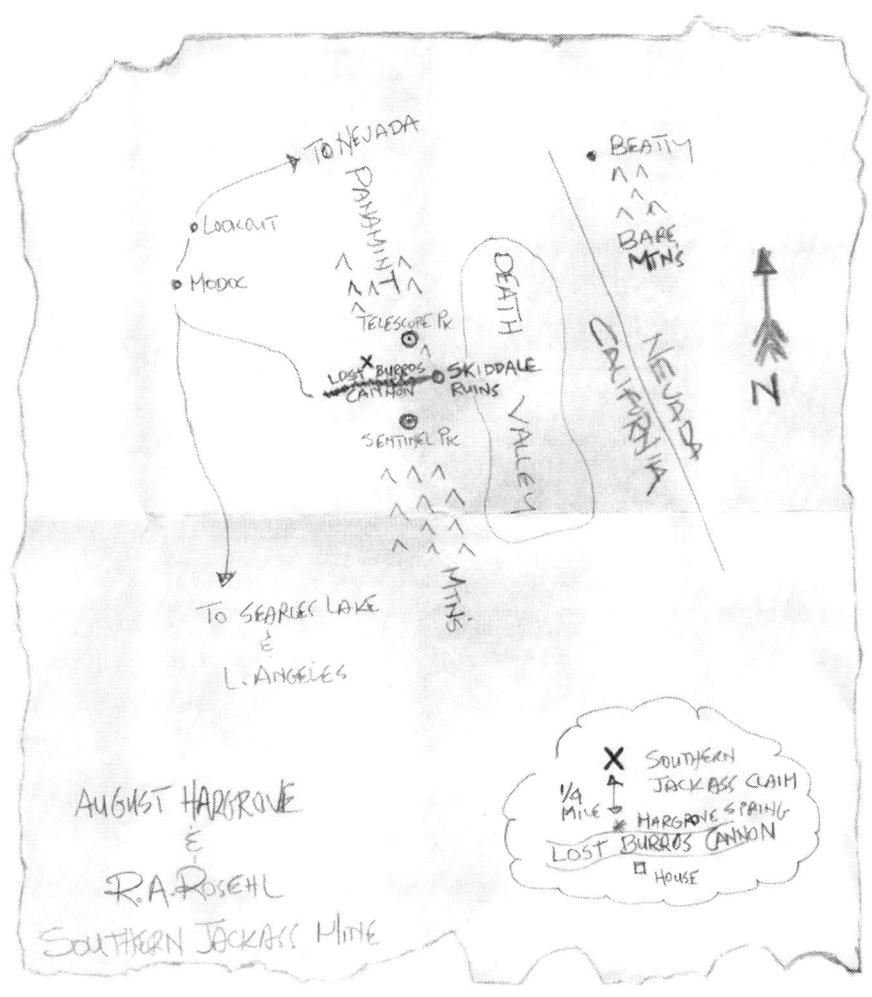

Clearly, the spot pinpointed on August Hargrove's and Dick Rosehl's map was a mining works—or claim—named the Southern Jackass. And all indications were that the Jackass was located in the Lost Burros Canyon, on the west side of Death Valley in California's Panamint Mountains. The two mining partners had even gone to the trouble to further locate the claim—or mine—one quarter of a mile north of Hargrove Spring. *Why had they drawn such an elaborate map?* Clint pondered. *Why was it so important to Dick Rosehl and Great-Grandfather Hargrove?* "Hmm," *Hargrove Spring—no doubt my great-grandfather's doing,* he figured. Clint was so intrigued, the excruciating headache was all but forgotten.

Carefully securing the rusty tobacco tin and all its contents, he very cautiously picked his path back across the barn loft and climbed down to the ground. As he did so a different sensation began to burn inside him. Gone were the lonely, sorrowful emotions that had driven him to the bottle for escape. Instead, he felt warm embers of excitement and a growing feeling for family, history, mystery, and adventure. In the short time it took Clint to snap a few last pictures of the old Hargrove barn, climb into his red Chevrolet pickup, and wend his way back to Asheville, he had made up his mind. He was going to try and re-discover his great-grandfather's old mine—the Southern Jackass—all the way across the country in California!

### (In the year 1883)

It was not long past sunup, and August Hargrove was already hard at it, wielding a double-bitted axe and hacking blazes into the sides of towering trees. The waning days of fall had ushered a blast of frigid air into the river valley, sweeping the last leaves from the tree limbs and causing the young man to work briskly in order to keep warm. The year was 1883, and August was working as a surveyor's assistant, in the extreme efforts to build a railroad westward through the rugged North Carolina mountains.

A link-up with another line out of Georgia was the object of the Western North Carolina Railroad. So far, the construction work had been completed only as far as Waynesville, more than a hundred rail miles short of the line's proposed terminus at Murphy. A small mountain village at the time, Murphy was located at the very southwestern tip of North Carolina, near the confluence of the Valley and Hiwassee rivers, and served as the seat of administrative governance and enforcement powers for Cherokee County.

The previous year saw the iron tracks of the W.N.C. Railroad laid as far west as the settlement of Pigeon River in Haywood County. At that wagon-fording spot on the east-west turnpike, Hack Hargrove had been hired as the railroad's station agent. Holding such an important and influential position, Hargrove had been able to secure the surveying job for his seventeen-year-old son, Augustus—or August, as he was known to everyone. And now the son was enjoying himself immensely, blazing a railroad route along the Valley River toward Murphy.

On this cold day, there was another hand laboring out ahead somewhere, helping August mark the path for the loggers to clear. The pioneer logging gangs, currently some ten miles or so behind the survey party, had been slowed somewhat by the early bout of freezing weather. Chief Surveyor Bill Matthews was still back at the camp, transcribing notes from the previous day's work, and several other men were simply trying to shake off the coldness before getting started. As soon as Matthews and his surveyors reached Murphy, they planned to haul themselves back in their wagons to the point where the graders had ceased operations for the winter. There, the survey crew would begin work anew with the more demanding and tedious duty of staking the centerline of the railroad, setting elevation monuments, and marking the cut and fills for the earth movers.

A good two weeks of trail-blazing work still lay ahead, but August reckoned they should make it to Murphy in time for a Christmas break. Just as he was savoring one of his mother's pumpkin pies and raring his axe high to chop a gouge into a huge hemlock, he heard the loud crack of a gunshot resounding through the thick woods. It was a fair ways off, but too close for comfort! *Who was shooting a gun so close to us?* he fretted. Before the echoing sounds had died down, August was hustling toward his axe-man buddy, Calvin, to make sure he was all right.

*Who in hell is shooting a gun around here?* he kept wondering, as he sprinted, axe in hand, toward a man he could see in the distance. Slowing down as he approached the stranger, August spotted a body sprawled on the ground. It was Calvin, he could tell that right away! And now, of all things, the other man was pointing the repeater rifle at August and hollering out to him, "Halt right there, mister, or I'll put a bullet through you too!"

August could not believe his eyes—or ears—as he slowed to a stop! *Me too? He shot Calvin? This man can't be much more than twenty years old,* August thought, as he quickly studied him. Not believing his friend could actually be dead, he managed to get out a challenge between his heaving gulps for air, "What happened? Did you shoot him? Is he—dead?"

"Reckon he is. Shouldn't ought to skeered off that buck deer I was stalking."

"He's dead? Let's see!" August screamed. Dropping the axe and ignoring the gun dangerously directed at him, he moved over and knelt at Calvin's side. Blood was oozing through a hole in the heavy woolen coat. He pressed a hand over Calvin's heart to feel for a beat or any kind of movement. There was nothing! Then he licked his finger and stuck it under his friend's nose to check for signs of breathing—nothing! He slapped Calvin's lifeless face two or three times and got no response. "He's dead," August pronounced lowly and slowly, as a sorrowful fury began to rise within him.

"Tolt ye, mister! Now don't ye worry none 'bout going to the law. My pa is sheriff in these here parts. He's going to figger it weren't nuthin but a hunting accident. Nuthin ye say can prove otherwise, neither."

August was still on his knees next to Calvin's corpse, not fully realizing his hand had found and palmed a good-sized rock. All he could think of was his dead friend and the nonsense spouting from the killer's mouth. There were no hints of remorse atall in the man's actions or words. *Did he mean to shoot Calvin?* That was the question confounding August's mind as a hateful anger erupted within him. Then the growing rage inside exploded into uncontrollable actions. He gripped the rock in his hand, sprung up from the ground like a mountain lion, and lit into the buckskin-wearing stranger before the man ever knew what was happening. August brushed away the rifle with one arm and with the other struck a powerful blow with the rock against the side of the killer's head, crushing it with one fatal blow.

Bill Matthews had immediately ridden to Murphy to notify the Cherokee County Sheriff of the terrible incident on the railroad right-of-way. Returning with Matthews to perform a proper investigation, Sheriff Buford Posey had been shocked to discover one of the dead victims was his own son. And from the beginning, he had not believed the assistant surveyor's version of the story.

The sheriff glared at August with a look of pent-up hatred. "Ain't believing yer story nary bit, Hargrove! That boy of mine never intentionally kilt that other man. No sir, he sure 'nough didn't. The way I got it figgered is that the two of ye jumped Lester—while he was hunting—fer some reason or nuther. Guess ye're goin' have to tell yer story in the courtroom—why ye went and done that. But it 'pears he fought back a sight. Must have shot this other man by defending hisself, before ye laid into him with that rock. That 'bout right, Hargrove?"

"No, Sheriff! You're wrong! I told you! Your son shot Calvin outright—said Calvin scared off a deer he aimed to shoot! That's what he allowed, anyhow. Why, he even threatened to put a bullet in me. Then we got into it, him and me, and I hit him 'bout the head with the rock. I sure didn't mean to kill him though, Sheriff!" August was excited and frustrated and afraid—at the same time. But the sheriff was not listening to him, or, worse still, did not believe his story. *What a mess*, August thought, realizing he was in big trouble now.

"Well, I guess a jury is going have to decide if ye're telling the truth or not, ye son-of-a-bitch. I'll be arresting ye here and now, Hargrove, for the murder of my son, Lester Posey," stated the high sheriff hatefully and barely able to utter the name of his son. Then stiffening again, he went on, "We'll just have to lock ye up and see what the judge allows about bail. If'en I were you, I wouldn't get my hopes up though."

# Chapter 2

## BUSTING OUT

Word of his son's predicament quickly reached Agent Hack Hargrove at the Pigeon River railroad station, and soon the news was circulating throughout the upper Pigeon Valley. August's close friend, Joseph Edmunston, thought his own father was joshing him when first told about the affair out in Cherokee County. They were in the barn at their Crab Orchard farm, hitching up a pair of mules to a wagon, when Rufus Edmunston broke the incredulous news.

"Son, Hack tolt me some bad tidings 'bout August this morning. Says he's been jailed over at Murphy on a murder charge. Word is he kilt another man." The patriarch waited a moment to let the message sink in before going on, "Didn't get too much more information, but the hearsay is that it was the sheriff's son out there—a Posey—who he supposedly kilt. Crushed his head with a rock, they say." That was about all Rufus knew about the bad business in Cherokee.

A slight grin came across Joseph's face as he cinched a leather harness strap. Glancing back at his father though, he saw only the look of concern—not a joker's face. "Yea—right! What? No, ye can't be serious, Pa! He's not in jail—is he?" As Joseph finished, the grin had disappeared and in its place was a puzzled look of astonishment.

"Ain't pulling yer leg none, Joseph. He sure 'nough has been put in jail, and they say he won't be let out before there's a trial this spring. Hack's took off out there again to see what he can do, but he says the sheriff and judge have got it in for August."

Rufus and Hack had been best friends their whole lives. They had even fought side by side against the Yanks in the late war. Theirs was the fastest of friendships and not much went unsaid between them. That very morning Hack had confided to Rufus some scarce details that were going around about the situation out in Murphy. It seems that Sheriff Buford Posey was building a strong case against August. Posey was allowing to his cronies—and anybody else who would listen—that the two railroad men had jumped his son and that Lester had been killed trying to defend himself. Hack knew it could not be true, because August told him exactly what had happened. His boy was not a liar and, for sure, would never lie to him.

Nonetheless, the sheriff's reputation and political connections held significant sway around Murphy and Cherokee County, and the elder Hargrove could not readily see how his son was going to get out of this bad scrape with the law. Rufus had sensed Hack's deep worries. Not since their days serving with the Haywood Highlanders during the war had he seen his old buddy "Hat" so nervous and agitated—and for good reason, apparently.

Shivering uncontrollably in the extreme cold and darkness, the gangly teen kept a close watch on the jailhouse across the street. It was a small stone house that had been reinforced and re-purposed as the county lockup. Concealed in a frigid public livery with his horse, Joseph Edmunston looked on, as some hardy folk moved between the town's two saloons. It was New Year's Eve, and the revelers were already starting to celebrate.

Earlier that afternoon, he had visited with August in his freezing cell, and they had concocted a breakout plan, believe it or not. For sure, this was not the reason Joseph had ridden his horse hard from his parents' Haywood farm, through snow and ice, to get to the distant Murphy. He had only aimed to visit his best friend and bring him some belated Christmas cheer, but those good intentions had quickly vanished upon meeting Sheriff Posey earlier that day.

"How can I be of 'sistance to ye, son?" the sheriff had asked upon Joseph's arrival at the jail. "Sheriff Buford Posey at yer service."

Moving into the dim room, Joseph looked toward the sheriff who had not bothered to get up. Instead, he remained in a reclined position with his muddy boots comfortably propped up on a battered desk.

"Uh—I came to talk with August Hargrove," Joseph finally stammered. Standing almost six feet and four inches tall, the stringy eighteen-year-old—almost nineteen—glanced at the sheriff and then around the large room. An iron stove in one corner burned red hot, barely keeping the inside temperature above freezing. Along a rear wall were two jail cells, one empty and the other housing his buddy, who he could see was standing anxiously with his face pressed against the rough iron bars that secured him. A slight smile spread across the prisoner's face.

"Didn't get yer name, stranger. Ye a friend of Hargrove?" the seated Posey queried.

"Yes sir, I'm his friend. Can I have a talk with him?"

"Ye have a name, mister?" Posey persisted, as he let his legs fall heavily and loudly to the floor and began sitting taller in his chair.

"Yes sir, I have a name—Edmunston. I'm Joseph Edmunston."

"Ye are, are ye? Ye from 'round about Forks of Pigeon where Hargrove hails from?" the sheriff grilled, while getting up, moving over closer to Joseph and staring up directly into his eyes.

"That's right, Sheriff. Mind if I step over and talk to August?"

"Holt right there, Edmunston! I'm goin' want to see if'en yer armed, now ain't I?" While searching Joseph's person up and down for a weapon, Posey added, "Don't believe he's goin' be yer friend too much longer, Edmunston. Ain't no way a jury will be swayed from convicting him of murder—murdering my son—no way atall. Ye might want to come back over here about March time when the court convenes. Then ye'll be able to see yer friend's neck get snapped by a rope—watch his hanging body wiggling while he dies good and dead. Soon's we're done with him, ye can take him back over to Haywood with ye, if ye like. That'll be in March, maybe April, like I said. Think ye may come back and visit us then, Edmunston?"

Joseph just stared unflinchingly at the sheriff without replying. When the body search was completed, Posey barked, "Okay, ye can go over and talk to him now, Edmunston. Ye've got ten minutes starting—right now!" and he took out a pocket watch and marked the time.

"I've nary chance of escaping the hangman's noose, Joseph. Sheriff's got everyone in town believing I'm guiltier than hell." August was convinced he was done for, and Joseph could see that his buddy was badly shaken. "I didn't mean to kill that man. Don't know what came over me, though, to make me smash his head in like that. You've got to believe me, Joseph. It wasn't intentional—ye believe me, don't ye?"

"'Course I believe you, August. Don't you fret about that," Joseph allowed, trying to reassure his distraught friend. "He killed the other man too, didn't he? Least that's what your pa said." That part had been worrying Joseph, and he was only trying to clear his mind of the other killing.

They were both talking in raised whispers so as not to be overheard. "He shot Calvin! The sheriff's son shot him dead, sure as I'm sitting here," August pronounced coldly and plain as could be. "Did it intentional, too—I know he did—'cause Calvin scared off a deer he had in his sights. He didn't show no shame or regret 'bout it atall. He even threatened to shoot me!" At that point August grabbed the iron bars with both hands, stiffened, and stared intently into his friend's eyes. "You believe me, don't you?"

"Shoot you too! You've got to be joshing me?"

"Ain't making this up atall. You believe what I'm saying, don't you? You believe me?"

"Damn right I believe you! We all do! Pa said that your father's going to get the best lawyer in Haywood County to defend you. We're all going to be here for you. Don't let yourself get down too much, August."

"No, Joseph, you don't understand! It ain't goin' be a fair trial. I've seen the judge and sheriff talking." He glanced over at Sheriff Posey and then continued, "It's done been decided between them two. Ain't no lawyer can keep me from goin' to the gallows. You've got to get me out of here, Joseph—help me escape!" August pleaded in a hushed voice as a blank look froze across his friend's face.

What could Joseph do? August—and Sheriff Posey—had convinced him that true justice would not be dispensed in favor of his friend. If he failed to help August—simply walked away and did nothing—then the doomed prisoner would surely be killed at the hands of the Cherokee County hangman. After only a brief moment of contemplation, the radical notion came over Joseph that he had no other choice. He had to do something! *I've got to do what I can. Can't let them kill him.*

"Escape! How in the hell are we going to do that?" Joseph whispered back. He cast a look at Posey and then back to August. "What you got in mind?" And for the remaining minutes of the visitation, the two of them tried to concoct some sort of bust-out scheme.

After several nervous and frigid hours of waiting and watching, the time had come for Joseph to make his move. Not long after midnight, he stole his way from the hide at the stable to the rear of the rock jailhouse. The streets were nearly deserted, and Sheriff Posey had left for home a couple of hours ago. Joseph had watched him ride away after turning over the prison security duty to a young man, not much older than the pair of Haywood conspirators. Realizing that necessity would require the deputy to use the outdoor privy at some point during the early morning hours, Joseph concealed himself behind an old wagon and waited in the dark for nature's call.

Gun shots rang out in the distance, and the faint sounds of boisterous laughter and talking could be heard. *At least somebody's having a good time bringing in this new year,* he noted to himself, as he waited for the deputy to come out and relieve himself. Another hour went by, and the freezing conspirator began to doubt himself and this crazy jail-breaking notion. While trying to wiggle his frozen toes, he was surprised by the abruptness of the jailhouse door slamming closed. Directly the deputy rounded the corner and entered the tiny outhouse. *It's now or never,* Joseph thought. He stretched out his cold limbs and limped quickly across the frozen mud to surprise the jailer.

"Get your hands up! Quick about it now!" Joseph ordered in a low yet determined voice, after flinging open the privy's plank door. He pointed the barrel of an old revolver—one that his father had brought home from the Civil War—at the surprised deputy, who was still sitting and doing his business.

"What—what ye mean, feller?" The deputy was dumbfounded and halted all efforts to relieve himself.

"Hurry! Let's go! Get them britches up, and let's get back inside. Don't try anything or I'll shoot you—I will!" Joseph tried to act as mean as he could, realizing that he would be hard-pressed to pull the trigger and shoot this young lawman.

"Okay, okay—let me get 'em on then," came the nervous reply. Spitting out a huge wad of spent tobacco, the deputy hurriedly hiked up his britches and pulled his suspenders over his shoulders in one movement. "This ain't right, mister."

As the Haywood conspirator hurriedly escorted the deputy back inside through the heavy door, August spotted them. "Over there, Joseph—hanging on the wall. The keys are over there!"

With one hand still holding the gun, Joseph pushed the deputy hard toward the rear cells and directed him again in as harsh a voice as he could muster, "Let him out! Now!"

Before fleeing out of the rock prison house, they tied up and gagged the young deputy and left him locked up in August's cell. By that time on the year's first morning, the streets were deserted, and the boys sprinted across the icy ruts to the stables, retrieved Joseph's horse, and high-tailed it out of the river town. And that's how they did it! That's how August busted out of the Cherokee County lockup.

Within a very short time, they found themselves traveling down a lonely river road in who-knows-what direction to an unknown destination. They had not planned the breakout that far. There had not been sufficient time to think the thing through beyond the escape. Neither of them had any idea what they were going to do now.

"Whew! I didn't know if you were coming, Joseph. You did right good though. Even scared me a little with that there mean talk you used." August was proud of what his friend had done for him. And he was even prouder to be out of Posey's jail and on the loose. But he was scared, just like Joseph was, and had no earthly idea where to go.

"What? You didn't think I was coming? I told you I would, August! You mean you didn't trust I was up to it?" Joseph retorted, feigning disappointment to his friend.

"No! No! I didn't mean it that way! 'Course I knew you would come. I was just getting a little scared something had happened to prevent you from coming—that you might have got found out or something. That's all!" August thought the world of Joseph Edmunston. They had been best friends ever since he could remember. Joseph was the most honest, upright, smartest person he knew. Truth be known, August had not believed Joseph could go against the law in this nefarious jail-breaking affair. But now that he was a free man again—thanks to Joseph—he was prouder than a peacock for what his friend had done for him.

"Well, I told you I would do it. Sure am glad I brought Pa's pistol with me though. Don't know how I would have gone about the thing without a gun. Say, where we going anyway? You know these here parts pretty good, don't you?"

"Not familiar with this country atall, Joseph. Ain't been beyond Murphy. Wonder where this here river—believe it's called the Hiwassee—wonder where it leads off to?" Then with a forced chuckle, he joked, "Guess we're 'bout to find out, ain't we?"

They took turns riding the horse that night and moved steadily along the road, hugging the right bank of the Hiwassee River. Since neither of the Haywood conspirators knew where they were going, their sole intent, of course, was to put as much distance between themselves and Sheriff Buford Posey as possible. For sure, they would have to make themselves scarce for a while. The sheriff was going to scour these North Carolina hills and valleys—and hell itself—looking for them. He would never rest until his son's suspected cold-blooded murderer was sent back to Haywood County in a coffin box.

Although the young men had no earthly notion where to go to evade the sheriff's manhunt, at least August had a slight chance of living now.

Joseph had given his buddy a reprieve from the hangman's noose, and the surveyor's assistant meant to make it an extended reprieve—one that would last for the rest of his life, ever how long that was going to be. So during the last cold, dark hours of the morning the young Haywood duo hurried downstream, talking and arguing and ciphering on yet another fateful plan.

### (In the year 2005)

That evening after Clint Hargrove arrived back in Asheville, an associate of his from Asheville School dropped by to see him. Claire Shook just happened to be in the downtown vicinity and thought she might pay Clint a visit. After all, she had not seen him in a week or two—well, ever since he was reprimanded and relieved of his teaching duties for the rest of the semester. So, the comely English teacher was just checking up on him to make sure everything was all right. At least that was her pretension.

"Claire! What brings you around here?" a surprised Clint offered. He did not let on that he was actually happy to see her. If the truth could be told, they both shared an infatuation for each other, yet they had not been able to break through the formal barriers of their professional relationship to let it be known. How could he not be drawn to this woman? Never mind that she was forty-four years old—seven years older than he was. She was absolutely beautiful in his eyes. At least an inch taller than himself, her thin athletic body was proportioned so precisely as to incite crazy sensations within him. Downright pleasurable feelings these were. Her glistening dark hair flowed just low enough to touch the shoulders, and her face was remindful of the ones that routinely graced the pages of *Vanity Fair*—the South American beauties, that is. At least these were Clint's figments, as he welcomed the intoxicating woman into his small condo.

"Just came by to see how you're doing. I was in the area. Everything okay with you?" Claire asked, noticing the empty glass on the lamp table next to his television-watching chair. It appeared to her he was sober enough.

"Yea, fine! Why, you worried about me or something?" he replied with a quizzical look.

"Nope—just checking, and I wanted to catch you up on a few things over at school."

Claire settled comfortably on the sofa near Clint's chair and began discussing mainly professional affairs, along with some scuttlebutt related to a couple of their teaching associates. Soon however, they were talking about lighter and more pleasant things, even some personal matters. Clint was still extremely excited about the treasure map he had found earlier that day, and he couldn't keep from sharing the news with Claire.

"You're not going to believe this, Claire! This morning I was over in Haywood at my family's place—the Hargrove farm—and I ran across an old mining map that my great-grandfather may have drawn up when he was out in California. It's at least a hundred years old—I'm sure of it! And the thing is, it's completely legible and understandable."

"No! You've got to be kidding! Do you have it here?" Claire was excited too, and Clint saw her genuine interest. That was another thing he liked about her. In addition to being a good-looking woman, she was as intellectually gifted as he was. Given this teasing hint of historical mystery, Claire became filled with curiosity and excitement—almost to the extent Clint himself had been aroused upon discovering the timeworn document.

For at least an hour, they poured over the map with Clint explaining what he knew about it and trying his best to answer Claire's probing questions.

"Have you searched maps on the internet to find these Panamint Mountains and this Lost Burros Canyon?" Before Clint could answer, she spotted an anomaly, "Look how it's spelled, 'c-a-n-n-o-n!'"

"Yep—looks like August was about as good a speller as I am," Clint joked. "Those Panamint Mountains and the Lost Burros Canyon actually exist! They have the same names today, Claire. They're located just west of Death Valley, like the old map indicates. I even found a vintage USGS map online, dated 1908, that shows a road leading up the canyon to the abandoned mining town of Skidaddle. See here on Great-Grandfather's map—'Skidaddle ruins.' It's the same old mining town!"

"Hmm—really? So it's an accurate map after all. Amazing—simply amazing! Why, I bet we could find it!" As she finished, she looked up from the table where the map was spread and stared straight into Clint's confounded eyes. "Don't you think?"

He really could not believe how excited Claire had become—or get over the determination in her expression. With a slight chuckle, he replied, "Now hold your horses, young lady. What's this 'we' business, anyway? I've already made up my mind I'm going out there and check it out. As a matter of fact, I'm planning on leaving this coming weekend. Going to drive all the way across the country in the old Chevy truck. Too bad some of us have to work, though—isn't it?"

"You are? Why, you crazy thing! Can't you wait for me? School will be out in three weeks. Then we can go together—both of us! I'll keep you good company, Clint Hargrove! I promise! Can't I go with you?"

Clint could not believe his ears—or his good luck.

# Chapter 3

## WANTED!

(In the year 1884)

Neither August nor Joseph had ever seen such a river as the one flowing serenely before them. After three freezing, grueling days and nights of hiding, riding, and walking down the icy Hiwassee, the fugitives now found themselves blocked by a broad river. They had left the towering mountains behind, dodged a small town or two, and now found themselves in this picturesque rolling terrain, confronted with their first real navigational decision since the rushed exodus from Murphy.

Over the course of the last few days, they had discussed at length their dire predicament and the options available to them. Joseph sensed that he was up to his neck in trouble for aiding and abetting a presumed murderer. Not a killer, mind you, which August certainly was, but a "presumed murderer," because there were no doubts in Sheriff Posey's mind that August had intentionally killed his son. Now Joseph himself had become a criminal for conspiring, aiding, and abetting the presumed murderer's escape.

The pair of so-called criminals figured the sheriff and his allies were bound to spin a spidery web through the Carolina highlands to catch them. No mere men could elude for very long the Cherokee lawman's quest for justice and vengeance—or so Joseph and August reckoned. Now linked together in this bad business, the two of them had ciphered and argued until at long last they agreed on a destination where the sheriff's web could never ensnare them.

"Got to cross this here river to get out West, Joseph. That's west, there," August confidently pronounced, while pointing directly toward the setting sun across the river."

"I know that's west! What? You think I don't know that's west? Any fool could figure that!" For some reason, Joseph had taken offense at August's helpful directions. Now August was hesitant to respond, but he did anyway.

"Sorry! Just trying to stir up some conversation, so's we can make a decision—whether to try and cross the river here or not. That's all. You ain't said a word in the last hour or so. What's on yer mind?" It was a question that August would wish he had left unasked.

After a few seconds of mulling, Joseph lit into his friend. "What's on my mind? Well, I'll tell you exactly what's on my mind, August. What's on my mind is that my life is ruined right about now. What's on my mind is that I may never see my mother and father and sisters again—that's what's on my mind! Anything else on my mind?" Joseph asked mockingly. He hesitated for a second or two to break the cadence of the protest, then continued, "Well, yes, I would say so, Mr. Hargrove. There is something else on my mind. Like how in hell are we going to make it all the way to Montana with no money in our pockets—not much anyway. Have you thought about that? Given it much thought, have you? We've only got one horse between us—that's a sight worrisome too, I'd say. It's a good piece, August, way out there to Montana! Yea, that's what's on my mind. You given it much thought atall lately?" Simmering frustrations, pent up for the past day or two, had finally erupted into this disagreeable outburst incited by an innocent query.

August was taken aback by his buddy's heated reaction and hesitated to respond. It was true that the two of them had finally decided to head for the Montana Territory. It had seemed to be the rational choice of few options. They could think of no other more backward or remote place in the country. Besides that, a passel of Hargroves had up and left Haywood three years before and migrated to Montana. Sure enough, August had kin folk out there in a place called Townsend, but that was all he knew about it.

Finally, August worked up enough nerve to say something. "Yea, I have. I've been thinking 'bout all those things too. Don't know how Ma and Pa are goin' to take this—or when I might ever see them and the others again." It was saddening to think about such things, and he paused to let the shot of emotion dissipate before continuing. "How-some-ever, Joseph, we said we were going to Montana—that's what we said—and I aim to do just that. Now are ye goin' with me or not?"

By now Joseph had calmed down somewhat and pulled himself together. "'Course I still aim to go with you. Never thought different, but you asked me what was on my mind and I guess—well, I guess I just lost it for some reason. Sorry to go off on you like that." Then looking up and down the expansive river, he allowed, "Don't know how we're going to get across to the other side, though. Maybe we should ride down to the next ferry crossing and see what they'll take for a ride across. Reckon?"

"Well, I don't see nary one of them big bridges, like the one they're building in New York—that Brooklyn Bridge, I believe they call it. Ye hear 'bout it?"

Again Joseph fought back making a sarcastic comment and simply allowed, "You mean the Roebling suspension bridge—yep, I've heard of it. Say, look down there a ways, August. See? Believe that there's a farmhouse—looks like. What do you say we go down and make some inquiries? It should be safe enough."

"Hmm, yea—sounds like a plan. Let's git!" And then they were on the move again, with August sore-footing it in front of the horse and rider.

*Knock, knock, knock.* Joseph looked around suspiciously, as August knocked on the heavy front door. It was a very small farm, set back from the river and above the flood plain—appeared to him. The house's log structure had been clad with unpainted, rough-sawn boards. Several roof shakes were missing, and some of the glazing in the window openings was broken. A stove pipe pierced one end wall, high up near the gable. In the dim gloaming light, gray smoke could be seen pouring out of it. All in all, the place was not much to look at, but it compared favorably with the familiar houses spotted throughout Haywood's Pigeon Valley.

"Jest a minute—hold yer horses! I'm a'coming!" They could tell the voice was that of an elderly person, or at least they thought so. But when the door finally opened, it was a middle-aged gentleman who greeted them, and he was standing on one leg with the aid of crutches. "What can I do for you men?" he at last asked, after looking the two strangers over real good.

August anxiously replied, "Hello, sir! We're just passing by. To tell the truth, we're not exactly sure where we are, and we was hoping you might be able to enlighten us." He glanced over at Joseph and then back to the man standing in the doorway.

"That so?" the one-legged man asked, as his mind worked to determine whether these two fellows were up to no good. "Ye want to step in out of the cold, do ye then? Can't afford to let all this good heat 'scape the house.

"Yes sir! Don't mind if we do," August thankfully replied, and then he and Joseph followed behind their host and stepped through the doorway into the warmer confines of the modest home. To one side, they could see a red-hot iron stove, and against the wall next to it, firewood was stacked almost to the ceiling. "Sure feels nice and cozy in here, sir—sure does," August offered as a plain-dressed woman quietly entered from a room in the rear of the house—probably the kitchen, the boys figured.

"Pull you up a couple of chairs from the table there," the man directed, as he set aside his crutches and awkwardly maneuvered to take his seat in a large wood rocker. "This here's my wife, Ellen, and I'm Tom Doughty. Can't get around much good anymore, I'm afraid. Lost this here leg at Chickamauga. Lucky to be alive though. I'm proud for that!"

As Joseph settled into the offered chair, all he could think about was his Grandfather Basil Edmunston's similar predicament. At least his grandfather had a prosthetic leg that allowed him to walk almost normally. Tom Doughty was not so fortunate. Finally, Joseph said something, "Pleased to meet you, ma'am, and Mr. Doughty. We're—I'm Joseph Edmunston and ..."

"And I'm August—August Hargrove." August figured he would jump in and introduce himself, since he had done all of the talking thus far. It had not dawned on either of these novice fugitives to consider using aliases, in order to frustrate the sheriff's future efforts to apprehend them. They were as innocent in conscience as they were in actions and simply appreciated the kindness offered to them by this crippled man and his wife.

Tom's headful of gray hair was neatly combed back from his face, and he possessed the look of hardened experience. "It's good to meet you boys. So you're strangers in these here parts, are you?"

"That's right, Mr. Doughty," August answered. "We're aiming to go out West, and was wondering what river this might be and how best to get across it." Just then, it hit August that it might not be prudent to be completely straight forward with his host. After all, they could not very well let on that they were criminals on the loose. So he added a made-up explanation for their travel plans. "We've got our minds set on doing some gold mining, sir. Going to strike it rich, I hope, somers out West." He could feel Joseph's eyes boring into him.

"Gold mining! Don't you think you're a mite late for that? Why, they must have it all cleaned up by now."

Joseph decided to help August out of the hole he had dug, "Still a lot of it to be found, we hear, Mr. Doughty. We're headed to—Virginia City." Joseph had heard of this western boom town, not fully realizing there were actually two of them with the same name.

"Which one you aim to go to?" the ever-inquisitive ex-Rebel soldier came back.

"Sir?" Joseph was puzzled by the query and looked from Doughty to August and then back to Doughty.

"Which Virginia City, son—the one in Nevada or the other 'en up in the Montana Territory?"

Trying to get his feet back under him, Joseph now understood where his host was coming from and immediately responded, "Oh yeah—I see what you mean, sir. We're going to the Nevada one, Mr. Doughty—out to Virginia City in Nevada.

"There were a slew of boys from my regiment that deserted us and run for it to them places. Left the rest of us high and dry, they did. Still think it's all been dug up by now. But what the hell, you may strike it rich! I wish you two boys luck and more power to you. Now, Ellen, could you get me and our guests here a cup of cider, please? You want some, boys?"

Of course the Haywood youths took Doughty up on the offer. Eventually, they each guzzled several cups while gulping down generous portions of Ellen Doughty's biscuits and molasses. During this enjoyable and informative stopover, the Civil War veteran offered up much wise counsel about the westward journey, and August and Joseph were all ears. He allowed that they should not try and cross this big Tennessee River that they had run into. Although there were several ferries spread out down the river, if it were him—he had told them, he would follow the river all the way down to Chattanooga, some fifty miles to the south. Why not sell their fine horse there and then take the trains all the way to Memphis, he suggested. From there, they could catch a ride on a river boat to New Orleans or St. Louis and then weigh their options on how best to proceed toward Nevada. That was what Tom Doughty said he would do.

And that is precisely what the two Haywood conspirators did. At Chattanooga, they sold Joseph's horse and old saddle for a good sum—enough to purchase train tickets to Huntsville, Alabama, with plenty of money left over. At Huntsville, the two buddies boarded the Memphis and Charleston Railroad and rode the cars through Decatur, Alabama, and Corinth, Mississippi, all the way to Memphis. In less than five days time from the chance visit with the one-legged Civil War veteran, they found themselves milling around the busy boat landings on the Mississippi River. Somewhere between Chattanooga and Memphis, the sinister vexations of Sheriff Posey catching up with them had curiously vanished. Instead, exciting dreams of gold and starting life anew in Montana filled their impressionable minds.

However, Sheriff Posey had not forgotten his son's escaped killer, and he was hell bent to find the fugitive, along with his shady accomplice. For three weeks, he and a posse of ten local men scoured the surrounding treacherous terrain on horseback, questioning travelers on the valley roads and turning the mountain towns and Indian villages inside out. On storefronts they tacked simple printed posters with an ominous "Wanted" and "Reward" heading, accompanied with text specially thought up by the sheriff to inspire vigilant behavior in the citizenry of the region.

# WANTED

**$100 REWARD!**

$100 in hard coin for information leading to arrest of AUGUST HARGROVE.

Hargrove is an escaped MURDERER from Cherokee County jail. He is a short man of stout build with reddish-blond hair and is 17 years old. Thought to be travelling with a lanky man by the name of Edmunston. Contact Sheriff Buford Posey in Murphy, N.C. if you have any information.

Copies of the wanted posters arrived in Haywood County by stagecoach within a week's time following the jail break. One was nailed on the Waynesville courthouse door and another to a prominent wall of the Pigeon River Post Office. Of course, the Hargroves and Edmunstons were distraught with these public notices highlighting the criminal troubles of their sons. Joseph's parents, Rufus and Emma—along with his twin sister Nancy Louisa and younger siblings—had been worried sick for him after his Christmas disappearance. Now, in this surprising and embarrassing manner, they suddenly learned of his complicity in August's escape from jail. Hack and Harriet Hargrove and a lawyer had actually been in route to Cherokee County to begin plotting August's defense strategy when Sheriff Posey's posters came to light. To be sure, all was not well in Haywood, and the Hargroves and Edmunstons struggled to comprehend and cope with the direful news about their beloved sons.

"I'm Sheriff Buford Posey, sir! Mind if I come in and ask you a few questions?"

It had taken the sheriff almost a month to finally carry out his searching down the Hiwassee River. At the confluence with the Tennessee, he and his deputy split up. Sheriff Posey was to ride south toward Chattanooga, down the left bank, while the other sworn lawman covered the far side of the wide river. The first house Posey had come to was the one-legged Civil War veteran's place.

"Glad to meet ye, Mr. Doughty. Sorry to bother ye like this, but I'm searching fer a 'scaped murderer."

"Ain't no problem, Sheriff. Mind if I sit down—go ahead and take a seat for yourself." Tom Doughty had to take the load off his leg, and he turned and backed carefully into his rocker.

"No sir—don't aim to stay very long. Got to keep at it, I reckon. Now, like I said, sir, I'm looking fer a murderer—or there may be two of 'em together."

"Two killers on the loose, Sheriff?" Doughty asked incredulously, as he looked over at Posey, while at the same time catching the glint of the lawman's gold badge. *Guess he sure 'nough is a bona fide lawman*, the veteran mused to himself. One could never be too sure.

"Well, no—that ain't jest right. There be just one killer. You see—he murdered my son Lester. There's another one might be with him who helped him 'scape."

"Hmm," the older veteran mumbled, as his mind thought back to about three weeks ago. He remembered the two likeable young men who had knocked at his door and then paid an overnight visit with him and his wife. *Couldn't be them, surely*, he thought, as he asked, "Can you describe them, Sheriff? What did they look like?"

"Neither one is twenty years old yet, I don't believe. The killer—that be Hargrove, August Hargrove—he's not too tall and about as stout as a mule, I'd say. Has a shock of hair with a reddish kind of straw tinge to it. That he does."

Tom Doughty's suspicions were verified. He already knew who this sheriff was looking for, and he could hardly believe it. They both had seemed like such good honest boys. But he held back from letting on to the sheriff, just yet. "And the other one, Sheriff—what about him?"

"That other one is tall and skinny—'bout six and a half feet tall and has a head of hair the color of summer hay. Right light it is. His name is Edmunston. These boys are a mean sort, sir. Have to be mean to do what they did!"

They had not seemed a mean sort atall to Doughty and his wife. As a matter of fact, they had taken a real liking to the young men. *Don't seem like them boys*, Doughty reflected to himself, as he decided to confess he had seen the two men. "I seen them, Sheriff, about three weeks ago, I'd say. They stopped by here to get some directions."

Posey perked up noticeably, and his eyes opened wider as he followed up, "They did? Ye sure 'bout that, sir?"

"Sure as sure can be, Sheriff. But are you certain they're killers? Didn't seem like killers to me. I'd sworn them two were upright young men. You sure 'bout this, are you, Sheriff?"

"Ain't no doubts, sir. Now, did either of them say where they might be headed? Think they might have crossed over this here big river?" Sheriff Posey's anxiousness showed. Finally, after a month of fruitless searching, he had discovered their trail, albeit somewhat cold by now.

Tom Doughty still held reservations about this business. *Could the sheriff be wrong?* he wondered, while mulling whether to tell him more. Deciding finally that the sheriff surely could not be wrong in this matter, Tom Doughty spilled the rest of what he knew. "They're headed down to Chattanooga, Sheriff. At least that's where I think they're going—planning on catching the trains to go out West. I recall one of them boys mentioning Virginia City. Said they were going to hunt for gold in Nevada's Virginia City."

Sheriff Posey could not conceal the smug look on his face, and his head nodded knowingly up and down as he listened to this new, vital intelligence. Finally, he had picked up the escapee's trail! Reinvigorated and reassured now of the killer's intentions, he left Doughty's with his mind racing and calculating the next pursuit tactics. Most definitely, a trip out west to Nevada was in the sheriff's considerations.

# Chapter 4

## Alias Mr. Hipps and Mr. Woody

It was back-breaking drudgery, but the young mountaineers kept their heads up and their backs bent to the work. They had hired themselves out to a wood-supply contractor and were unloading cordwood from mule-drawn drays and stacking it on the Memphis levee. Several large steamboats were landed at the low side of the sloping levee, where the waters of the mighty Mississippi River lapped. Long gangplanks joining the vessels with the expansive stone-paved landing area were busy with men—Negro and white, but mostly Negro—treading back and forth from ship to shore and vice versa, toting and pushing and pulling valuable cargos and supplies.

The two fugitives were absolutely lost amidst the masses of horse-pulled drays and draymen, mule-pulling teams, rough-looking roustabouts—either working or trying to look busy, hand carts and trucks, cotton bales covered in ice, sacks of cotton seed, barrels of pork, dozens of brand-new wagon wheels, great piles of unseasoned lumber, stock animals, and other such cargos as one would expect to encounter on a bustling Mississippi River steamboat landing.

As soon as August and Joseph finished unloading the drays, they joined a parade of roustabouts carrying as much fuel wood onto the riverboat's main deck as there was room to put it. In a very short time, this same load of wood would fuel combustions within the ship's several boilers, producing steam and powering the giant paddle wheels that drove the huge river-going vessel. It was mighty hard and dirty work, carrying the heavy cordwood, and the boys labored briskly with their small crew to get the job done. But the boat's firemen and engineer cursed and jawed at their every move, even finding fault when they took a breather now and again. One especially loud stoker slouching nearby tried to prod them out of a restive break.

"Ain't goin' to git them holds filled up dogging it like that, boys. The captain aims to be underway in lesser than an hour, I hear tell. Better get yer asses moving and try to keep up with them blackies."

The engineer, who was inspecting the goings-on, spat out a glob of brown tobacco drool onto the water's surface and chimed in, "He ain't shitting you nary none, men. I aim to be getting up a head of steam right short-like, as per the pilot's orders. He says he don't like the looks of the water stage and is a'feared he won't be able to pass over the sandbar 'bove the city a ways. So if'en you want to earn full pay, there's two more holds got to be filled up and quick. Get moving!"

As it turned out, it took another full hour and a half to charge the ship's holds with wood. When that time was up and with winter's darkness falling quickly over the landing, the boat's bell rang a departure signal. Steam escaping from a variety of relief valves and leaky fittings began hissing and whistling in the night air. Then the gigantic wheels on opposite sides of the ship began turning ever so slowly, churning the river water into splashing torrents.

The evening was cold, and the pair of exhausted fugitives sprawled on the freezing paving stones, gazing in wonderment at the departing craft. They watched the amazing steamboat—freshly supplied with firewood, cargos, and passengers—work its way into the powerful currents and begin steaming up the river for Cairo. Lanterns and candles lit up the ship's three decks, shining like a layered birthday cake. The boys watched these glowing, flickering lights grow dimmer and dimmer and then slowly disappear around a bend.

"Four more days, Joseph, and we'll ride one of them big boats out'a here. Can't wait to get to St. Louis. Can you?" As August talked, he began slowly raising himself off the ground and painfully stretching out his sore limbs.

"No, can't wait neither. This wooding work is 'bout to get me down, though. It's just our second day, and I'm hurting like hell!"

"You ain't the only one. Oww! I can't even straighten up good without hurting a sight. Come Saturday, Mr. Reinhart will owe us ten dollars each for helping him out. With what's left over from selling yer horse and this here twenty dollars we're goin' to make from wooding, then that ought to do it—be 'bout enough to get us to Montana. He'll be good for it, don't you reckon?"

"He seems like a decent sort of man. I don't doubt—hold on! Here he comes now!" Joseph warned, jumping to his feet and standing at attention as his boss, Will Rhinehart, approached them.

"Thanky, men, for your steady work. Didn't think you were going to get it all on the boat in time. Sure couldn't tolerate some other contractor taking our business with the Anchor Line," Rhinehart said, referring to the prominent shipping company. He reached out his hand and gave each of the new employees a stout shake. About fifty-some in age, he stood somewhere between Joseph and August in height. Although his dress and stature were those of a businessman, not a laborer, you would not know it by the way he treated his employees. Aloofness did not run in the man's blood, and he was very approachable and easy to talk to.

"The others have already gone home to get some rest. We've got those other two boats to supply tomorrow, you know. You two staying nearby somewhere?" Rhinehart knew nothing about these young men he had hired the day before, but they sure looked and acted like decent sorts. An unexpected, busy January schedule of boat landings had forced him to boost his team of roustabouts, so he had given the two white boys a job on the spot, hoping they could keep up with the Negroes.

"We've not got a place to stay," August answered without reservation or embarrassment. "Slept in a pile of cotton and straw behind the warehouse over there last night," he added, while pointing toward a plain brick building standing in the proximity of the towering customs house. He and Joseph looked at each other and then stared back at their boss, not knowing what he would allow about their poor circumstances and worried he might become suspicious of their criminal status.

"That so!" the surprised Rhinehart responded. Without hesitation or evident forethought, he put this proposition to his new employees, "Well, why don't you come home with me? Got a visitor's room at the front of the house. The heat's no good in it, but it's got a bedstead and tick, and we can scare up some blankets or quilts to keep you warm. What do you say, men?" Will Rhinehart liked the looks of these two, and he certainly was impressed with their efforts on his behalf over the past two days.

Joseph and August were flabbergasted at the unexpected generosity of their employer. They glanced at each other with half-open mouths and then back to Rhinehart. Joseph was still unsure whether they should take up the offer but went ahead and asked, "That sure is mighty nice of you, sir, but—but are you sure you can take us on?"

"Wouldn't have asked if I wasn't, son. Come on, both of you. Hop up in the wagon, and let's go see what they've got cooked up for us tonight."

The entire Rhinehart family was in the parlor basking in the heat from the yawning fireplace, when Will and his two young employees walked in on them. At once, all eyes were drawn to the strangers. Standing bareheaded side-by-side, holding floppy felt hats in their hands, Joseph and August still carried dirt from the levees on their heavy winter clothes. They stared in turn from Mrs. Rhinehart, to the two teenage sons, and then to the most beautiful female human being either one had ever admired—at least in some time.

They were utterly gawking at her, spellbound and besotted with the most foolish thoughts in their heads and looks on their faces. As Rhinehart made the introductions, first his wife and then his twenty-year-old daughter, Eugenia, the most amazing thing transpired. She smiled at the two young men who were sweat-stained and bedraggled after their hard day's work. Why, she even seemed to show a semblance of interest in them. The young Rhinehart sons, however, acted either indifferent or bothered by the outsiders' intrusion. After all, these were not guests—anyone could see that. They were only dirty dock roustabouts, who their father had seen fit to bring into their home, for some inexplicable reason. So after quick nods of their heads in Joseph's and August's direction, one quickly buried his head in a book, and the other resumed a whittling project.

"Where you fellows from?" Eugenia asked politely to break the ice.

The boys talked on top of each other trying to impress her. "North Carolina," Joseph allowed.

Before his buddy could say more, August blurted out, "In the mountains, miss—we're from the mountain part."

"Well, I haven't been that far east yet," she added, while glancing toward her father and mother, then to August and lastly at Joseph. She was enamored from the start with this tall, blond stranger. *Wonder what he's like,* she mused to herself before going on, "But Father has promised to take me to New York, as soon as the great bridge is opened. We'll walk across it at night and gaze upon the city, all lit up by electricity lights. They say the buildings rise so high that your ears pop from simply walking up the flights of stairs. We're still going there, aren't we, Father?"

It was easy to sense Rhinehart's discomfort, as he squirmed and wiggled and groped for a reasonable comeback to his daughter's pointed query. He searched his brain for the right response—one that would not let her down or commit him to more than was possible to deliver. Finally, he responded, "Yes, yes, dear—just as soon as the Roebling bridge is opened, we'll try to go there. Or I still say, you should just travel up to St. Louis with me one of these days and see that Eads iron structure spanning the Mississippi. Can't get much grander than that, and I do believe your curiosity would be satisfied. They say it's one of the wonders of the world. Truly, it is!"

"Ah, ah, ah, Father! You're not going to back out on us again. We're traveling to New York, and you might as well set your mind to it," Eugenia replied determinedly and not about to let her father off the hook. Just then, a Negro male servant entered the room and announced, in an unusually deep voice, that the evening's dinner was ready to be served. Neither of the guests had eaten much of anything the entire day, and the tantalizing smells emanating from the adjoining room were creating rumblings inside their stomachs. Suddenly, before a startled Joseph knew what was happening, Eugenia pertly moved to his side, took hold of his arm, and proceeded to lead him toward the dining area, as the rest of the family and August followed them.

The Rhineharts became quite taken and impressed with the two young roustabouts who shared dinner with them that evening. The exceptions being, of course, the wood contractor's withdrawn sons, who were polite enough but continued to keep to themselves. Certainly, August and Joseph were enjoying this evening. They counted their blessings to be entertained in such a high manner by amiable hosts and a young lady whose beauty fascinated them to no end. Mr. Hipps and Mr. Woody—these were the aliases the fugitives had invented—ate their fills while enjoying the conversations immensely.

Mr. Hipps' curious speech was one of the early topics of discussion. August explained the Scotch-Irish origins of his dialect and how his and Joseph's families pioneered the remote mountain region of western North Carolina. But he was very careful to steer away from the mention of place names, like Haywood County or Forks of Pigeon or Pigeon River. The fewer details he revealed to his hosts, the less they would be able to tie him back to his criminal past—or to Sheriff Posey.

For some reason that Mr. Woody—or Joseph—could not adequately explain, he spoke with a far less "mountain" dialect than his friend. Left unsaid was the fact that both he and August were well-educated, having received their primary schooling at small local schoolhouses and later graduating from a more advanced academy in Waynesville. Joseph told Eugenia and her parents that he and August were working their way to Nevada, where they wanted to try their hands at gold mining, of all things. He admitted to their total lack of mining experience and to the fact that it was a risky venture; but it was a challenge, he explained, that both of them were determined to give a try.

"So in a week or so, you boys will be departing for St. Louis?" Rhinehart asked in bafflement.

August thought he had better explain this delicate matter to his boss, "Yes sir, that's 'bout the size of it. We figure that the twenty dollars you're going to owe us and what we already have in our pockets will be enough to get us to Virginia City—where we're headed."

"Well, I didn't realize that you were going to be with me for such a short time. Fact, I was hoping I might come to depend on you two boys. Some of those niggers of mine are strong and can cut and handle timber better than most, but damn it to hell, they're not dependable. I've lost a ton of business on account of their drunken sprees. And it looks like I won't be able to count on you two, either." Will Rhinehart's disappointment was self-evident, and Joseph tried to make amends for any communication failures on his or August's part.

"We're awful sorry, Mr. Rhinehart. Guess we didn't figure on you needing us longer than this week's time. If it's putting you in much of a bind, then we might be able to stay on longer and help you out. I reckon there'll still be gold out West for us to discover, and we sure wouldn't want to let you down or anything." Finishing up, Joseph looked expectantly at August, "That not right, August?"

Well, Hipps—or Hargrove—was trying his best to keep up. The sudden attention thrown his way surprised him somewhat, but he gathered his wits about him and responded, "Yep, reckon we can sure 'nough stay on longer if you're needing us to, Mr. Rhinehart. All you have to do is say the word, and we'll keep on wooding those big steamboats for you." August's glance shifted from his boss to Joseph, where he saw a pleased look flushing across his friend's face.

Will Rhinehart was not the only Rhinehart that wanted the youthful roustabouts to remain in Memphis longer. "Oh, Joseph, it would be so good if you and August could delay your departure for the West. Stay with us here while you work for Father, and then we can get to know you better," Eugenia reasoned. Not only was Joseph smitten by the young hostess, but she had taken to him as well, it seemed. Beauty and innate forces were at work here. The two young people were drawn to each other with a natural curiosity and attraction meant to ensure the survival of the human species.

Interaction at the dinner table that night had definitely spawned the possibility of a closer relationship. Eugenia had been pleasantly pleased—as had Mr. and Mrs. Rhinehart—with Joseph's and August's display of gentlemanly comportment and social manners, as well as their obvious high intellects. And unquestionably, she had been impressed with the exceedingly tall, blond, and handsome Joseph Woody—or Edmunston, that is.

His entire life, Joseph had heard people carry on about how his grandmother, Julia, had been the most beautiful belle in the Pigeon Valley. With the exception of hair color, Eugenia reminded Joseph of his grandmother—so much so, that he was beginning to feel homesick pangs. Taller than most girls with whom he was acquainted, Eugenia's bodily curves and proportions stacked and meshed so delightfully as to increase his pulse rate and set astir the hormones and adrenalin inside him. The color of her hair, worn loosely piled atop her head with only a hint of bangs, matched the dark brown stain of a walnut. Truly, she was the picture of perfection, sitting straight and proper in her long, black satin dress directly across the table from him and August.

The Rhinehearts' home was situated in a newly sprouted suburb of Memphis, where other upper middle-class families were gravitating. There was nothing grandiose about the house atall. But it was spacious and filled with stylish furniture and adorned with tasteful wallpaper, artwork, and other finery. Between mouth-filling bites of the beef stew and boiled potatoes that had been served, August was impressed enough with the quarters to remark to his hosts, "If you don't mind my saying so, I believe this is the most beautiful house I've ever had the pleasure to dine in."

"Oh, Mr. Hipps, you're so kind. We've only been in the house for a little less than five years. It's quite a bit more house than our old one, too," responded Mrs. Rhinehart, as she looked to her husband and back to the guests. She then went on to explain how her husband's business had prospered over the past ten years, and within a few minutes, the two guests reckoned they knew quite a bit more about their boss than they ever expected to know.

Rhinehart had remained mostly quiet and thoughtful, while his wife was carrying on the discourse about the house and his business. He liked these two hard-working boys, and figured he could not afford to let them get away. So he continued to press them. "Sure could use you boys for the next month. If the river stays ice-free and we can continue to cut and haul wood over those bad country roads, we've got a hefty schedule lined up. That front room is yours to use until you decide you have to go. How's that sound then? What do you say?"

The highlanders cut swift glances toward one another and seemed to come to the same conclusion—they ought to help this man who was being so kind and generous to them. "Don't reckon we're in that big a hurry, sir. If you need us, then we'll stay on," Joseph replied, while immediately sensing Rhinehart's appreciation and seeing the contentment in Eugenia's face. August Hipps—if anyone noticed—was outwardly expressionless. But pangs of doubt and fear permeated his insides—fears of being captured by Sheriff Posey. He had not counted on being waylaid at Memphis for an extended period. *Hopefully, we're not making a big mistake,* he worried, while watching Eugenia and Joseph goggling at each other. *Now what's he got that I ain't?* he fumed.

# Chapter 5

## Keeping on Getting It

Two weeks had passed since that initial dinner engagement with the Rhineharts. In that time, the weather had turned bitter cold, and snow and ice covered large expanses of the steamboat levee. But the river had not completely frozen over and remained navigable, thus ensuring steady work for August and Joseph. Day after day, they toiled among the rabble of the landing area—the roustabouts, steamboat men, merchants, contractors, draymen, passengers, loiterers, and pathetic vagrants. Winter's cold bite seemed to have no effect on this shipping industry, with precious cargos always in a constant state of motion between ships and shore. The fugitive highlanders had by now adjusted uncomfortably into the hierarchical scheme of things, where they fit right in at the bottom of the ladder and pay scale.

Although the dreadful hard work was tolerable for the most part, it became more and more difficult for them to ignore the constant hounding and insults thrown their way, usually by riverboat employees and a few slackers prone to bullying ways. In particular, a couple of rough warehousemen, who frequented the landing every day, had singled out Joseph as an object of their taunts and ridicule. Whether it was because of his unusual good looks or his gangling manner, Joseph did not rightly know why these crude men picked on him so. But every day, the two roughnecks heckled him with the meanest words and hateful scorn imaginable. They were out of control, and Joseph had tolerated about as much of their rude behavior as he was going to.

A favored method of loading fuel wood onto the big riverboats was to employ a wheeled handcart, as Joseph and August were doing on this day. Their tandem-team approach had Joseph holding onto and pulling the cart handles, while backing precariously across the plank stage bridging the gap between the riverboat and levee. At the same time, August pushed and steadied the heavy load while guiding his buddy. However, August was not the only one who was offering instructions today. One of the warehousemen who had been bedeviling Joseph on a daily basis happened to be loafing onboard the boat the boys were loading, and he was showing his colors.

"That's the way, men. Easy does it. Better not drop a stick of that firewood, mind you. Moving a bit slow, ain't you? Them niggers move a sight faster than you two!" As the warehouseman gouged them, cackles of laughter arose from a fireman and the engineer standing nearby. Then, believe it or not, just as Joseph was laboring hard to pull the load of wood up the landing stage and onto the boat's deck, this same warehouseman purposely stuck out his foot and tripped him. Instantly, the blond lad fell hard and awkwardly onto the deck, while the cart with its load of wood spilled over into the Mississippi River. August looked on in disbelief, as the many bystanders roared with laughter at this bout of misfortune that had suddenly become the wooders'.

Needless to say, Joseph was absolutely furious. In no time, he was on his feet and in the warehouseman's face, challenging him, "You tripped me on purpose! Didn't you? What did you go and do that for?"

The warehouseman, much older than Joseph and a good deal stouter, wiped the grin off his face and snarled back, "What you mean, trip you? I didn't trip you up, towhead. It's them big feet of your'en. You must have tripped over them big feet!" Another round of laughter ensued from the growing crowd of onlookers.

"You did, too! I know you did! I've had enough of your meanness! You're a damn bully! That's all you are—a damned bully! Put 'em up!" It was an instinctive challenge, and before even realizing what he was doing, Joseph held his fists up in a fighting posture. "Come on—get 'em up, bully!"

The warehouseman may have been a bully, but he was no coward. "Okay, how's this towhead? What you going to do about it?" goaded the roughneck, as he drew up his own fists to protect himself and began moving his head from side to side in the manner of an experienced pugilist. But at that moment, a couple of men barged in between the brawlers. It was the captain and one of his pilots, and they were not about to allow a physical altercation on their steamboat. "Hold up, men! Hold up right now! No fighting allowed on my ship. Take this dispute elsewhere—hear!"

Joseph's and the warehouseman's intentions and hard looks at one another did not ebb a whit. Nodding their heads slowly and menacingly, they seemed to understand what to do next and began making their way to shore to continue this bad business. August was distraught with fear for Joseph. Although the warehouseman was not nearly as tall, he was obviously stronger and likely much more experienced in bare-fisted brawling.

A host of bystanders followed the combatants off the boat to where a large gathering was already forming. Suddenly, August spotted the second warehouseman who had been badgering them relentlessly. This man sidled up next to the one facing off with Joseph and appeared to be offering his support. When the second man began to slowly circle around Joseph, August jumped in front of him and gave him a stiff shove. "You stay out of this, you son-of-a-bitch! It ain't your fight. If you want to have a go at somebody, here I am!" This man was about the same age as the other, but nowhere near as strong. After looking August over real good, the warehouseman could tell right off he was outmatched in physical strength—and probably mental fierceness as well.

"I ain't part of this show, Red! Let 'em fight then," the man replied hatefully, as he settled down a little and became much less threatening.

"Okay, you stay back away from 'em. If you interfere, you'll have me to deal with!" August was dead serious. Turning back to see what Joseph was up to, he called out a helpful caution, "Careful, Joseph! He acts like he's done this before!" Joseph had only been in a couple of scrapes, neither one being very serious. But his father, a veteran of the Civil War, had been involved in a good many fist fights and free-for-alls. Rufus had taught his son how to defend himself, and this coaching was about to be put into practice.

The warehouseman continued to constantly move his head and circle around his young opponent, looking for an opening or opportunity to launch a punch. Joseph nervously held his arms and hands in front of his face, just waiting to counter any attacks. Then—*pop, pop!* In quick succession, the warehouseman's left jabs struck Joseph hard in the face. He was addled by the blows and retaliated by launching a wild right haymaker of his own. It missed the target entirely!

*Pow!* Another left jab stung Joseph, and then came a hard right punch—POW! It knocked him completely down onto the stone pavers. He was shocked and momentarily dazed—it had all been so sudden! His opponent did indeed know how to fight. *I've got myself into a real fix this time,* Joseph worried, as he struggled on the hard ground to regain his senses and defend himself against his opponent's kicking.

"Get up, Joseph! Get up!" August encouraged, his support being muffled by the chants from the bloodthirsty crowd.

The rabble relentlessly pulled for Joseph's whipping, chanting in unison, "Finish him! Finish him off!"

August cast an alert eye toward the second warehouse bully to be sure he was keeping his distance and, as he did so, he happened to spy Will Rhinehart pulling up in a wagon. "Damn!" August cursed at no one in particular.

Joseph was still striving to get up, while the vile antagonist kicked him with his boot, trying to land a punishing and decisive blow. Once, twice, three times, he rared back his leg and booted at the young man's head, savagely attempting to crush it. He held no reservations about the lethal consequences. Joseph was down, but he was not out of it by any means. On the third kicking attempt, he grabbed the warehouseman's leg and latched onto it like a bulldog, twisting and pushing and pulling the muscular limb, all the time ignoring the pounding blows raining down on his head and body.

While Joseph battled to topple the warehouseman, he suddenly heard August cry out loudly, "Watch out, Joseph! Watch him—he's got a knife!" Sure enough, the man had unsheathed a large bowie knife from under his belt. Hopping on his one free leg, he struggled to contort himself into a position where he could plunge the dangerous weapon deep into Joseph's body—anywhere. But before he could do so, the youthful roustabout caught hold of the warehouseman's other leg and yanked both of them out from under him. The man crashed so violently onto the rock-paved levee that his fearsome weapon was knocked loose from his grip. Then, before the onlookers could utter moans of disappointment, the two combatants were rolling around on the ground in each other's brutish clutches.

Both of them were gouging and biting in efforts to wound the other. Joseph suffered a painful chomp to his ear, and he feared he might have lost it. They wrestled and tumbled over the ground, fighting like two wild animals locked in mortal combat. After only a minute or so of such viciousness, the two fighters became utterly exhausted—the warehouseman more so than Joseph. Somehow, Joseph managed to cock his long arm back and fire a powerful fist punch directly into the man's face. *POW!*

It was an extremely effective blow, and he felt the man's resistance melt away. *Now or never,* the lad figured, and with lightning bolt swiftness, Joseph grasped the warehouseman's bald head with both hands and slammed it against the hard stone paving, time and time again. *Slam, slam, slam.* He kept doing it until the man's limp, unconscious body moved no more.

The end of the brutal affair came so suddenly that the spectators were left with their mouths gaping open in a strange silence. But when Joseph rose to his feet and stretched out to his full height, the crowd came to life again, hooting and hollering for their new champion. He could not give a damn for this fickle crowd's show of appreciation, as he stepped over toward his friend.

During the latter part of the fray, August had been forced to tackle the other warehouseman, when at the last minute the man made a move to intervene. Joseph found his buddy still sitting on top of the captive, who was sporting a bloody nose. Slowly, August got up off the man and let him go check on his unconscious cohort.

"Well, I guess you took care of that one, didn't you, Joseph!" August said proudly.

"Yea—well, maybe now those two will stop their foolery. We'll see," Joseph replied. "Hopefully, he's not dead. We don't need another killing to account for. One's bad...," and then from behind him, all of a sudden, he felt a hand placed on his shoulder. Turning in surprise to see who it was, he saw his concerned boss, Will Rhinehart, looking worriedly at him.

"Are you okay, son?" Will asked him.

"Yes sir. I reckon I am. I didn't start the fight, Mr. Rhinehart. That bully tripped me on purpose and made us spill the whole cart of wood in the river. Didn't he, August?" Joseph was awful worried that Rhinehart might think he was a troublemaker or—worse still—fire him.

"That's right, sir! Those men are bullies, and for some reason they've had it in for us. Been calling us names and such."

"Don't you worry now, boys. I know those two, and they're no good—a real bad sort. But you're sure you're all right, Joseph? I think I'll take you home and let the women folk look after you for the rest of the day. That ear sure looks pretty messy, and I swear your face is getting blacker as I talk to you here. What do you say?"

Well, what else could Joseph say? Given a choice between Eugenia's company and that of August and the rough levee roustabouts, he knew which he preferred. "Appreciate it, sir. Guess I could use a little female attention!"

Ever since the wounded warrior had trudged into the Rhineharts' house, he had received constant attention—and love, one might say. Mrs. Rhinehart and Eugenia bathed Joseph with soapy water, treated the several facial cuts, smothered his skinned knees and elbows with an iodine solution, placed a gauze wrap over his ear, and promptly put him to bed. The ear looked so bad that the doctor was sent for. Eugenia lodged herself at Joseph's bedside for the rest of the evening, caring for his every need and lavishing attention that few patients receive—or deserve.

"Oh, Joseph, what am I going to do with you? I let you out of my sight for only a brief moment, and see what happens?" Eugenia had been highly distressed to receive her new beau in such poor shape, especially when she learned he had been involved in a savage brawl. Over the previous two weeks, they had become quite close and enamored with each other. Although their acquaintance was brief, their affection had grown strong. It was so strong, that Eugenia had already professed her devotion for the handsome house guest.

Joseph truly believed he had stumbled upon the only person in the world who could make him happy. Certainly, they both were still young—Joseph having just celebrated his nineteenth birthday, and Eugenia being a year older—but they were not too young to love. That is what they both felt for one another—love. They were sure of it. So sure were they that discussions about sharing a life together had already begun.

Besides, what else did Joseph have to look forward to? His involvement in the jailbreak episode had doomed any real chances he had for a normal life. That's what he had come to believe, anyhow, while fleeing with his partner, the escaped criminal known as August Hargrove—or Hipps—out of the North Carolina mountains. He was doomed for all eternity—or at least the rest of his life—to toil on the steamboat levees or bury himself in dark underground holes hunting for elusive veins of gold or silver in Montana. That's what he had believed was in store for him, until that fateful evening when he first gazed upon the beautiful face of his boss's daughter.

Now it all made perfect sense to Joseph. He would ask Will Rhinehart for Eugenia's hand in marriage one day. Surely, the astute businessman would have no qualms with taking him on as a son-in-law, and who knows, maybe one day he could even see fit to offer Joseph other opportunities in his wood-supply company. Once Joseph had the father's unreserved approval, he could pop the delicate question to Eugenia, real easy-like. He had no real doubts about her feelings toward him, or whether she would take him as a husband—no doubts atall.

But there was one thing related to all this romantic business of his that definitely perturbed him. Seeking Mr. Rhinehart's sanctioning and, subsequently, asking for Eugenia's lovely hand in marriage were easy matters to deal with—pieces of cake—compared to this other thing that bothered him so. What about August and the plans they had made together? How was he going to break the news to August?

"Marry her! You're going to get married?" August sought clarity because he did not believe the words he thought he had just heard.

"That's what I said! I'm going to marry her! It's already been decided, August. Eugenia already said she'll have me." Joseph spoke so determinedly that August could not help but understand his buddy. But his reaction was not at all what Joseph had feared. August took off the worn leather gloves he was wearing, stepped over next to the wood-filled dray where Joseph stood, spread his arms out wide, like the wings of an eagle in flight, and then wrapped Joseph up in a huge bear hug.

"Damn it to hell, congratulations, feller! I couldn't be happier for anyone!" August was genuinely pleased, and it showed. When they broke their embrace, Joseph could see that his friend's smiling face was glistening with tears, and he grabbed August, and they hugged again.

"Thanks, August! I was hoping you would understand and not be too aggravated at me for breaking my promise to you." Directly, they broke from hugging and backed off to look at each other. "I told you I was going to Montana with you, and here I am up and getting myself married in Memphis—I hope. I meant to go! I did! I promise you, I did, August!"

August wiped his face with one hand, dried the same hand on his pants leg, removed his felt hat and slapped it against his thigh a couple of times, replaced the hat on his crop of reddish hair, and then replied to his best buddy of all time, "I know you meant to keep your promise, Joseph. Ain't no doubts 'bout that, far as I'm concerned. I'm happy for you! Eugenia's a catch, she sure 'nough is. I don't blame you one bit. If I could ever find me a girl like her, I'd latch on to her, too. Believe me, I would!"

They carried on like this for a few minutes more, before rejoining the team of roustabouts working in the freezing weather to load another steaming riverboat. For the rest of the day, August pondered his friend's good news and the implications. It was now late February, going on two months since their arrival in Memphis. August had been nervous all along about the extended stay, but he had remained in the employ of Rhinehart to help the contractor out, and, also, because he knew Joseph was highly satisfied with his current prospects. There were no doubts in his mind that Sheriff Buford Posey had not forgotten him. Knowing the sheriff's determination to see him hanged, August believed no stone would be left unturned in the sheriff's pursuit to apprehend him again. He knew exactly what he must do.

August figured Joseph could take care of himself for sure, as evidenced by the fist fight with the warehouseman and his new situation with Eugenia Rhinehart. As long as his friend kept the alias 'Woody' and separated himself from August, he could easily lose himself in Memphis and never be discovered. August realized that he must get away from Joseph and allow his friend to build a new and happy life for himself here. Convinced there were no other reasonable options, he told himself, *I've got to keep on getting it and put as much distance between myself and Joseph as I can. Got to find Montana and my kinfolk.* And very soon, that is what August found himself doing—keeping on getting it.

# Chapter 6

## A Swedish Beauty

Somewhere on the Mississippi River, between Cairo, Illinois, and St. Louis, Missouri, the riverboat plowed ahead through strong currents and growing sheets of ice. August Hargrove sat uncomfortably and discreetly at a small table in the corner of the vessel's expansive saloon, which stretched almost two hundred feet in length. He was onboard the northbound *City of Cairo*—one of the Anchor Line Company's workhorse steamboats—and was busy drafting a letter to his family. Undoubtedly, the Hargroves were worried sick about his welfare and whereabouts.

It was after midnight, and the lady passengers were conspicuously absent among the throng of well-dressed men occupying the grand carpeted space where August was writing. Some of these first-class passengers occasionally cast a disparaging eye in the direction of the coarse-looking individual scribbling away in the dark corner. They realized that this interloper was obviously a deck passenger and therefore out-of-bounds in the cabin deck's saloon. Little did they suspect, the sorry-looking young man was an escaped prisoner on the run, trying to write a long overdue missive to his parents.

Using scavenged pencil and paper, August was actually in the process of scratching out two notes—one to Joseph's grandfather, Basil Edmunston, and the other to his own dear mother and father. Concerned that Sheriff Posey could have coerced the postmaster at Pigeon River to monitor the incoming mail to his father, and possibly even that addressed to Joseph's father, August had decided to mail his letter to Basil instead. He fully realized he was not supposed to be up on the cabin deck, so he hurried to eke out these painful notes.

> March 2$^{nd}$, 1884
> Dear Mr. Edmunston,
>     This is August H. writing to you. I used that name Hipps to post this letter in order to conceal myself from the law who are bound to be after me, especially the Cherokee sheriff. Don't be worried about _____. He has gone to calling himself Woody. If you have not heard from him, he is doing just fine and has found himself a real nice girl named Eugenia. He got himself a paying job too. Hope you and everyone else at the Forks are doing fine and if you don't mind too much, please pass along the other note I enclosed to my mother and father. I would appreciate it very much.
>
> Thankfully yours,
> August

Folded neatly and meant to be contained in the same envelope, the other message he wrote was to his parents, Harriet and Hack.

> March 2$^{nd}$, 1884
> Dear Folks,
>     Hope you have not been worried much about me. No need to. I'm about as well as could be expected given the situation I got myself into. I got to ride on a train and am on a big steamboat now writing this letter. Have left _____ behind where he is fine. He found himself a pretty girl.
>     If you are wondering why I did it, I just figured I had to. They were going to hang me for sure which was not right. I'm an innocent man. That sheriff had it in for me and there was no way I was not going to be hanged. So I broke out of that jailhouse and _____ helped me.
>     Please don't worry yourselves anymore over me. I'm heading out west to see our kinfolk in _____. Don't know if I will ever be able to come

back to the mountains and be with you but you can be sure of one thing. I'll be thinking of all of you. I love you all very much. I surely do.

Love always,
August

August did his best to leave out incriminating details, such as names and his Montana destination—just in case the letters fell into the wrong hands. As he was finishing up and tucking the envelope into his coat pocket, one of the cabin passengers sauntered over toward him. The man was tall and well into his forties, maybe even fifties, August reckoned. He was decked out in a dark top hat, white dress shirt closed at the top with a stringy red tie, and brown dress coat and trousers. Light given off by kerosene lamp fixtures glimmered off his highly polished black shoes. Indeed, the mustachioed gentleman was impressive-looking, and August could not fathom why the man might want to talk to him.

"Hello, sir! Henrik Stenson here, and who might you be?" The gentleman spoke with a noticeable accent, as he removed his hat and stuck out his hand toward August.

August quickly jumped up and out of the chair he was sitting in, took off his floppy hat, and shook the man's hand stoutly. "August—August Hipps, sir. Pleasure to meet you." August, who was dumbfounded and unsure of the man's intentions, anxiously awaited the next words.

"No, son, the pleasure is all mine, I can assure you. I've been watching you, ever since you came in and sat down here in this corner. Believe I've seen you before—down below. You would be a deck passenger, I presume?" Although the man was getting a mite personal, he maintained a curious smile on his face and a pleasant air about him.

*Now why in the hell does he want to know that?* August worried to himself. "That's right, Mr. Stenson. I'm booked as a deck passenger." For some reason, August felt inclined to give the man even more personal information. "But Captain's letting me help wood the boilers and clean-up manure after the stock to reduce my fare."

"I see! That's a good thing to do—an excellent thing." Stenson nodded his head up and down as he said this, all the time smiling and looking August over real good, as if sizing him up. The boy had a good honest look about him. From all outward appearances, anyway, the young man should be able to stand his own in a confrontational situation. "Going all the way to St. Louis?"

*What? Now why in damnation would he want to know that for?* August fretted, before answering, "Yes sir." Again, perhaps from nervousness, August gave out more detailed information than was called for, "Then, I'm going to catch a train to Omaha—in Nebraska—and see if I can find a way to go out West toward Montana on the Union Pacific."

The stranger hesitated for a second or two before responding, "That so! We're going—that is, my wife and daughter and I are going to California, by way of Omaha and the U.P." Not knowing where this conversation was leading, August just kept quiet and tried to show his interest. "Saw you writing before, I believe. Are you educated, son?"

*The inquisition continues,* August mused before answering, "That's right, Mr. Stenson. I've been schooled most of my life, I reckon—as far back as I can remember."

"Hmm," Stenson uttered, sensing this might just be the man he needed. "Son, I've been looking for someone—it's a very long way to California, and I desire to hire a man that can assist us and offer protection against undesirables and dishonest people we may encounter in route." The Swedish immigrant had taken notice right away of the strawberry-haired youth and his obvious physical stoutness. The fact that he was also literate impressed him enough to conclude this young Hipps man could replace his valet, who had suddenly taken sick and was left behind in a Cairo hospital bed. The unfortunate servant had apparently come down with cholera—not an uncommon disease along the river corridor, albeit more usual in the summertime.

A gentleman sitting at a card table across the big room hollered out above the din, "Stenson, are you in?"

Henrik turned and waved the man off, "No, give me a few minutes over here," and then he looked back at August and continued, "As I was saying, Mr. Hipps, I'm looking for someone to accompany us to California. I hold a majority ownership in a mining venture in Skidaddle, near the Death Valley. We'll make our home in Los Angeles, and I plan to travel back and forth to Skidaddle to manage the affairs of the mine. There's not much going on there at this time, I'm afraid." Stenson paused to gather his thoughts before outright asking, "So, what do you think? If you're not in too big of a rush to get to Montana, would you like to work for me and escort my family to Los Angeles?"

*Rush? There's no rush atall to get to Montana,* August thought. Besides, here it was the dead of winter, when this big steamboat can barely navigate the Mississippi River ice flows. *What would Montana be like now—the North Pole?* August liked this man, Stenson. He had been pleasant and polite. And, to tell the truth, August was partial to the idea of heading to California, so he could have a look. Without much more hesitation than it took to think these thoughts, he replied, "That's mighty good of you to offer me the opportunity, sir. You just want me to accompany you and your family to California—carry your bags, keep the roughnecks away, and things like that? Is that about the size of it?"

"That's correct, Mr. Hipps. There won't be any hard work associated with the job. But there will be responsibility, and, of course, your loyalty and courteous behavior will be expected. Think you are up to the task, young man?"

"Yes sir! I'm up for it—sure am! If we can just settle up on the wages, I'm ready to start whenever you are." August's anxiousness showed, which pleased Stenson. The two of them agreed on a salary that was much higher than August could have expected—or imagined. Once that was settled, they agreed on a meeting time the next morning for the new security guard-slash-valet to assume his responsibilities. Then, the employer rejoined his card game, and his new employee walked out of the saloon's aft door, feeling much better about himself than when he had skulked in.

August had slept that night on the foul-smelling main deck, buried in a cramped crevice between a cotton bale and some wood crates. This bright cold morning found him huffing and puffing and sawing cordwood into smaller pieces. The fireman had allowed that the lesser-sized chunks were not only easier to handle and chuck into the firebox, but they burned much better too. Sweating profusely while working alone in a small confined area, August was lost in his thoughts and oblivious to the time of day. Then, out of the blue, he was jarred back to the real world by someone calling out his name.

"Mr. Hipps! Mr. Hipps!"

Turning quickly, he saw that it was Mr. Stenson yelling out to him. His new boss was trying to be heard over the pronounced mechanical and splashing noises of the starboard paddlewheel. *Damn, eleven o'clock already!* August cussed himself, as he let go of the saw and moved toward Stenson and the two well-dressed ladies at his side. Brushing himself off with both hands, he started to shake his head back and forth and apologize, "Sorry, Mr. Stenson! Plum lost track of the time. I told them I'd be working up until eleven o'clock. Just wanted to finish this last load was all." Not only was August still breathing hard, but he was nervous, and it showed.

During the awkward explanation of his forgetfulness, he looked from his new benefactor to the tall elegant woman next to him and then to—to the most ravishing blonde girl he had ever seen. *She must be about my age*, he figured, *or maybe a tad older*. The girl was indeed so beautiful that the young steamboat wooder was taken aback, and he blushed and stammered out, "Hello there."

"Hello," the beauty replied politely, while her blue eyes locked on the sturdy young man in front of her. His coarse clothes were filthy, and an old floppy felt hat covered his head and almost hid his face. But she could make out enough to be favorably impressed with the ruffian—his gay brown eyes and reddish hair showing from under the hat's brim. It was an honest, kind face she looked at, and she liked it.

Henrik Stenson graciously accepted August's apology, "No problem, Mr. Hipps! We've got plenty of time between now and this evening when we reach St. Louis for you to get started. Now, let me introduce you to the fairer side of the family." Twisting to face the ladies, Stenson announced, "This is my wife, Pernilla, and my daughter, Hanna." They both curtsied in a friendly way, while August smiled and started to stick out his hand to shake theirs, before thinking better and pulling it back hurriedly.

"Real pleased to meet you both—ma'am—miss," offered August as he looked from mother to daughter. "Sorry 'bout the way I look. I'll be a sight better once I get cleaned up. I promise I will." August was clueless about what he should say to them, as clearly demonstrated by this utterance.

Mrs. Stenson tried to put him at ease, "I'm sure you will, Mr. Hipps. Please, don't worry about the way you look. In Sweden, where we're from, men who do strenuous labor like you've been doing are looked up to. There's no need to be embarrassed, I can assure you."

"You look fine, sir, just the way you are. But might you take your hat off so we can see you?" Hanna asked as she and her parents chuckled.

"No problem, miss. Sorry 'bout that," and August immediately reached up, removed the hat, slapped it against his leg, and let the Stenson women look him over real good from head to toe.

"Now that's better, Mr. Hipps. We can see you have potential now," came Hanna's joking assessment. Her comment was met with laughs from both Mr. and Mrs. Stenson. Although August laughed along with them, he was not quite sure whether the joking was good-natured or derisive. Still, he managed to take the comments in good form.

"No, I don't reckon I'm much to look at, miss, but you can trust me. That you sure 'nough can." Although such self-deprecating nonsense might serve him well in some instances, such as this one, August certainly did not mean it—or believe it. He felt proud, and rightly so, of his above-average good looks, and knew he was stronger and more athletic than most. Also, he had the Hargroves' good common sense and his mother's keen Yankee intellect. Strangers like these Swedes—or anyone else outside of the Carolina highlands—might not take his words seriously, since they were spoken with such a curious accent and unfamiliar dialect. But August was a sincere man— deep down—and usually spoke with insight and specific purpose in his own jovial mountaineer manner. Nonetheless, to most people not raised in the southern Appalachian Mountains, he still sounded like an oafish hillbilly.

"You can even trust me enough to call me by my given name, if you don't mind. August—you can all call me August." That alias of his—Mr. Hipps—did not seem natural atall. He was not used to it yet, and it made him think of Sheriff Posey and the bad business in Cherokee County.

"Okay—August it is then," Hanna jumped in. "We're just about to have lunch in the saloon, August. Would you like to come and join us?"

Although it was a nice gesture, August knew he was not supposed to climb up to the cabin deck. His trespass the previous night had gone unheralded and unchallenged for some reason, but he felt uncomfortable taking the risk again. His new employers might be embarrassed if someone happened to take exception to his presence there, and create an untoward incident. "Oh, I'd better not, miss. I'm not allowed on the cabin deck."

However, Henrik Stenson would have none of that and intervened. "Don't worry, August! I spoke to the captain's mate and have already taken care of things. You're a cabin passenger now, and Hanna's right! Why don't you come up and share some food with us? We can all get to know you better. You and I can discuss your responsibilities and the things we'll need you to do for us. Sound okay with you?"

*Got a right good ring to it,* August thought. "Yes sir! Sounds good to me! Got me a real hankering for something good to eat." Seeing their puzzled looks, he hastily added, "I'm right hungry, sir."


For the rest of the afternoon and into the early dark hours of the evening, the *City of Cairo* steamed against the powerful Mississippi River current, plying its way through thin layers of ice toward St. Louis. August had eaten his fill at the delightful luncheon with the Stensons, and afterwards he and Henrik spent a couple of hours alone talking business.

"Be especially watchful, August, when we are in large groups," Stenson coached. "What comes to mind is the riverboat wharf where we will land, the railroad stations, at dining and hotel establishments, and the town streets. Those are the places where thieves and drifters congregate and are prone to prey on travelers. You should stay real close and watchful for us in those situations—and all of the time, actually. Understood?"

This was Stenson's first overland train trip to the western United States. Like most American citizens who lived east of the Mississippi River, stories of the Indian wars, Wild West mining and railroad boomtowns, and six-gun shootouts resonated within Stenson's mind. After immigrating to Pennsylvania at the beginning of the War Between the States, his timely investments in iron-ore mines and a steel mill had transformed him into a wealthy mogul. In fact, he was rich enough now to speculate in an undeveloped, unseen gold mine in California, while leaving his eastern enterprises in the hands of others to manage and operate. But he was understandably nervous about traveling through the West with Pernilla and Hanna. Thus, he had felt inclined to hire August to protect his family.

"You can count on me, Mr. Stenson. I'll stick real close to all of you and provide protection for you." Of course in saying this, August fully realized his charge included protecting Hanna too. That was a perk too good to be true in his estimation, and he intended on taking every opportunity to stay real close to her. Matter of fact, he got real close to Hanna not long after the meeting with her father wrapped up.

Hanna invited August to step outside of the saloon onto the promenade and take in some fresh air with her. Wrapped up in blankets and standing side by side, they leaned against the deck railing and peered over at the tree-lined icy banks of the river. She kicked off the banter by asking, "So you're a mountain man, are you?" That subject had been discussed at length during lunch, and August was surprised at the question.

"Sure am—from North Carolina." With difficulty he held back on giving her more substantive details.

"You're a long way from home, all by yourself. Do you know anyone in Montana?"

"Had a buddy with me, but he stayed on in Memphis. I decided to keep going. I've got kinfolk in Montana and aim to look them up." August was a little uncomfortable giving out this personal information, so he decided to try his hand at redirecting the exchange. "Hanna, I know it's not right to ask a girl how old she is, but I'd say we're near about the same age. You 'bout nineteen or twenty, are you?"

"Well, I'll say, Mr. Hipps, if you don't have a lot of gall. How can you be so presumptuous to make such an inquiry?" Hanna retorted with a stern piercing glance at the inquisitor. But she could only maintain the ruse for a few seconds, before bursting out in laughter. "Okay then, August, I'll humor you. I'm twenty-one. So does that make us close to the same age—you 'reckon?'"

*Well, I'll say! She's three years older than me,* August ciphered instantly. "We're the same age all right—twenty-one." *What's one more lie going to matter,* he thought. *At least she won't think I'm just a young'en.*

For almost an hour, they braved the cold weather and talked and laughed. Although August knew he was no match socially for Hanna, he fell for her just as hard as Joseph had fallen for Eugenia, if not harder. Every glance met by hers sent flutters of excitement vibrating throughout his entire being.

Interestingly, Hanna revealed to him she had been engaged once. However, six months ago, her betrothed had gotten cold feet, for some mindless reason, and had set sail for Europe a day before their wedding date. She was still not over this humiliating and heart-breaking experience, but August seemed a good soul with whom she could confide her innermost feelings. Besides, she was taking a liking to her new security guard. He was interesting and, well, she kind of liked him.

# Chapter 7

## FULL STEAM AHEAD

Forward progress on the riverboat *City of Cairo* had slowed dramatically in the past hour or so. Only twenty miles shy of St. Louis, near Chesley Island where the river narrowed substantially around an alluvial bar, ice nearly bridged the channel from bank to bank. The riverboat's pilot had been advised at Cairo that the river was freezing up, but he was gambling on making it to St. Louis first. Steaming at almost full power, the boat's massive-timbered bow crashed loudly through the ice, cutting a path for the giant paddlewheels to budge the craft through. But the farther north it travelled, the ice grew thicker and thicker, and the headway diminished proportionately.

Although it was almost midnight, most of the passengers were awake and making preparations for the landing and disembarkation at St. Louis. August and Mr. Stenson had joined the ladies in their cabin berth, and the party was chatting away, mostly about the increased noise from smashing through the ice and the noticeable decrease in the boat's speed.

"Don't worry, girls. We're almost there. Won't be long now," Henrik affirmed, trying to ease their tensions.

"Oh, dear, do you think we can make it before the boat breaks apart?" Mrs. Stenson fretted.

August thought he might be able to ease her distress. "Don't you worry, Mrs. Stenson. I had a chance to study how this boat's built when I was wooding and cleaning up after the stock. It's framed good and sturdy so it can't be damaged when it hits a snag or the bottom. This ice won't be a problem atall."

"That's right, girls. These boats are designed very strong," Stenson offered, hoping he and August were right. But it sure seemed to him things were getting a little too rough.

Above them in the pilot's house, seasoned men were beginning to show varying degrees of tenseness, as the thickening ice threatened a successful passage. The captain and both pilots were gathered there along with their assistants, and while the duty pilot wrestled to get control of the large wheel, the others offered their advice freely.

"You're going have to turn back, ain't ye, Jim?" asked one doubtful riverman.

The captain, a more optimistic type, chimed in, "No—keep on steaming ahead, Jim! We're almost past this narrow neck part. We'll be free of the ice 'fore you know it. Need any help steering?"

"Nah, I've got it," Jim replied. Then he gave stern orders to his assistant, "Holler down in that speaking tube for full steam ahead. Tell him to light those boilers up!"

In the boiler room two decks down, the message was received loud and clear by the duty engineer and fireman. They looked at each other nervously while shaking their heads, knowing the four boilers were at full steam and then some. Both of them realized that the aging boilers' cylinders could not withstand much more pressure, so they respectfully elected to ignore the pilot's orders.

However, after only a minute or so had passed, another screaming hollow sound came out of the speaking tube. "God damn it! Give me everything you have, I said! Full steam ahead!" Realizing the pilot desperately meant what he said, the two men reluctantly started putting things into motion. The fireman heaved more wood into the fire compartment, while the engineer adjusted the water supply, glanced at the safety valves, and adjusted several other valves to speed up the engine and the boat's paddlewheels. Then they backed away and watched apprehensively as the needles on all four of the boilers' pressure gauges slowly climbed into the red zone.

While downing a glass of sherry with the Stensons, August felt the rumbling of the wooden ship's structure first. In less time than his brain could process this odd sensation and work out there might possibly be something gone awry, he felt the floor under him heaving violently. It was only after he and the Stenson family were flying through the air that he heard the terrible booming sound of an explosion. *Damn—the boilers have blown up!* was the first intelligible thought that raced through his mind, with the recognition he was weightless and suspended helplessly in the air. Seconds later, August landed hard on top of Hanna, where they found themselves lodged at the edge of the promenade. Part of the railing was still intact and had prevented them from tumbling overboard. He spotted Henrik sprawled in pain nearby, but nowhere did he see Mrs. Stenson.

Luckily for them, they had been situated a good distance away from where two of the boat's boilers' steam drums had violently ruptured—and where now a raging inferno and pure mayhem ensued. Screeching steam escaping from the breached equipment and piping, frightful cries in the night, beef cows bellowing, and men and women's loud voices resounded across the terrible scene. Fires were breaking out all over the craft, as it listed more and more to port while rapidly sinking hard by the stern onto the shallow bottom.

August looked out over the glimmering ice and water at the hundreds of men, women, and children fighting to stay afloat in the strong current. Some were grabbing at burning pieces of boat debris or cargo floating by. Others tried to hang onto the thin layer of sheet ice extending to the river banks. *Where was Mrs. Stenson?* he worried, as he got to his feet and began helping Hanna get up.

"Are you okay, Hanna? Did you hurt yourself?" She looked like she was in one piece.

"I guess so. Don't think anything is broken," she said and began frantically looking around for her mother.

"How you doing, sir?" August asked after quickly moving over to the father's side.

"I believe I'm okay, son. But where's Pernilla? I don't see her anywhere!"

"Me neither! The fire's going to reach us here soon, sir. Can you help Hanna get down below, where we can get ourselves off this boat before it burns up? I'm going looking for Mrs. Stenson." There was no telling where she could be, and August was definitely concerned.

"Go right ahead, boy! I'll get Hanna down to the water."

Most of the outside stairway was gone, so August leaped onto the top of a bale of cotton and scrambled down to the main deck. Immediately, he began prowling and searching through the scattered cargo, splintered timbers, and the dead and wounded stock animals and passengers, while all the time trying to avoid the intense hot flames lapping up every combustible object on board. Finally, he heard a woman's faint cry for help coming from under a jumbled pile of sawn lumber near the bow of the boat. Rushing to uncover the hapless victim, he found her to be badly bloodied but alive and able to move on her own. Alas, it was not Pernilla! August helped the poor woman get out of the tangled mass of wreckage and, eventually, was able to hand her over to a trio of men who were working to save their fellow passengers. Then he instantly resumed the search for Mrs. Stenson.

The entire aft end of the riverboat was now submerged up to the main deck, and the raging fires had engulfed nearly half of the superstructure remaining above the water. August hustled toward the conflagration to see if Henrik and Hanna had been able to make their way off the cabin deck. He saw them quickly enough but discovered they were in a dire way. By some unfortunate quirk of fate, the fire had encircled and trapped the father and daughter, preventing their retreat from the upper cabin deck level. It appeared to August they were awaiting their doom. *No–this won't do atall*, he judged, while desperately seeking some way to reach them. He spotted one of the boat's collapsed crane poles. It was lodged against a section of promenade railing at the cabin level and sloped downward, dipping into the water. For someone with the climbing ability of a monkey, it might possibly offer a path to the upper deck. That opportunity was apparently good enough for August, who figured he would try to shinny up the wooden pole.

Without further consideration or concern for his own well-being, he made his way directly to the fallen mast, wrapped both arms and legs around it, and began to worm his way up to where the terrified Stensons waited for him. They had seen August coming and were screaming out—trying to alert him to their perilous dilemma. The young security guard shinnied and wriggled high enough to finally be able to grab hold of the railing and pull himself up the last couple of feet. He crawled onto the severely tilting promenade and, wasting no time, ripped one of the thick satin saloon curtains from a large window, wrapped it around his head and body, and then plunged through a wall of fire. He had never felt such extreme heat before. During those few seconds it took for him to penetrate the scorching blazes, he thought he was done for.

Somehow August made it through, although in the risky undertaking he suffered painful burns to his arms and hands. Undaunted and without stopping to assess his wounds, he ran directly to the Stensons to offer his assistance.

"You made it, son! We couldn't get down! We're trapped, I'm afraid," was Henrik Stenson's depressing greeting. He had seemingly given up on escaping, resolved to a certain sizzling end to his and Hanna's life.

"Oh, August, how are we going to get down from here? Look at you! You've burned yourself terribly!" cried Hanna, frightened of dying and equally concerned for August's blistered arms.

The Stensons' new security guard/valet realized the situation was dire. The fire was swiftly closing around them on all sides, save one. *We can jump for it!* August instantly determined. He knew there was no other way. "We're jumping!" he hollered above the noise of the holocaust. "Here, Hanna—come here and hold on! Can you swim? That's okay—we'll jump together!" With that split-second decision, August took hold of the beautiful girl and then urged her father, "Come on, sir! Follow us! There's no other way!" Holding tightly to Hanna's hand, August led her to the edge of the lofty precipice.

"You ready for this?" were his grave words. The lapping flames were reaching them now. Without really receiving Hanna's response, other than a determined look, the two of them leaped hand-in-hand off the cabin deck and plunged toward the freezing water of the Mississippi, some fifteen feet below them. Henrik very reluctantly jumped after them.

"Ahhh," screamed Hanna, as she and August landed with a hard smack against the water's surface. And then there was just blackness and freezing cold wetness engulfing them. Kicking and fighting the water with their arms, they regained the surface together. "Can ye swim, Hanna?" a hopeful August asked as he tried to get a breath of air.

"Yes—yes, I can swim! But Father can't! You have to save him, August!" Hanna almost screamed out as she gulped and tried to breathe.

"Okay—see if you can get to that sandbar over there! The ice shouldn't be too thick," August directed, while treading water and nodding his head in the direction she should go. Right away the frightened girl started paddling through the cold water, flotsam, and ice, realizing that she had to hurry or suffer certain death from freezing.

In the meantime, August had located and was trying to subdue Henrik Stenson, who was flailing his arms wildly in a terrified effort to keep his head above the water. It instantly became an actual life-and-death struggle between them! Henrik locked hold of August in desperation, instinctively trying to keep his head out of the water to breathe. He clasped his arms so tightly around August that the rescuer could not move, let alone swim. They both were sinking! August finally broke loose from Henrik's death clutch and did the only thing he knew to do to save them both. He cold-cocked Henrik! Raring back one of his blistered arms, he let loose a hard punch to his employer's face, and then another. Upon addling him sufficiently, August caught his boss's shirt collar with one hand and started swimming and dragging him to dry land.

Once they finally reached the island sanctuary, Hanna and two other nearly drowned passengers lugged the passive Henrik Stenson out of the ice and water. There were several other lucky survivors stranded on that crowded sandbar, and a few of them were in the process of getting a warming fire going.

"Hanna, I'm going back to look for your mother," August announced once he was able to catch his breath.

"Oh, August, where is she? Have you seen her? I'm so afraid!" Her distress was manifest.

"No, I've not seen her—but I'm going back to try and find her. Wish me luck that I don't turn into an icicle first," he responded in all seriousness, realizing that it was a very risky endeavor.

The boat was only about fifty yards off the little island, and August paddled himself over to it as quickly as his numbing arms and legs could power him. He swam against the current and through the broken ice, to where he could easily distinguish details of the wreck under the light of the raging inferno. By now, the entire superstructure was either burned up or burning, and the towering twin chimney stacks had buckled and collapsed into the river. The bow, however, was still riding partially above the surface of the water. There were many passengers still clinging to the exposed wreckage, timbers, flotsam, and tangled ropes that remained. In the flickering radiance, he spotted a lone woman barely holding to a rope that dangled from the flaming ruins of the boat. She resembled Pernilla, and the shivering rescuer thought it could be her. *It had to be her*, August told himself.

He knew he had little time left. His legs and arms could barely move now because he was so cold, and it seemed to him that his mind was slowing too. Splashing as fast as he could through the icy water, he struggled to reach the woman. *Is it her? It has to be her!* August fretted, as he approached close enough to make an identification.

*It's her! It's her!* He could see that it was Mrs. Stenson right away. She was caught in the heavy rope lines—the only thing that had prevented her from slipping into a watery grave, as hundreds of others had done that fateful evening. The woman's eyes were open, but her body was lifeless. August suspected she might not have long to live.

It was said that the explosion and almost complete destruction of the *City of Cairo* was the first such incident to have occurred in years on the Mississippi River. Approximately two hundred and sixty persons lost their lives in the terrible tragedy. They were either killed by the extreme shock of the exploding boilers, burned to death by the blazing inferno, or drowned in the freezing river's currents. Two days after the newsworthy incident, four lucky survivors were counting their blessings inside The Sisters' Hospital, one of several St. Louis medical establishments hosting victims of the disaster.

"No ma'am, doctor says these here burns look worse than they are. Got to keep the bandages on for two weeks, he said." August held out his heavily wrapped arms so Mrs. Stenson could look at them.

"Dear boy, I'm so sorry! I hope it's not terribly painful," Pernilla replied. She herself had barely remained amongst the living, after August saved her from the burning wreck and icy Mississippi. Pernilla was on the verge of succumbing to hypothermia, when August and one or two survivors on the small island—or sandbar—placed her near their burning fire and lay down close against her body. Then they proceeded to hug the nearly frozen woman snugly to transfer their warmth to her. Although August had little body warmth left in him, he lay shaking in misery against Mrs. Stenson until another man relieved him after a half hour or so.

"No, it's not too bad, ma'am. I reckon I can stand it," the new security guard/valet replied.

"You saved us all, August! Had it not been for you, the three of us would not be here now," Pernilla went on vehemently. While resting and recovering in the hospital, she had given the horrible events and near-death experience a lot of thought. With absolute conviction the Stenson matriarch believed August to be their savior.

"You know you saved our lives, August. Don't act like it's nothing to you. We're so grateful Father found you—and hired you," Hanna added with strong, heartfelt emotion.

"Ah—it ain't nothing, Hanna. Jest wanted to help is all."

"Help you did, son. Had it not been for you, my family and myself included would most certainly have perished," offered Henrik Stenson, as he nursed a tender black eye. "We can't say enough about what you did for us. I'm indebted—always will be indebted to you."

About that time a fidgety reporter, nosing around the hospital for survivors' stories, interrupted their bedside conversation. Informing them he was from the *St. Louis Post-Dispatch*, he requested that they squeeze closer together so he could make their group image. Then, while a photographer hastily worked, the newspaper man took down everybody's names and got selected versions of the terrifying events they had experienced. Needless to say, the Stensons lavished due praise on the personage of their savior, one

Mr. August Hipps, and the columnist could not write fast enough. As Henrik feigned some far-fetched excuse for how he came by the shiner under his left eye, August twitched and turned and fretted over this unwanted publicity.

*This is no good—no good atall,* he told himself, feeling uncomfortable with the whole thing. There was no telling who might read about him and see his engraved likeness. He did not like it one bit, and when asked for his account of the rescues, he just shrugged the man off.

Two days later, the Stenson family along with their security guard/valet, whose arms were still wrapped in bandages, boarded the train in St. Louis and rode across the state of Missouri to St. Joseph and from there on to Omaha, Nebraska. August—sporting a new suit, shirt, and boots that Henrik had purchased for him—was feeling his oats despite the burn wounds. At Omaha, the jumping-off place to the Pacific, Mr. Stenson paid one hundred dollars apiece for four first-class tickets, all the way through to Sacramento.

Even before the party of four had finished freshening up, the conductor's boarding cries could be heard echoing throughout the huge depot. Moving along with a throng of passengers—almost one hundred and fifty of them—August and Henrik escorted the beautiful Stenson ladies onto the loading platform, where they found a monstrous steam engine awaiting them. It was bellowing gray smoke from its huge stack, and behind it was hitched a great line of Union Pacific rail cars. In very short order, August and the Stensons stepped aboard their fine Pullman palace car. As the train's bell clanged continuously and its whistle shrieked loudly, the overland journey to California got underway.

# Chapter 8

## RIDING THE RAILS

*Look at me,* August fancied, as he gazed out the car window at the snow-covered Nebraska prairie whizzing by. The land seemed to go on forever. *Wish Ma and Pa could know I'm riding this train to California. It would make them feel a sight better and not worry so much,* he speculated, as the speeding palace car streaked down the tracks through the dusky light. From time to time, he caught silvery glimpses of the Platte River meandering behind a screen of trees—cottonwood trees, one of the porters had told him earlier. *Almost as pretty a sight as the mountains back home,* he pondered, *but not near as pretty as her.* August had turned to stare at the beautiful Hanna Stenson seated directly across from him. And to his surprise, he found her staring back.

He had thought it to be too far-fetched to find a girl as beautiful as the one Joseph had hooked up with. But Hanna Stenson was Eugenia's equal in looks and then some, he figured. However, he held little hope that she might entertain amorous notions toward him. He was their hired guard after all. Not only that, they thought he talked funny. Little did he realize, the stunning girl was actually warming up to him.

*Oh, how she's blessed with physical beauty,* August dreamed. The Norse goddess had her flaxen hair fixed tightly in a pile on top of her head, with ringlets spilling from under a small black bonnet. She was taller than August by a couple of inches at least, and her slender build, covered from nape to shoe top with a stylish scarlet and black dress, revealed a pleasing womanly form that stirred his insides real good. While August was relishing these stirrings and all manner of other fantasies, Hanna interrupted his delusions.

"Four days and nights—what are we going to do with ourselves all that time, August Hipps?" Hanna asked, referring to the schedule to reach Sacramento. For most of that entire time, they would be in continuous motion riding the rails through Nebraska; the territories of Wyoming, Utah, and Nevada; and then into California. It was an extremely long passage of almost eighteen hundred miles. However, there would be frequent stops along the way to take on or disembark passengers, deliver and pick up the U.S. mail, charge the tender with water and coal, replenish the supplies of food and drink, and occasionally slip onto a side track to allow eastbound traffic to speed by. But for the most part, during these short stops, passengers stayed on board and whiled away their time in one way or another.

As daylight waned this first day, Henrik Stenson sat next to August, reading the *Harper's Weekly*, and Pernilla was perched beside Hanna, doing some knitting. The kerosene lamps located along the car's high ceiling had been lit and adjusted to cast a dim light over the cabin's interior.

"Look out the windows, I reckon," August responded at last, after giving it plenty of thought. "There's some real beautiful country we're heading into, they say. Our porter is right worried about crossing the California mountains though. They are the Sierra Nevada Mountains, he called them. Says that means 'snowy mountains' in Spanish, and he's afraid we might run into some trouble. Word by the telegraph is that there's a big storm brewing! That's what he said."

"Oh no! But that's a long way down the road, August—three days from now. What about between now and then?" Hanna may have been somewhat less excited than August, but she still was very much looking forward to this train adventure. And she especially wanted to get to know August better and see if he was as nice as he appeared to be.

"Well, we could eat for one thing. 'Bout that time, I'd say," he replied with a sheepish grin, while rubbing his tummy with one hand. "It's almost dark out, and to my belly that's a sure sign to start growling."

"Oh, August, you can be so funny," Hanna laughed out loud. Then, not so tactfully, she asked her parents, "Mother, Father—August says his belly is hungry. Would you like to accompany us to the dining car and see if we can find something there to satisfy it?"

"Well, it's getting to be about that time, isn't it?" Henrik replied, putting down his paper. "What do you say now, dear—hungry?"

Pernilla perked up and dropped the unfinished shawl onto her lap, and with a growing smile she responded, "Don't mind if I do. I hear the food on these Pacific trains is wonderful. Why don't we go and see?"

Inside the luxurious Pullman dining car's walls, covered with walnut paneling and appointed with splendid ornate carvings, waiters hustled back and forth to attend to the diners' beckons and calls. Beef steak was the main course for this evening, and August managed to devour more than all the Stensons combined. Afterward, Pernilla sauntered off to the parlor car to chat with a lady passenger she had become acquainted with, and Henrik found his way to the smoking compartment, to enjoy a cigar with some gentlemen he had only just met. August and Hanna returned to the palace car, excited and eager to exploit their alone time and begin to satisfy their curiosities about each other.

Sitting in opposing plush-cushioned couches—the very ones the porter would soon transform into a large sleeping berth—they engaged in some light-hearted banter at first. Hanna teased August about his hillbilly accent. He poked fun at the scared look in her eyes when she jumped for her life off the riverboat. But very soon, their playful jabs and jokes gravitated into a more serious conversation.

"Nah—I never had a real girlfriend, don't reckon," August responded to a probing query from Hanna. "Guess one or two of 'em were a mite partial to me, making a fuss and all. But there never was a special one that I ever liked much."

"Hmm—that's interesting. A good-looking boy like you—why you must have been the biggest catch in the whole valley where you lived! What was the name of that place you're from, August?"

"The Pigeon Valley—it lies high up on the Pigeon River." *Won't hurt to divulge a little more secret information,* he supposed. "No, can't say I was much of a catch for those female anglers," August answered with a slight grin. "Joseph—he was my best friend—he had girls after him all the time. But I just never found one to my liking—that's 'bout it, I reckon. How 'bout you, Hanna? You 'bout to get over that ex-fiancé of yours? All I can say is that he must have a big hole in his head to give you up." August was starting to probe a little himself.

"Oh yes—I think I'm getting over the hurt. I'll never know what came over him or why he abandoned me." Although it did not show, Hanna was not entirely sure she was completely purged of the deep love she had held for her former beau. "Father says he must not have been much of a man to do what he did." Then she added with a chuckle, "Father was furious—madder than me, I believe."

August did not know exactly what to say after that, and his emotions stumbled out along with his words, "Well, I'd never leave ye at the altar, Hanna!" Then he thought a little clearer and quickly added, "Not that I would ever have a chance with a girl as fetching as you are, or anything like that."

With a cute grin, Hanna tenderly eyed the embarrassed young man across from her and teased, "You never can tell—can you now, August? You seem to be a pretty fair catch to me, even though you do talk strangely."

Somewhat taken aback, August was about to stammer out a reply when the porter inconveniently interrupted them. It was time to begin making up their beds, so he proceeded to convert their two couches into a sleeping platform for two. Then he pulled down the overhead bed, which was fitted neatly against the car's sidewall above the windows. *Damn, that's my luck for you,* August brooded to himself. About then Hanna's parents sauntered in, and before long the four of them were re-situated and sleeping comfortably under warm blankets, oblivious to the motion, constant vibration, and jolting of the car.

The next day, as the train continued rolling through Nebraska's snow-covered prairie lands and Great Plains, the passengers were awestruck by the vastness of the country. Only as the evening hours set in could they sense their train beginning its steep climb up the towering heights of the Wyoming Territory's Rocky Mountains Range. While they slept tucked under extra blankets, the Union Pacific locomotive pulled the long string of cars to the highest elevation on the transcontinental line—eight thousand and two hundred feet above sea level—and then began its long slow descent.

Come morning, August and company awoke to the startling views of the Great American Desert. Never before had he or his traveling companions viewed such stark desolation as this landscape presented. They beheld vast, white alkali barrens, pocked with scrub brush and spreading as far as the eye could see; curious towering rock croppings sculpted by the elements into fearsome forms; spectacular mountain crags unlike any other on earth; and deep canyons with precipitous walls extending vertically to heavenly heights. These wonders of nature smothered the insignificant little train as it puffed and passed them by. August's curious eye also caught the numerous coal pits visible along the way, these being excavated and exploited by the railroad to feed its growing herd of insatiable steam engines. For hours on end, the party of four—as well as most of the other passengers—simply sat back and stared in wonder at this strange new western world.

Early that evening, after jouncing across more than a thousand miles of rail that had traversed the contrasting extremes of plains, mountains, and desert, the train screeched to a halt at Ogden, Utah—the western terminus of the Union Pacific's railroad. All Pacific-bound passengers were required to disembark and re-check their baggage on the cars of the Central Pacific, which would carry them the rest of the way to the west coast. August, Hanna, and her parents dined quickly in Ogden, before hustling back to the station and boarding their luxurious palace car, just minutes before the iron wheels began rolling westward yet again.

By then, darkness had descended outside, but the car's interior was brightly lit by the overhead oil lamps. When the elder Stensons abruptly begged leave from August and Hanna to fulfill their social obligations in the parlor car, the young friends found themselves in each other's good company playing a board game—checkers, of all things.

"No, can't move 'em that way, Hanna. Got to move your pieces slant ways along the black squares. That's right—now you've got it, girl." It was a game August grew up playing with his father and anyone else he found slacking around Deaver's Store back in Forks of Pigeon. Hanna seemed to be enjoying learning the game, and the two of them became so engrossed with each other, the hours slipped by before they knew it.

"He said you were a man that could be relied upon, one that he could trust with his life," Hanna eventually confided to her opponent, almost in a whisper. "Really, that's what he said."

August looked at her kind of stupefied, while not believing his ears. "He said that! Well, I don't know why he would say something like that 'bout me."

"No? That's odd, silly, that your memory could be so short. You only saved his life—what—a week ago? Not to mention mine and Mother's!"

"Yea, but that wasn't anything. Anybody could have done it. So, he said he could trust his life with me, huh?" August was feeling awful proud that Henrik Stenson had said that about him.

"That's not all. He even mentioned that he was going to talk to you soon about staying on with him—us," Hanna disclosed in a low voice, so she would not be overheard by the other passengers. "Said he's going to try and convince you not to go to Montana. He hopes you'll agree to work for him steady."

"What? You're joshing me now, Hanna! I know you are!" August was incredulous. He knew it could not be so. "Stay on and work for him? He wants me to?"

Then Hanna started chuckling and tried to simmer her companion down, "Whoa, August. Don't get too excited now—or say anything to Father about what I just told you. Let him approach you about it first. He—we weren't sure you would want to stay in California and work for us. Don't let him know I told you—please! Promise me, August, that you won't say anything."

August could see the anxiousness in Hanna's eyes, and he was not about to let on anything to her father. "Course not, Hanna! Don't you worry—I'll play dumb about it, I promise."

"Shhh—here they come now," Hanna warned under her breath.

The Stenson parents, flushed and acting rather lively from the effects of a few libations, settled into the velvety-soft cushions and related some fresh news they had learned.

"Word is there's a major storm brewing in the Sierras ahead of us," an antsy Henrik stated. He did not seem nervous, just a little concerned.

And Pernilla added, "The conductor didn't seem too troubled with the situation. He told a few of us ladies that it's a regular occurrence in the winter. Says the train should be able to plow right through the snow."

"That's right, dear. It shouldn't be a problem," the husband added quickly, trying to reassure his little entourage—and himself. "One of the men, a Mr. Wilson Ralston, who's a vice president of this Central Pacific road, was telling us that if it gets bad enough, the train will take on more engines and a snow plow at the Truckee roundhouse to pull our train across the summits. Suppose it will be tomorrow night before we reach that station. Until then, it should be clear sailing."

August was certainly not bothered with this weather forecast. It snowed all the time in the western Carolina mountains, where he was from. Why, sometimes it would snow a sight, and there could get to be six to ten inches of accumulation on the ground. But that never bothered him a bit. He just waded right through the stuff to get to wherever he needed to go—the outhouse, spring, barn, school, store, mill, and places like that. Deep down, August figured those Sierra Nevada Mountains up ahead, the ones he had heard so much about on this trip, could not be too much worse than the hills he was from. So with his mind fussing with the notion of an impending job offer and hardly any apprehensions atall for the coming snowstorm, he dropped off into a sound sleep in the overhead berth.

"What? Thirty feet! You've got to be joshing me!" reacted August to the news the next day.

"Serious as a heartbeat, sir," the train's conductor replied in defense of his unbelievable report that more than thirty feet of snow covered the high mountain tops they were approaching. He related that the plows were having difficulty keeping up with the storm, and there could be ten-foot drifts covering some sections of the railroad near Truckee. "When we get to the station tonight, we'll have to take on four more locomotives and a plow to get us through to Summit, at the top of the divide. That is, if it doesn't get any worse. Long sections of the track—about fifteen miles or so—are protected by snow sheds, thank the Lord!"

A dumbfounded August looked from one Stenson to another, as they all silently absorbed the trainman's sobering intelligence. *Thirty feet–that's impossible!*, thought the security guard/valet as he looked out the window at the desolate Nevada landscape they were moving through. All day long and into the evening hours, the cars sped steadily westward without incident toward California, abuzz with excitement and talk of mountains and snow.

Soon after midnight, most of the passengers were awakened from their sleep by the clamor of activity at Truckee station. A huge snow plow and additional engines and tenders were being connected, one after another, to the front of the train. The noisy sound of steam blowing off to relieve the boilers was continuous, as coal, water, and supplies were being taken on. Travelers, curious about all this commotion, peeked out of the car windows, only to be greeted by the blurry whiteness of a blizzard lit up by the station's numerous gas lights.

When the train began to move again, ever so slowly with its bell clanging and its whistle screeching, August and Henrik attempted to peer out their upper-berth window. However, only the falling sheets of snow just outside the car were visible to them. Beyond that was total blackness. Gradually, the train's speed picked up as it ran through the extensive snow shelters that protected the railroad. Upon exiting each of these timber structures, it was a different story though. Progress was slowed to a crawl, as the plow bulled a path through the deep drifts covering the tracks. But it kept moving forward, creeping along through banks of snow as high as the train itself and then speeding through the railroad tunnels and the sturdy timber snow sheds.

At this rate, August calculated they might actually get through the worst of it by sunrise. It was fifteen miles from Truckee to the Summit station at the crest of the mountains. From Summit, the train could simply roll downgrade out of the mountains into the valley of the Sacramento River. *If we can just make it to Summit, then everything will ease up*, August worked out in his head. Suddenly, a few minutes after he reached this hopeful conclusion, all hell broke loose!

Just as the front part of the train had cleared a snow shed, one powerful punch of nature smothered it on its tracks. An avalanche of snow and ice sliding and tumbling down the mountain, completely covered the giant plow, six locomotive engines, tenders, baggage car, and a passenger car that had exited the shed. As ill-timed as one could imagine, the entire mountainside of snow above the railroad, piled in layers thirty to forty feet deep from the long winter's storms, had let loose. Driven by the force of gravity, this immense cascade of snow and ice destroyed evergreen forests, pushed and carried huge boulders and trees, and swept over the crawling train's path.

Without warning, the car August and the Stensons were riding in began moving and shaking violently, and the ground and tracks under them trembled as well. Crashing noises toward the front of the train could be heard, while kerosene lanterns fell from the ceiling, breaking and spilling fire throughout their car. Both August and Henrik were thrown from the overhead bed hard against the car's ceiling, before tumbling heavily onto the floor. Although August had never been through one, this had to be an earthquake, he deduced. His first instinct was to look for Hanna, and almost instantly he saw her. She was on fire!

His left arm, still bandaged from burns, hurt terribly but differently, and he had also suffered a hard knock to his head from the fall. Realizing his arm must be broken, August was not fazed in the least. After managing to right himself and get to his feet, he immediately jumped to the aid of Hanna, whose nightgown had caught fire and was completely ablaze. First he stripped a blanket from the bed. Then he stretched it out as wide as his good burned arm and broken arm could reach, before diving on top of the Norse goddess.

"Don't worry, Hanna. I've got you! You're going to be okay, girl!" August cried out as the flames licked and scorched his face. Furiously, he wrapped the blanket around her, smothering the fire in the process.

In mere seconds, August had saved Hanna, and in even less time had pulled them both into the safest corner he could find. By that time, the ground and car had stopped shaking, and the only noises to be heard were the awful cries of injured and distressed passengers. Taking notice that Henrik and Pernilla were moving and apparently okay, August joined two other stout-hearted, clear-thinking gentlemen in putting out the several fires that were still burning inside their car.

The darkness was overwhelming once all the fires had been snuffed out. Sounds of crying and yelling and muffled voices persisted, as the passengers, including August and the Stenson family, tried to assess their fate and chances. A few candles had been found and lit, so there was sufficient illumination to take in the scenes of destruction and provide assistance to those in need.

In a couple of hours, daylight could be seen penetrating a few places where the shed's roof had been ripped away. The Stenson party had been lucky! Although the interior of their car was a jumbled scorched mess, it had remained upright on the tracks. But the passenger car ahead of theirs was on its side, and beyond that was the end of the snow shed, where all was engulfed in darkness, snow, and rock. To their rear, the remaining train cars were upright and relatively intact, with only fire damage. Beyond the last car, for more than half a mile, was black emptiness, where the timber structure had done its job and protected the road. One of the porters, exploring all the way back to the far end of the snow shed, had discovered that it was open and the tracks intact.

Luckily, there was a doctor amongst the stranded passengers, and he was able to give August's left arm some expert attention. One of the small forearm bones—the radius—had been broken, and the doctor reset it, much to August's discomfort. The doc also concocted a makeshift splint for the arm and smothered an ointment over the first-degree burn on one side of his face. Thank goodness, the Stensons had made it through unscathed, and even Hanna was no worse after her scare.

The broken arm failed to keep August down. He worked with Henrik and a crew of gentlemen and railroad men, assisting the other injured passengers and setting up several camp sites outside the cars with fires, bed cushions, and blankets. Since the telegraph lines had likely been destroyed by the avalanche, they figured it would be sometime before another train was sent from Truckee to rescue them. Until then, they would have to stay warm and make do.

"Well, you did it again, didn't you, August?" Hanna asked while looking him over with a knowing smile—almost a loving one. She and her parents were sitting with him around a popping fire inside the snow shed, trying to stay warm. They each had blankets wrapped around them and, given the circumstances, were not too bad off.

"What you mean?" replied the young security guard sheepishly.

"You saved me again, silly! It's getting to be quite a habit of yours, isn't it?" replied Hanna as her parents looked from her to August, while smiling and nodding their heads approvingly.

"Uhh—well, I wouldn't say that. All I did was snuff out that fire that got on you. It wasn't nothing atall. You didn't even get yourself burned."

"What? Why I would be a pile of ashes now if you hadn't been there, and you know it, too! Don't be so modest. If Father hadn't found you and hired you, all three of us would surely be dead. Wouldn't you say so, Father?"

"I believe you're right, dear. It was indeed fortuitous that August crossed our path, very fortuitous! You had the right look about you, son. Don't know what it was. In fact, I'd like to talk to you about a business opportunity when we get somewhere that we can talk in private—whenever that might be.

"Yes sir," August replied, looking from Henrik to Pernilla and then Hanna. She returned his foolish grin with a teasing look. *How quickly things can change*, he thought. *From a jailbreaker running from the law to a "business opportunity." How lucky can I get! That Sheriff Posey ain't never going to find me now.*

# Chapter 9

## Opportunities and Possibilities

Three days had passed since the avalanche had so inopportunely crashed across the path of the Central Pacific train. The snowstorm had finally abated, and crews of Chinese workmen were still busy digging out the railroad cars from under the mountains of snow, ice, and debris. Another train had promptly been sent to the snow shed to bring all of the surviving passengers back to Truckee. In all, it was estimated that sixty-five people had been buried alive and, of course, an extensive rescue effort was underway to try and save them.

In the meantime, August and the Stenson family had been put up in the Cardwell House, one of two first-class hotels in the remote station town. There, they were content to wait it out until the tracks were cleared and their westward journey could be resumed. The railroad was sparing little expense in comforting the rescued passengers. Most, who had survived the ordeal, were counting their blessings that the resilient snow shed had saved their lives. Amongst them were August and Henrik Stenson, who had just sat down at a table in the hotel's busy saloon.

"Sure was a good thing the railroad built such hefty snow sheds, Mr. Stenson. Now I can see why they need 'em." August was just trying to be social and thought this a good way to get up a meaningful conversation with his boss.

"It sure was, August. I should tell you that I'm an engineer by academic training. Studied mining engineering for three years in Stockholm, and if anyone can appreciate the massive timber design and construction of those shelters, I certainly can. The expense the railroad must have incurred—why, they surely expended ten thousand dollars or more per mile of track to build them. And can you imagine the work required to keep them in a good state of repair? I doubt you noticed it, but those heavy wooden support columns were bolted into the rock cuts. It's no wonder the shed was able to withstand such tremendous forces!"

"That so?" August offered, while trying to think up a smart response. "I thought it was an earthquake or something like that. Sure did feel like an earthquake, the way the ground was shaking and our car was pitching all over the place." With his right hand he gently rubbed the broken left arm secured in a sling.

"How's that arm feeling, August?"

"Oh, I don't know. Don't guess it hurts too much. Never had a broken bone before. Have you?"

"No, can't say I have."

There came a pause after that, which caused August to think hard and worry about what to say next. But Henrik beat him to it and broke the silence.

"How would you like to go into the mining business with me, August?"

Even though he had been forewarned about the possibility of a business opportunity, August was jolted into an entirely different mindset by the question. He had it in his head that Henrik Stenson simply wanted him to continue as the security guard/valet, after they reached Los Angeles. "*Mining business?*" *Me? What do I know about mining?* These were the foremost thoughts that raced through his addled brain.

"I don't know too much about the mining business, sir. Guess I can't say I want to go into the mining business until I'm right sure what you've got on your mind." It was not the most positive or informed answer he could have given his boss. Nonetheless, it was an honest one and the best he could do under the circumstances, given his limited knowledge of mining.

"Well, I didn't think you knew much about mining. But I expect you could learn, couldn't you?"

*Now he's talking,* August thought. Things were clearing up somewhat. "Yes sir! I expect I can learn mining."

"Yes, I'm sure you can. I believe I've mentioned to you before that I've acquired some mining assets. It's a place named Skidaddle in the Panamint Mountains near the Death Valley. Believe it or not, I bought the property sight-unseen. Rather a foolish thing to do, you might think," at which point Henrik began chuckling. "Pernilla certainly thinks so! But I've made one fortune in the steel industry, August, and I was looking for a place to invest some idle funds. My agents, geologists, and assayers have advised that there is significant revenue potential in Skidaddle—several claims have already been made and are being worked as we speak. What I'd like to do is take you under my wing, and we'll both go out there to Skidaddle. I plan to build an infrastructure to remove the ore from the ground, crush and screen it, and then ship it to the port at San Pedro, near Los Angeles. From there, we can sell it to foreign entities at the highest price. They say there's already been promising veins of silver ore discovered in the region. I have my suspicions there's gold there as well. You can help me do this! What do you say?"

The wealthy entrepreneur hesitated for a moment to assess how August was taking the pitch. Henrik had to be sure there was no misunderstanding. A lot was at stake, and he intended, over time, to place immense responsibilities on the stout youth's shoulders. Stenson truly believed this would be a life-changing opportunity for August, so he sweetened the offer.

"You can live with my family in Los Angeles, and we'll travel back and forth to Skidaddle to manage things, as needed. And I'll make it worthwhile financially for you too. Now then, what do you say about that? Don't believe you're ever going to have such an opportunity as this, son."

Neither did August! It took very little ciphering on his part to decide what he wanted to do. "I don't know what I've done that makes you feel so confident in me, Mr. Stenson. I'm just a mountain boy with no experience like this here atall—mining. But I'll tell you one thing. If you place your confidence in me, then it'll be well placed. I can guarantee you that, sir! There won't be nobody else that'll work harder than me to get your money back out of that Skidaddle mine hole, wherever that is. Ain't nobody wants to work for you more than me—you can count on it. So, guess what I'm trying to say, sir, is that I'll take you up on your offer to learn the mining business."

Over the next few days, the passengers stranded in the wintry railroad town of Truckee waited and whiled away their time with the few social pursuits available to them: reading, conversing, parlor games, gambling, and short excursions to the local shops and eateries. Henrik Stenson captured much of his young associate's spare time in long discussions about the particulars of mining engineering. August, for sure, was interested and attentive. For hours on end, he listened, asked questions, and sought understanding on the methods involved in extracting ore from hard rock and the processes used to refine it into precious metals.

They studied a current map of California, searching for the location of the ever-elusive Skidaddle, but to no avail. However, the Panamint Mountain Range bordering the western edge of the Death Valley was prominently shown, as was the Southern Pacific Railroad through the Mojave Desert. There also appeared to be wagon roads crossing the Mojave and penetrating deep into the Panamints. Naturally, August was happy to take breaks from the tedious study, especially to spend precious time with Hanna.

"You think your family will be upset that you're not going to Montana?" Hanna inquired, as she and August braved the cold and took a walk out toward the railroad's roundhouse on the outskirts of town. Truckee's Main Street was covered with a thick layer of crusty snow and ice, and they tread carefully, with Hanna hanging onto his still-bandaged, good right arm.

"Don't reckon they will be. They don't even know I was coming. There was a bunch of Hargroves—uh, I mean Hippses—who left from home to settle in Montana." *Damn*, he fretted, *I've got to keep my name straight.* "My Uncle Alfred and Frank—Hipps—were among them, and so was Cousin Thomas. He was a real good friend of mine. Don't reckon any of them Hippses will miss me, though."

"Well, we're happy you changed your mind. Father says once things get up and running at Skidaddle, he hopes, one day, you'll be able to superintend the whole operation. He's counting on you, August. He wants to make you rich!"

Surprised by the revelation that he might be a superintendent, a wide-eyed August responded, "Superintend! Well—I don't know too much 'bout that. I don't even know what gold or silver ore looks like. But I'll take the 'rich' part," he finished with a grin. They both laughed, as Hanna held tightly to August when they tread over a particularly nasty section of ice.

After safely crossing over the patch, Hanna unexpectedly stopped and scrunched closer to him, being very careful with his broken left arm. With her face blushed from the cold and just inches from his, she smiled and breathed the words, "You're such a strong, handsome man, Mr. Hipps. I really haven't thanked you properly for saving my life—twice." Then she pressed her freezing face and mouth toward August's and gave him a lingering peck on the lips. Pulling back just far enough to see into his eyes, she finalized the sweet gesture with these tender words, "Now then, I hear you might be living with us too. Have you thought about all the possibilities that might mean for the two of us?"

*Whoa! Damn her eyes are blue—'possibilities!' Wonder what she means by 'possibilities?'* He could not imagine what she meant and tried to get his feet back under him after being startled with the kiss. "What do you mean, Hanna—'possibilities?'"

Still clutching him firmly and pressing close enough to sniff his manly smell, Hanna wasted no time in answering, "Possibilities—who knows what might happen with us living so close together. If you get to liking me as much as I think I like you, then anything is possible. We might decide to—well, we could become romantically entailed, couldn't we? What would you think about that possibility?"

Stunned and struggling to come up with a coherent answer, August babbled back, "Entailed? You and me—entailed? What you mean?"

The seriousness in Hanna's expression disappeared, and her rosy lips formed into a little grin as she went on, "We could get to know each other much better, couldn't we, Mr. Hipps? We might even declare our intentions to—well, maybe one day we could get married and have a family of our own. That's what I mean by 'entailed.' Understand?"

He understood all right! His face became flushed redder than Hanna's lips—not from the cold, but from the blood surging through his body and the adrenalin and hormones rushing to seldom-visited places. Hanna's definition of 'entailed' was exactly the way he would have defined it, had he not been so flustered. He liked entailed and wanted nothing else but to be entailed with Hanna. So there was no babbling in August's reply.

"Yea, I think I understand you now. You mean you like me that much? I—I think you're wonderful—beautiful! And I like you a sight—more than anything else in the world! But I never thought you might get to liking me too. Just look at you—and look at me! Why, I'm just a poor ole mountain boy! Are you saying you might have me one day for—for a husband?"

That was what Hanna meant, believe it or not. Her companion today, who talked so differently, had grown on her in the two weeks or so she had known him. There were subtle things about August Hipps, besides his propensity for heroic antics, that made her want to stake a claim on him. Besides the obvious physical attractions—his rugged stoutness and handsome features—she found him to be unusually kind and considerate. However, she could still not help from comparing August with her ex-intended. It had been such a passionate and torrid affair and had ended so abruptly and unexpectedly. How could she not still hold feelings for him, too? Perhaps, he might come to his senses one day.

Backing off a little and pulling August along with her, Hanna began walking again and replied to the delicate query in a good humor. "I'm saying I'm glad to hear you like me too, August!"

It took hundreds of Chinese railroad workers eight days to clear the tracks just west of Truckee Station. Several of those poor souls who had been buried alive by the avalanche had, in fact, been saved. Nonetheless, fifty-seven lives were lost in the freak accident that had become front-page news in the eastern papers, along with the tragic tale of the Mississippi steamboat sinking. One reporter from the *Leslie's Weekly*, snooping around Truckee for sensational stories, discovered that the Stenson family and Mr. August Hipps had miraculously survived both disasters. So he made it his business to pull a few bare facts out of the party and to telegraph a two-column editorial to New York for immediate publication.

No matter how hard August tried to keep a low profile, notoriety seemed to follow him these days. He worried about the likelihood of Sheriff Posey reading about him in some journal, but then figured that could never happen. Besides, how would the sheriff know who August Hipps was? Still, such reasoning did not allay fears of him being apprehended and hung for a murder he did not commit. There was no denying he had killed that man—the sheriff's son—or any doubt that it was a terrible thing. But the deed had been committed in a retributive fit of rage and in fear for his own life. Unfortunately, no Cherokee County jury would ever see it that way, though. Sheriff Posey had tainted the case with malicious misinformation that was bound to send him to the gallows. When at long last their train left the Truckee station, August had considered his situation ceaselessly and was more resolved now than ever. *I've got too much going for me now to get caught. Can't lose Hanna—never!*

The passage through the remaining snowy Sierra Mountains was extremely difficult and tedious, requiring a plow engine. Some fourteen hours after leaving Truckee, the train conveying the Stenson party finally reached Sacramento, California. At the capital city's new railroad station, August and the Stensons swapped over to the Southern Pacific road and headed southward on another long journey of five hundred miles, more or less. This last stretch passed through snow-capped mountains pierced by tunnel after tunnel, yawning canyons, vine and fruit lands, expansive grasslands supporting huge stock ranches, fertile valleys and lush farmlands along the San Joaquin River, and the arid plains of the Mojave Desert. At long last, almost two weeks after leaving Omaha, they reached the thriving city of Los Angeles, their destination and home to around twenty-five thousand people.

When not residing and working at the remote Skidaddle mining town, August would live in Los Angeles with the Stensons. Far removed from his troublesome legal problems, he could make another go at life here in California. It was to be a new beginning for him and a chance to make something of himself. The Cherokee County sheriff would never be able to find him now.

Sheriff Posey's resourcefulness and his reach was underestimated by August, it turned out. Only a week earlier and half a continent away, the lawman was prowling the waterfront at Memphis, searching for his son's killer. After learning from Tom Doughty, the Civil War veteran, that Hargrove and his accomplice were headed for the Nevada gold fields, the sheriff had wasted no time. His burning desire to apprehend the fugitive killer led him first to Chattanooga and now to this Mississippi River town. For two days, he scoured the boat landings, streets, and various hotels and bars, trying to turn up a lead as to the whereabouts of August and Joseph. After talking to the local police and questioning countless town citizens, he had come up with nothing so far.

One more day was all the time the sheriff could afford to spend in Memphis. Pressing business and court appearances back in Cherokee County required his return. If he came up short in finding Hargrove today, there was only one thing left to do—go out to Nevada. But Posey figured he would not be able to break away from his sworn duties to make that long journey until late summer, four or five months from now.

On this final morning, he sat alone at a table in the hotel restaurant, sipping a cup of steaming black coffee and brooding about where to start looking. When a folded *Harper's Weekly* paper, left behind by a previous customer, caught his eye, he offhandedly picked it up and gave it a quick gaze. Immediately, the prominent front page headlines of a riverboat tragedy jumped out at him.

### *CITY OF CAIRO* EXPLODES ON MISSISSIPPI RIVER AND SINKS! HUNDREDS OF LIVES LOST!

Included with the details of the tragedy were several survivor stories, including two or three engravings of some of the lucky passengers. One of these pictures in particular caught the sheriff's attention, and he squinted his eyes for a closer study. An image credited to the *St. Louis Post-Dispatch* came into sharper focus, showing a woman resting in a hospital bed with her family huddled around her. Pernilla Stenson was the name of the patient and her husband and daughter were identified in the caption as well. A fourth person hailed as a hero in the incident was standing beside the beguiling young daughter. That man's name was August Hipps.

Sheriff Posey blinked rapidly several times and squinted his eyes even harder, his nose almost touching the paper. There was no mistaking about it! "It's him!" the sheriff muttered aloud. "I've got ye, Hargrove! I've got ye! Ye're not going to get away from me now, no matter how fer ye run!"

# Chapter 10

## BIRTHING SKIDADDLE

Back in Haywood, the fugitives' families were still as distraught as ever over the fate and well-being of August and Joseph. Basil Edmunston—Joseph's grandfather—had received the notes August had written aboard the *City of Cairo*. As luck would have it, the boat's United States mail had been salvaged after the sinking, and the Edmunston and Hargrove families had read the water-stained missives over and over.

In addition, Joseph's Great Aunt Folsom Mann had received a newsy missive from the missing nephew. Folsom—or the Bee Woman as most people in the region knew her—had recently lost her husband, Horace Mann the miller. Receiving the letter from Joseph had lifted her from a bad bout of doldrums, and it plainly showed when she rushed over to the Edmunstons' to break the news.

"Hello, hello everyone!" were the Bee Woman's first bubbly words as she scooted into the house. "I've news from Joseph!" she continued loudly, while hurrying excitedly past Rufus, who stood holding the door open in bewilderment. In no time, the entire Edmunston clan was swarming around the Bee Woman, much like her beloved honeybees. Handing the precious letter over to her nephew, the excitement could not be contained, "Here, Rufus—read it aloud for all us'ens! Hurry now!"

Rufus's nervousness was plain to see, as he unfolded two small bluish sheets of stationery and began reading his son's words.

March 13th, '84

Dear Everyone,

   I sent this letter to you, Aunt Folsom, for obvious reasons. August and I thought Sheriff Posey might have someone watching the mail and we don't want him to know where we are. I'm going by the name Woody now so as to be extra sure he does not catch me. Hope you are doing tolerable well and please give this letter to the family when you are done.

   Hello, Everyone. It's your favorite criminal Joseph Woody writing to you from the mighty Mississippi River town of Memphis. Now isn't that a mean name—Woody? August is using the name Hipps and has headed on to Montana to join up with his kin folks, if he can ever find them. I stayed on here because I met a girl I'm going to marry, I hope. She's the prettiest thing you ever did see. You all would like her so much. I know you would. You should see her needlework. It's almost as good as yours, Louisa. Her father is a good man and I reckon he's taken a real liking to me. He liked August too and he's got me doing all sorts of work in his timber business. They are even letting me live in their front room. We plan to get married in the summer.

   I expect it best if you don't try to write back to me. Never can tell about that sheriff. Just know that I'm doing finer than I ever could have hoped for. I'm happy, and I'm going to be all right. You don't have to worry after me. I'll write ever now and again to catch you up. I love each and every one of you—Mother, Father, Louisa, Lizzie, and Tom! And you too Aunt Folsom!

I'm very sincerely yours,
Joseph
P.S. Please let August's folks know about him. Thanks!


   Joseph's informative letter was dated and not accurate on all accounts. Of course, August had bypassed Montana and found his way to Los Angeles, where he had caught his own pretty girl, it seemed. However, his current circumstances greatly limited the amount of time he was able to spend with Hanna Stenson. Her father was keeping August busy with the colossal efforts to consolidate the small independent rock mines scattered around remote Skidaddle into an organized mining works.

Stenson's agents had purchased several thousand acres of land and acquired most of the claims of the many miners who were trying to blast the ore out of their mine holes. An engineer had been brought in to oversee installation of a steam-powered stamp mill for crushing and processing the ore. It was being built on a hillside, in order that the ore-bearing rocks could be pulverized by the stamps at the uppermost level with the residue falling or flowing by gravity through various other washing, screening, and filtering processes located at lower levels. Of course, these milling processes required water—lots of water—but there were no sources of this life-sustaining and critical resource at the higher elevations of those arid Panamint Mountains. So water had to be pumped up to Skidaddle!

August busied himself surveying a route for the new pipeline that would supply water to the mining works. At the source, a well point was tapped into a shallow underground aquifer. Fortunately, it was a veritable artesian well that spewed copious quantities of water without having to be pumped out of the ground. Low rock walls were quickly laid up to contain the water in a large fountain that August dubbed the "Hargrove Spring." In less than two months' time, steam-driven pumping equipment and piping—shipped over from Los Angeles—were installed and feeding water from the Hargrove Spring up to Skidaddle.

Contracts were signed with hundreds of miners to extract gold and silver-bearing rock from the existing hard rock mines as well as to exploit new veins located by Stenson's geologist in the surrounding terrain. By summer's end, the mill was crushing and refining ore by the tons. Wagonloads of processed ore rolled out of Skidaddle every other day under heavy security, headed to the ports near Los Angeles to be sold to Mexican entities. On the return trip to the mines, these same wagons hauled coal from the nearest Southern Pacific railyard to fuel the boilers that produced steam and powered the mill and pumps. In surprisingly little time, the Skidaddle Mining Company became a complex and highly functional operation.

In the first months after August and Henrik Stenson arrived on the scene, neither a town nor decent living quarters for the miners existed.

Squalid camps with makeshift lean-tos, huts, and tents sprouted up every day in close proximity to the mines. Along with the booming influx of miners, enterprising men as well as contemptible sorts clamored and clashed to establish business ventures. More often than not, they simply squatted on mining company property, pitching huge canvas awnings fronted with wooden facades to attract and pull in customers. One such illegal establishment was a saloon and bordello that sprung up not long after Henrik Stenson and August had gotten things going in Skidaddle.

With seemingly no order or laws to control the growth of the wild boomtown, Stenson soon realized that something had to be done. His company engineers, accountants, and mill operators could not be expected to keep the peace in Skidaddle. They were already overwhelmed with running the mill and meeting the production demands of the company. So the shrewd Swede turned to the only man he knew who had the time and determination to do something about the situation. He decided to have a talk with August.

"August, that killing at the Thirsty Miner last night—how many does that make so far?" This question was posed to August as he and Henrik ate their lunches in Stenson's cramped office.

"Expect that's 'bout the third killing at the saloon since we came here," August replied, spooning some soup into his mouth and hardly looking up.

"No, I believe there's been five, August, by my count! We're going to have to do something, or you know what's going to happen? This whole place is going to blow up in our faces! It's getting to where it's not safe to show our heads outside these office doors," Henrik fumed. "I would never allow Pernilla and Hanna to come anywhere near Skidaddle. What do you think, August? What can we do?"

August was surprised by the query. He knew that Mr. Stenson counted on him for certain things—certain duties and tasks. But seeking his advice on how to change the state of law and order in Skidaddle might be a tad beyond his capabilities and expertise. Leastwise, that's what August thought, and he had to ponder right hard before responding.

"I reckon it might be time we found us a lawman who can simmer things down 'round here. We've got some men hanging around that ought not be here—troublemakers and drunks. Everyone of 'em ought to be run out of town, I do believe."

Henrik had been thinking along those same lines and was glad to hear the young protégé echo his sentiments. It would make it much easier to recruit August into the new responsibility he had in mind for the boy.

"I agree with you one hundred percent! Yes sir, I do. But who? Think you can find someone that could straighten things out around here? I'll pay him a salary and build a jailhouse, if that's what it takes." Henrik paused for a moment to let August take all this in and then continued, "And we can let him work for you. What do you say to that?"

Heaving such a responsibility on an eighteen-year-old's shoulders was right much, and August hardly knew what to say. But Mr. Stenson needed something done—they all needed something done. And to be completely truthful, August had already been contemplating the matter. He knew a man—an independent miner—who had impressed him greatly. Maybe this man would be suited for the job.

"I might know somebody who can do it, sir. Don't know if he will want the job or not, but I'll try and persuade him to."

"Fine! That's just fine! See if you can get him, August! Let's turn Skidaddle into a real little town. Tame it! That's what we have to do—tame it! Just tell me how much it's going to cost me!"

Near the Hargrove Spring—Skidaddle's vital water source—a lone miner was attempting to extract ore from a rock face in Lost Burros Canyon. It was his own private claim, and its still relatively shallow hole was following a promising quartzite vein packed with both gold and silver mineral occurrences. Dick Rosehl had discovered this pluton outcropping the previous year and returned to it a few months ago to begin working it.

"Hello, Mr. Rosehl!" August hailed from outside the man's small rock hut. Although summer had ended, it was still plenty hot, and the plank door was left wide open. August had formed a friendship with the Civil War veteran, Rosehl, while developing the Hargrove Spring pumping infrastructure. "You in there, Mr. Rosehl?"

In just a matter of seconds, a hulk of a man suddenly appeared and made his way through the narrow doorway, stooping so as not to hit his head. He was easily over six feet tall and built as stout and husky as his visitor. A wild crop of gray hair hung to his shoulders, hiding his ears. "Hello there, August! What in the world brings you down this way? Just was having me a bite—you hungry?"

"Oh no—no sir, Mr. Rosehl. Just wanted to talk to you 'bout something I've got on my mind. Reckon you've got time to hear me out?"

"Now what did I tell you about that 'mister' business? I won't talk to you unless you call me 'Dick.' Is that understood?"

August had forgotten Rosehl's previous admonitions. "Yes sir—Dick—understood!"

"Now come on in, and let's hear what's on your mind. You can talk while I eat. Hope it won't take us too long. I've got some drill holes ready to blast."

During previous conversations, August had been able to pry enough information from Rosehl regarding his personal experiences during the Civil War to develop a healthy respect for the man. Although a somewhat reserved individual now, Dick had been a young captain with General Sherman's Union forces that had wrought a swath of destruction and terror through the South. He still carried his Colt revolver holstered on his side, and August had no doubts the gun would be put to good use if need be.

Rosehl was the man August was counting on to help him tame Skidaddle. It took all of his people skills and at least two hours' worth of talking to convince Dick to give it a try. But finally the man had relented, persuaded not only by August's smooth nudging but also by the promise of a healthy paycheck each week. And there was one further enticement that was thrown in at the last minute—a life-insurance policy.

Realizing that Rosehl was a widower and had a daughter living in Los Angeles, August sweetened the pot by assuring Rosehl that the Skidaddle Mining Company would take out an insurance policy on his life. Their agreement was that the policy would be structured such that an award of ten thousand dollars would be payable to the daughter in case of Rosehl's death by causes directly associated with his professional duties as Skidaddle's sheriff. It would turn out to be an absurdly expensive policy, and August would later have a lot of explaining to do with Mr. Stenson. But it was a necessary expenditure to secure the right man for the law enforcement job, and August was absolutely convinced that Dick Rosehl was the right man.

"We'll round us up a vigilante force to back you, Dick. Course, I'll be helping you too. And I've got to organize the town property—lay out plots and a street and such—and establish some rules and regulations. You know, things like that. Me and Mr. Stenson figure on giving out operating licenses, and we mean to help the men build places to live, like you've got here. Some of 'em have their families with them. 'Spect we'll need to get a school started up soon, too. Going have to find us a teacher, though. You any good at teaching?" August asked, while not being able to resist cracking a smile and giving away the jest.

Being a sincere and thoughtful man, Dick just raised his eyebrows and retorted, "The sheriffing work will be enough to keep me busy, August. It's a good idea—the school. Say, you got a badge to give me to wear?"

No sooner had Dick lodged the question than August fished out a shiny silver badge from his pocket and proudly pinned it to Sheriff Dick Rosehl's shirt.

A veritable renaissance erupted in Skidaddle that fall—one which birthed a true town. Two streets were surveyed, with rental plots laid out along each side for the establishment of stores and other businesses. A hundred or more tiny allotments were identified on a hillside overlooking town, where the miners began constructing more suitable living quarters for their families. For the Chinese work gangs, contracted to exploit the company's most productive and profitable mines, a sizable area was set aside for their camp and families. Pipelines with several taps were provided for these residential facilities, so that buckets could be filled with clean water pumped from the Hargrove Spring.

Also, operating licenses for the Thirsty Miner saloon and its adjacent brothel were drafted by a company lawyer. Opening and closing hours were established, and legal regulations regarding health and cleanliness, rowdiness, noise, guns, and more were set down. Only after the threat of immediate eviction from Sheriff Rosehl did the ornery saloon proprietor sign the twelve-month license.

A sturdy jail was constructed from which the sheriff could conduct his business. Striding up and down crude wooden sidewalks bordering the dusty streets, the hatless Sheriff Rosehl was an impressive sight with his silver badge gleaming and his long gray hair flopping in the breezes. Needless to say, the quiet sheriff quickly earned the respect of the town's citizens.

It took August and Henrik Stenson all of seven months to get the mining business sorted out and running smoothly and to finally establish some semblance of law and order in Skidaddle. Smoke now billowed continuously from the steam plant's high brick stack, and the ten-stamp mill pounded and washed and screened incessantly, refining the excavated rocks into a rich, highly marketable ore. Wagon trains loaded with precious cargos were constantly in motion between Skidaddle and the port at San Pedro. During this entire time, while the vital birthing work was going on, August desperately longed for Hanna. He missed her so much.

Their romance had been an infrequent and long-distance one for sure. Between April and the present month of October, August had returned to Los Angeles only twice. It was no wonder, considering the extraordinary amount of work at Skidaddle and the long treacherous journey between the mining town and Los Angeles. A one-way trip took a full day and a half of travel by horse-pulled conveyance and train. From Skidaddle, a one-day grueling coach trip across the desolate Panamint Valley and through the waterless and vast arid expanses of the Mojave Desert just gained the nearest railroad station. From there, an eight-hour train passage to Los Angeles was left for the parched traveler. Certainly it was not a trip for the faint-hearted, but it was a trek that both Henrik and August looked forward to. It offered them a rare chance to bate their yearnings for the beloved Stenson women.

Their carriage, driven by a Chinaman and with the Stensons' Chinese valet sitting at his side, at last pulled under the porte-cochere of the grand baroque mansion on Orange Street. Sitting impatiently on the expansive and ornately trimmed porch, the beautiful blonde Stenson women teemed with excitement. Hanna rushed and greeted August as he wearily hopped out, giving him a warm hug. He had not seen his Norse girlfriend for three months, and pent-up passions gushed between them. Pernilla, of course, was no less overjoyed to see her husband, and she hurried into Henrik's arms and planted a lingering kiss on him. It was the happiest of reunions, dampened only by the unspoken recognition that the miners would once again be off to the Panamints in a matter of a few days. So during these infrequent visits, close companionship and efficient use of time was the rule.

The very next day August and Hanna giggled and laughed profusely while hopping around in the shallow waves breaking along Santa Monica's sandy beach. The barefooted Hanna was having to hold her long, wine-colored dress above her knees to keep it from getting soaked. August, who had shed his suit coat and shoes and managed to roll his pants legs up, held Hanna securely by her free hand as they frolicked in the cool ocean water. It was a delightful fall morning, and the couple was taking full advantage of their brief time together—and their escape from Sunday worship and parental oversight.

Finally tiring from their wading exertions, they flopped down on a blanket and let out huge sighs of relief. Before long, they were sharing picnic snacks and engaging in enthusiastic discussion. "Father is so proud of the job you're doing in Skidaddle, August. He says that you and Mr. Rosehl have almost got the town tamed. Don't guess you can ever tame a mining town, but he says things have improved greatly."

"Dick's done it all by himself, I reckon. Can't take credit for his sheriffing. He's had to pull his revolver a few times on some of those rowdies at the Thirsty Miner—but he ain't shot nobody yet. Most of 'em know by now he means business. Did you know he was a Yankee during the war?"

Hanna's mouth was full of bread and grape jam, causing her to shake her head back and forth. She was not aware Rosehl had been a Union soldier.

"Yea, he was in right-smart fighting with Sherman's army marching down from Tennessee to take Atlanta and Savannah. Don't reckon he ever ran into my pa though. They—Pa and Joseph's father—Mr. Edmunston—were

Rebels. They were with the Haywood Highlanders but never went down to Georgia." August had spoken many times of Joseph to Hanna, and she knew all about their close friendship. As a matter of fact, they had even talked of travelling to Memphis to visit with Joseph and Eugenia one day.

"Oh, I almost forgot to tell you! Earlier this week a man called at our house looking for you. He was carrying a news picture of all of us in Mother's hospital room, taken after that horrible steamboat explosion. Said he recognized you in the photo and had clipped it from a weekly journal. Mother told him that you and Father were working in Skidaddle." Hanna did not seem too concerned about it as she added with a slight smile, "He said he was an old acquaintance of yours from North Carolina."

*What!* August thought, as his heart began to race and it slowly dawned on him who this "old acquaintance" had to be. "Did he give you his name?"

"Posey—Buford Posey—I believe that was his name. Do you know him, August?"

He stared at Hanna and fretted in stony silence, while puzzling over how in tarnation the sheriff had found him all the way out here in California. "Yea, I think I remember him."

# Chapter 11

## Last Sheriff Standing

Back in Cherokee County, Sheriff Posey had chawed on the matter all summer long. The news-journal likeness of Hargrove with the Stenson family was the best clue he had to go on so far. Not only did the caption identify the Stensons by name, but the brief accompanying article went on to tout the good fortune of the "Los Angeles-bound steel tycoon" and the circumstances of his family's rescue. The reporter had given the name of the Stensons' savior as August Hipps and described him as a companion of the family. But the sheriff had no doubts that the man identified as Hipps in the picture was actually Hargrove. And he suspected that Hargrove was not headed for the Nevada gold country after all, as the Tennessee war veteran, Doughty, had led him to believe. Posey had worked out in his mind that if Hipps was the Stensons' companion, then by all rights he should be Los Angeles-bound too.

That was how Sheriff Posey had finally ended up on the Stensons' doorstep in Los Angeles—that and no little amount of sleuthing via telegraph messages with the railroads and the County of Los Angeles. After a few days respite to see the Pacific coastal region, he headed directly for the Skidaddle mining town. Two days of arduous travel later, the sheriff climbed down out of the stagecoach.

*Skidaddle? What in hell kind of name is that?* he wondered, brushing clouds of dust off his clothes and looking around at the poor excuse for a town. Plank storefronts lined both sides of the streets for about fifty yards. Posey noted that the places were not much more than shanties, with the exception of the Thirsty Miner and a sturdily built log building. "Hmm," the sheriff mumbled as he read the sign nailed over the log structure's door. The huge words SKIDADDLE JAIL were painted in white over a dark background. *Better to see at night*, Posey reckoned, as he walked toward the open door.

"Yes sir! How can I help you, stranger?" the seated Sheriff Rosehl asked, as he looked up from some paperwork on his desk.

"Howdy, Sheriff. I'm Sheriff Buford Posey from Cherokee County," said the mountaineer lawman as he opened a coat breast and revealed a shiny gold badge pinned to his denim shirt. It was a six-pointed star with the words "Sheriff" and "Cherokee County" neatly etched into it.

"Cherokee County—where might that county be located, Sheriff?" Rosehl had obviously never heard of the place.

"North Carolina, Sheriff—way over in the western tip-end of the state. Our court business is done in the town of Murphy. That's where my jail is—smack-dab in the middle of the mountains, we are."

"Is that so?" Sheriff Rosehl was puzzled over what this North Carolina sheriff might be doing in California. He had come a long way for some reason. "Well, that's a pretty far piece from Skidaddle, Sheriff. How is it you've come to be in these pretty Panamint Mountains of ours?" Rosehl's mouth formed a grin, as he looked curiously at the other sheriff.

"Well, sir, I've come a'looking fer a killer that might be somers in these here parts. I've heard tell he might be." Then Sheriff Posey's hand dipped into a front coat pocket and pulled out the worn, folded clipping from *Harper's Weekly*. "It's this 'en here, Sheriff," Posey pointed out after unfolding it. Using his finger as a pointer, he went on, "It says his name is 'Hipps.' But that ain't right. I know him as 'Hargrove.' He's a killer, Sheriff, and he killed my son. He sure 'nough did."

Sheriff Rosehl studied the picture hard, and there could be no doubt about it atall. The images were of his bosses, August Hipps and Henrik Stenson. *Killer—August's no killer! What's this man's game?* were the first thoughts that rushed through his confused head. "Well, let's see here. That man is our president—Henrik Stenson. He's the owner of Skidaddle Mining. Sure is. He's in Los Angeles right now, taking a few days off. But this other one—the one you say is Hargrove—can't say I recognize him." Pausing for only a brief moment, the sheriff then finished emphatically, "No, don't know that gentleman. You say he's a killer—that one?"

Sheriff Posey could not have been more devastated! He had been dead certain he was on the verge of nabbing Hargrove. *The Stenson lady allowed Hargrove was in Skidaddle. That's what she said!* This was what flashed through Posey's mind as he angrily rebutted the Skidaddle sheriff, "No, ye're wrong 'bout that, Sheriff! This here man, Hipps, he's here somers. I know he is! Take another look…The Stenson woman back in Los Angeles allowed he was here. What ye lying to me fer? Huh?" By this time Posey's face had grown beet red, and he had puffed himself up like a courting gobbler.

Sheriff Rosehl kept his head about him, rising up and walking around the desk, so he could look his accuser in the eyes. No way was he going to let on about August to this hick sheriff until he knew more. The two sheriffs were close to the same age. Rosehl was not much taller than Posey, but he was a good deal stouter. So when the Skidaddle sheriff approached him, Posey felt threatened enough to let out some hot air, deflating his stature somewhat. He even backed up a step or two, while flipping his coattail out of the way to reveal a holstered revolver. All at once, a heightened level of tension filled the air, as the two lawmen faced off against each other. It was absolutely crazy how things had gotten out of control so quickly!

A gunfight was the last thing Sheriff Rosehl contemplated—or wanted—and he tried to talk the crazy North Carolina sheriff down. "Now that's a mighty serious accusation to make, Sheriff, to somebody you don't even know. And I'd think twice about pulling that gun, if I were you." The stress was apparent in Dick Rosehl's voice, but at the same time he stared coolly and resolutely into Sheriff Posey's eyes. "I won't hold it against you though, Sheriff, if you simmer down and hand over that weapon. Can't have you losing your temper again and pulling on me, can I? Let's have the gun! Slowly does it." Both sheriffs were extremely edgy by now—Posey noticeably more than Rosehl. Like two kegs of black powder, their fuses were lit, and they were both set to go off. Any sudden movement by either one would surely spark deadly fireworks.

Just then, someone busted through the open door hollering out, "Hello, Dick! We need to talk!" And almost immediately the percussive blasts of two pistol shots resounded loudly through the log structure. Smoke and a screamed curse word filled the air, as one man tumbled heavily onto the stone floor. With blood gushing from a shoulder wound but still pointing his smoking gun, Sheriff Rosehl stared down at Posey, who was gasping for air. Then he looked through the smoky haze at the intruder, who stood motionless just inside the doorway. August's timing could not have been worse.

"So that's 'bout all there is to tell, Dick. I've been running for my life ever since that day it happened. He meant to hang me one way or 'nother for accidently killing his son. You understand I hope—don't you?" As August finished relating his tale of woes to Sheriff Rosehl, he gave a hateful glance toward the lifeless form of Buford Posey lying under a coarse blanket on the jail floor. The body was growing stiffer by the minute.

With intense remorse, August had spilled his guts out to the sheriff, leaving out no details of what had happened back in Cherokee County. Skidaddle's sheriff sat in befuddled silence the whole time, looking at August with an empathetic expression, broken ever now and again with the sudden raising of his brows or a look of utter disbelief. Finally, heeding August's prompt, Rosehl spoke.

"They didn't leave you much choice, did they? Don't doubt a bit you didn't mean to kill that sheriff's son—he had it coming to him anyway after shooting your friend and threatening you. But for the life of me, August, I can't understand how this sheriff tracked you down all the way across the country!"

"Damn if I know! Thought I was clear of him when me and Joseph got to Memphis. Sure as hell didn't think Posey would cross the Mississippi and this whole wide country looking for us—me!" As an afterthought, he added, "Wonder if he caught Joseph?"

Sheriff Rosehl was not worried about Joseph. He was more concerned about August's fate and what could be done to continue hiding his dark secret. "What are we going to do, August?"

"You ain't turning me in, are you?"

Stupefied, Rosehl's response jumped from his lips, "What! What do you mean 'turn you in?' Course I'm not! I can't—you're too good a friend for that. And besides, you're not guilty, are you?" The sheriff was convinced his young friend was not guilty, but he wanted to hear August say it one more time.

"Hell no, I'm not guilty! I told you everything, Dick—everything!" After a brief pause, August almost pleaded for the lawman's understanding. "You don't figure I'm guilty, do you?"

"Nope," came Rosehl's immediate response. "If you're guilty, then that Southern Jackass claim of ours is full of gold. Now what are the chances of that?" the sheriff asked with a wry smile forming on his face, obviously convinced their claim near the Hargrove Spring—the one he and August had partnered on—was just another worthless hole in the ground.

Things lightened up a bit after that, and August felt a sense of relief come over him. "Then I'm not guilty for sure."

A moment or two of understanding passed between the two. Then the sheriff allowed, "You're still August Hipps, far as I'm concerned. We've got to go on acting like this man never came here to Skidaddle." Saying that, the sheriff walked over to check if the door was still securely locked, and then he took a peek out the window. "He was alone when he came here. Nobody's come snooping around yet, so I guess they ain't too concerned 'bout those gunshots. You leave it to me to clean up this mess. I'll take care of it."

"What you aim to do? I can help you."

The former Yankee captain, who killed his share of Rebels during the war, could not have been more emphatic in replying, "No! You don't need to know! I'll take care of this myself. Sheriff Posey never came here as far as I'm concerned. And they sure as hell won't ever find him when I get through. Now go on—go on about your business!"

He was now scarred for life by the accidental killing of Lester Posey, with a false charge of murder lodged against him and this latest deadly encounter with Buford Posey at the Skidaddle jail. Nevertheless, August felt a newfound sense of relief and freedom when the haunting threat of the Cherokee lawman was extinguished forever. Heeding Sheriff Rosehl's counsel of going on about his business, August did his best to cleanse himself of the Posey affair. He buried himself in his work, tackling problems and issues related to the administrative affairs of the town.

Taking full advantage of his agreeable personality and innate way with people, August was able to resolve many sticky disputes and complications before involving either Sheriff Rosehl or company lawyers—or even the distant county court. In reality, August was more like a youthful mayor than anything else, although not in an official elected capacity. Trying to get a new school organized, seeing after the booming town's limited infrastructure, and helping settle contractual infractions were just a few of the responsibilities that were to keep him busy until Christmas.

The holiday season could not come soon enough, far as August was concerned. He was actually planning to pop the big question to Hanna on Christmas Eve and get himself entailed. It was a question he figured he knew the answer to, but could not rightly be sure until he heard the words "Yes, I will marry you, August" from his beautiful girl's mouth. That would be such sweet music to his ears. He could not wait to get back to Los Angeles!

Festive greenery and garlands hanging from the platform structure, throngs of excited travelers, and two merry carolers greeted August when he stepped out of the car. The air was a bit chilly, and the afternoon sun still burned low on the horizon. He glanced around for familiar faces, but there was no one awaiting him at the railroad station—except the Stensons' Chinese driver who had been sent to pick him up. August was somewhat disappointed, but he kept his head up. *Ah, that's all right. Going to see her directly*, he thought, as he gave his bag over to the Chinaman and followed him to the carriage.

It was only a short ride to the Stensons' grand house. Henrik had returned to Los Angeles a couple of weeks before, ostensibly to take care of a business entanglement with one of the ore brokers. So August expected his boss might even be on the porch, alongside the beautiful Stenson women, to welcome him home. When the carriage pulled to a halt, however, there was not a soul outside waiting—not even Hanna.

He was somewhat puzzled but not dismayed. Probably, he was more annoyed than anything else. Strangely, August had not received a letter from Hanna in the past two weeks. The two of them had been religiously writing to each other for months, and there were few days that he failed to receive a chatty missive with her expressions of affection for him. She had been smitten by her mountain boy, it seemed to him, and he had fallen in love with her. *Where is she?* he fretted.

"Hello, dear boy! Welcome home and merry Christmas to you!" Pernilla wrapped her arms around August and gave him a huge hug as he entered the house, even before he was able to shed his heavy coat. "It's so good to see you!"

"Hello, Mrs. Stenson! Good to see you too!

"August—come on in! You don't look too worse for the wear, after that long mule trip from Skidaddle." Henrik offered a hardy hand shake and an appraising look before continuing, "Damn hard trip that is!"

Both of the Stensons' outward show of happiness while welcoming August home was genuine. He was a part of their lives now, and he had earned their love and respect. Sure, he had saved all of their lives a time or two, but that was not the reason—not at all. They had discovered in this young man what they believed was a vein of golden goodness and character, and a soul that was honest and dependable to a fault. He was almost too good, and they tried desperately to conceal the uncomfortable secret they were holding.

"Where's Hanna?" August asked, as he looked around and into the house. He neither saw nor heard her anywhere. *Strange, what's gotten into her?* he thought. Then he saw the masks of happiness melt from the Stensons' faces, and their worried glances dart back and forth at each other.

"Come on in first, August, and get comfortable. We've got something to tell you about Hanna."

"But I thought she was over him! How could she? After what he did to her..." The words of shock spilled from August's mouth as first Henrik and then Pernilla explained the unthinkable. Their daughter's old flame had unexpectedly come to Los Angeles and beseeched Hanna to give him another chance. Against the Stensons' wishes and admonitions, she had left with him a week ago on a train bound eastward to Pittsburgh to try to work things out.

"We know, son. It's not what Pernilla and I wanted or wished for Hanna." Henrik was shaken too. "Peter has professed to Hanna—and to us—that it was the biggest mistake of his life—what he did to her. He begged her and us for another chance to show how much he loves her. But against our wishes, she decided to return east with Peter and spend Christmas and the New Year with him and his family." Then with a sigh, Henrik finished, "That's it! That's all I can say, August."

"Here, August. Hanna left this for you. Why don't we remove ourselves, dear, and let him read it alone," Pernilla suggested as she handed over a small envelope.

"Okay, fine." Henrik's head was hanging as he walked his wife out of the salon, leaving August to himself to sort out the letter Hanna had left him.

He was flabbergasted and heartbroken at once. Never had he seen this coming! For the past months, he had only heard wedding bells and seen happiness in his and Hanna's future. *How could I have messed this thing up so bad? Damn, that's all I'm good for!* Thinking harshly of himself and trying to hold back the tears, he opened the letter and began reading.

*December 15, 1884*

*Dearest August,*

*I don't know what to say to you or tell you how sorry I am to disappoint you like this. Everything happened so quickly and unexpectedly, it almost seems unreal. I won't bore you with all the details, but Peter has convinced* me that he loves me now more than ever and that he has always loved me. He says it was the biggest mistake of his life to leave me and I believe he means it. We're going to spend the holidays in Pittsburgh and see if those wonderful feelings we once held for each other can be revived.

You are such a good person, August Hipps, and I truly know that I felt a love for you too—and still do "I reckon." It's no wonder, after you swept me off my feet with your acts of heroism on the river and railroad. We both know I would not be here if not for you—nor would my parents be. I felt for you more than you'll ever know, but it seems to me that fate has intervened to guide me in another direction. It's so hurtful to write these words—I can't go on and must stop. Please believe me when I say I loved you too!

Take care of Mother and Father (I know you will) and keep up the good work. Father says you and Sheriff Rosehl have turned Skidaddle into a real town now. I can just imagine you with a six-gun hanging off your belt. Ha! Good luck to you, August! I wish you only the best the world has to offer. You deserve it!

Lovingly yours,
Hanna

The two tiny pages of neat handwriting delivered the biggest disappointment of August's life. Hanna, the girl of his dreams, had dealt him a blow he would never forget and probably would never get over. Stuffing the pages back into the envelope, he suddenly realized his life had been drained of all meaning. There were no future prospects for him atall. Even the Sheriff Posey business had never affected him like this. *What kind of Christmas is this going to be?* the sorrowful and lost highlander fumed, wiping the tears from his watery eyes.

# Chapter 12

## Free at Last

In May of 1885, after almost nine months of operation, the mining town of Skidaddle continued to boom, with the reverberations reaching throughout southern California. The population had grown to more than eight thousand people of all sorts: miners, mill workers, wives, children, merchants, a doctor, a blacksmith, whores, drunks, drifters, speculators, Chinamen and other foreigners who could speak very little English but knew how to wield a pick and shovel. Through the efforts of the hardy miners, steady quantities of ore-bearing rock were being removed from the ground and processed at the stamp mill. Whenever one hole in the ground played out, another quartzite vein unfailingly was discovered nearby. In less than a year, Henrik Stenson's risky venture had become wildly successful.

Of late, Stenson was spending more and more time in Los Angeles managing product sales and exports. He had also begun discretely working to find a buyer for his mining enterprise. After all, he was an entrepreneur and not above making another quick fortune before his mines played out. In his absence, he left the Skidaddle mining operations under the control of the superintendent. Sheriff Dick Rosehl was keeping things simmered down in town, while August did his best to keep folks happy and look after their welfare.

Administrative problems and issues of all natures usually came across August's desk to resolve first, before involving Sheriff Rosehl or the courts. He bowed his back and worked relentlessly to clear these up as expeditiously as possible, in some measure as a distraction from the mopes and bouts of depression he was still experiencing from Hanna's rejection. August was in his office—actually, it was Mr. Stenson's office—on this sunny spring day with two sticky matters before him. A petition had been gotten up by a sizable religious contingent, demanding a venue for a place of worship, and August was fretting over a suitable site to construct a small church. More pressing, however, were the revisions he was contemplating for the Naked Lady's operating license. This bordello, which sat adjacent to the Thirsty Miner, had doubled in size over the past several months, and the soiled doves were literally pulling customers from the streets into their beds. Sheriff Rosehl had sought some assistance from August—not the lawyers—in resolving the sordid situation, but thus far nothing had been resolved.

Speaking of the sheriff, just at that moment he sauntered into the office to make August aware of yet another issue that had cropped up. "Hello, August. Looks like you're hard at the paperwork. Don't envy you one bit."

"Howdy, Sheriff! Good to see you. I'm glad you came in, because I wanted to chat with you 'bout that Naked Lady business. Might have an idea that could help us. Think you can spare the time?"

"No can do! Sorry, but we've got bigger problems, I'm afraid. You know those twin Rego brothers—ones that robbed a bank in Sacramento and are wanted for murder somewheres over in Nevada?"

"No—don't believe I ever heard of 'em."

"Well, I believe they've showed up here in Skidaddle." The sheriff's usual confident bearing appeared to be one of unease now, so August's attention was duly aroused. "They're dangerous, and they're over there at the Thirsty Miner and packing guns. Came in with a couple of other vaqueros pushing a small herd of steers. Need you to back me up, August. I'm going over there now to arrest the four of them. Don't doubt those other two are outlaws, too. I'd appreciate your help!"

It would not be the first time August had stood next to the sheriff in a difficult situation. As he pushed back from the desk and reached for his Colt revolver, the nervousness showed. "Yea—no problem, Dick. Let me strap this here gun on, and I'll help you round up those desperados. Say they're dangerous, are they?"

"They're meaner than dangerous. You'd better watch yourself! They've had a lot more gun practice than you have. Let me do all the talking and threatening. All I need you to do is stand behind me and watch my back. Hear?"

"Got it! I'll be right behind you—you can count on it." August wished it was going to be a free-for-all brawl instead of a potential gunfight. He could stand his ground against most men in a battle of brawn and fists, but pulling and shooting a revolver at another man was an entirely different proposition. Hours of practice with the sheriff down at the Hargrove Spring had hewn August's skills in quick drawing and shooting at stationary targets. But as of yet, he was untried in overcoming jittery nerves and drawing against live targets that shot back. Walking down the street with Sheriff Rosehl, August pondered if that time might not have come.

Dirty ragged miners, shiftless vagrants, and all sorts were loitering outside of the Thirsty Miner. When they spotted the sheriff and August walking toward them, they began to scatter. Wagons and horse traffic in the dusty street slowed and then halted. The scantily clad doves next door to the saloon spied the strapping lawman and his stout young colleague headed their way, and they fluttered for their nests. Inside the watering palace, the piano continued to blare away over the usual noisy din of loud talking and profanity-laced arguments.

As soon as Sheriff Rosehl and August walked through the open doorway, the music stopped, and the many boisterous conversations ceased. Men in various degrees of intoxication rose up from their chairs or backed away from the bar and hastily beat it for the back door. The piano player and several ladies-of-the-night scurried along after them. A few curious patrons fled to the corners of the establishment or behind anything that might offer adequate cover. There they eagerly awaited, hopeful and excited that they might witness a shooting or other scenes of violence and carnage.

The Rego brothers and their compatriots stayed put, standing at the bar throwing back shot glasses of rye whiskey. They were easy to spot, being the only gun-toting customers in the place. The sheriff had been sent for after these men had refused to check their weapons at the entrance gun closet—it was one of the regulations contained in the Thirsty Miner's business license. All four of the wild men turned to look at the approaching lawman and his cohort, their smirking grins revealing rotting and tobacco-stained teeth. The sheriff's shiny silver badge shone prominently, and his hand had seemingly grown a gun that pointed directly at the rowdy vaqueros.

"You men—one at a time—I want you to take out your weapons and put them on top of the bar. You first!" said the sheriff in a low commanding tone, as he nodded to the closest Mexican to him—the only one wearing a hat. "Easy does it now!"

August stood a few feet away from Sheriff Rosehl—not behind him but next to him—and watched the four gun-slinging vaqueros carefully. Every few seconds, he cast his eyes all around the saloon, doing his upmost to ensure the sheriff's safety by watching his back. These four Mexican cowboys were a poor sight. Scraggly beards covered their bronzed faces, and dark hair hung in greasy strings to their shoulders. They were dressed almost alike in ragged shirts and pants, cow-hide chaps, and plain boots with spurs. But only one of them was wearing a hat—a soiled, light-colored sombrero—and he appeared to be the spokesman for the group.

Backing away from the bar slowly, the grinning Mexican with the sombrero tried out his smooth-talk on the sheriff. "What is matter, Sheriff? We make no trouble here. All we do is wet our whistle just a tiny bit. You have no problem with that, do you?"

August could feel the tension in the room escalating, and his stomach began to roil. Sheriff Rosehl appeared to be as cool as ever though. "No problem with that, mister. But I've got a problem with you wearing that six-shooter in this saloon. Like I said before, remove your gun and put it on the bar—use your left hand! You other men there, stay still!"

"Now, Sheriff, why will I, Miguel Rego, give my gun to you—huh? How then am I to protect against all these men who want to robar nuestro dollars?" As Rego talked, he started waving his arms around, indicating the many dangerous characters slinking in the dark corners of the saloon. But it was a trick, a sneaky ploy to distract the sheriff and catch him off guard.

Rego was quick, lightning quick, and in the moment it took for his abrupt quick-draw movement to be registered and processed in Sheriff Rosehl's agile mind, the Mexican's gun was flashing loudly and violently. But Rosehl had not been fooled in the slightest. His Colt also blasted away. In mere seconds, both

Rego and the sheriff lurched backwards and fell heavily to the floor. Rego, fatally wounded, groaned in agony while Sheriff Rosehl tried to right himself.

The bout of nervousness August had felt was washed away by this swift deafening action. He instantly realized that his partner had been shot and the other bandits were going for their weapons. Instinctively and at once, August went for his Colt. His hand expertly jerked the revolver out of the holster, just as he had tirelessly practiced. In one swift motion he cocked and leveled the weapon at the nearest Mexican, and then pulled the trigger, and again, and again, and again—*bang, bang, bang, bang!*

Two of the vaqueros were hit and tumbled hard to the floor. But August himself had been shot by a well-aimed bullet! His chest hurt and burned like hell. He couldn't stand on his feet and, before he knew it, he was sprawled on the dirty floor. Two of them—he saw them fall. He had gotten them for sure! *The other one—what about the other one?* He was not sure he got him, and the uneasy thought flooded through his mind as he attempted to raise himself up to find that last Mexican.

But he need not have bothered. The other Rego brother was still alive and stood directly over him, snarling and pointing a six-shooter directly at his head! *This is it! Sorry Ma and Pa, I love you!* August's last thoughts were of his family. He would never see them again and be able to explain everything—

*Bang!* With the loud report, August jerked in anticipation of being summarily executed. *Strange,* he sensed his head had not been blown off. And then the damn Mexican tumbled on top of him, bleeding and convulsing and dying a horrible death. August struggled under the dead bandit's body, trying to figure out who was dying. His wound hurt terribly, and he was losing buckets of blood. Then he caught a glimpse of Dick Rosehl. The sheriff was still pointing a smoking gun at the Rego brother who was lying on top of August. *Dick's a good man,* and with that last thought August felt a sudden faintness rushing over him. His vision was blurring too—and quickly. Everything around him was fading into darkness. Then there was nothing.

"Hello, son," whispered the sheriff. "How do you feel?"

The light was blurred at first and then gradually a familiar face began to take form. August blinked several times to bring it into better focus. There could be no mistake about it. *Dick—it's Dick! Where am I?* These notions flashed through his mind until his sight blurred again from the tears welling in his eyes.

"Don't know. Did I get shot? Where've you been, Dick? Are you okay?" The muffled and slurred words came slowly.

"Yes, you got hit. So did I! Doc says you're going to be fine though. Are you hurting bad?"

"Not bad, don't reckon. Where am I? What's happened?" August was trying desperately to look around, even attempting to raise his head off the pillow. But he had a strange light-headed feeling about him. And he felt surprisingly good.

"Now don't move too much, August. Me and the doctor have got you in my place, here at the Hargrove Spring. Doc has patched you up real good. You're lucky to be alive!" The sheriff, with a gunshot wound in the arm, along with a couple of miners and the town doctor, had wheeled August to Rosehl's home in a wagon.

"The bullet passed all the way through your chest and out your back—just below the left shoulder."

"You saved my life, Dick. I remember that."

"Had to, son, after you shot those other two off me. You saved my life— you sure enough did!"

"I did?" August did not remember that part very well. Something was not right though. He felt awful strange. Actually, he sensed little or no pain. "Funny, I don't hurt none atall."

"Here's Doc Wrigley, August. He wants to talk with you."

The doctor slid in by the patient's side and took his hand, squeezing it as he talked. "Don't you worry, August. We'll have you back up in Skidaddle in no time. You're lucky! The bullet entered your pectoral and travelled straight through and out your back, without affecting your vitals. There's a good-sized exit wound in your back though. I fixed it up. Do you understand me?"

August was still coherent and comprehended what the doctor was saying. He just nodded his head for the doctor.

"Okay, good! I've given you quite a dose of morphine, so that's why there's no feeling of pain. Going have to do that for a while, I'm afraid."

"Morphine! You mean I've been drugged?" the patient mumbled.

Doc Wrigley exchanged looks with the sheriff before offering his reassurances, "It's only morphine, and you need it! You're going to have to stay in bed for a week or—"

"Damn, I've been drugged," he mumbled before asking, "How's Dick? Is he—okay?"

"The sheriff's going to be fine. Don't you worry about him. He was shot in the arm. Sheriff Rosehl's in much better shape than you are, August. But don't concern—"

"Ohh—I've been drugged, Dick—drugged. I feel—I feel so good..." And after another minute or two of such nonsensical babbling, the patient fell asleep and was soon gallivanting with the angels again.

"A letter's come for you today!" The sheriff had ridden down to the Hargrove Spring to check on things with the convalescing patient. August was leaning over the kitchen sink with half his face still lathered in soap, attempting to shave off a scraggly reddish beard with an ivory-handled straight razor.

"Just trying to clean up a tad." It had been almost two weeks since the encounter with the Rego brothers. His wound was healing relatively well, considering the large hole behind his shoulder. The offending bullet had entered just over the top of his left lung, shearing off a small piece of shoulder bone but missing other vital organs and arteries. Luckily, no severe infections had set in, and he was recovering as well as could be expected.

"I'll leave it on the table so you can read it when you get through. Looks like it's from a Mr. William Hargrove at Pigeon River. Kinfolk?"

August flinched with the unexpected announcement and nicked himself with the razor. "Ouch," he muttered from the sharp sting, while thinking, *finally, they wrote me back.* He was relieved to get the letter from his father at long last. Almost four months ago, during the heights of his depression, he had posted a letter to Joseph's grandfather, Basil. Since then, not one word from the family had come his way.

"Yea, sure is."

"Good—hope it brings good tidings. Well, I've got to get back. I'll see you this evening. Going to try to clean up some of that business of yours that's been let go since you got hit. See you later," he finished, cracking a slight smile.

"Yea—see you later, Dick. Oh, don't forget to bring some milk if you can find it."

August scraped off the rest of his beard and hurried to open the letter. He was barefooted and bare-chested, wearing only a pair of pants and a white linen bandage wrapped around his entire upper torso. Pulling a chair to the table, he sat down and began reading carefully.

April 29th, 1885
Dear Son,

    *Congratulations on the mining job, boy. You've done well! And who would ever thunk you would take up mining! I figgured you'd do right good in something but never knew it would be mining. Sorry to hear about that break-up with the girl. We won't say no more about that.*

    *First things first though. We only got your letter last week. It got miscarried somehow, and Basil and Rufus carried it straight down to us when it finally come to them. We have good news to give you—real good news—about that Cherokee County killing. Nobody's heard from that no-good Sheriff out there, ever since he went out west searching for you. It seems they now have a witness thats come forward who seen the fight. He's a farmer who was hunting in them woods and he says he saw the whole thing. He told the Judge he saw that Posey man shoot straight at your friend, and he testified Posey was aiming a rifle on you. Well apparently this farmer is right well respected in those parts and can be believed. The judge has dropped all charges against you, August! You're a free man now! You can come home whenever you want to! Joseph's in the clear too. We can't wait to see you!*

    *Joseph got himself married last summer and is still living in Memphis. He and Eugenia have a son now. They've named the new baby Basil after* his grandfather. Appears Joseph is making himself into a timber man and is moving right up in his father-in-law's company.

Your mother and Beth are doing right well now. Beth and her family have moved down to Flowery Garden and they seem to be doing good as most. Your Mother is bearing up much better now that she don't have to fret none about you. I'm still the agent at the railroad station. Don't see myself going away anytime soon. It's getting busier and busier with the timber men coming in and all. We have five cars or more a day of logs and rough lumber headed for Asheville and beyond. Them timber barons are buying up our mountain forest land to beat. That section of railroad you was working on out at Murphy is still under construction. I suspect it will be at least a couple more years before they finish it up.

We're proud of you August! You and Joseph did what you did because you had to. Weren't no other choices, far as I can see. You keep up the good work out there in Skidaddle with the mining company. Come back to visit or stay as soon as you can. We want to see you!

Guess you saw we addressed the letter to your new name, August Hipps. Hope you don't have to keep that name anymore.

*Your loving Mother and Father*

Taking note that his father had scribed the letter and his mother had bothered to sign it, August tossed it up in the air and let out a whooping cry of joy, "Yay! I'm free! I'm free! I'm free at last!"

# Chapter 13

## Return of the Prodigal

By the onset of summer, August had made considerable gains toward full recuperation. There was a small pockmark high on his chest and a good-sized scar on his back, everlasting evidence of the bullet's entry and exit wounds. However, most of the hurting had subsided such that he could work again. During the withering daytime hours, he kept watch over things in the mining town with the sheriff, and in the sultry evenings, he and Rosehl picked away at their mining claims.

The business with Hanna had created no rifts in his relationship with her parents. Their official relationship, as well as personal friendship, remained as fast as ever—maybe faster, although the boss was spending far less time in Skidaddle. When August received a summons from Mr. Stenson to come to Los Angeles, it came with neither surprise nor concern. The young unofficial mayor of Skidaddle took it only as an invite to visit, and he relished the opportunity.

Before August crossed the Orange Street house's doorstep, Pernilla grabbed and hugged the poor boy so hard that she felt him flinching from pain. "Oh, August, I hope I didn't hurt you!" It had been all Henrik could do to keep Pernilla away from Skidaddle when she heard about August's run-in with the Rego brothers. But he had not been able to stop the many basket loads of fresh fruit and bread that were sent to the Hargrove Spring hospital quarters.

"No—I'm okay, Mrs. Stenson. I'm fine. It's so good to see you!" And then he grabbed her and gave her a kiss on the side of her face.

Henrik was no less enthused to see his young protégé and helped his wife usher their guest into the house and get him settled. The rest of that afternoon and evening was taken up with social niceties, small talk, discussions of the going's on at Skidaddle, the latest news regarding Hanna, and a couple of subjects of a more profound importance.

Come to find out, Hanna had recently returned to Pittsburgh to start planning her and Peter's fall wedding. Things had worked out for them, it seems, and they were both ready to make a fresh go of it. August finally 'fessed up to the Stensons about the bad business in Cherokee County and even showed them his father's letter. Pernilla and Henrik were absolutely flabbergasted and unbelieving! They grilled August for explanations about everything concerning the matter. Eventually, the Stensons' respect and even sympathies for August grew higher than ever, when they realized all that he had gone through.

Henrik had been harboring some explosive news of his own throughout this long vetting of August's past. Actually, it was the reason he had called the boy to Los Angeles in the first place. When he could no longer hold back sharing the fateful news with August, he decided to break it slowly and plainly. "Now, I've got some good news for you, August. I think you're going to like what you hear," stated Henrik with obvious excitement. "Please, come on over here, and let's sit down. We'll tell you what's happened in your absence."

The three of them nestled down in comfortable cushioned chairs as Henrik started. "I can't help worrying about you out there in Skidaddle, August. It's such a forlorn, lawless place. Uh—I'm sorry for that. I misspoke! It's not an entirely lawless place anymore, thanks to you and Dick. You two have done an admirable job bringing order to Skidaddle! Can't adequately give high enough praise for what you both have done. People don't have to fear for their lives now when they walk down the streets. What I meant to say was—maybe you might want to move back here to Los Angeles with us.

I've sold the mining company!" With that pronouncement, Henrik reared back and looked closely to catch August's reaction.

Well, understandably, August was dumbfounded! Still, he bounced up out of his chair to shake Henrik's hand, while acting like a stuttering fool. "Congratulations—I reckon! I don't really know what to say! What—what you mean, sir, you sold it? You sold Skidaddle?"

"That's right, August! I sure did! And just between us, I've made another fortune!"

"But why, sir? We've only been operating for a year or so. Why did you sell it now?"

"That's a good question! Let me see now, how can I best explain it? Why don't you sit down there and let me try." Henrik—and Pernilla—watched August flop back onto the couch as an expression of incredulity grew ever broader across his face. "Well, it's like this, son, we've done all of the hard work now, and the mines and stamp mill are very productive and profitable. The value of our company, based on existing profits and future potential, is extremely high. But, as you know, there's always an inherent risk in the mining business," he added emphasis by pausing and looking for understanding.

However the look of disbelief was still washed across August's face, so Henrik continued, "Catastrophe looms with each rising sun, August! You can never know what's going to happen, and heaven only knows when the mines will play out! About a month ago, I met with a man from a San Francisco conglomerate, and he made me an offer that was simply too attractive to ignore. All capital and operating debts will be assumed, this fine house of ours will be paid off, and a substantial profit for our mining company will go into the bank. In a million years, I could never have hoped for more out of this Skidaddle financial venture—and so quickly!"

"That mean, sir, I won't be working in Skidaddle any longer?" the dumbfounded August asked. "What about the sheriff?"

"I'd like for you to come back here and work with me. Pernilla and I like living here in Los Angeles. The weather is so much nicer than Pittsburg. And I'll tell you what, August. I'll pay you a hefty salary if you do. I'm looking for other business opportunities, and I'd like for you to continue on with me here."

After a brief interlude of silence, August offered, "Can't see no problems with moving back here, don't reckon. I'm glad for you, Mr. Stenson—making out so well with Skidaddle. You deserve it! You gambled and it paid off! What about the sheriff then? I'm worried about him."

"We both deserve it! Don't play down your role in all this. As far as Dick is concerned, there'll always be a need for a sheriff in Skidaddle. I know he's your good friend, and I'll make sure the new owners take care of him. He's a good man, sure is!"

"Yes sir, he is! I appreciate it! So will Dick."

A lot of hard good-byes were said over the next month or two as August turned over his Skidaddle duties to the new owners. Miners, mill employees, town's people, business owners, and even the ladies of the night were disappointed to learn he was giving it up. The hardest farewell was the one shared with Sheriff Rosehl. The two of them had developed an incredibly tight bond—one akin to that of a father and son. So, understandably, the breakup of their partnership was difficult, but they got through it. Dick Rosehl stayed on as the sheriff of Skidaddle, and the transfer of the mining operations to the La Fortuna Mining Company came off without any serious complications.

By early fall, August had moved back to Los Angeles and was shadowing Henrik Stenson in his search for potential new business ventures. However, a growing itch to go back east for a visit soon became too strong to ignore. Realizing it must be scratched, August begged leave from his new duties—whatever those were—and headed back home to see his family and friends. And, as quick as that, he found himself on a train scooting northward through California and then eastward bound on the Central Pacific road.

Who could have foreseen such a miraculous turn-of-events? Less than two years ago, the two young men were fugitives from the law when they chanced upon the Rhinehart family in Memphis. Now, here they were reunited again, each with promising circumstances, and one with a beautiful wife and baby to his credit.

"Hello there, little Basil. Why, you're going be taller than your pa—yes you are," August said in as sweet a voice as he could softly whisper. The squirming blond baby's eyes were glued on the strange man holding him, and everyone else was watching the amusing pair with interest. Basil was six months old and big enough to prompt August's remark. "He's such a pretty and healthy baby, Eugenia. Congratulations!"

"Thank you, August. We're so happy—the three us. I can say with certainty, if it weren't for you, Joseph and I would never have met," and they all had a good cackle over the wise crack.

"You're welcome then, Mrs. Edmunston. Glad to oblige! It's about the only good thing I've done in the last couple of years," and with that, another hardy chuckle was had by all.

The three-day stopover in Memphis passed quickly. A once-tight friendship was rekindled. August reacquainted himself with the Rhineharts and learned much more about their timber and riverboat-wooding business. He also found out that Joseph's father had written his son, telling him that there were no more legal difficulties to worry about. And just as August had been hiding his past from the Stensons—and everyone else—Joseph had concealed his from the Rhineharts. Only days before their baby was born, he revealed the dark secret to Eugenia and her parents. Not only did they help him bury the troubles for good, but Eugenia proudly adopted Joseph's true name—Edmunston.

When the stopover in Memphis came to an end, the parting proved to be difficult. Promises to write more often and visit occasionally were made, and then August found himself riding the rails again. His circuitous route dipped into Alabama before passing through Chattanooga and on up to the east Tennessee rail hub of Morristown. From there, it was a relatively short passage along a twisting line that penetrated the North Carolina mountains to reach Asheville.

Taking full advantage of the first class ticket his boss had purchased for him, August sat on a comfortable couch and peered out the window at the passing countryside. Directly across from him were a couple of gentlemen with their noses buried in newspapers. The early morning sun glared harshly in August's eyes, and he had to squint right much to get glimpses of the lazy French Broad River slipping by.

Through the glare, he could still make out the towering mountains rising steeply from the banks of the river. The hardwood forests blanketing the mountainous terrain were awash in the brilliant colors of fall. With the exception of dense evergreen stands high up on the mountain tops, vast living canopies were painted with rich hues of yellow, gold, orange, and deep scarlet. August had suspected he would never again see the natural splendor of his native highland country. Looking upon these sights filled him with a pleasurable homesickness.

"I say, sir, would you happen to know the name of this big mountain river we can see below us there?" The question caught August somewhat by surprise, and he turned toward the fellow seated across from him. He was in his late thirties, August guessed, and slight of build. Thinning black hair and spectacles had August guessing the man might be a banker or such.

"Yes sir—that there's the French Broad River."

"French Broad, is it? Does it extend all the way to Asheville?"

Taking only a second or two to remember, August replied, "Yes sir, it does. And from here it flows down to about Knoxville and joins up with the Tennessee River, I believe." Memories of the veteran, Tom Doughty, flashed through August's head at the mere mention of that big river.

The bespectacled man mulled this new intelligence over for a few seconds then chimed back, "By the way, the name's Reginald Whitney, sir. I'm from Cincinnati." He reached out and offered his hand in a friendly manner. August, likewise, clasped the man's hand in his iron grip and replied, "August Hargrove at your service. I'm heading over toward Pigeon River ways. It's where I hail from."

"Glad to meet you, August." Whitney retracted his hand and made a show of squeezing it into a fist. "Quite a grip you have there, Mr. Hargrove. Oh, this is my valet, George Abbott."

The elderly man sat still and simply nodded his head toward August, hardly changing his stoic expression. August, however, reached over and jabbed out his hand, forcing Abbott to come out of his shell. "It's good to meet you, Mr. Abbott!"

"You too, sir." Abbott said as he shook the stranger's hand, even managing a friendly smile.

August and Mr. Whitney gradually entered into a relaxed banter, each querying the other to learn more about their fellow passenger. From these exchanges, August learned that Mr. Whitney was not a banker—far from it. He was the son of a Cincinnati, Ohio, lumber baron. In addition to a supposedly secret mission in Asheville, Whitney was scouting for timber resources. From the lumber man, August learned that the industrial revolution, a booming furniture industry, and the railroad's insatiable need for construction materials and boiler fuel were driving lumber barons like Whitney's father into the mountain wildernesses.

"So, August, you say there are virgin forests close by where you live in Pigeon River?" Reginald asked. They were on a first-name basis by now.

"As far as your eyes can see, Reginald. You need to come over, and I'll show 'em to you."

"Well, I might just take you up on that." Then he revealed the nature of his other business in North Carolina. "I'll be meeting up with George Vanderbilt this evening at the Battery Park Hotel. It's supposed to be a hush-hush meeting, I understand. He has a vision of building a large country estate, and his agents are quickly buying up vast tracts of mountain farmland and forests. Father has close ties to the Vanderbilts. He's been asked to assist in appraising the timber resources on the properties they've already purchased and those they still seek to control."

"Sounds like quite an undertaking. How long you figure it'll take to do the work?"

"Not quite sure. I'll know more after tonight's meeting with Mr. Vanderbilt and the agents. I've set aside two months to get my work done, so we'll see."

"Well, when you're done with Mr. Vanderbilt, come on over to Pigeon River, and I'll show you around some real pretty country. What you say?"

"I say fine and dandy, August. I'll telegraph your father at the railroad station, and let you know when to expect me. Will that work for you?"

"That'll work. We'll treat you real nice, you can count on it."

The Pigeon River station platform was crowded with folks who had made the trek down the river to meet August. His small family clan was there—parents, Hack and Harriet, and sister Beth and her family. The Edmunstons had shown up in force, including Joseph's parents, Rufus and Emma, and his grandparents, Basil and Julia. The elderly Folsom Mann—the Bee Woman—had even shown up. And there were many other old friends of August's, bearing names such as Osborn, Cathey, Terrell, Shook, Long, Burnette, and Moore. The scene was one of utter chaos, confusion, hugging, and crying for several minutes as the masses welcomed home the prodigal.

Hack held tight to August with one arm wrapped around him and his other hand ruffling his son's hair. "Good to see ye, son! It's real good to see ye!"

Harriet's crushing bear hug lingered and lingered, with Beth simply trying to find a place to hang on. "Oh, August, we're so happy to see you again," his mother said, sniffling and crying, unable to hold back her emotions.

She was not the only one having a hard time containing pent-up feelings. August found the huge reception and just being with his family once again to be profoundly overwhelming. After using his shirt sleeve to wipe away welling teardrops, he was barely able to reply, "I'm glad to be back with you, Ma—real glad."

# Chapter 14

## A Christmas Token

(In the year 2005)

"Hello, Aunt Nannie. Hope I'm not disturbing you."

"No, not atall, Clint! Been expecting you. I'm glad you could come."

Clint Hargrove had kept fairly busy while waiting for his friend, Claire Shook, to finish her teaching responsibilities for the semester. He had poured over maps of California's Panamint Mountain region, plotted out the cross-country road trip to Panamint Springs, California—the nearest point of civilization to the Lost Burros Canyon, made reservations at an inn there, bought camping supplies, and researched property holdings in the vicinity where he reckoned his great-grandfather's old mine might possibly be. This afternoon he was paying a visit to his late father's sister, to see if she could shed more light on August Hargrove's mystery mine.

"You not having to work today, August?" Nannie asked, as she led Clint into the kitchen area of her house.

"Uh—no, not today, Aunt Nannie. It's exam week, and my day was freed up." Clint was too ashamed to let his aunt know he had been suspended from work in order to sober up. The last thing he wanted was for the family to find out. Only the evening before, he had fallen off the wagon once again, so he was trying to keep a good distance back from his Aunt Nannie. A whiff of his breath might give away his dark weakness.

"Oh, good for you! Now then, you just have a seat here at the eating table, and I'll go get something I've found that could be of some interest to you."

"Sure thing!" Clint's eyes roamed around the kitchen while he waited for his aunt to return. There was an old Hoosier cabinet against one wall, still being used for storage, it appeared. *Wonder if she still keeps her flour and sugar in that thing*, he was pondering just as Nannie walked back in.

"I rummaged through some of my old Hargrove things last night, and this is all I could find that might help you. It's a very old letter to August," she finished, plopping a yellowed envelope in front of her nephew.

Clint immediately began examining it, first looking at one side and then the other. "Hmm—addressed to August Hargrove at Canton, N. Carolina," he read aloud, "very intriguing, Aunt Nannie! And I see it's dated October, 1898, and—hmm—looks as though it was posted from Dick Rosehl at Ballarat, California. I remember seeing that place on the old maps too."

"Go ahead and open it up, son. Take a look. There's an old letter!"

Clint opened the envelope and took out a single sheet of stationary. He could easily detect that it was indeed an old letter, noting that it had been scrawled with a pencil on both sides of the paper. Wasting no time, he began trying to decipher the handwriting.

*Skidaddle, California*

*October 23rd, 1898*

*Dear August,*

*I know its been a right smart while since I wrote and I'm sorry about that. Ever since you were here last year I've been trying to get back around to working that old Jackass claim of ours. About two weeks ago I drilled and blew out a big chunk of rock right over that small vein we could see. Well, damn if it doesn't look to be promising. It's gold and it sure enough looks to be widening out as it disappears into the rock. I'm going to keep following it and I'll let you know if it might be worth your time to come out here and give me a hand with it. You never can tell.*

*Weather is finally cooling off a little. Its getting mighty lonely now that most of the diehards are finally moving out. The mining company has removed all of the valuable lift equipment and stamps out of here—everything that the fire didn't destroy or ruin. There are a few men, some with their families, who keep scratching around trying to make a living. But they won't be here too much longer. Let's hope the Southern Jackass won't peter out like all those others. Maybe we'll both make our fortunes in gold one day. What do you say about that?*

*You take good care August and don't be a stranger in these parts. You've got the gold fever just as bad as the rest of us. You only hide it better. I'll let you know about the Jackass after I've dug it out a little deeper.*

*My Sincerest Wishes,*
*Dick*

After painstakingly working his way through Dick Rosehl's awkward scribbling, Clint glanced over at his aunt, who was watching him closely. Aunt Nannie was the keeper of the Hargrove family history. Her mind was a fierce trap that latched onto and never seemed to forget the stories and details of her ancestry. These she could readily recall and share with interested kinfolk, such as Clint. Nannie had an idea that this letter might be important and exactly what he was looking for.

"There was a mine then! It's the Southern Jackass—the one on the map! This is great, Aunt Nannie! It's what I needed to validate this crazy trip I'm planning to make."

Validation was good. But the trip was by no means dependent on his finding this long-lost letter. Clint was going no matter what. He desperately needed to get away and find some purposeful challenge or distraction in his life. And there was Claire. He was highly anxious to spend this time with her, so he could get to know her better—and who knows what else.

"Well, it sure enough appears that the old map you found might be exactly what you thought it was. It shows the same mining claim that Dick Rosehl writes about in this here letter. You never can tell—he might have found a right smart amount of gold in it. Is that about what you allow, son?"

Nodding his head, Clint hurriedly replied, "Right! That's what I think! But don't get me wrong, Aunt Nannie. I'm not driving all the way across the country in hopes that I'm going to find a rich gold mine. That's the last thing in the world I believe! But, still, I want to go out there and see that country—see what those Panamint Mountains are like. Hike up to where the Skidaddle ruins are shown on the map. Why, I'll bet we can still see something of the old mill and the town itself. Maybe we can locate the Hargrove Spring! That would be something—a spring named by your grandfather and my great-grandfather. I doubt we will, though."

Clint paused briefly to catch his breath and to let Aunt Nannie interject something—her approval or understanding, anything—into the conversation, but she was not of a mind to do so just yet. So he fired back up again. "Probably won't be able to see anything but a pile of rocks and rattlesnakes though. But if we do find the spring, then we ought to be able to locate where the mine was—roughly. It should be about a quarter of a mile away. That would be where Dick Rosehl is likely interred. And I've been thinking—and Claire thinks so, too—that we might want to leave a marker or monument identifying the spot as his final resting place. Great-Grandfather Hargrove would appreciate it—I'm sure he would. I'll try and contact the property owners to see if they would have a problem with us doing that."

"Well, I'll say! Good going, Clint! Glad to know you've got your head in the right place, and you've thought everything out so well." The smile on Nannie's face stretched from ear to ear, and her enthusiasm was manifest. "We've all wondered for a long while now about Grandfather August Hargrove's doings out west. I expect you're going to learn a lot on this trip. And it'll be a grand experience for both you and your lady friend. One of these days you're going to take my place as the keeper of the deepest Hargrove secrets. You know that, don't you?"

Then, as they looked knowingly at each other, Clint responded with a grin, "Looking forward to it, Aunt Nannie! You know I am."

### (In the year 1885)

The time had passed quickly for August. For more than two months, he had been doing some well-earned slacking. Many of his days were spent simply catching up with his folks and the rest of the highlanders along the upper Pigeon River. But at times, he was not beneath showing a little industry, like helping Hack and some other neighbors mash up their sorghum cane harvest and cook it into the sweet, sticky syrup called molasses. Hog-killing time had also come and gone. August lent a hand to Rufus and Basil Edmunston, slaying and butchering more than thirty fat beasts to fill their smokehouses with bacon hams.

Twice August had telegraphed Henrik Stenson, begging for more "vacation" time to spend with his folks. Stenson had willingly obliged, since he had not found any capital investment opportunities that suited him just yet. A few days after Thanksgiving, however, a surprised August found himself on the receiving end of a telegraph request from California. Seems Hanna had indeed gotten herself married, and she and her husband were spending several months abroad to see the sights and seal their love for one another. Henrik and Pernilla Stenson were wondering if they might not be able to spend the Christmas holidays with the Hargroves in North Carolina. Hack had already read the telegraph when he gave it to August and stood by to watch his son's surprise change into excitement.

"Well I'll be! Did you see this, Pa?"

"Yep, done read it. Wouldn't be no problem with us, son—no problem atall. We'll find a place to put 'em up. 'Sides, I mean to thank them Stenson people for all they've done for you. I can't wait to meet the man—and her too."

Expectations were high in the Hargrove household, and excitement abounded as they prepared in earnest for the Stensons' visit. Poor Harriet almost worked herself to death—cleaning the house, putting things in order, and planning the meals—so that she could make the well-heeled guests feel right at home this Christmas season. Although August tried his best to put everyone at ease, explaining that the Stensons were just regular folks and would not want to be treated special, it did not matter much. Harriet—and Hack—still fussed around to make things just right for August's wealthy benefactors.

At last and on a frosty afternoon, August found himself loitering on the wooden platform at the railroad station, anticipating the arrival of Henrik and Pernilla Stenson. Directly, he heard in the distance the faint sound of a train's whistle, and before he knew it, the steam locomotive was pulling to a stop at the Pigeon River station. After several more minutes of waiting and a lot of commotion, the Stensons eventually exited their car; whereupon August hustled over and greeted them with big hugs.

Hack was not far behind him, and his son did the honors. "Mr. and Mrs. Stenson, this here is my pa, Hack Hargrove. Pa, this is them, Pernilla and Henrik Stenson."

"I'm pleased to meet both of ye! Heard a lot 'bout ye from the boy here. He's spoke some mighty good things 'bout ye." Pernilla gave Hack a soft hand to shake, and he took it, squeezed it lightly, and gave the beautiful woman a polite head nod to acknowledge his high honor in meeting her. After that, he and Henrik had themselves a firm hand shake.

"Me and Harriet are mighty happy ye're goin' be spending Christmas with us," Hack welcomed. "We ought to be able to accommodate the both of ye without much trouble in our place, up the river a ways." As Hack finished his invite, a shortish man dressed in a suit and bowler hat sidled up behind the Stensons. He was certainly a strange-looking fellow. Why, Hack even thought his skin appeared to be a tad yellowish.

"How kind of you, Mr. Hargrove!" Pernilla replied. "We're so happy you will be welcoming us into your home. Henrik and I have been looking forward to it so very much. August has told us all about you and your wife and daughter. We can't wait to meet them! Can we, Henrik?" she finished with a sweet look at her husband.

"No, we can't wait! We appreciate your hospitality, Mr. Hargrove! I hope that's not too much of an inconvenience. Oh—Mr. Hargrove, this is our valet, Jee Man Sing. Would it be a great imposition if he stayed with us too?"

By this time, Hack had already figured out who this strange-looking little feller probably was. Weren't many service people employed around Pigeon River, especially of this variety. But there were still a few Africans around, of course, who provided mostly manual labor for the farmers and merchants.

Hack could not recollect ever seeing a Chinaman in these parts. *Hell,* he thought, *this might be the first Chinaman ever to set foot in Haywood!*

"Why, sure thing, Henrik! Won't be no trouble atall! We'll find a place somers other for this man to bed down." Then Hack reached over and offered his hand to the valet. "Pleased to meet ye, sir! Hack—Hack Hargrove's the name." The significance of the extended hand was not immediately understood by Mr. Sing. But he quickly picked up on the intention, and put down the bags and gave Mr. Hargrove's hand a manly shake.

Blazing flames danced in the stone fireplace of the Hargroves' modest frame house, barely warming the freezing room. A kerosene lantern hanging from the ceiling overhead shined its dim glimmering light over all those gathered around the crowded hearth. In the corner of the room, a good-sized evergreen tree was propped up and trimmed with all manner of crafted ornaments and decorations. Tiny candles attached to the sturdiest boughs were alight and flickering with yellow flares. On this cold Christmas Eve, these miniature conflagrations served to warm the spirits of the Hargroves and Stensons, if not their bodies.

The conversation they engaged in also seemed to have a thawing effect. In short order, the two families became closer and began to share feelings in freer and more personal terms. The essence of Christmas infected both hosts and guests, who reveled in the good times and stories that were being told. Such was the spirit, when Henrik and Pernilla spoke about a certain person's heroic escapades out West. Hack and Harriet sat on the edge of their seats, harkening to the words, while glancing from the Stensons over to their son and then back. Embarrassment glared from poor August's red face, as he listened to the talk about the lifesaving incidents on the riverboat and train.

The Hargroves' pride in hearing about these acts of heroism could barely be contained, and Hack was able to offer an understanding comment, "Knew ye had it in ye, boy. Ye're a Hargrove, ain't ye?" Then he went on to express a real heartfelt sentiment to the Stensons. "Guess ye've heared all 'bout the bad business the boy got himself into. Well, we can rest easy now that he was able to save his own life—just like he did yers."

There was no end to the questions an uncomfortable August tried to dodge, as his family sought to understand his heroic antics. Pernilla, bless her heart, shared her version of the Skidaddle shootout involving the now-deceased Rego brothers. Of course, that brought on another round of inquisition. But, finally, attentions were diverted back to the real reason everyone was huddled before the Hargroves' hearth that evening. It was Christmas Eve after all, so at the very time Saint Nicholas was working his way around the world, the Hargroves and Stensons began exchanging Christmas gifts.

The California guests had very thoughtfully carried with them lavish presents for each of the Hargroves. And the Stensons, in turn, were treated generously as well, receiving hand-crafted items from the Hargrove women. A colorful woven shawl draped comfortably over Pernilla's shoulders, and Henrik was overjoyed to fit his cold hands into a pair of knitted woolen gloves. Perhaps unnoticed by some, these practical presents were actually worn for the rest of the festive, albeit frigid, evening.

"We thought we were coming to the South," Henrik joked, "not the frozen Arctic." His humor was appreciated and, even before the laughter subsided, he raised his cup of hard cider to offer a toast. "Let me express my and Pernilla's sincere and honest sentiments to everyone on this eve of the Savior's birth." After a slew of hardy "hear—hear's" and everyone had taken a big gulp of cider, Stenson took the floor again. "Now if you will allow me, I would like to say something else to my good Hargrove hosts." He paused for a moment to gather his thoughts and foment the anxious audience. "You should know that the best decision I ever made in my entire life was to place my trust in a down-on-his-luck young man, one who was sitting alone in the corner of a riverboat writing a letter to his parents."

August slowly rocked in his chair, wondering, *Uh oh, what now?*

"I can assure you," Henrik went on, "it was the wisest thing I ever did. Not only did he save our lives and the life of our daughter, but he worked himself to the bone at Skidaddle to ensure the success of that venture—and he almost gave his life for it."

All of this was still such fresh news to the parents, sister and her husband, that their eyes widened, and their mouths gaped in astonishment. As Henrik continued, they were still giving quizzical looks toward the red-faced August.

"All of you know what kind of young man August is, so I'm not going to embarrass him further, except—" Henrik reached inside his coat pocket and pulled out a small piece of folded paper. He struggled to open it with his gloved hands but finally was able to. "August, Pernilla and I offer this small token of our gratitude for all that you have done for the Stenson family. We love you like our own and are ever grateful that you stumbled into our lives. Cheers, everyone!"

August had never been so embarrassed in his whole life. After taking another swig of cider, he took the piece of paper from Mr. Stenson and was just going to stuff it in his pocket—but Henrik insisted. "It's okay, August. Take a look and see if it meets with your approval. We wouldn't want you feeling slighted."

The redness in his face was still glowing as bright as the burning yule log when he snuck a peek at the inscription on the little document—a bank check. He could hardly believe what he read. Looking up at Henrik and Pernilla in astonishment and then turning toward his family, he stammered in bewilderment, "Ten thousand dollars!"

# Chapter 15

## Scouting the Big East Fork

"His name was Whitney—Reginald Whitney," August explained. "We met on the train and got to talking about these mountains and the untapped wealth he says they hold. Timber and mineral resources were primarily what he was interested in. He was raving on and on about our virgin forests, swollen with them centuries-old hardwood trees. Said they were here just for the taking. He wants to see 'em for himself, and I invited him to come over." Pausing for a second or two to catch if Hack and Henrik Stenson were following him, he then continued. "According to Mr. Whitney, now that the railroads have penetrated these southern Appalachian Mountains, it won't be long before the wealthy capitalists sweep in and begin buying up everything they can get a title to—or steal."

The three men were in the Hargroves' front living room talking, and Henrik Stenson was on the verge of actually becoming excited. He was learning more and more about the investment opportunities that existed in the North Carolina mountains for deep-pocketed speculators, like himself. But all of his enthusiasm had no effect on Hack, in the slightest.

"Last thing we need in Haywood is a bunch of Yankee carpetbaggers destroying our forests. No offense, Henrik." Hack's words were spoken to his guest with about as much reserve and politeness as the former Rebel could muster. "But ye're right 'bout one thing, August. Them woods of our'en are chock full of giant trees—sech as walnuts, chestnuts, oaks, poplars, hickory—trees sech as that. Got us a sight of evergreen hemlocks and balsams too—and them spruces. Why, I reckon there be some trees that five men linked up can't reach their arms around!"

"No offense taken, Hack! No sir! I understand where you're coming from. Would you believe we brought our own carpetbag or two with us on this trip?" Following that well-aimed quip, laughter filled the room.

After more than a week's time lodging with the Hargroves, the host and guest had taken a shine to each other; the same could be said for the growing friendship between Harriet and Pernilla. Even Jee Man Sing, the Chinese valet, was fitting in rather well to his new rustic circumstances. A corner of the barn had been made quite comfortable for him to sleep in at night, with its own kerosene lantern and stove.

"They grow 'em like that up on the Big East Fork!" August pitched in. "That's what I told Whitney. Heard from him the other day! Says he still wants to come out and see for himself, but he's been delayed with all the work he's doing for Mr. Vanderbilt." Rising from his chair, he poked up the fire and threw on another hickory stick. "The Edmunstons' property is full of them big trees too. But Mr. Edmunston and Mr. Basil don't cotton to cutting 'em down unless they're needed for something other." August was, of course, referring to Joseph's father and grandfather, who owned a sizable tract of land on the East Fork River.

"You thinking of another business venture, Henrik?" Hack had gotten quite curious about the matter.

"Oh, you never can tell. Sounds like it might be worth my time to explore around here and get a feel for the resources and business potential myself. After selling off those Skidaddle holdings, there's a large sum just sitting in the bank. Need to invest it somewhere, don't we, August? Sure can't wait too long, or someone else will jump in and beat us to it."

"Yes sir. If you say so—I reckon. Why don't we set out tomorrow up the East Fork and do some exploring, like we talked about? I'm sure the Edmunstons will put us up and maybe they can guide us where to go on up the river. What you say, sir?"

"Rufus would be more than happy to host ye, son. And he can take ye way up by the Shining Creek. Most of that wild land is still held by either the heirs of Robert Love or the State University. May have a few squatters on it, though. Henrik, don't believe I ever mentioned it to you, but before I got the railroad agent's job at Pigeon River, I held the County Surveyor position for a few years. Know this Haywood land fairly well."

"Well, I'll be!" Stenson reacted, being quite impressed indeed with Hack's previous professional experience. "August, if Pernilla offers no objections, I think I would like to take a look with you up on—what did you call it—the East Fork?"

"That's right, sir. It's the East Fork of the Pigeon River. Reckon you can sit a horse for the trip?"

"We'll see about that, if you've got an extra one. Guess we can leave Jee out of this little excursion. Don't you think?

"Yes sir, Mr. Stenson. I think probably it would be best to leave him here. The bad roads and snow and ice might make it difficult for him to keep up with us on foot. 'Sides, I don't know what those East Fork folk would allow about Jee—or them wolves and panthers, either." At which point all three men had a good laugh.

August and Henrik got off early the next day, traveling at a slow pace until the guest got a hang for the horse's gait. Also, the roads were icy and dangerous, further hindering their progress. They made their way by Deaver's Mill at Forks of Pigeon, and around noontime rode into the Edmunstons' farm on the lower East Fork River. Although pushing sixty years, Julia and Basil were both looking pretty good for their age—especially Julia. Her blonde hair showed some streaks of gray, but she was still as sprite and beautiful as ever. Captain Edmunston had kept himself in fairly good shape too. As he led the travelers into the Den—his log home, it was hardly noticeable that he wore a prosthetic leg.

The amiable visit proved to be not only relaxing and restful for the fatigued horsemen but also extremely informative. Basil shared with them that most of the lower portion of the East Fork valley still belonged to his family. His grandfather had received the land as a state grant, just after the Cherokee Indians were pushed out. Way on up above them on the East

Fork, above where his son, Rufus, lived at the Crab Orchard farm, there were several other settlers farming along the river and the feeder creeks.

"The further up the East Fork you go the wilder it gets and the less clear the land titles become. You'll see," Basil explained. "Uh, Henrik, you mentioned before the possibility of maybe building a sawmill to cut up the trees. That would seem to make sense to me—saw up the huge trees in the forest, haul the lumber down to the railroad at Pigeon River, and then ship it through Asheville to buyers outside these mountains. Don't know too much about it, but I hear the furniture makers are setting up shops down about where the mountains flatten out."

"You're right there, Mr. Edmunston!" added Henrik. "I met a lumberman on the train—August, you met that Mr. Whitney—well, they say there are furniture factories springing up along the railroads in Carolina to take advantage of the abundant lumber resources here in these mountains."

"Henrik, you can call me Basil. If you're a friend of the Hargroves, then you're most certainly a friend of ours. I ought to tell you, I'm mighty stingy with my timber. I've discussed it before with Rufus and Hack about building a larger sawmill on the river. But we never figured out how to raise enough capital to do it. I've always been leery of mortgaging my own land for such a risky venture. Not much of a business man, I reckon." Chuckling a little, Basil went on, "Say, don't know if you noticed it, but I've got a little mill on the creek at the foot of the hill. Used it to saw all the oak lumber for my son's house up at the Orchard. Still piddle around with it sometimes. August, you've seen the mill, I'm sure."

"Yes sir, Mr. Edmunston. I've seen it. But I don't reckon I've ever seen it running and sawing timber."

"Ha! That's a good one! Ought to tell you, then, about a little flaw my mill's got." Cracking a smile of embarrassment, Basil continued, "You see, me and Blaylock—he was my builder—didn't cipher things out exactly right. The water wheel and gearing are not sized correctly, so the confounded mill won't run unless we get enough rain and water to flood the creek and turn the wheel." Basil gave out a hardy chuckle, slapped Henrik on the back, and joked. "If it comes a monsoon, fellows, and you ever need any sawing done, you know where to come!"

After the laughter died down, August shared a notion with the others. "Might ought to use steam power, if we get around to building a bigger sawmill. Don't you reckon, Mr. Stenson?"

"Certainly do! Like we used to drive those big stamps at Skidaddle—that ought to do it."

Basil listened appreciatively as August and his new Stenson friend discussed the motive forces that would be needed to drive an industrial sawmill. He had always dreamed of building one of those on the East Fork. Now here was his son's son's best friend and a carpetbagger discussing how they could make it happen. *Maybe they can do it. Hope Stenson's got plenty of money and can tolerate the risk,* he thought to himself as he listened to their ideas.

Just before nightfall, August and Henrik rode into the Crab Orchard farm, higher up on the East Fork, where they found Joseph's mother and two sisters at home.

"I'm sorry, Rufus isn't home right now. He's off in the woods somewhere trying to round up a bunch of stray steers," Emma explained, as she and her daughter, Nancy, welcomed the visitors and began helping them shed their heavy overcoats and hats. "August, it's so good to see you! What a surprise! And you must be Mr. Stenson. How do you do, sir? I'm Emma, Emma Edmunston."

"Pleasure is all mine, I can assure you Mrs. Edmunston." Henrik privately appraised the beautiful woman, as he lowered his head slightly in an abbreviated bow. "Please, call me Henrik!"

Emma was a fine-looking woman, all right. Although well past forty years old, she still presented herself with the same grace and beauty that had swept a young Rebel soldier off his feet. And her daughters were no slouches either. Teenager Lizzie bounced out of the kitchen just about then, still wearing an apron and with one side of her face smeared with flour.

"Hello, I'm Lizzie. Please excuse the smell. I was just chopping up an onion," the younger sister announced with a laugh, as she presented her hand for Henrik to take. Turning to her long-time friend, she expressed with pleasure, "It's so good to see you again, August!" Then she crowded up and gave him a big hug. "Now, if you'll please excuse me for hurrying, I've got something in the oven that needs tending to right away!" With that said, she turned and rushed back into the kitchen.

August chuckled along with everybody else, as his attention was drawn briefly to Lizzie's sister, Nancy. There was something about her that—well, she seemed so much more mature and beautiful now. Those emerald-green eyes were just as enchanting as ever. *She's sure gotten pretty since...*

"Please, August, you and Mr. Stenson come on in and make yourselves comfortable," invited Emma. "I'm sure Rufus will be dragging in shortly." Then she and Nancy helped the guests get settled near the warm fire, and for the next half hour or more, they engaged in a friendly chat until Rufus finally joined them. The ladies were soon excused to fix some supper, and the conversation gradually took on a different tone.

"For years we've talked about building a larger water-powered sawmill on the river. Reckon Pa told you his mill won't run unless the creek floods," Rufus said with a grin. "'Sides not having the cash money to build one, neither of us can hardly see our way free to cut our own trees. Been a whole slew of tenants run off for chopping down trees without good reason."

Henrik and August related their experience at Skidaddle with steam power, suggesting the technology was proven. But Rufus was not readily convinced, outlining a whole host of concerns. "A sawmill operation high up on the East Fork—I don't know about that. Can't imagine the manpower and stock you'd have to supply and feed. Might be dealing with fifty head of oxen! Just dragging those big trees out of the woods and getting them to the mill—how would you do it? Then you've got a long-ass haul over bad roads to the railroad at Pigeon River. I don't know, Henrik. It'd cost a sight of money to overcome all those problems and get a large mill started." Rufus' skepticism was self-evident.

Nonetheless, Henrik was not one to be dissuaded easily from a promising venture. "Well, Rufus, it's like this. I've got to invest some capital somewhere. Can't afford to let it sit idle in the bank. Got to put it to work, and me and August thought a lumber mill up this way might produce a good return on our investment. That not right, August?"

August had a healthy respect for his father-in-law's judgment and business acumen, but he had his own reservations. "Not real sure I know enough about sawmilling yet, sir. Reckon I'm goin' have to learn up on it before deciding one way or other. And I'd sure like for us to get on up the river and scout the land for timber. Give it a real good look. Don't you think we ought to take a look at that Love property Mr. Basil spoke of? He seemed pretty certain it might do and thought those Love heirs might be partial to letting go of the mineral and timber rights. We can't cut the timber if it don't belong to us."

"That's right, son! First things first! I want to see this East Fork forest land there's been so much talk about."

"It's a good idea, August," Rufus added. "I'd like to go with you, but I'm afraid I've got some pressing court business in Waynesville to take care of tomorrow. You can manage, can't you?"

"Yes sir. Me and Joseph's been all over those mountains. And I brought along Pa's old Colt revolver, just in case we wake the bears and snakes," August shot back with a confident grin, gingerly patting the holstered gun on his hip. "You remember it, don't you, Mr. Edmunston?"

"Yep, I remember it, son. I sure do," Rufus replied, as visions of August's father confronting a Union cavalryman flashed through his mind.

Patches of snow and ice covered the narrow wagon road along the bank of the East Fork River. These were the places where the sun never shined, but the horses trod right over the treacherous footing. August and Mr. Stenson had spent the night at Crab Orchard and awoke to embrace this glorious morning with the temperature hovering near the freezing mark. They rode and rode up the brawling stream, trying to reach its upper headwaters. Passing Big Pisgah Mountain rising on their left, the horses plodded a few miles further before wading through a boulder-strewn spot where two creeks emptied into the river. At that watery junction, lit by the glimmering sunlight shining through the forest's winter nakedness, the travelers spotted a small cabin up on a high overlook. Thinking it might be best to stop and make inquiries before continuing on upstream, they reined their horses toward the rustic shelter.

It was an old log structure, and gray smoke spewed from its rock chimney high into the clear sky. Although the roof shakes seemed to be in tolerable condition, the mud chinking was in dire need of re-daubing. August's sharp knocks at the door were soon answered, and he stood back as an older woman, far beyond Henrik's age, opened the door and peered out at them.

"Can I help ye?" the haggard-looking lady asked sharply, while still holding the plank door ready to shut in the visitors' faces, if need be. Her silver-colored hair fell wildly around her face, and her lower lip bulged from a large pinch of snuff trapped against her teeth.

"Yes ma'am. Hello—I'm August Hargrove, and this here is Mr. Stenson. We're heading on up the road a piece—higher into the mountains. We were wondering if we might be able to ask you or your husband a question or two 'bout this land 'round here. We don't mean to bother you none, though!"

"Hargrove, huh? I know me some Hargroves down 'bout the Forks."

"Yes ma'am. I've got kin folk down there. My folks are Hack and Harriet Hargrove. They live just below the Forks, not too far."

The woman just looked at August for a few seconds and then toward Henrik. All of a sudden, she turned her head and called out, "Charlie! We've got visitors—Hack Hargrove's son." With that announcement, the lady opened the door a little further and motioned with her head for the visitors to come in.

Just inside the cabin, a tall gangly man dressed in a pair of dark wool pants and flannel shirt stepped over to meet them. One of his cheeks puffed abnormally from a wad of tobacco he was chewing on. While pushing back a shock of gray hair with one hand, he offered the other to his visitors along with a friendly greeting. "How ye fellers doing? I'm Charlie Hardin. Come on in now—come in and find yerselves a place to sit, why don't ye. Now, what can I do ye fer?"

There were not enough chairs to go around, so August stood with his back to the fire, facing the others. Come to find out, Hardin knew Hack fairly well and had even known August's deceased grandfather, Columbus. After a brief exchange of small talk, Henrik got down to the crux of their visit. "Mr. Hardin, we've been told there's plenty of wild land somewhere up here that is privately owned by the Love family. Could you tell us where that might be?"

"Well, sir, this land of mine we're sitting on used to be the Love's. Some time ago, my wife's father got himself a deed to these five acres. Named this here creek after him—Crawford's Creek. Sally was a Crawford," he pointed out, glancing over toward the old woman. "Everything else up the river, for more than ten miles, thereabouts, it ever bit belongs to the Loves—or the government—on both sides. Why, I reckon the Loves' land goes all the way up to and past the Shining Creek. Them other pole cabins you seen 'round here—squatters live in 'em. Sheriff can't seem to run 'em off though. They keep coming back."

"Guess it's right hard to uproot a squatter once they get planted good," August observed. But he thought he remembered at least one other shack much further upstream in a wilder country. "Uh, Mr. Hardin, what about on up the river? Are there more squatters living higher up, between here and, say, the Shining Creek?"

"Reckon there be one more, son. Way up high yonder, ye'll find a Ashe family squatting up there. Jack Ashe is his name—a bear hunter. Best ye'ens don't cross him. He's meaner ary rattlesnake, I tell ye." Hardin looked first at one and then the other visitor, while steadily working the wad of tobacco in his mouth. "Why, he tracks them bears down on foot—don't use dogs like the rest of us'ens. Sells the hides to fureigners lodged in them fancy hot-spring hotels over about Waynesville and Asheville. Ye best watch out for Ashe and not cross him. He ain't nary good atall!

# Chapter 16

## MOLLY

The farther the two horsemen rode up the river, the narrower and more treacherous the icy wagon path became. They rode all afternoon through the snow drifts blanketing the magnificent virgin forest, amid towering poplars and great trees whose staggering girths astounded Henrik Stenson. Encountering a small creek gurgling and splashing into the East Fork, they pulled back on their horses' reins and came to an abrupt halt.

Henrik shook his head in wonderment as he gazed into the leafless forest surrounding him. "Can you believe this, August? Look at all of these gigantic, beautiful trees. They're so immense! Goodness, I would hazard to guess some may be as old as five hundred years—don't you think—or older? Look at them!"

August had pulled up beside Henrik, and he started glancing about too, but not nearly so enthusiastically. "Yes sir. Guess they've been here a right smart time. Reckon God must have planted them when he created these here mountains. Had to! Don't believe there's ever been any loggers in these here woods, unless the Indians hacked one or two down with their tomahawks, for some reason or other."

"I don't see how a man could cut through such huge trees! It's beyond me. But I suppose they can work those long crosscut saws all around the tree and eventually saw clear through the trunk. Must take hours and hours to do it, I would think."

While they were idling about admiring the forest, August caught a slight whiff of wood smoke, causing him to extend his searching gaze to take in a much broader expanse of the forest. Soon he spotted the source of his sensual arousal. Perched way up on a high knob, overlooking this same little branch their horses were slurping from, he saw a crude log hut.

"Up there, sir! There's a cabin—see! I can smell its fire."

Henrik glanced quickly toward August and then looked in the direction he was pointing. "Oh yes—yes, I can see it."

"Thought I remembered a cabin somers around here! Wonder if that's the Ashe place."

"Might as well go up and find out. Don't you think?"

August had a funny feeling about it. Old Hardin had warned them about Ashe, and August knew how contrary mountain folk could be if they were riled. But darkness was settling around them quickly now. Maybe it would be a good idea to go up and introduce themselves and see if there was some sort of stock shed where they could camp for the night. Perhaps they could pay Ashe—or the occupants—for some cooked food to eat.

"Suppose we could, sir," August finally answered, as he patted the holstered revolver on his side for reassurance.

*Knock, knock.* After tapping lightly at the door, a suspicious August looked around him. *How can anyone live like this?* he wondered, hoping no one was at home. Guinea fowl were still moving about and pecking for food, obviously curious about the late visitors. Several curing bear hides nailed to trees and the sides of the cabin could be seen. There was a fire burning inside—no doubts about it. In the gloaming light he saw feint traces of smoke escaping from the mud and stick chimney. Also, through gaps in the stacked poles forming the walls of the cramped structure, he could detect a flickering light. August knocked again—louder. *Knock, knock, knock.* Moving back from the door and glancing over at Henrik, he wondered, *Where the hell is Ashe?*

"Who's there? Who is it?" came a soft fearful voice from inside.

August was somewhat surprised that Ashe had not come busting out of the door with his fists balled up, spoiling for a fight. "Uh—it's me, August

Hargrove. We're just looking around these here parts and wondered if we might camp nearby. Don't aim to trouble you none. We can pay if you care for us to." Then he hushed and waited. After a long moment, he heard the latch being moved, and then the door wobbled slightly and gradually swung open.

It was a girl who stood just inside the threshold with her head bowed down, as if studying her bare feet. August was taken aback and could not say anything at first. She was young for sure, sixteen years old or so, he reckoned. Her raven-black hair was cropped just below the ears, with short bangs that he could see in the feint light. "There ain't nobody home. He's gone off hunting." The girl's words were soft and trembly, almost scared.

August barely heard what she said. Moving in a little closer, he hurriedly tried to mollify the girl, "Don't you worry, miss. We don't aim to hurt you—not atall! Don't be afraid—please!" He looked anxiously at the girl to catch her reaction.

Slowly the girl's head rose until she was at last looking directly at August. Her face was expressionless, perhaps ashamed. He perceived it as a look of shame, not timidity or nervousness, and it immediately dawned on him that something was amiss. One of her eyes was almost swollen shut, with a huge black bruise framing it. There was a large red welt on the other side of her face. *Poor girl!* August fretted. *She's been hurt somehow—been in some sort of accident!*

"Are you okay, miss? Appears you've been hurt somehow. Can we offer our assistance? I can put some salve on those bruises of yours."

The young lady continued to stare directly at August. As her lips tremored slightly, she responded, "He ain't home! Better you git 'fore he comes home. He don't much like folks coming 'round here."

August was literally stunned at the situation, and he hesitated at first. Gathering his wits about him, he responded in as soothing a voice as he could muster, "Who's not home, miss? Is this the Ashe place? Are you Jack Ashe's daughter?" By this time Henrik had dismounted and walked over to see what was happening. The girl did not take her eyes off of August, as she nodded her head up and down. Her peering dark eyes, set above prominent cheek bones, seemingly had a mesmerizing effect on him. *The girl's beautiful,*

August mused. *Must be part Indian!* "This is Jack Ashe's daughter, sir. He's not home, she says."

"How do you do, miss? I'm Henrik Stenson. Pleased to make your acquaintance." With that polite introduction, Stenson took off his brimmed felt hat and bowed before the bewildered girl. August detected her unease and worried desperately about what to do. In addition to being barefooted, she was wearing a tattered dress fashioned from sacks. An old knitted blanket, draped around her neck and shoulders, hung loosely down to the packed dirt floor of the cabin. Being so far away from the fire, the poor shivering girl was absolutely freezing to death. August intuited this and noticed through the open door that the low fire was on the verge of extinction.

Suddenly, he announced, "You're freezing, girl! Let me see if I can build that fire up for you!" And without asking permission or any further to do, he barged by the girl, straight into the cabin, and began poking at the fire. Looking around for more firewood, he could find none. In fact, there was very little else in there. So ignoring the girl's protests and Henrik's stupor, he rushed back by them and began searching outside for a stash of wood. Finally discovering a few sticks near the guinea coop, he carried them back inside and began stoking the fire until it was roaring.

"Now, that ought to do you awhile, miss," a contented August allowed to the girl, as she and Henrik moved up beside him to warm themselves. "Anyhow, it should keep you warm until your father gets back, I would think."

"That's a fine fire you built, August. Now, why don't we leave this young lady and find ourselves a comfortable place to rest tonight—back down there near the trail? Don't you think that's best?"

August could feel Henrik's discomfort, and he understood. If the truth be known, he was extremely uneasy himself. But he was also troubled with the idea of leaving the girl there by herself. He had the awful suspicion there was something afoul about the whole situation, but he had no idea what it was—what was wrong with the girl. He fretted over leaving her there alone, but they had not been invited in. Actually, the girl had warned them off. No telling what Ashe would do, if he found two complete strangers inside his cabin with his daughter—alone. August imagined what the man might do, and it was not very pretty.

Reluctantly, he responded to Henrik, "Yes sir, you're probably right." And then he looked into the girl's enchanting eyes again and began to apologize, "I'm so sorry to have bothered you, miss. We're going to leave now, and I hope you'll be all right. Do you want me to round you up some more firewood?"

The girl's face began to reveal a pained expression and returned August's stare with an equally intense one of her own. Then, with a slight quivering of her lips and tears beginning to stream down her battered face, she responded, "Please take me with you. Don't leave me here with him. He's going to kill me! I know he will! Please! Please help me!"

Dumbfounded, the two men just turned and looked at one another, not knowing what to say or do. Neither could believe his own ears. *I knew there was something wrong here, had to be*, August realized. With little time to weigh the ethical and moral considerations—let alone the legal ones—they both reacted to the girl's plea for help with understandable empathy.

"Let's go then! We'll help you—won't we, Mr. Stenson?" August replied. "We've got to hurry!"

Henrik just stood there for a second or two in shock. But there was no way he could deny this young girl his assistance. "Yes—yes—damn right, we'll help her! I'll get the horses! You get her ready to go!"

Hugging this kind man provided a wonderfully strange and secure feeling, the poor girl thought, as she straddled the horse behind August and wrapped her arms tightly around him. Trying to put as much distance between themselves and Jack Ashe as possible, the three of them travelled through the freezing night to reach the Forks. At last, just as the first glints of the morning sun began spewing over the mountains, they made the Hargrove place.

After eating some breakfast, the girl sat among the others—the Hargroves, Stensons, and Jee Man Sing—and tried to warm herself in front of the fire. She remained quiet and listened, while her hosts chatted about the trip and the wonders of the East Fork mountain forests. Now and again, she glanced around at the strangers surrounding her, but her stare would always home back on August's kind face. Being around this stout handsome fellow made her feel safe. Something told her that he would never hurt her, ever.

Eventually, the cold and fright slacked off, and the girl grew more easy in her new surroundings. She became comfortable enough to begin divulging the most horrific details of her life with Jack Ashe. Molly was her name, and she was seventeen years old, she thought. Several years ago, her mother, who was Cherokee, had disappeared without a trace. Family members had come inquiring after her, as had the Haywood Sheriff. Jack Ashe had claimed the woman was not legally his wife, and she had just up and walked out on them. Per Ashe, she simply had gotten fed up with their meager circumstances and had returned to her people, deep in the Snowbird Mountains. Since then, Molly had not seen her mother—nor had anyone else, for that matter.

The bruised face that she shamefully tried to hide from August came courtesy of her father. Molly allowed how Ashe regularly beat her and abused her in the vilest manner possible. Whether liquored up or not, he vented his frustrations by hitting her—sometimes with a stick—or by laying into her with a leather thong. Her hosts were astounded by the scars and wounds she reluctantly revealed to them, including a permanent deformity in her left arm. Seems Ashe had broken her elbow when he was roughing her up once—twisting her arm real hard in order to force her to do things she was set against doing. Left untreated to heal on its own, the elbow was never the same again, greatly limiting the use of her arm. But that was not the worst of it!

In the last few years, Ashe had regularly overpowered Molly and sought from her a relief for his bestial lust. Night after night, he forced himself on his daughter and dared her to deny him the female comfort she could provide. If she resisted, he let her have it with either a powerful blow from his hand or a cutting lash from the leather strap. Trapped like an animal in the squalid cabin, she was made to service her father on demand and satisfy his fleshly desires.

Moreover, Molly told them how she had recently noticed a peculiar abdominal discomfort and had been suffering inexplicable bouts of queasiness and even intestinal sickness. In her worst dreams, she worried that she might have been impregnated by her father, a nightmarish scenario simply too horrible to contemplate. Molly was savvy enough to realize that Ashe could not be allowed to suspect such a thing had occurred. She knew he would not stand for it. People would work out that it was his baby. They would know he had had his way with his own daughter. Molly had absolutely no doubts that if her father discovered she was pregnant and carrying his baby, he would not hesitate to kill her—just as he had killed her mother.

Oh, Ashe had never fooled Molly one bit. She had believed all along that there was something sinister about her mother's disappearance. The mother and daughter had loved each other dearly, and Molly was convinced her mother would never have abandoned her. Ashe had gotten rid of her mother—Molly was certain of it.

The sexual abuse and the dire consequences of a potential pregnancy ultimately drove Molly to avail herself of the rescue opportunity. Instinctively, she felt the handsome man who had knocked at her door could be trusted. More importantly, she believed by the looks of him he could stand up to her father and would not be intimidated by him. Simply put, she thought August could save her.

Henrik and Pernilla, along with their Chinese valet, returned to California in late January. Before leaving, Stenson gave August instructions and full authority to proceed cautiously and advance the East Fork sawmill project as he saw fit. The necessary communications were to be handled through telegrams, letters, and such. "Keep me posted" had been the boss's final words, and in the week or so since, August had been a nervous wreck, fretting and wondering how in hell he was going to advance a sawmill. Where would he get one of those things? What about logs? Where and who would harvest them? What would he do with the sawn lumber? These were fairly basic questions that had to be worked out in order to advance a sawmill, and they required sensible answers—answers he did not have. Where was he to start?

If that was not enough to keep him occupied, he had an even tougher situation to deal with. There was little doubt now that Molly's father had impregnated her. In a tearful session around the Hargroves' popping and crackling hearth, the poor girl had confessed to her hosts that she did not care to have the baby. She was noticeably dead-set against the notion. Her rationale was plainly obvious. It was not because of the potential adverse biological consequences—she knew nothing about that—or the shadow of immorality that would be cast over her and the child for the rest of their lives. Neither of those reasons was why she did not want the baby. Molly simply could not tolerate the thought that she was going to give birth to another Jack Ashe, even though she had the man's blood running through her. She was horrified with that realization and wanted nothing to do with it.

After days of deliberation, arguing, and praying, the Hargroves finally concluded that they must intervene and help Molly resolve this dilemma. Such a thing as they had in mind was hardly condoned by the church or the righteous people of the community, and certainly the law would not allow it. But in this instance, August and his family saw fit to shun these moral attitudes and conventions and do what they thought was right for Molly. So they sought the assistance of the only person they knew who could possibly help her.

# Chapter 17

## Futile Warning

"Molly, this here is Mrs. Folsom Mann. She's a real good friend of ours, and she's going to help you, like we talked about. Bee Woman is what most folks 'round here call her, though."

Earlier that day, August had hitched a couple of mules to a wagon and ridden through the snow up to the Bee Woman's place on the Big East Fork of the Pigeon. She was almost seventy years old now and had moved back—along with myriad critters—into a tiny log structure on the Edmunstons' Crab Orchard farm. Her husband, Horace Mann the miller, had passed away only a couple of years before, and August found her sitting alone close to a blazing fire. Usually, a possum or polecat, or sometimes a black snake, could be spotted hiding about, but August wasted no time looking for them. He had important business to discuss with the Bee Woman.

He meant to solicit her services, since she was known by the locals to be the best healer and midwife in the county. After nervously explaining the situation as best he could, he beseeched the woman to return with him to see Molly. Well, Folsom was not much inclined to turn someone down who was in dire need of her special healing powers. So, after quickly stashing a few items in a small basket and hopping in the wagon next to August, she returned with him to the Hargroves' home.

It was uncanny how the two women, so far apart in years, took to each other so quickly. Probably, some unknown affinity was at play that made them almost immediately sense a closeness in their relationship. "Hello, dear girl. Can't say how sorry I am ye're suffering under such circumstances. Ain't right that ye are! Do you want me to help ye, Molly?"

They were alone together in one of the cold upstairs bedrooms. Molly was wrapped in a blanket and on the verge of shivering. "Yes ma'am—August says ye might be able to do away with this baby that's growing inside me. Can you sure 'nough do that?"

"Yes, I believe I might be able to make it go away, dear girl. Ye're right sure it's what ye want, are ye?"

"Please, Mrs. Mann, make it go away as quick as ye can. That's what I want ye to do. Make it go away! I don't want this baby inside me no more!" Molly's normal soft-spoken voice had disappeared, and she left no doubt atall what her wishes were.

"Well now, we'll see then what we can do. Ye're sech a purty girl, Molly. Ain't nary need fer you to suffer with sech a worrisome thing. Better ye jest lie down there and cover up good, dear. I'm going to make up a special tea that's goin' to relieve you from yer torment. That sound okay?"

"Yes ma'am—I appreciate any help ye can give me."

"Okay, then, let me see if I can fix ye up, Molly."

And with that said, the Bee Woman went to work. Carefully descending the steep stairs, she found the rear kitchen where Mrs. Hargrove was fixing supper. The contents of Folsom's basket were quickly emptied onto the kitchen table. Then, using a small soapstone mortar and pestle, she proceeded to pound dried rosemary and peppermint leaves, willow bark, and a very special plant until the mixture had been reduced to a fine powder. Next, she poured the contents from the mortar into a small pot of boiling water, threw in a pinch of snuff, and mixed in a large glob of clover honey. That was all there was to the steaming concoction that she hurriedly and carefully carried back up to Molly's bed.

"Mixed ye up my special tea fer ye to drink. Hope it don't taste too sharp. It's still hot, so be right careful, Molly," cautioned the Bee Woman, as she fed the syrupy tea to the girl, spoonful by spoonful. "Once ye're done drinking it, I want ye to rest in bed awhile. Okay, my dear girl? That's it now, drink it down."

Molly nodded in understanding, as she continued to slurp the honey-laced tea. As soon as she drank her fill, she lay back in bed, and the Bee Woman placed another quilt over her. "Ye'll bleed a sight down there where you make water. Don't ye be surprised none," Folsom allowed. "And ye're goin' to feel a lot of uncomfort and queeziness in yer belly fer awhile—but ye'll get over it. No need to worry yerself 'bout it!"

Slowly, Bee Woman backed away from the bed. "Well—reckon that 'bout does it fer my healing treatment, Molly. Ye take care, now, and I'll come back and check on ye in a day or two. Ye might have to drink another batch of my tea. We'll wait and see."

A huge smile grew over Molly's face as tears welled in her eyes. Then in a wink, she threw back the covers and jumped out of the bed, hugging the Bee Woman as hard as she could. She loved this queer old woman for some reason and was sure that she was soon going to be without her father's child. "Oh, Mrs. Mann, thank ye so much! I know ye've fixed me good, and I ain't no longer goin' have his baby. Thank ye—thank ye so much!"

August sought the law's assistance with the Jack Ashe business. A couple of weeks or so after the Bee Woman's healing visit and Molly's nausea, pains, and bleeding had diminished, August brought the sheriff to the Hargrove home to talk with the girl. After listening to Molly's story, the Haywood Sheriff was somewhat sympathetic to her situation. However, he did not think an arrest was warranted or that a strong legal case could be brought against Ashe. The girl was over ten years old—the legal age for consensual sex in North Carolina—and it would only be her word against his if they took the thing to court. But the sheriff did allow that he or his deputy ought to ride up to Ashe's and set things straight with the man.

So it was that on this cold February day August found himself riding in the van, ahead of the sheriff's deputy, climbing the steep mountain slope to Jack Ashe's place. They found him there, outside his little cabin, splitting sticks of firewood into kindling. From the looks of him, he had imbibed his fill of ardent spirits, as he was tottering so badly that he was barely able to wield the axe.

"Hello there, sir. Are you Jack Ashe?" the deputy hailed from a short ways off.

Ashe lowered his axe, turned and looked toward the visitors with an indignant frown. "Who wants to know?" He was a big burly man, dressed in clothing fashioned out of animal hides. Most of the hair on his head had disappeared over the years, but his unruly black beard grew like a bush around his face.

"Swift—Deputy Sheriff Swift from Waynesville. Are you Jack Ashe?"

August just looked at the bear of a man who was drunker than a skunk. The weight of the revolver holstered on his side was a confidence booster for sure. It brought back memories of Sheriff Rosehl and similar work back in Skidaddle.

Ashe sneered at the two mounted men as he approached them closer. "Yea, I reckon I am. What ye aim to do 'bout it?"

Deputy Swift glanced at August and then back to Ashe. "Don't aim to do nothing 'bout it, Ashe. Keep yer distance there! Don't come any closer now!" Pausing for a moment to make sure his words were heeded, the deputy continued, "We've come to talk to you 'bout yer daughter. Do ye know where's she at?"

Jack Ashe gave both men a threatening look, as his mind rushed to comprehend what they could be after. "She ain't here! Don't know whur she's run off to! She's got a whupping coming to her when she gets back!"

Still sitting his horse, August was beside himself and could not hold back his fury. "I'll tell you where your daughter is, Ashe. She's at my place nursing all those beatings you gave her. Molly told us all about what kind of father you are—how you treated her. What are you—some kind of animal?"

The rage was noticeably boiling up inside Ashe too. August and the deputy watched anxiously to see if he would be able to control himself. He stood up as tall and straight as he possibly could, gripping the axe with both hands now. Wobbling on his feet with his hairy face twitching and his mouth drooling spit, his reply came in a low voice at first, then building to a holler, "She's mine. Molly's mine. You ain't got no right to have my girl! You hear me, mister, god damned ye!"

There was no hesitation in August's reply. "No right! Reckon it's you, Ashe, who has no right to beat your own daughter and have your way with her! You ought to be ashamed! She wants no part of you—never wants to see you again!"

"No! She can't do that! You can't do that! She's my daughter! I want her back!" Then Ashe suddenly began to move toward August, raring his axe back to take a swing.

*Crack!* "That's enough, Ashe!" The sound of Deputy Swift's pistol going off stopped the outraged man in his tracks.

Jack Ashe had no idea who to attack—the one shooting the gun or the one firing stinging insults at him. He looked at the deputy, whose gun was still smoking and aimed high in the air and then back to August. Trying his best to utter something intelligible, he burst out, "I'll get her back, mister! Don't ye worry none 'bout that! You ain't goin' stop me! Ain't nobody goin' stop me!"

"You stay away from her, Ashe! Me and the sheriff will lock you up if you try to get her back. You're not going to hurt your daughter anymore—or have your incestuous way with her." The deputy was firm, and Jack Ashe sensed the lawman meant business. Nevertheless, they could never keep his daughter away from him.

"Don't rightly know what ye mean by incest...somethin'-other. That don't mean nothing to me. But I never hurt that girl! I'm gittin' her back!"

"You heard what I said, Jack! If you come around her, me and the sheriff will lock you up! Can't make it any plainer than that." The deputy's patience was waning.

So was August's. "She's scared to death of you! That's what she told me, and she won't be having anything else to do with you! You'll have to go through me to get her, Ashe! I wouldn't try it if I were you." August emphasized his intentions by patting his trusty revolver with his hand. "'Spect we're done conducting business here! Reckon, deputy?"

"Yea, reckon so. We'll be seeing ye, Jack. Remember what I said! Don't want any trouble out of you. Best ye leave that daughter of yours be. She's way better off now where she is."

Futile was the deputy's warning, because it fell on deaf ears. Sloshed and seething mad, Jack Ashe staggered back and forth, watching the strangers ride off. Given his drunken state, comprehension of what had just transpired was limited. He understood one thing though. He wanted his daughter back. He needed her. The man—that young son-of-a-bitch—said he had her, and Ashe aimed to get her back from him, one way or the other.

### (In the year 2005)

The red Chevy truck was almost ten years old, but you would never know by the way Clint pushed it. In the sweltering heat, he and Claire rode west along Interstate 40 all day long, first through the Pigeon River Gorge and then across the entire width of Tennessee. Their trip was interrupted only by a short stop for gas and a couple of breaks to accommodate human necessity. When they finally reached Memphis, Claire was dozing with her window wide open.

"Wake up, Claire! We're crossing the Ol' Mississipp!"

Slightly startled, she glanced out the window. "What? Oh—oh my—it's so big! Isn't it?"

"Yes, it sure is!" Unmindful of his great-grandfather's brief experience wooding steamboats almost directly below them, Clint added, "See that riverboat down there—used to be hundreds of them plying up and down these waters." In silence, Claire gazed down at the boat and then all around, marveling at the height of the bridge they were crossing and the size of the river.

"Say, I'm getting a little tired. Do you want to take over and try your hand at driving the truck? Guess we're about two hours from Little Rock. We can find a motel there somewhere near the interstate. Want to try it?"

"Sure. Always wanted to drive a truck—especially such a nice one!" Their two smiles could not be helped.

They made it to Little Rock and, after having fast food for dinner, checked into a Hampton Inn. Interestingly, the two friends shared a room together with double beds. Although not official full-fledged sweethearts or anything, they were teachers after all—being such, they were possessed with good sense and rational ideas on how to stretch a dollar. Nevertheless, after choosing their beds and turning in, the two pooped travelers leaked some telling feelings from their hearts.

"I had a good time today, Clint."

"Me too. Appreciate you helping out with the driving."

"Well, I didn't do too bad, now did I?"

"I thought you drove just great, Claire—when I was awake, that is."

"Ha! Did you know that you snore?"

"Oh no! I did? I'm sorry about that. I'll try to keep the noise level down tonight." Although they both had a chuckle, Clint was embarrassed.

"How far we going tomorrow? I'll drive longer if I have to."

"Believe we'll need for you to. Maybe we can get all the way to Albuquerque. It's about twelve hours away, I think."

"Sure, I'll do what I can." Then Claire decided to make a leap. "Think you can do me a favor, since I'm going to help you drive?"

"If you don't need a million dollars, I'll see what I can do. What you got?"

"Uh—I may want to scoot over a little closer to you tomorrow. What would you think about that?"

Clint's hesitation in responding was not due to his pondering whether Claire's request might or might not be a good thing—absolutely not! Actually, he was so stupefied and excited at the same time, he did not know what to say.

Claire asked again, just in case he had not heard her the first time. "Think you might allow me to sit a little closer to you? Surely, you don't think your Chevy would be jealous." She was not entirely sure that her secret affection for Clint was shared. This two-bed compromise was not a promising indication that he intended to make their trip more than a treasure hunt—not at all promising. Although thoughts of the cross-country adventure and hunt for Clint's great-grandfather's gold mine had truly piqued her curiosity—even excited her—she hoped to get more out of the trip. Claire sincerely wanted to let her feelings for Clint be known and possibly learn if the romantic interest was mutual.

*Did I hear right?* Clint struggled to interpret the words he had just heard from this beautiful woman, the one lying in the darkness in a separate bed, mere feet away from him. *Could it be that she likes me too?* he fretted. He held his breath and waited a moment longer. *Can't let her see how nervous I am.* "What—sit closer to me? Ha, that's a good one, Claire. You mean like we're watching a drive-in movie or something?"

"Yea, something like that."

*Damn! What now?* "Well then—sounds okay to me. Matter of fact, I believe I'd like that, Claire!"

"Me too!"

Early the next morning, after ingesting complimentary breakfasts, the two travelers found themselves speeding westward again, along I-40. But it was an entirely different ride than yesterday, because Claire had eased herself over and was now seated snuggly beside Clint. Simply feeling her pressed against him caused all manner of sensations to run through his body—not excluding ones of a highly erotic and sexual nature. Claire smelled delicious too—she sure did.

"Boy, you smell good this morning, Claire!"

"So do you, cowboy! We're heading to Oklahoma, aren't we? Then I guess I'll let you be my cowboy."

"Giddy-up!" he yelped, as they both had a good chuckle. Then, when Claire slipped her hand over on his thigh to rest it, he almost yelped again.

Everything was going just as Claire had hoped and as Clint could ever have dreamed of. However, things were about to take an unexpected turn for the worse. A little less than three hours down the road, near Fort Smith, Arkansas, Clint pulled into a truck stop for an "emergency." While he hustled off to find the bathroom, a leering truck driver parked nearby watched intently, as the beautiful, long-legged Claire climbed out of the red Chevy and began topping off the gas tank. The lurid rhyming ditty painted on the door of his truck was a good indication of what kind of man he was— and what might be running through his filthy mind—*I like beer, I like pot, I like a woman, Who likes it on top.*

However, there was more than filthy thoughts rooted in the ogling truck driver's head, much more. Before Claire finished pumping the gas, the man had hopped down out of his truck cab and jogged over to have a quick chat with the pretty lady.

"Hello there, ma'am!"

He startled Claire, and she immediately challenged, "What do you want? Who are you?"

The man was a good ten years older than her and lanky with slicked-back greasy brown hair. A yellow snaggletooth showed when he replied, "I want you, darling! How 'bout you and me go have us a good time over there in my truck. What do you say?" The driver did not seem perturbed atall that Clint might return anytime. His behavior was highly irrational.

Claire was beside herself and looked nervously around in desperation, hoping to see Clint coming to her rescue. *Where's Clint?* "Go away before I scream!"

"Now, don't you do that, darling," and the man made a sudden move to grab her and pull her back to his truck. "Shssh, shssh! Don't scream, darling! We're going to have us a good ol' time—me and you!" Trying to subdue Claire with one arm, he held his other hand tight over her mouth, as a look of determination and hunger grew across his face. Then he began dragging her back toward his truck.

While Claire kicked and desperately fought back, she fearfully wondered, *Where's Clint?*

# Chapter 18

## A Killer on the Loose

**(In the year 1886)**

Winter's icy grip on the Pigeon Valley and its inhabitants had begun to ease somewhat. Around the Hargrove homestead, the warmth of the vernal sun's rays had stimulated many of the trees to burst into colorful bloom. Flowering redbuds, wild crabapples, and mountain dogwoods, among others, flecked the hillside in pink and white. But these trees were not the only things blooming with the arrival of spring. Molly Ashe, whose belly had been fixed by the Bee Woman, was also beginning to blossom, revealing a stunning natural beauty and pleasant personality. As her shyness—and her welts and bruises—began to disappear, she started to take an intense interest in helping her hostess around the house, as a way of earning her keep. This included learning the intricate craft of weaving, which occupied her full attentions on this fine spring morning.

"There you are! Been looking for you," August called out to Molly, as he entered a shed attached to the back of the house. It was a lean-to enclosure built especially to house Harriet Hargrove's large wooden loom. Molly was sitting at the cumbersome contraption and busily weaving away, using the last bit of spun wool left over from last year.

"Hello there, August. Almost finished with the blanket yer mother started," Molly returned in a polite low voice as she looked up from her work. She fought back showing any emotions—especially her affections toward him. These she had harbored ever since being rescued from her father's imprisonment.

"Yep, looking good, Molly, real good!" August tried his best to show an enthusiastic interest.

"Ain't as good as yer ma's. See here how my edges don't line up good."

"Well, it looks right good to me, Molly. Can't see no difference atall," August lied, as he studied the area where Molly pointed. In fact, he could easily make out the difference in workmanship, but he was not about to let on about it. The girl was learning good from his mother—learning how to weave and cook and other things—and he certainly was not going to dampen her spirits. "Say, Molly, I've got to meet someone down at the Pigeon River station this afternoon. You want to accompany me down? We'll pick up some supplies while we're there."

August felt sorry for Molly. That frightened look he had seen in her eyes when they first met still haunted him. But over the past weeks their relationship had gradually evolved beyond his being solely a custodian/care-giver. They had become good friends and were developing quite a close attachment to one another—too close, really, for August's comfort level. A strange feeling was beginning to affect him, and he was doing his best to shuck it off. Thinking the peculiar feelings he was having for Molly were similar to those ones he had felt for Hanna, he continually reminded himself, *Hell, that can't be—no way! She's only seventeen years old!*

The hurt he had felt after being jilted by Hanna still burned hot inside. He had loved her dearly and had no intentions of losing his head—and heart—to another female, especially to such a young one. No matter how strong the self-rebuke, though, the special feeling persisted.

"What do you say, Molly?"

"Me? Ye want me to go with ye?" Molly could hardly believe it. She had never actually been to a town—neither to Pigeon River nor to Waynesville—and she was suddenly elated.

"Would love to have yer company! Nothing would please me more."

"Well, then, in that case I think I might just go with ye!"

The buggy rolled and bumped down the river road, jostling the two passengers in the single seat to no end. August and Molly took comfort from the beaming warm sun and each other's company.

"Say you've never been to town before?"

"No, never have. Been to Deaver's Mill, up at Forks of Pigeon."

"Well, I believe you're in for a real treat today. You're going to see more people than you've ever seen in your life." August gave the leather reins of the mule team a stiff jerk to gain their attention. "We'll head to Hampton's Store to look around a little and let you see what you think of that place. After that, reckon we can drive down to Thompson's Mill and get Ma's flour, before heading for the station. Sound okay?"

"Sounds fine! Mrs. Hargrove said to be on the look-out for me a sunbonnet. Goin' need one pretty soon now." Molly grinned as she spoke.

Directly, they reached the fording place above the railroad bridge and splashed across the languid stream, as the water level reached almost to the buggy's axles. "Hold on!" reacted August as the wagon lurched up the embankment out of the river. "You okay?" he asked with a concerned look at his pretty passenger.

"Whew—yep, I'm okay, I guess."

"That's the worst part, Molly. Sorry to rough ye up like that."

Holding on to the seat as hard as she could, Molly smiled as August secured the reins with his left hand and rubbed the girl's shoulder softly with his right. She thought it felt right good—what he was doing to her—but wondered why he was doing that.

Rolling by the few business enterprises astraddle the rutted dirt street, Molly looked on in fascination at the horse and wagon traffic and all the people milling about. They rode past the livery stables and blacksmith shop on the left and the hotel on the right. In front of Hampton's Store, which carried a general variety of dry goods, August pulled over and locked the brake on the buggy, as one of the pedestrian passersby took the reins and tied the mules off for him.

"Thanky, sir," August hollered as he hopped down and hurried around to help Molly. He led her across the plank walkway and through the doorway of Hampton's, where she stopped in her tracks. Mesmerized, she stared in amazement at the shelves upon shelves stocked with the most wonderful things she had ever seen.

"Oh my goodness!"

"Isn't it something, Molly? Come on, let's find you a sunbonnet."

---

The 3:30 p.m. train from Asheville was right on time. As it rolled to a stop at the station, the platform was filled with noise and smoke. August and Molly waited and watched from a distance with heightened anticipation. Then, out of the clamor and clouds of steam, August spotted Reginald Whitney walking briskly toward them. His valet, George Abbott, was toting a couple of heavy carpet bags and trying to keep up.

It seems the work Reginald had taken on with the young Vanderbilt gentleman in Asheville had evolved into a much larger project than originally anticipated. However, as Whitney had telegraphed, he needed a break and wanted to scout the virgin forests August had praised so highly. So, August intended to carry the Ohioan into the deep reaches of the East Fork River Valley and see what the lumber baron allowed about those woods.

Hack and Harriet put the strangers up for the night, and early the next morning August, Reginald, and George Abbott set out on their trek into the wilderness. The two horses the guests had rented from the Pigeon River livery were not exactly lively, so August kept his steed's reins taut to match the slow pace. It took the better part of the day to ride up the river past Basil and Rufus Edmunstons' property to the place where the little Crawford's Creek and Hungry Creek emptied into the East Fork. There, they chose to camp for the night.

"That's Charlie Hardin's place," August replied to a comment Whitney made about the primitive log cabin above them.

"Incredible that people can live their entire lives in such a poor place as that." Reginald continued. "How in the world do they even survive? Huh, George?"

After a second or two of reflection, the valet countered, "I was raised in a house in West Virginia not much better than that one, sir. We were proud of it, as I'm sure those folks are."

August was impressed with the valet's remark, raising his opinion of the man substantially. "You're right, George. People 'round here don't have much, but they're mighty proud of what they've got."

After eating the cold bacon and cornbread that Harriet had prepared for them, their chatter gradually turned toward the task of building August's sawmill.

"Mr. Stenson and I have a lawyer in Waynesville working on acquiring timber rights to all this forest land, on both sides of the river—more than ten thousand acres, I reckon. We were thinking about building the mill somers 'round here on this flat spot. The road's tolerable down the river, and we figured to haul the sawn boards in large wagons all the way to the station in Pigeon River."

"Not a bad spot for a mill. What's your market for the lumber, August?"

August stared at him for a long second or two, before stammering, "Sir?"

"Your market—who do you plan on selling the lumber to?"

"Oh, that market! Why, I don't rightly know, sir."

The Ohio lumber man did not offer his very first thoughts to the naive young companion sitting across the campfire from him. He could only wonder to himself how in the world it was that this likable young man had been charged by a wealthy benefactor to build a sawmill. "Well, before you invest a substantial sum of money, I would advise that you first find buyers for your lumber. The furniture industry here in North Carolina is on fire at the present. Factories are being built as we speak. Perhaps you could pursue that outlet—or there are others, too. The railroads need crossties and timber for their trestle bridges. The building industry..." Reginald paused to see if the message was being received and processed. Apparently not reassured, he decided to offer his assistance in another manner, "Tell you what, August, I can help you on that end. I just met the owner of a new furniture company out of Lenoir—in the eastern foothills. I'll talk to him and try to arrange a meeting for you. How's that sound?"

The firelight reflected from August's wide-open eyes, and his excitement was evident. "You will? Why, that's sounds fine to me, Reginald—just fine!"

Then for the next couple of hours, Reginald expounded on logging and sawmilling practices—cutting timber, transporting logs to the mill, sawing logs, and producing lumber. The subject of transporting the logs took up the bulk of the conversation. As explained to the novice lumberman, only if he was able to haul the logs out of the woods and get them downstream to the mill expeditiously and efficiently could his lumber company be successful. August learned how huge logs were commonly hauled on skids pulled by teams of yoked oxen. Of course floating them down the river was a preferred method of transport too, but none of these mountain streams was large enough or deep enough to make that a feasible alternative. Another option, if the grade was suitable, was to sluice them out of the mountains and alongside the shallow stream beds through wooden slides called flumes.

Whitney told him how splash dams were sometimes used to flood small streams, so that the raging water could carry the logs to the mills. Steam-powered portable sawmills and large band mills were talked about, as were the difficulties involved in hiring an adequate work force—employees such as sawyers, teamsters, and loggers. It was not the first time August had been exposed to the techniques and science of lumbering, but it seemed to have more of an effect this time. For hours they talked, with even George adding his useful thoughts occasionally. And the whole time, until he could no longer hold his eyes open, August was weighing ideas and trying to figure out how to advance his and Henrik Stenson's East Fork sawmill operation.

The next day broke with a heavy mist shrouding the East Fork forests. They had gotten off to an early morning start and were plodding up the river through a dark enchanting wilderness. Finally, the sun broke through the lifting veil and lit up the way for the explorers, revealing nature's primeval forest in all of its richness. Almost every five minutes or so, Reginald would proclaim his profound wonder at the immensity of a poplar or the density of a particular stand of chestnut or hemlock trees. And as they gradually gained elevation and the flow of the headwaters diminished, he became flushed with excitement to witness the spruce and balsam thickets grow ever larger. This rich diverse forest that August was leading him through rivaled the tracts he had been surveying for Vanderbilt. In his mind, he began appraising the value of these vast timber resources and entertaining thoughts of some sort of partnership with August. Maybe together they could tap and extract the wealth these magnificent trees represented.

Unbeknownst to the three horsemen, they were not alone in the thick wilderness. Well out of sight and paralleling them on foot was a lone figure, breaking from one tree to the next and carefully keeping out of sight. Jack Ashe's repeater rifle—his ol' bear slayer—was slung over his shoulder as he tracked along, watching the strangers and weighing his options. He had spotted the three riders over an hour ago and had been certain he recognized one of them. There could be no mistake about it. Good fortune had brought his prey to him, and he meant to slay that damn insolent smart ass who had taken Molly away from him.

Ashe had learned who the man was that had stolen his daughter. On one previous occasion, he had even traveled down to Forks of Pigeon and stalked both August and Molly, but circumstances did not avail an opportunity to either inflict harm on the kidnapper or snatch his daughter. Now, he was in his element. No one knew these mountains and woods like he did. Being an expert marksman, he figured he could sharpshoot that stout son-of-a-bitch and then make off into the deepest wilderness recesses, places where few bears and no men ever ventured. That was the plan Jack Ashe hurriedly hatched, and now he was searching for the opportunity to carry it out.

August and his guests had just ridden past Ashe's cabin. Although it could not be seen through the leaving trees, August knew exactly where it was. An uncomfortable feeling came across him as he thought about Jack Ashe and the meanness embodied in the man. *There's no telling what he might try to do to get Molly back*, he thought, realizing for the first time that he might have led his two companions into harm's way. *Wonder where Ashe is right now?*

On one occasion, August thought he saw something moving in the trees above them and a short distance off. He stopped and gazed in that direction for a minute or two, but could not make out anything unusual. *Surely he wouldn't try to shoot me*, was a thought that ran through his head more than once. *No, never! Not even Ashe could be that cold-blooded!*

The horsemen kept riding along for another mile or so until their path crossed over a small stream. There they stopped and let their horses crowd close together to slurp up the trickling creek water. While remaining mounted and stopped, August felt a bit uneasy and began looking around and behind him. His antics caught Reginald's attention. "What's the matter,

August? Afraid some beast's going to charge out of these trees to get you? Ha, ha!"

There was no chance to reply. At the same moment Reginald was joshing him, August felt a powerful blow and sharp pain run through him. Then he saw Reginald's mouth suddenly gape wide open. As the Ohioan slumped forward in the saddle, a loud cracking noise could be heard far off in the distance, undoubtedly the sound of a gunshot. Instinctively, August winced and his hand moved quickly to his side, where blood was already oozing through his coat. Reginald was crying out in horrific agony, as he desperately clung to his horse's neck.

"Sir! Sir, what's wrong?" George Abbott had dismounted and was at Whitney's side in no time, getting him down off the horse. "Here now, sir. Let's get you out of this water. Lie down over here."

"I've been shot, George. It's—it's my stomach. I've been hit."

August was hurt badly himself, and the blood was spewing from a wound in his side, but he managed to dismount and move to the aid of his friend.

"He's been gut-shot!" George cried out to no one in particular.

"Ohh! I'm hurt! I'm dying. I know—I am," were the last coherent words that came out of Reginald's mouth. From that point until he breathed his last breath more than an hour later, he lapsed in and out of consciousness while suffering inordinate pain. August's wound was not nearly as bad as his hurting had led him to believe. In short order, he and George were able to staunch his own flesh wound, and then they tried desperately to ease Reginald's agonizing death pains.

It did not take a genius to work out what had happened. From the very first moments that August had flinched from pain and heard the distant gunshot, he knew. He knew that Jack Ashe—damn him to hell—had tried to kill him. A single bullet must have grazed him before burying in Reginald's belly. And with that realization, he began blaming himself for the great tragedy that had befallen Reginald Whitney.

When news of Whitney's murder was picked up, it was not only the local rags that published the horrible tale. Major news outlets across the country, especially those east of the Mississippi River, fed the story of a crazed killer on the loose to a surprised and outraged public. Reginald Whitney was a man of high social status and wealth, and the taking of his life by an unknown sniper in the middle of western North Carolina's remote mountains garnered attention at all levels of society, everywhere.

People from far and wide gathered at Haywood County's courthouse in Waynesville to organize and be assigned responsibilities to quickly hunt the killer down. Posses, comprised of concerned citizens, sheriffs and deputies from Haywood and surrounding counties, and even a force of eleven men from Cincinnati, were sent off into the wilderness areas surrounding the Pigeon River headwaters to search for and find the likely culprit, Jack Ashe.

August and Hack, along with Rufus Edmunston and George Abbott, participated as well. They rode into the deepest and darkest hollers, circumvented the laurel hells, and crossed crags and ridges looking for signs of the killer or his hideout. All the way to Devil's Face Mountain and its rocky bald—a place of historical significance in Edmunston and Hargrove family lore—they searched. But the posses turned up nothing, and after several weeks the search was finally called off. The killer had vanished like a ghost into the wilderness without a trace, and there was little else anyone could do about it.

August still blamed himself for what had happened, although he and George had been thoroughly questioned and their story accepted without suspicion. However, August knew better. It was his fault for leading Reginald into the crazed man's habitat. Everyone knew Jack Ashe was a dangerous character. August knew it. Molly certainly knew it. *But what could I have done differently*, he kept asking himself? *Reginald had been so keen to survey the forest, and it was a free country*, or at least August told himself so. He had no business telling Reginald that they could not explore the deepest regions of the East Fork because Jack Ashe might be waiting behind a tree up there to get them. Hell no, he would never do that! But he should have taken some precaution—done something to prevent this tragedy—and that was what haunted him.

Molly, unexpectedly, was a rock during this period. Although the idea that her father had killed a man—and had tried to kill August—brought an immense amount of pain and shame to her, she did not let it get her down. She had lived and suffered through terrible things at the hands of Jack Ashe and had ceased to think of him as either a father or a human being. Her mental and physical scars shielded her from any sympathetic or personal feelings toward the man. She hated him without remorse, and was going to do her best to prevent his savagery from affecting someone close to her, as she tried to do today.

"Shouldn't blame yourself, August. No matter what ye think, it weren't yer fault." Molly could not see August. He was feeding the mules, and the cow she was milking blocked her view. So the soft-spoken girl had to up her vocal range to be heard.

"Don't see it that way," August allowed. "Shouldn't have been up that high where your—his cabin is."

"Don't matter none. Ain't nobody would've figgered he would try and shoot ye like that. I've been worried sick he were goin' to come down here to fight ye to get me back. Been 'specting it fer a long time now."

He moved around to where he could get a good look at Molly. Her silky sable hair was pulled up and covered with a new blue bonnet. As she sat on the stool squeezing away at the cow's saggy tits, August could not help from thinking, *What a picture of loveliness. Getting prettier ever day.* "Me too, Molly! I've been worrying and waiting for him to show up. Figured we would have it out in a fair fight, if that could ever be possible with Ashe."

"He's a good fighter, all right—always getting in fights. But he's got a big knife. I've been afraid he'd cut ye with that knife of his. I surely have!" She had turned to look at him now through her sirenic, walnut-tinted eyes, while keeping a steady flow of milk directed into the pail. "Don't believe I could bear seeing ye get hurt."

August just stared at her, not really knowing what he ought to say. He truly felt affection for the girl, but he had to fight it off. *Hanna was enough. Not going to let another one get to me.* That was all he could think about.

"Don't you worry none, Molly. He's not going to hurt me. I won't let him hurt you either!"

# Chapter 19

## Conflicted

The sparse foliage remaining on the trees glistened in the sunlight, with red, orange, and yellow hues still plainly visible. Stiffening cold winds out of the north hinted at winter's approach. On a patch of low ground near the river, August and the man riding with him could see dark gray smoke billowing from the stack of a portable steam engine. The incessant noise of spewing steam, rotating mechanisms, racing leather belts, and a spinning saw blade slicing through poplar logs muffled the sound of the brawling stream. Could it be that on this bottom adjacent to the East Fork River, just opposite where Ugly Creek poured in, there was a sawmill works?

To say that August Hargrove had advanced his and Henrik Stenson's sawmill venture would not do him justice. Good fortune was his ally, for a change. With the financial backing of his benefactor and plenty of grueling field work by himself and the surveyors, their Waynesville lawyer had been able to secure timber rights to almost twenty thousand acres of forest land bordering both sides of the upper East Fork River. Stumpage contracts with the Love Estate and the State of North Carolina permitted Henrik Stenson's East Fork Lumber Company to cut and harvest any standing or fallen trees lying within the agreed-upon boundaries—all for $0.75 per acre.

Back during the summer, Stenson had returned for a brief business visit to help August with a few key decisions. Upon his first trip to the proposed sawmill site, or Ugly Camp as it was called, he had a chance to meet the company's first two employees.

"Mr. Stenson, these are the men I was telling you about. This here's George Abbott and this one be Mr. Claude Johnson. Fellers, this is Henrik Stenson, our boss and the owner of the company." August made it all sound so formal.

To make a long story short, August had offered both these men employment during his trip to Ohio, where he attended Reginald Whitney's funeral. George, of course, was out of a job, and August learned that the former valet had previously worked as a sawyer for the Whitney and Son Lumber Company. Not only that, but Abbott had a nephew who was a first-rate sawmill superintendent. The man had recently been laid off from the Whitney company for lack of work, so August hired them both—sight unseen, in nephew Claude Johnson's case.

Claude was a rougher sort than his uncle and was the first to stick his hand out to greet the big boss. "Pleasure meeting you, Mr. Stenson!"

"Glad to know you, Mr. Henrik, sir." George very politely offered, as he shook Stenson's hand too.

"How do you do? Yes, good to meet you, sir!" Henrik returned their hardy handshakes, but he was still not sure in what capacity the men had been hired—or at least, he could not keep them straight in his mind. But he trusted that August had vetted them and had hired two responsible and skilled men into the company. "Now men, I want you to know—I'm not the boss! August is the boss, and I trust you will do what he says!" Henrik said it in a way that left no doubt he meant it. "In two weeks, I'm going back to California, and he'll be running the show here. Now, is that understood?"

Both new employees nodded. "You can count on it, Mr. Henrik!" George assured him.

"Ain't no problem on my end, sir," Claude chimed in. "Done found it out, me and August can work together. I ain't goin' have no problems whatsoever taking my orders from him." Claude looked over toward August and then back to Henrik. He had already made up his mind about his youthful boss. Although a good fifteen years younger than himself, Hargrove was smart and a good listener. The choice of the sawmill site had convinced him of that.

August had originally chosen the spot near Charlie Hardin's cabin to build the new lumber operation. However, the new sawmill superintendent had convinced him otherwise. Not only did the Ugly Creek site offer as much level acreage, but less than half a mile upstream was a perfect place to construct a high dam. There, where the river narrowed for a short stretch and poured through rocky escarpments—described as a throat by Johnson—hundreds upon hundreds of floating logs could be impounded behind a dam. From this manmade storage impoundment, the enormous logs could be fed, as needed, via a flume to the sawmill. August had immediately seen the wisdom in the man's argument, as had George Abbott, and readily agreed to the venue switch.

After these first awkward introductions, the men began to feel a bit more comfortable and at ease, as they all sat together under the rustic shed that Claude and George had thrown up. The shelter had actually been their home for the past few weeks, while they familiarized themselves with the land and timber resources. As a consequence of their diligence, they had been very influential in helping August formulate a plan to get a small sawmill up and running. It was this plan that August was anxious to lay out for Henrik at the company's first meeting.

"That's why we chose this ground for the mill, sir. We can slide the logs straight from the dam through a flume to our mill here." Claude might have been a backwoodsman, but he spoke to the owner of his company with pluck and confidence. "Ain't goin' be a problem to build a dam in the spot us and August picked out. Twenty feet, or such, should be high enough. You see, sir, our idea is this—while we're sawing smaller logs with a portable mill and building up our workforce, August will be getting us wagons and oxen and getting our big machinery in here. We aim to use that first lumber we saw to build the dam and flumes. 'Spect we can get to sawing and selling a little poplar, too—that's right, ain't it, August—poplar?"

"Let's wait and see, Claude. Mr. Stenson found us a buyer. They want rough sawn boards, but I reckon he forgot what wood they wanted." With the hint of a smile, August finished, "But we can check on that, right, Mr. Stenson?"

"I'll look into it, sure will. For the life of me, I can't remember what variety of wood the man desires. One of my lawyers in Pittsburgh travelled down to Lenoir, after August told me of his conversation with the late Mr. Whitney. He was not successful there, but he did find a prospective buyer in a place called Hickory. The company is the Piedmont Furniture Company and, by all accounts, is an up-and-coming business."

"The furniture companies in Ohio can't find enough poplar," George popped in. "Mr. Reginald has—uh, sorry…" Abbott paused for a few seconds to regain his composure. "Sorry, Mr. Reginald had started to move into the West Virginia mountains to cut it."

"Poplar will be better for our business. It's lighter and floats good. Saws easier too. Won't matter none, sir. We'll saw whatever you give us." It made little difference to Claude what they sawed. He just wanted to get started sawing and get on with the plan.

"Mr. Henrik, I told August about a used portable mill I know of up in West Virginia. It has a Geiser engine that's not been run much, I hear. Believe it's been for sale for almost a year now, so I'm sure the company would give us a good price."

Henrik looked over at August, who nodded his head that it might be worth checking into. "Well, George, I'll leave that up to you three to work out. If it will get us started, then I'm good for it." Then Stenson raised up to stretch and announced, "August, I like your plan. Now, could you and Mr. Abbott and Mr. Johnson here take me up to that 'throat' that was referred to? I'd like to see the place you've chosen to construct the dam. And, maybe, you can also explain more about that slide, or 'flume,' and how it's going to work."

"Yes sir, Mr. Stenson! It's this way. We can walk there."

Since that first company meeting during the summer, the portable sawmill had been purchased and started up, and Ugly Camp was teeming with activity. As August rode into camp with a companion on this brisk fall day, he surveyed all around him. Certainly, there was no shortage of manpower. Late fall in the mountains meant that the corn was cribbed, grass crops reaped, sorghum mashed, apples picked, stock gathered, and hogs butchered. Men, whose work at home was done until the coming spring, could stand the additional income, and George Abbott and Claude Johnson knew how to put them to work.

All day long, farmers manning huge crosscut saws felled poplar trees of a size that could be handled and sawn in the little Ugly Camp mill. Teams of oxen were kept in constant motion, pulling the logs out of the wilderness along rough paths to the mill. Once there, the mill workers under Abbott's supervision rigged, pulled, pried, and rolled the logs onto the sawmill carriage that fed them into the hungry steam-driven saw. Trimmed poplar boards were directed either downstream to be sold or were toted upstream, to be used in the dam and flume construction, which was well underway.

Every day at least two heavy wagonloads of lumber were hauled down to the Pigeon River station, bound for the Hickory furniture factory. One shack after another was built at Ugly Camp, and the skeleton of a new, larger mess hall was being erected. August had a right to be proud of the progress that had been made, but to no one's surprise, the enterprise had yet to show a profit.

Selling two wagonloads of poplar lumber a day did not generate near enough revenue to offset the wages, stumpage obligations, expenses, and capital investments. One such investment was a new and much larger steam engine and sawmill, which was currently being fabricated in Chattanooga. Until the coming spring, when this equipment was scheduled to be shipped and installed, the financial hemorrhage was likely to continue for the East Fork Lumber Company.

The man riding into camp with August was the company's new accountant, Everett Clinard. Turns out, this is his first day on the job, having been hired to see what he could do about balancing the debits and credits and staunching the excessive monetary outflow. His was plainly an unenviable task.

"I've got the Geiser running full out, and we're sawing the logs as fast as they come in, August. Might be able to get a little more out of this mill, but we'll need more logs coming in." George Abbott laid it out as plain as he could, while looking at August and then Claude for understanding. Everett

Clinard was listening in on the meeting, but George figured he was clueless about what was being discussed.

"What about it, Claude? Can you supply him more logs?" August asked, as he looked over toward his superintendent.

Johnson struggled to hide his aggravation from the boss man, his uncle, and the new bookkeeper, who kept frowning and looking over the top of those infernal wire spectacles toward him. "We've done been over this, men! I simply can't count on these farmers 'round here to show up for work. They ain't dependable, I tell you. Still believe you should let me call in them woodsmen from Maine I was telling you about. 'Sides, we're going have to do something to get more good men in the woods. Come spring, when we light up that new mill, we'll need three times, or even four times, more logs to keep it running. What are we goin' do then? I'm telling you, we're goin' have to reach out and bring new blood in."

August had been hoping to delay recruiting more outsiders until they absolutely needed them. But it appeared he could not put it off any longer. "How long will it take to get them outlanders in here, you think?"

"A month, maybe—we can telegraph 'em tomorrow."

"Okay then, I'll send for them. How's the construction coming along?"

"'Bout got the dam built. Taking a lot more rocks to fill in between them timbers than I figured. She'll be strong, she sure will."

"Is the flume going to be ready?"

"That's still the plan. I figure by Christmas we should have enough water behind the dam to float the logs and start scooting 'em to the mill. Then we'll start work on building another flume up the river."

The accountant, for some reason, showed an interest at this point. "Excuse me, Mr. Johnson. Am I to understand that it will be another flume you will be constructing?" This astute man's imagination was not yet harmonized with the dreams of these lumbermen he was meeting with. Instead of valuable logs flooding down a flume, all he could visualize were dollars flooding out of the company's coffers.

"That's right, sir. As our loggers work their way up the river, we'll extend the flume up to reach them. Can't express to you how much more efficient it will be to transport them logs through a flume. Ox-skidding them big ol' logs would break us. Couldn't never keep our new mill running at capacity by using them beasts—too hard—way too hard to keep 'em fed and working!"

"Mr. Clinard, by next summer, we should have that new mill from Chattanooga started up. Then, if all goes well, we'll triple our production and have a steady stream of lumber wagons moving down to the railroad." August's confidence was manifest. "Mr. Stenson's lawyer is looking for other furniture makers for us to sell to. That's our plan. Until then, we'll just have to keep our costs down as much as we can—right, men?"

"Couldn't put it any better, August. I'll keep our mill running until then and try not to blow up the Geiser," George said with a chuckle.

"We need to get those Maine woodsmen in as soon as possible, August. You going to see to it for us?" Claude urged.

Before he could answer, Everett Clinard spoke up, "More employees, is it? I'm going to need an up-to-date listing of everyone employed by the East Fork Lumber Company, as soon as you gentlemen can get that to me. And if I could impose on you further, I'll want to see your labor records and all outside expenditures by 1:00 p.m. each and every Thursday. Now then, gentlemen, that shouldn't be too much to ask—I don't think."

Claude and George stared expressionless at the accountant and then turned toward August with quizzical looks. *What—what are you looking at me for?* August thought to himself. It was Skidaddle all over again, and the headaches were endless as the boss of the East Fork Lumber Company struggled to get the enterprise off the ground.

Snow before Christmas was an unusual occurrence for the Pigeon Valley region. The day before, a white powdery blanket several inches thick was deposited across the high North Carolina mountains, and August was finding the road to Pigeon River to be extremely treacherous. Molly, as usual, was at his side keeping him company as he drove one of the lumber wagons down to meet the Stensons at the train depot. Henrik and Pernilla were coming early for an extended Christmas visit, and, rather than impose on the Hargroves, they had made arrangements to stay at the Penland House in

Pigeon River. August had learned that Hanna was traveling with them, and he was not atall looking forward to seeing her or meeting her new husband.

"So, do you know Mr. Stenson's daughter, August?" Molly was curious, after having heard the Hargrove womenfolk talking about her.

"Yep, I sure do. Got to know her when I met the Stensons out West. She's a beautiful girl, you'll see! And she's a lot different than you. She's got real light hair—blonde hair! And she's tall! You're taller than I am, Molly, but you should see her! She's taller than you are. Yep, she's tall all right."

Molly did not say anything for a minute or so, just looked at the snowy landscape as she mulled August's words over in her mind. Then she spoke up. "Do you think I'm purty, August? I know my hair ain't a purty blonde color, but I think it's purty, don't you?"

August blurted right back, "Sure I do, Molly! You're real pretty!" *I've stepped in it this time, as usual*, he chastised himself. "Molly, I didn't mean for you to think I thought Hanna was prettier than you. I think you're beautiful! Course I do! Your black hair is beautiful—way more beautiful than blonde hair. Don't you worry none 'bout that!

She was worried. She could not stand to think that she might lose August to someone else. Although he acted as if he liked her at times, he had never come right out and said so. No one could have been kinder or sweeter to her than he had. Sometimes, when they had been together alone, he looked at her like he wanted to take her in his arms and kiss her. But he had never done that. He had not even told her he had feelings for her. Neither had Molly expressed her love for him, but how could he not know?

"I'm not worried. I can't wait to meet Hanna and her husband."

*Yea, me too,* August mocked to himself as he prepared the team to ford the Pigeon. "Hold on, Molly!"

The river was low and not frozen over, so the crossing was uneventful. When they pulled into the station, they found the Stensons, along with their valet, Jee Man Sing, already waiting there for them and being fully entertained by Hack. There was a lot of hugging to go around, and Hanna seemed to be particularly happy to see August. Of course, the parents were overjoyed to see both August and Molly again, but, strange as it seemed, there was no husband anywhere about.

"So, Hanna, where is he? Where's your husband?" August could not contain himself. He was curious about this man who had stolen Hanna from him.

"Oh, he didn't make the trip, August. I'll tell you about it when we get to the boarding house." August was puzzled, as he looked away from the beautiful girl to her parents, who tried to mask their frustration.

"And who might this be? Is this your sister?"

"Oh, sorry—no, this is Molly! She's a friend of the family. Molly, this here's Hanna."

"Well now, I'm very pleased to meet you, Molly. If you're August's friend, then I hope you'll be my friend as well."

"Pleased to meet ye, ma'am," Molly replied as she stared at the most beautiful person she had ever seen.

Soon the pleasantries were dispensed with, and they all headed for the Penland House, on the other side of the river. Hack had found someone with a buggy to carry Henrik and Pernilla over there. Hanna rode with August and Molly in the lumber wagon, along with Jee and three large trunks of belongings in the back.

"Oh, Molly, I'll have to tell you the stories sometime of how August saved all of our lives, time and time again. He couldn't help himself. Ha, ha, ha!"

Molly kept quiet while August reacted, "Now, don't you start that! You don't have to listen to her, Molly. Wasn't nothing atall."

"Was too! Remind me, Molly, and I'll tell you all about it."

"Okay, ma'am, I will."

In less than ten minutes they were unloading and moving into the large frame boarding house overlooking the Pigeon River. August was keen to Molly's situation and kept his eye on her to make sure she was not uncomfortable. She seemed perfectly fine. *So what about the husband?* he wondered, but he did not have to wonder very long.

Henrik and Pernilla invited Molly to have some tea and a snack with them, while Hanna visited with August for a short spell. They explained how their daughter had a lot of catching up to do with August.

She sure enough did and got right to the point. "We're not together anymore, August. I thought I knew him, and he seemed like he had changed.

But I could not have been more wrong. He was not true to me. I learned that he was with another woman—she had followed us to Europe on our honeymoon. Can you believe that?" Hanna started patting away the tears with a kerchief.

"Well—well, I don't know what to say, Hanna. I'm sorry—I'm real sorry it didn't work out. You mean you're not married to him anymore?"

"Father's lawyers have filed for divorce, and they're gathering proof of his infidelity. They say it will take a while to get a divorce from him. Oh, August, how could I have been so foolish?" The tears were unstoppable now.

"I'm so sorry. Hope everything's going to work out for you, Hanna. I really do!"

"Thanks, August. All I could think of when this was happening was that I gave you up to marry that man. I loved you, too—so much! You know that, don't you?" Hanna was almost heaving with distress.

This conversation was going in a completely different direction than August was prepared to go, and he tried to get it onto a different track. "That was a long time ago, Hanna. Don't cry now. Things have changed since then. I was hurt so bad—I can't go back there. You'll never know how much I was hurt. Please, please stop crying. Besides, I may have already found somebody else. I don't know for certain, but I'm waiting to see. I want to make real sure of it first."

"What?" Hanna was stunned, and her heaving and crying quickly abated. She had thought—and with good reason—that August would accept her apology and receive her wishes to rejuvenate their old romance with open arms. August had loved her deeply, and she knew it. Who? Who could have won the heart she had broken? "There's someone else? Oh, I see. Well now, that's a horse of a different color then. I see."

There was not much else of consequence said between them, and soon August begged their leave from the Stensons to let them get settled. He wanted to make it home before dark and felt Molly and he should get going. On the way back up the river, Molly slid over close to him to keep warm. He put his arm around her for a minute or two to see if that helped any.

"What did you think of Hanna?"

"She's more beautiful than anybody I've ever seen. Her mother said you and her were real close once." After a prolonged pause, Molly then asked, "How close?"

August was totally confused about his feelings for Hanna. He had been so surprised by her turning up like this and the news she brought. The last thing he wanted to do was lie to Molly about it. He had to have someone to confide in. "We were very close. Truth be known, I almost asked her to marry me. Before I could, she up and ran off with her former fiancé and married him. Now, come to find out, they're split up and getting a divorce."

Molly strained to look at August and see his face. He had such a serious look, and she could also see the hurt in his eyes. "'Spect you loved her a lot."

"Won't lie to you, Molly—I did. But I don't love her anymore. Tell the truth, I don't rightly know how I feel about her at this moment. I'm pretty much conflicted about how I feel." August shied away from elaborating more on his conflict, while worrying to himself, *Should I tell Molly how I feel about her?*

Molly wondered and worried about August's conflict too, but she let it go. They both let it go, which made the ride home in the cold and snow a rather dreary one.

# Chapter 20

## August's Choice

During the week leading up to Christmas, August and Henrik spent much of their time up on the East Fork seeing about sawmill business. These extended absences left Pernilla and Hanna with ample opportunity to visit with the Hargroves and spread their Christmas cheer. Molly became quite friendly with the Stenson mother and daughter, and like everyone who got to know her, they were soon struck by Molly's sweetness. And it was not very long before Hanna came to realize who she was competing with for August's affections.

"He has this habit for saving people. I hear he rescued you too, Molly." Hanna had decided to confide in Molly, while the girl was churning in the kitchen. They were comfortable in each other's company by now, with Molly having taken a real liking to the Swedish beauty. Reckoning that she was not nearly as beautiful as Hanna, she completely understood why August had fallen in love with her.

"Yea, he got me out of the woods—sure did." Molly kept the dash in motion, vigorously stirring the thickening milk. She was fretting over whether to mention something that was on her mind. But she had to know. "August told me he loved you."

"We were both in love, I'm sure of it now. He kissed me so sweetly—we even talked about getting married." Hanna could never believe that Molly, as innocent and uncultured as a newborn in the wild, might wrest August from her. She had been made aware of the girl's situation—abusive father and all—and felt that August's attraction to Molly was stimulated purely out of pity. Thinking it best to make sure Molly knew her place in the pecking order, Hanna laid it on thick. "I believe that deep down inside him he still loves me as much as ever, Molly. Just you wait and see, we're going to be together again. I know we are."

Molly kept churning away and mulling things over as the conversation stilled for a long moment, if not the stirring. She knew where she came from and who she was. Obviously, there was no comparison between herself and Hanna, whose polished manners, striking blonde looks, and fetching womanly features no man could resist. However, she was of a mind that those things really mattered very little. She knew who she was and how she felt, and she secretly reasoned she could love August anyway—whether he loved her or not. Nobody could keep her from doing that.

By Christmas, more than two acres of water was backed up behind the completed dam at Ugly Camp, and logs had been slipped through a flume to the sawmill. However, all logging operations were shut down, and the local men had hurried back to their homes and families for a short holiday break. The Hargrove house was filled with a passel of folks on this Christmas afternoon. The Stensons, of course, were there, along with George Abbott, Claude Johnson, and a few of the imported lumberjacks from Maine. They were crowded throughout the house on the festive occasion and making merry, while Hack and Harriet busied themselves with their hosting duties, including keeping everyone's cups filled with cider.

August was unusually jovial, and for good reason. His sawmill business was progressing tolerably well, and Henrik Stenson was pleased with everything he had seen and heard. Hanna appeared to be as happy and hopeful as ever. Of course, she was still ravishingly beautiful, just like the old days—before she had forsook him and gotten herself married. Topping things off, Molly was seemingly having the time of her life, moving from person to person and enjoying the company and the cheerful spirit of the season. It was, after all, her first Christmas celebration, and as August watched her from across the chilly room, he pondered about how much she had matured in the past year—*so beautiful and poised now*. Harriet and Beth had been teaching her to read, write, and cipher, and her speech was becoming noticeably more refined. *Funny how she doesn't seem so young anymore*, he mused. Although Molly did not know her age precisely, they figured her to be about eighteen years old by now.

Regarding his conflicted romantic feelings, August thought he had things just about sorted out. Hanna still loved him, there was no doubt about that. She had taken every opportunity to let it be known. But August had not fallen for her beguiling charms, after all. He had hardened toward her and had been able to resist a strong urge to give her another chance. Besides, he was convinced more than ever that his true affections were felt for Molly, and he was not going to let Hanna come between them.

Anxious to convey these feelings and get them out in the open, he figured it was time. He had waited long enough, and it was Christmas! Why not give himself a Christmas present? *Well, it's now or never, August. Let's see what you've got in ye, and don't mess this one up*, he challenged himself while moving over to talk to Molly.

"Merry Christmas, Molly! Looks like you're enjoying yourself."

"Oh, I am, August! It's wonderful! Merry Christmas to you!"

"You like my new hat," he laughed as he used both hands to pull the stocking cap down over his ears.

"Why, yes I do—looks good on you."

Molly had knitted it herself, and ever since August opened his present the evening before, he had not taken it off. "Fits real good—see? One of those Frenchies, Jacque Pelletier over there, liked it so much he tried to buy it off me." Laughing, he suggested, "Might be able to sell these hats up at Ugly Camp this winter. You make 'em, and I'll take 'em up and sell 'em for you."

"Really! You think somebody would buy 'em?"

"Course! Do me up a few, and I'll guarantee to get you some spending money."

While August tried to think how to steer the talk in the direction he was aiming, Molly pointed out, "Hanna sure is purty tonight."

Glancing over to where his former flame was gleefully enjoying the company of his mother and sister, August mumbled, "Yea, reckon so. But you too! You look stunning tonight, Molly! Sure do."

Molly was caught off guard. She had not expected to hear him say that. Why, she was not exactly sure what August meant by "stunning." Looking wide-eyed back at him she replied, "You mean, I look purty, too, August? You think I'm right purty?"

Grabbing Molly gently by the arm, August glanced around him and then led her back into the kitchen, which surprisingly was deserted for the moment. It was time to get down to business. "Course I think you're pretty, Molly. I think you're the prettiest thing in this world! Always did think you're pretty, ever since we found you."

"You do?"

"I'm telling you the truth, Molly—how I feel about you. 'Sides that, I believe I've fallen in love with you." There, it was out now. But August could not stop. "I don't love Hanna anymore, like you think. I'm over her—plum over her! You're the one I have feelings for—you, Molly! I love you! I'm sure of it—right sure!"

She could hardly speak—or think. The words would not come to her, and the tears began to well up. With her watery brown eyes staring directly at him, she tried to respond, "But Hanna—what about her? She still loves ye, August. Ye can't love me over Hanna, surely ye can't."

"Don't matter none that she loves me. I've quit loving her for you, Molly. It's you I want to marry one day. Can't you see? I sincerely love you and want you to be my wife!"

Her face glistened from wetness as she continued to rub the tears away. "What? Marry me?"

August quickly looked around to check if anyone was coming. Being assured of their privacy, he hurriedly explained, "That's what I said. I want to marry you! Do you think you could have me for a husband?"

Molly could not believe her ears. Never would she have expected August to ask her that. Could it be possible he wanted her to marry him? But then another thought slinked into her mind, squashing her excitement. It was such an ugly notion, making her realize he could never marry her. Bowing her head, Molly replied in a low sorrowful voice, "You can't marry me now, August. I'm tainted bad—you know that. My father had his way with me. Surely you don't want me for a wife! I'm not pure no more."

"Don't matter none, Molly! I don't care about that, and neither should you. That's all over now. I know I want you! I want you to be my wife more than anything else in this whole wide world."

"Well, what do we have here?" came a sudden voice from the doorway. It was Hanna! She had become suspicious when she noticed they were both absent from the festive goings-on and had gone looking for them. "The party's out here—why, Molly, dear girl, are you all right? It appears you've been crying." Hanna's obvious concern was sincere.

While Molly tried to dry away the tears, August hurriedly explained, "We're just talking here, Hanna. Molly got all emotional for some reason," and he managed a forced grin and chuckle. "Didn't you, Molly?"

"Reckon so. Don't know why," she replied with a sniff or two. "I'm okay though."

"Good! August, Father and those sawmill men were asking after you. They're talking business on Christmas Day. Can you believe that?"

"Okay, Hanna, I'll be right there—tell them for me, would you please? Now, could you give Molly and me just another minute to finish up? I'm a'coming."

"Of course! Then maybe we can talk afterward—after they get through with you. Think so?"

"Right—sure—we can talk after while."

As Hanna turned and walked away, August drew close to Molly and pleaded from the bottom of his heart for her to understand. "You've got to believe me, Molly. It's you I want! I want to live together with you for the rest of our lives. Please say you'll marry me. Please!"

Molly felt his genuineness, though she could not understand why he had chosen her and not Hanna to marry. It was beyond her. But there was one thing she did know. She loved August Hargrove with all her heart and soul, and nothing could please her more than being his wife, if he wanted her. "Yes, I'll marry you, August. I love you more than you can ever know!" And after hearing that, August's eyes lit up brighter than the setting winter sun outside. He wrapped his arms around Molly, pulled her in close, and kissed her as passionately as he knew how. And Molly—sweet Molly—kissed him back, while feeling the most pleasurable of sensations.

By late January, the Stensons, including the heartbroken Hanna and Jee Man Sing, had returned to California. News of August's and Molly's engagement had gotten out, and although Hack and Harriett had been somewhat surprised at first, they quickly warmed to the idea. Just as soon as the weather turned, August aimed to use some of the Skidaddle money he had squirreled away in the bank to build a house for Molly. Hack meant to gift them a piece of Hargrove land up the river, and August could not wait to get construction started. He hoped it might be ready come summertime, when they planned to be married.

At Ugly Camp, the freezing weather had not slowed things down appreciably. Claude Johnson had approximately sixty men in the woods—counting the northern lumberjacks—felling huge trees. Several pulling teams of oxen were kept busy skidding logs to the mill's pond. A crew of carpenters worked like beavers, building a timber and plank V-shaped flume up the river from the log pond. Their objective was to catch up with the loggers as soon as possible and then keep on going. Sliding the logs downstream through the flumes was the answer to the crucial transport problem Reginald Whitney had preached to August about. It was definitely Johnson's preference over the slow, burdensome ox teams that had to be constantly fed and cared for.

George Abbott kept the Geiser engine and portable mill at full throttle, even during a significant snowfall a couple of weeks previously. He and his men had devised an ingenious arrangement of timber slips and snatch blocks and to move the floating logs from behind the dam through the flume and into the mill's log carriage. Then—after a log was chocked tight in the carriage—steam-driven pulleys, leather belts, and clever mechanisms fed it time after time into the whirling circular saw. In addition to a deafening shrieking noise and clouds of sawdust, the process severed boards of exact thickness from the mother log.

Once a board was cut and fell free, men standing by instantly grabbed it up, bucked it to the proper length, and ran it through the edger to trim the ragged lengthwise edges. Two or more men were kept busy either loading the sawn boards in wagons or stacking them nearby. In all, counting the engineer running the steam engine, George had fifteen men working with him at the mill to fill the furniture factory orders and to supply planks to support the flume construction.

Every day for the past week, Hack had watched at least three heavy wagonloads of green poplar and hickory lumber being unloaded and stacked onto rail cars at his Pigeon River station. It was a sure sign that his son's East Fork Lumber Company was running at full production. August was having to spend the greater part of his time at Ugly Camp these days, keeping a lid on things. That is, he was constantly dealing with irregularities that the company accountant, Mr. Clinard, brought to his attention; trying to keep his bull-of-the-woods, Claude Johnson, and the sawmill superintendent, George Abbott, working together harmoniously; and hiring and firing men to support the logging operation. The demands of the job were keeping August and Molly separated most of the time, allowing them to visit with each other only at night in their dreams and on Sundays.

The day was clear and cold, and the edges of the East Fork waters were beginning to freeze where they lapped against the rocks. After riding a couple of miles above the mill, August found his bull-of-the-woods standing and watching two men laboring to fell a poplar tree. Each lumberjack stood on springboards set into opposite sides of the tree trunk, as they pulled and pushed a crosscut saw through the living tower. Sweating and laboring with a coordinated rhythm that slowly, but steadily, opened a kerf deeper and deeper into the tree, the men bantered back and forth as if their arduous, dangerous work was nothing more than a lark.

"Hello, Claude. Is it leaning yet?" August called out, bending forward himself and clinging to his horse as it climbed up the steep slope under the tree. Johnson had sent for him earlier that day, via one of the teamsters sledding logs to the mill.

"Nah—been at this one the better part of two hours now, I reckon. Should have it on the ground in a couple more. Got a team working its way here—it ought to be able to get to this one."

"Looks like you've got men felling on both sides of the river today. Are they just cutting the poplar?"

"Yep—it's closest to the river. Ought to tell you about something, August. It's why I sent for you. Care to move out of the away over there, and I'll tell you what's happened."

August hopped down, leading his horse and following Claude to a safe spot, out of the way of the work. His curiosity was aroused about what might be up.

In a matter-of-fact manner, yet showing some concern, Claude allowed, "Pelletier and his crew have been staying in a log hut they came across near here. Said it was vacant and didn't appear to be anybody else around. They've been staying there near on a week now."

Immediately, the hair on August's neck rose, along with his suspicions. Jack Ashe's old place was across the river, about a mile upstream. *It's about that damn Jack Ashe*, he knew it. "Well, that's pretty convenient. What about it?"

"Twice now, somebody's taken a shot at 'em—trying to scare 'em off. Whoever it was, the men don't think he was aiming at 'em. Leastwise, he's not nicked one of 'em yet. You got any ideas about that place or who could be shooting at our men?"

Of course August had an idea. "Sure do! I've got a notion who it might be. Let's go talk to Jacque and find out exactly where that place is. I want to make sure of what I'm thinking."

"Okay—but while you're at it, we've got something else we need to run by you."

"No problem, Claude. What is it?"

"Better let Pelletier and those Frenchies explain it to you. They've got this crazy plan of how to wash the logs downstream—flood 'em down, they say. If what they say works, we wouldn't have to build the flume so far upstream— just have to skid our logs downhill to the river. The flood would do the rest.

Mind you, August, I've never seen it done myself! It's called a 'splash dam'—that's what we'd have to build. Care to hear 'em out?"

"Hmm—don't guess it would hurt to listen, right?"

"Make 'em feel good that the boss man will listen to what they've got to say."

"Let's go then."

In little more than ten minutes of awkward dialog, laced with heavy mountain and French Canadian dialects, August found out all he needed to know. It was just as he had suspected. The Maine loggers were squatting in the squatter Jack Ashe's abandoned place. It had to be Ashe who was doing the shooting. August related an abbreviated account of the sordid Ashe story to the men and asked them to find other shelter for the time being. He assured them Ashe would be found, as soon as the sheriff was alerted and got a posse together to track the killer down.

Deep inside, though, August was not as sure of apprehending Ashe as he let on. His future father-in-law was still alive! And for some reason, the fiend had come out of hiding. That fact alone had ominous forebodings. The man was undoubtedly dangerous, and anyone coming within his gun sights could be his next victim. However, August had even greater fears. Ashe would certainly be able to find Molly sooner than later, and there's no telling what he would do to her. As he pondered the prospects, realizing there was no way he could protect Molly from his Ugly Camp quarters, a sinking eerie feeling came over him.

# Chapter 21

## Taking a Stock to Things

Indeed, Jack Ashe was still alive! Month after month, while sequestered from the human race, he had been damning himself for killing the wrong man. How he had missed such an easy shot aimed at Molly's kidnapper, he had agonized over incessantly. But he figured not to miss the next time. There was no call to take Molly away from him, and that young stout son-of-a-bitch was going to pay for it.

Ashe had judged that the lawmen would surely have given up on finding him by now, and he was on the move. Their posses had not even come close to discovering his whereabouts in a little cave squeezed between folds of rock and hidden amongst a laurel hell growing for hundreds of yards around it. And those loggers who had moved into his place—he had no intention of killing them. He just wanted to encourage them to move on somewhere else. In fact, he harbored no real grudges against them atall, except that their logging activities were encroaching closer and closer to his patch of woods. However, Ashe had a notion that Molly's kidnapper was somehow tied in with this logging work, and he did not like it one bit.

Ashe had seen him more than once riding around on a horse, all high and mighty like a Confederate general or something, talking with the tree cutters. An easier target could not be found, but it was not time to kill him yet. Soon as he shot the son-of-a-bitch, he would be forced to hightail it out of the country, probably for good. And he was certainly not going to leave without Molly. He had to get her back first!

Hack and Harriet were against it from the start. The elder Hargrove tried to convince his son that they could look after Molly, but August would not be swayed. Until the sheriff rounded up Jack Ashe, he was going to keep his fiancée close by so he could protect her. There was a spare room in back of Everett Clinard's office at Ugly Camp, and Molly moved in there.

The sawmill men, loggers, Clinard, and the cooking crew working in the new mess hall certainly had no objections. Molly became the center of attention at Ugly Camp. If not helping Clinard with something or other, she was visiting with the cooks or helping serve hot food to starving loggers. Usually, she wore one of her stocking hats to keep her head covered and her hair held back. Loose-fitting denim trousers and a flannel shirt worked fairly well to conceal her womanly form. But heads turned toward her anyway, seeing as how food was not the only thing the men were hungry for. The quiet girl's beauty could not be hidden nor escape their gawking eyes.

This day was just breaking, and the sun's rays had begun to leak over the mountains. August found Molly already busy at work, assisting the company accountant. "Morning, Molly. You helping Mr. Clinard keep the figures straight, are you?"

"That she is, sir," the accountant jumped in. "She's a delight to have around, and I don't know what I'd do without her fresh eyes. Going to need to get me some new spectacles though." Only in his fifties, Clinard's steadily diminishing eyesight was becoming a real handicap for him. But he and Molly had found a way to help each other, as it turned out. She could see the letters, words, and numbers, and he tutored her on interpreting and reading them better. For more than a month they had teamed up like this, and the arrangement seemed to be working well for both of them.

"Hello there, Mr. August. I see you're not out in the woods already," Molly said, as she moved over and gave him a big hug.

"Heading that way, girl. Wanted to see if you had a hankering to give me some company."

"Hmm—don't know. It's still pretty cold out."

"No—it's not bad atall. Come on! I'm going all the way up to Shining Creek to check on the construction. Let's go!"

Molly hesitantly looked toward Clinard. "Think you can spare me?"

"Sure I can. Go—go on! I'll be just fine, Molly."

In little more than twenty minutes, Molly had donned some warm clothes, they had saddled up their horses, and were joyfully riding up the river. It was a good six miles upstream to the construction site, and August figured they could make it there before noon.

On the way up they chatted about a variety of things: Mr. Clinard's peculiarities, the new families that were moving into Ugly Camp, the preaching building August was contemplating, a severe injury suffered by one of the woodsmen, a belligerent run-away ox, and on and on. In particular though, August spoke enthusiastically about the project he was heading up the river to inspect.

"It's called a 'splash dam.' The boys from Maine put me up to it. They say we won't have to continue building the flume further up the river."

"Not sure I understand. How will you get the logs to the mill?"

And with that question posed, August spilled out all he had learned about splash dams. He explained how Claude Johnson had a crew constructing another large dam across the East Fork, just below Shining Creek—where they were headed. Pelletier and the other outlanders swore that if the large quantity of water contained behind this dam was suddenly released in a torrent, felled logs piled up along the river's banks and in the stream itself would be washed all the way down to the mill. It was far simpler than constructing ox paths, wagon roads, and miles of flumes. After much debate and deliberation, August had given Claude the go-ahead to stop the flume work and construct a splash dam.

"Our plan is to flood the logs down to our mill pond by the time the new mill gets up and running—maybe in June. Ought to have plenty of logs cut and dragged to the river by then. The creeks will be swelled by the spring rains, and our splash dam should be plum-full of water. 'Spect it'll work like a charm, Molly—if those Maine boys know what they're talking about.

Anyhow, it'd better work, is all I can say. I didn't let Mr. Stenson know anything about it. Just figured I'd surprise him."

Molly rode and listened patiently, leaving August to expound on the benefits of this splash dam project and convince himself, once again, he had made a sound decision for the company.

"So, what do you think, Molly? Think it'll work?"

"Oh, it sounds so promising, August. I hope it'll work just fine, for your sake." Pausing for a moment and hoping to change the subject, she then asked, "I've been meaning to talk to you about the house. Do you think we could go down and see it—maybe this weekend?"

"Sure we can! Don't see why not. They've got it in the dry now, and you can see what it's looking like. I'm sending ol' Blalock plenty of lumber to go into it, too. We can stop by on the way to Ma and Pa's."

"Oh good—then I can't wait!"

"Me neither! Can't wait to live there with you, Molly. By that time, surely the sheriff will have your father rounded up. Then we can move into our new house."

"He's never going to leave us alone until he gets me back—and does those awful things to me again. I'm so scared he will, August. I know he will!"

"Well, it'll be over my dead body that he touches you again. I've been talking to Claude, and we might get some of the men together and go searching for him ourselves."

In a couple more hours, they reached the construction site where the new splash dam was taking shape. There appeared to be more than a dozen men sawing and hewing and hoisting logs and rocks into place. A team of oxen could be seen pulling additional logs out into the shallow water. These were to be worked and fitted together to form the walls of the dam, now jutting six to eight feet out of the water. His bull-of-the-woods was doing more working than supervising, August noted, as he led Molly out into the stream.

"It's looking good, Claude! Been a lot of progress made since last time I was up."

"Hello there, miss," Johnson politely offered while removing his floppy hat and ducking his head slightly. "It's getting there, August, I reckon.

Thought the hard part was over, once we got them big oak sill logs founded deep under the river bottom. Ha—that weren't nothing compared to hoisting and filling rocks in between these log walls we're raising. Damn Frenchies—sorry, ma'am. They said it's the way they did it up yender in Maine."

August thought the men's design should work. They were stacking up hemlock logs—one on top of the other—to build two walls across the river, set about thirty feet apart at the bottom. The upstream wall sloped toward the downstream wall and was being covered with a double layer of planking. Logs laid crosswise joined the two walls and locked them together, forming cribs into which the men were placing large rocks and boulders in an extraordinary effort to add stability and strength to the dam. It was this rock work, or fill, that Claude was complaining about.

"The higher them walls get, the harder it'll be to heft them rocks into them cribs. Taking us 'bout three times longer to build than it ought."

"Yep, looks like you're building it railroad-strong, Claude. I see the opening for the fall door taking shape over there. It's way bigger than I thought it would be."

"That'll be the weak point in the dam for sure, August. But we're building the door—it's a gate actually—as thick and wide as we can, so that when it flops open, we'll let enough water out to flush all them logs down to the mill. The smithy's making us plenty of iron fittings and pins to help hold the dam and gate together. Still haven't figured out a clever way of latching the gate closed, while we build up the water behind it. Going to be a right dangerous thing to throw it open. We might have to blast it open, like they ended up doing in Maine!"

"I'm sure you and those Frenchies will come up with something," August said with a chuckle. "Them new men we hired working out okay? Saw a lot of logs pushed into the river on the way up."

"Once they got started, appears they're fairly productive. Got most of our teams cutting poplar wood now. Course it's lighter, so it'll float better when we flood the river."

That made sense to August. Everything he saw and heard made sense to him. "So, you still think you'll be done and ready by the time our new mill gets going?"

"If the good Lord's willing and we get enough rain, don't see why we can't be ready by—how's the end of May sound? Will that make you and Uncle George happy?"

"I'll say it will! That should do it—fill up that log pond and then some. We should have plenty of logs to supply our new mill we're getting."

Claude wanted to share something else on an unrelated matter. "Uh, August, since you asked me to keep you informed, one of our men thought he saw somebody up at that cabin where Molly's fa...uh, sorry, Molly. It was up there at that cabin where they got shot at.

"That so!" He had been trying to keep that sore subject tucked into the very back of his mind, hoping he could at least enjoy this little outing with Molly. But when they rode near Ashe's place earlier that morning, the bad vibes had returned. Although not mentioning it to Molly at the time, he wondered if they were being watched.

"Thanks, Claude. I'll let the sheriff know." August had given up on the possibility that the sheriff would ever apprehend Ashe. He could not see it happening. Poor Molly was frightened to death of her father, and for good reason. Ashe would strike again. There were no doubts about it. He had to protect Molly from that son-of-a-bitch. And if they were ever going to be able to settle into their new house and live a normal life together, free of worry from a crazed killer, he had to do something about Ashe! But what could he do? There was only one thing to do. He had to go after Ashe!

The sun had just dipped below the horizon, and visual details of the near woods surrounding him could barely be made out in the gloaming light. Varying shades of gray and black could be distinguished, shifting eerily as the wind blew through the trees. It was bitter cold out, and August had long since given up on moving his fingers and toes to make sure they worked. That hurt too bad. So he just scrunched in a tight ball inside the hollow cavity at the base of an old oak tree, while surveilling Jack Ashe's little cabin situated fifty yards or so below him.

For the past three evenings, he had tucked himself away in hiding, peering over a mass of rocks and waiting for Jack Ashe to show up. He had not gone to the sheriff to report the recent sightings, figuring there was no use. So now, August was all set to ambush Ashe himself. That is, if the son-of-a-bitch ever showed up. Highly doubtful of his method and chances, August stewed and shivered with one not-very-positive thought running through his mind: *Ashe's not stupid enough to come back here.*

Two more hours slipped by, and it was black dark out. What light there was came from a slither of moon hanging low in the night sky. *Damn it, Ashe—where are you?* August fumed, as he berated himself for not being able to catch the man. However, just as he was ready to call it a night and beginning to stretch out his frozen limbs, he heard something.

*What was that?* It was not a loud sound, but it was out of the ordinary. Definitely, it was not the shuffling of a coon or possum through the leaf cover on the forest floor. It sounded more like a dead limb breaking. He froze still and listened intently.

*Snap!*

*There it is again.* As August remained still in his hide, he heard the distant sounds of advancing steps. Almost immediately, he ascertained it was not the noise of a cautious animal making its way carefully through the woods. No—they were the muffled sounds of a human walking fearlessly and steadily in his direction. Had to be!

Within a minute, he was sure of it. *It must be Ashe,* he thought, as he strained his eyes to detect any movements around the cabin below. He could not see anything, but directly there was another distinct noise—*probably the door being forced open,* he judged. Then, after a minute or so, a dim light could be seen between the chinks in the logs. Suddenly, there he was! Ashe was silhouetted behind a burning candle held in one hand and walking outside toward the wood pile left by the loggers. *He's going to build a fire,* August worked out. While crouching as still as possible and watching, his mind worked furiously to plot his next move.

There was no need to over complicate this thing, he figured. His father's old Spencer repeating rifle—the one taken off a dead Yankee cavalryman—gave him boosted confidence. All there was to it was to sneak up to the log hut, kick open the door, and get the jump on Ashe. If he resisted or made a move, then he would be left with no other choice but to let him have it. A more effective plot could not be thought up, August reckoned.

*Bam!* The loud noise of the cabin door being kicked open scared Ashe to death, as he lie freezing on the floor next to the low flames in the fireplace. He had not been there long enough to get the fire going good or warm himself up. Then, before he knew it, there's Molly's kidnapper busting in and pointing a long gun directly at him.

"Get up, Ashe!" ordered August, as he moved closer to the pathetic figure huddled on the earthen floor. He kept the repeater leveled directly at Ashe.

Ashe slowly rose up and gained a sitting position without saying a thing, just staring with burning hatred at the man holding a gun on him. Then he spoke as mean as can be, "What have ye done with her, boy!"

"Don't know what you're talking about, Ashe. Going have to take you to the jailhouse, where you rightfully belong. That man you killed was a friend of mine!"

"I didn't care none 'bout him. It was you I was after! What have ye done with Molly! Have ye turned her against me?"

"Get on your feet, I said! Don't know any Molly! Best you forget her too, Ashe!"

"Ye know her! Ye took her! Where is she? She's mine!"

"Up!" August said, as he gave the culprit a hard kick to get him on his feet. "Don't you worry none! You're not going to need anybody when ol' Satan opens the doors of hell to let you in."

Next to the fireplace August spotted Ashe's rifle but not the big knife Molly said he carried. As the man rose to his feet, standing almost a head taller than his captor, August racked his brain about what to do next. Turns out, the details of his plan to apprehend Ashe had not been thought out beyond this point. Now, he allowed it would be too dangerous to try to walk Ashe back to camp in the dark. That would not do, since he had to keep his eyes on the man and see him at all times. He could not see him good in the darkness, and Ashe could simply bolt off into the dense wilderness and escape. But then again, August figured the man could not run if his hands were tied and his feet hobbled. However, he could not very well tie-up Ashe without putting down his rifle. And if he did that, it would surely lead to the free-for-all, life-and-death struggle that August had always contemplated since rescuing Molly. What was he to do?

For some reason, memories of Hack's fireside tales invaded August's mind at this critical juncture, especially the one involving those Bugg desperados his father and Mr. Edmunston dealt with during the war. In a similar circumstance to the one he now found himself in, *what was it that Mr. Edmunston had done?* August's recollection of the story began taking form in his mind, until he was convinced that it was what he himself had to do too. *That's what Mr. Edmunston did!* And it was exactly what he would do!

August did not have to put his Spencer down. Instead, he deliberately lowered it, aimed at the top of Ashe's foot and pulled the trigger. *Bam!*

Just like that, he shot a bullet through Jack Ashe's foot, and the man immediately hit the floor writhing in pain. "Ahhh—god damn ye! Ye shot me, damn ye to hell!" The wound was terribly painful, yet it was not more than the tough ornery woodsman could endure. Ashe clamped his hands as hard as he could squeeze around the bloody hole in his boot, in an effort to stop the pain and gushing blood. August felt no sympathy atall for Ashe, while standing over him and watching him suffer. All he could think of was what Ashe had done to Molly. Directly though, he figured it might be necessary to help the man staunch the blood flow, lest he pass out—or worse. Spying a bed quilt he could use to wrap the foot, he stepped away to grab it.

This merciful act was not lost on Ashe, who instantly reached inside his boot top and pulled out a long knife—the mean-looking one Molly had warned about. Ignoring the horrific pain, he was up in an instant lunging toward August, who had momentarily turned his back to Ashe.

August heard him coming, but his reflexes were not quite fast enough. Perhaps it was because he had not yet thawed out good. But he flinched just enough to make Ashe miss his target. Instead of taking the knife thrust in the spinal area of his back, August was stabbed several inches over, just under the left shoulder. The eight-inch knife easily pierced through his woolen overcoat and sunk to the hilt into his body. Even with a gunshot wound in his foot, Ashe moved like a wildcat. He was not through by any means. As the Spencer rifle fell onto the earth floor, he jerked the knife out of August's back and reared his arm high, getting ready to stab his hated victim again.

"Ahhh!" Screaming at the top of his lungs from outrage and agony after being stabbed, August sensed the danger and threw his right arm backward—just in time to deflect the next thrust. Somehow, he managed to make Ashe miss with this follow-up attack. Nonetheless, he received a deep cut in his right forearm while fending off the knife, and blood was now spurting forth from both wounds.

Ashe was not feeling so sprite himself. He, too, was losing blood from the large bullet hole in his foot, and the pain was almost intolerable. Not only that, he was literally spent after the tremendous exertions to stick his hunting knife into August twice. Both men now stood hunched over and facing each other, as they gasped heavily for air. Eyeing each other in the firelight and gathering all the energy at their disposal, they feinted this way and that, either trying to discover a weakness to exploit or waiting for the next attack.

Out of the corner of his eye, August saw the Spencer lying on the dirt floor. Ashe, still in possession of the bloody hunting knife, saw it too. Among the other thoughts flashing through August's mine just then, was that he had better do something quick. He was losing lots of blood, especially from the terrible wound to his left shoulder—in the same place, by the way, that the Rego brother had shot him. *Got to do something—whether it's right or wrong. Starting to feel mighty weak,* he told himself as he moved in closer to Ashe.

"Where's she at? Tell me! Huh? Ye're never going to live to see her again, once I carve ye up and leave ye hanging from a tree." Ashe's threats were spoken in the vilest manner possible, leaving no doubts of his intent. He meant to kill Molly's kidnapper here and now and skin him like a bear!

August paid no nevermind to the hateful rhetoric. Certainly, he was not afraid of Ashe, but then again the man was dangerous. The bleeding shoulder was hurting awful, rendering his left arm practically useless. *Got to do something. Is the Spencer cocked?* He was not sure, and it was too dark to get a good look at the gun.

"I'm going to make Molly my wife, Ashe. What do you allow about that?"

Such a rage came over Ashe by the mere mention of Molly's name and this man saying he was going to take her for his wife, he could not control himself. In one sudden, violent movement, he lunged and stabbed the knife toward August's chest. But he missed! August was too quick this time! By quickly dodging and using his good arm—the one that was a bloody mangled mess, August had warded off the knife thrust. Ashe was now exhausted and slow, hobbled by pain and a useless foot. Instinctively, August moved like a flash of lighting toward Ashe. Without even thinking and still shielding himself with his wounded arm, he stomped his boot down hard on top of Ashe's bloody foot.

"Ahhh—ahhh!" The cries and screams were deafening, as Ashe dropped the knife and fell onto the floor in immobilizing agony. Writhing and hollering to high heaven, he did not even see the next blow coming. August's boot caught him full force in the face, crushing Ashe's nose and mouth and sending him sprawling. In an instant, August picked up the Spencer with his "good arm," pointed it at Ashe's head, and pulled the trigger!

Nothing! There was no loud cracking sound of exploding gunpowder. The gun had not been cocked after all. There was no cartridge in the chamber. There was nothing!

"Damn!" With only the one good arm, August could not readily cock the lever to load the gun, so he did the only practical thing that came to him at that confused moment. He grabbed hold of the barrel with his working arm and began swinging the gun like a club, with the heavy wooden stock striking Ashe in the head time and time again, until his flinching stopped. *There, that's for Molly you miserable son-of-a-bitch!*

Feeling dizzy and weaker by the moment, it dawned on August that he was about to pass out. *What if he's not dead?* he fretted, as he hurriedly began looking around for some suitable hog-tying material.

# Chapter 22

## SEEDS OF DOUBT

Claude Johnson, Pelletier, and two other Frenchies arrived at the gruesome scene just past midnight. Well aware of the ambush operation, Johnson had rounded up some men and gone looking for August when he failed to show up at the Shining Creek camp as expected. They found Jack Ashe lying sprawled on the dirt floor and hog-tied near the fire's still-warm embers. He was trembling from the cold and moaning lowly from insufferable pain. When Claude stripped back the blanket covering August, he gave him a quick shake, checking to see if his young boss was still alive. The body was definitely stiff! Whether this stiffness came from being graveyard dead or nearly frozen, it was impossible to tell.

"August! August! Wake up, August!" There were no signs of life as Claude gave the stony face a couple of hard slaps. August just lie there as still as could be with his eyes barely shut. There were no movements whatsoever or signs of breathing.

"August! Can you hear me?" Right away, Claude had detected the dark blood stains on the dirt next to August. It did not look good. In order to see, hear, or even feel a hint of life, he leaned in close with his face only inches away from August's. "It's me, August—it's Claude! Can you hear me?"

A few seconds passed, and then Claude saw it. He saw an eyelid flutter. There were no doubts about it. He saw a flutter for sure. "August! August! Can you hear me?" Claude watched closely as both eyelids now began to move slightly. And then he heard a muffled sound come from the frozen lips. "What? What did you say, August?"

Claude saw both of August's eyes barely open and his lips move almost imperceptibly. And then he heard it again. He heard a feint mumbled word, and there could be no doubt this time what it was. The word August had spoken was "Molly."

Claude's eyes opened wide, lighting up in the darkness as he jumped back up and barked an order. "Jacque, ride down to Forks of Pigeon and bring the doctor back to Ugly Camp! August's been hurt bad, but he's alive—for now! Go! Hurry! We'll carry them both down there and wait for you!"

Molly's room in the rear of Clinard's accounting office had become a veritable hospital for going on two weeks now. Unbelievably, August had clung to life despite the attending doctor's frequent dire pronouncements that the patient was about to inhale his last breath. Somehow, someway, August refused to succumb to death's best efforts to claim him.

The knife wounds had been cleaned and sutured, but just as the doctor predicted, they had become badly infected. Much to August's agony, Molly nursed the festering wounds constantly, cleaning and repacking the horrendous cuts as best she could and changing the linen bandages relentlessly. And she had good help with her tireless and passionate endeavors. Hack and Harriet came up to Ugly Camp almost every day to look in on their son and to do what they could—as did another elderly visitor.

Folsom Mann found the energy and gumption to make daily visits to the logging camp to lend her own special healing powers to the cause. Although she appeared to be growing feebler with each passing day, Hack hauled her up in a buggy every morning and took her home at dark. Often, the Bee Woman overrode the doctor's strict orders and instructed Molly on concocting and applying herb and honey pastes over the wounds. During August's sporadic periods of consciousness, honey-laced liquors were dripped into his mouth, and vapors from boiling honey broths were fanned into his nose. Whether these singular treatments had any positive

## August's Treasure

effects was disputed amongst family, friends, and certainly the doctor. But one thing was indisputable. August Hargrove survived the awful ordeal, and that was what mattered.

Outside of August's little room at Ugly Camp, the early blooming dogwood and wild cherry trees signaled that spring was nigh upon the mountains, though biting cold winds begged to differ. The morning sun shone brilliantly through the window glazing, as Molly sat bedside holding August's hand and watching him lapse into and out of a sleepful state. The fevers he experienced those first few weeks after the stabbings had subsided for the most part. Now he was in the throes of mending, which the doctor had warned could take months.

When August's eyes opened, Molly reached over and pushed back the shock of strawberry-red hair that blocked his view of her. The sunlight streaming from behind his nurse made her seem surreal—almost ghostlike. A bright lightness framed her shadowy body and when she spoke to him, the words seemed to be those of a goddess.

"Good morning, Mr. August. Have a good sleep?"

*It's just Molly*, he had to tell himself. *It's my beautiful Molly.* "Morning, Molly. Wow, don't you look beautiful sitting there in the sun like that."

"Why, thank you. Mighty nice of you to say so. How do you feel?"

"It still hurts bad in my back, every time I move. Reckon I'm going to need to drink some of Bee Woman's good tea. It always makes me feel better, that's for sure."

"Well, I reckon she'll be here directly. If not, I'll fix you some. But you should eat something first."

"You know what I need, Miss Molly? Huh?"

Molly just gave him a quizzical look.

"I was wondering if you could give me a big ol' whopping kiss! Reckon you could see fit to kiss me, Molly? I do believe that's what the doctor ordered, don't you?"

"Like the Christmas one we had when you asked me to marry you?"

"Yep—give me one of those! That should do the trick!"

And then Molly leaned over and moved her face close against August's. She felt his warm breath and scraggly beard, as they locked lips and tasted each other for only the second time ever. The passion and love that flowed back and forth between them was like nothing they had ever known. During these last weeks of intolerable pain and anguish, August had dreamt of just this experience—this opportunity to know and feel Molly's love. He had her back now, and he meant to hold on to her and treat her right. And Molly—well, she thought nothing in the world could match this taste and sensation, and she intended to do her nursing and womanly best to see that her man made it through this bad spell.

*No good fer nothing*, Ashe thought while casting a disgusted and sorrowful eye toward the bandaged foot. The shuck tick he was lying on was wallowed flat and hard by this time, almost as hard as the stone walls and floor of the cell he had called home for the past several weeks. He was right about the foot though. It was not much good for nothing. But at least he had a stunted foot to gimp about on. More than once, he had refused to have it removed, as he fought off and survived serious septic bouts. Though truth be told, the doctor and sheriff would just as soon have buried the foot, along with Jack Ashe.

Ashe was not about to give up and die. He still had too much to live for. Molly was ever present in his conscious thoughts and dreams. He had to get her back and he would—if he could ever bust out of this damn jail. There was another reason he had to escape. Word was that Molly's kidnapper was not dead, and Ashe was none too happy about it. He thought he had finally killed the son-of-a-bitch who took Molly away from him. One more chance was all Ashe wanted. Next time he would kill him for sure.

Very soon, Ashe would be tried for the murder of Reginald Whitney. The sheriff had already advised him to man up for his hanging, for that was what he had coming. Time and time again, Ashe told them what had happened. It was that young, stout son-of-a-bitch he aimed to kill—the one who took Molly—not that other man. But no one, it seemed, would listen to reason, not even the lawyer defending him. So he figured to bust out some way or other, before the hangman hung him dead. With his days numbered, he spent every day, all day long, either ciphering on an escape plan or dreaming of Molly.

Winter was all but forgotten now. The looming mountains over the Pigeon Valley and its upper watersheds were ablaze in a riot of spring's blooming colors. With each day, the sun's arc reached higher and higher into the heavenly sky, thawing the ground and giving life to God's gardens and creatures. Among these creatures, August Hargrove stood out especially. He was rejuvenated with exceptional vigor and spirit, akin to that enjoyed by most young men—at least those who had not recently suffered a near-death knife stabbing.

Back in the saddle finally, after many weeks of convalescence, he rode up and down the East Fork valley, overseeing the logging work and surveying the hundreds and hundreds of poplar logs that had been felled, bucked, and strategically positioned at the river's edge. Of course their plan—his plan—was to flood every last one of those logs down to Ugly Camp's log pond with a raging torrent of water, loosed from the company's huge splash dam near Shining Creek. Today, August was on his way up the river to check on the status of the dam and strategize with his bull-of-the-woods.

Upon reaching the site, he sat on his horse in the middle of the stream and gazed upon the impressive structure. Already, an ocean of water was impounded behind the log walls, although a considerable amount could be seen leaking through the many fissures in the dam. The structure was about twenty-two feet high, maybe a little higher, and almost sixty yards wide, anchored into steep rocky embankments on either side of the river. A monstrous timber flop gate in the center was held closed by four large prop poles embedded deep in the stream bottom and leaned at an angle to support the gate. These were not ordinary poles. They were oak tree trunks approximately eighteen inches in diameter. Claude was building the dam railroad-strong, or at least August thought so.

As he splashed through the shallow water to where the men were working, he could see that more prop poles were being set to support the entire dam wall. *Don't remember that being talked about,* he thought. It sure seemed a little odd to him, even excessive.

"Good day, Claude! Got things going mostly your way?"

"Hello, boss! Going okay, I reckon. Feeling spiffy, are you?"

August was a little surprised at the personal nature of the question. "Yep, feeling right good, thank you." Then with a chuckle he added, "Can't complain too much—I'm still breathing. Say, what's up with them extra prop poles?"

"Insurance, August. Me and Jacque and the men got to worrying if we had another big rain, our dam might give way. I can sense the pressure on it—I can, I tell you! The sooner we cut this water loose and wash our logs down to Ugly, the better I'll feel about it. We'll be ready to blow the gate next week, at the rate it's been filling up."

Blowing the gate was the clever solution Claude had come up with to open the gate. Deep bore holes had been drilled into each of the four prop poles, about two feet above the water's frothing surface, and these were meant to contain sticks of dynamite. By exploding these charges at once, the prop poles would be blown away, allowing the flop gate to instantly fall open as the tremendous water pressure pushed against it. And through this giant breech in the dam, the raging water would pour through. That was Claude's engineering solution, and he could not wait to blow the gate open.

"Surely, you don't think that dam will give, do you?" August had thought it was plenty strong enough.

"Well, it should be all right, but you never know. Come down and take a look over here."

Hopping off his horse a little slower than usual, August moved over closer to Claude. "What is it?"

"Put yer hand down here and feel. See if you can feel anything!"

Truthfully, August was more than a little nervous to be hunkering at the base of the dam, with water spewing out from between the logs and literally drenching him. But he dutifully placed his hand against the wall where directed, and tried to feel something.

"Feel it?"

"Feel what? I don't feel nothing! I swear I don't," August allowed as he gave Claude a curious look.

"You can't feel it moving?"

"Moving! No, I can't feel the dam moving! Are you crazy?"

"Well, I do—so does Jacque! I believe them big oak sill logs are giving some. Not too sure we've got them anchored good enough, August. We've got to let this water go next week when it begins running over the spillways. Can't wait any longer, especially if we get more rain!"

"'Spect that won't be a problem—none atall. There's plenty of logs along the river, so we should fill up Ugly's log pond and then some. George says it'll take that Chattanooga engineer another two or three weeks to finish erecting the new mill. Till then, he can just keep the old Geiser steaming. No, I don't see a problem with doing the flooding next week."

"Don't believe we should wait any longer. Mr. Stenson on his way, is he?"

"Last I heard, he is. He should be here early next week, and he might be staying until the new mill is up and running. He seems nervous about supplying that new customer we got—the one from down about Lenoir. Bet he'll be happy to see Ugly's log pond full of logs!"

As the soaked August moved away from the wall and its mini-waterfalls, Claude cut him a suspicious eye. "You tell him yet 'bout this dam?"

With a sheepish expression growing over his face, August replied, "No— no I haven't. Why?"

Taking a few moments to respond, Claude shook his head back and forth and then said in a low voice. "I don't know, August. Maybe you ought to have told him. It was a big decision you made to build this dam. The more I think about it, the more risk I see—I mean things that could go wrong. Still, them Frenchies say it's going to work. We'll see, I reckon."

*What? Risk? What risk?* It was the first he had heard of such notions from his main man—his bull-of-the-woods. It had crossed August's mind that there was some inherent risk in this splash dam venture, but Claude and the Maine lumberjacks had convinced him it would work without a hitch. Now, here was Claude planting seeds of doubt—telling him that the dam's foundation was shifting, that he'd better hurry or else, and that he should have told

Mr. Stenson because this was a risky undertaking. *Course the damned dam was going to work! It had to work!* he told himself before snapping at Claude.

"What? What risk? Why are you telling me it's risky now, Claude? Four months! Four long months you've been building this dam! This is the first I've heard from you that it's a risky business! What risk are you talking about?"

Claude wished he could have held his tongue, but his many burdens were beginning to weigh heavily on him. Keeping the men busy, productive, and safe; having to make design decisions and changes to the dam on a daily basis; growing unease and doubt creeping into his head; the likelihood there was a foundation problem; and August's near-death encounter—all of these things were bothering him to no end, and he had to find an outlet for his frustrations. Finally, Claude had felt that August was healthy enough to hear him out—share with his boss some of the nagging doubts he was having with the splash dam plan.

"I really believe our foundation is slipping, August! Just discovered it though! That's why I haven't sprung it on you before. But I think it'll hold up until next week. The risk is…Well, I've been wondering—it's been keeping me awake at night—what'll happen once we blow the gate open and let that twenty-foot-high wall of water go. What's going to stop it?" Claude paused to see if August wanted to jump in.

"What do you mean 'what's going to stop it?'"

"You see, what I'm thinking is—that wall of water—well, it ain't goin' be no problem washing all them logs down to our pond—no problem there, as far as I can see. But what then? How we going to stop 'em? That big surge of water might be too powerful for Ugly's dam to handle, even though it's miles downstream. I'm afeared of washing Ugly's dam away, August!" Claude stopped there, figuring he'd said enough.

August surely had not thought of that. He had only recently been trying to get back into the swing of things. Certainly, studying the potential downstream impact of his company's splash dam scheme had not entered into his recent considerations. It should have! Even with his inexperience in such matters, he should have been keen enough to think through this entire

## August's Treasure

operation until there were absolutely no doubts it was going to work. *Wash Ugly's dam away! Could it?* he now fretted.

"Nah, not that far down, Claude! The river valley way down there's much wider—don't you think? The water will be flattened out by then and lose all its power. Has to be!" This was the first thought he had, and he was not totally convinced of its validity.

"Maybe you're right, but I'm not sure. Neither one of us has ever done anything like this before. What I was thinking was that we need to build us some insurance. So just in case, I want to take the men down there tomorrow and begin propping the dam up, using big prop poles like these ones here. And we should open up the emergency spillway to allow more water to pass through the dam down there. Reckon our log chain ought to hold?"

"Hold! Ain't nothing going to break that heavy chain—them links are thicker than my arm—you know that! It'll hold as long as them big hemlocks are standing—the ones it's anchored to. Don't you reckon?" August was not totally convinced.

"Hmm—you're probably right there. The chain shouldn't be a problem, don't reckon. It ought to hold back all them logs from going over the dam. That's what it's designed to do!"

"Well, it'd better is all I can say! We've got a lot riding on this splash dam business—both of us. I can't afford to let Mr. Stenson down, so let's make it work, Claude! We've got to!"

Their eyes exchanged sober stares as Claude nodded in agreement. "We'll make it work, August."

# Chapter 23

## The Damned Splash Dam

The town of Waynesville was deader than a church graveyard and the only sounds to be heard were the barking of an old cur dog and the pouring rain. Daylight was yet hours away, and the old man keeping watch at the county jail was having a hard time staying awake. Going on five months now, he had held this special deputy's job of guarding the prisoners, and he still was not accustomed to staying up all night long. That was his only job, the sheriff had instructed more than once. "Stay awake and make sure the prisoners don't get up to nothing," was exactly what the old man was told. And that was what he dutifully set out to do every evening when his shift started. But, sure enough, when the ruckus started tonight he had nodded off once again.

The old deputy jumped to his feet with a start, awakened by an awful screaming noise below, and he rushed down the narrow basement stairs to check on his prisoners—both of them. One was a drunk who had been locked up earlier that night. The deputy found him passed out on the filthy bed tick, snoring and mumbling away. It was the other one who was pitching fits. That man was lying on the hard rock floor holding his neck, while screeching and wailing to high heaven.

*What the hell...?* thought the deputy as he looked on and tried to understand what was the matter with his prisoner. Jack Ashe was the prisoner's name.

"I can't breathe! Awk—awk—awk! Can't...breathe! Awk—awk," Ashe coughed and choked and yelled loudly, almost at the same time. He certainly seemed to be in the throes of a dying fit or something.

*Why, he's dying for sure! Can't be a show he's putting on*, figured the deputy. In all the days he had been at this job, Ashe had never said more than a few curt words to him. *What the hell's wrong with him?*

For more than two minutes, the deputy watched Ashe writhe and scream in pain, surely dying of something other. The old man could not decide what to do. Was Ashe putting on, or was he really dying? It was hard to tell for sure, though it would be nearly impossible for anybody to feign good enough to trick the deputy. His advanced years did not automatically make him a fool. He could certainly tell if somebody was actually dying. So, after studying Ashe's struggles to breathe and live and listening to the awful sounds of death and a man's dying pleas for help, the deputy made up his mind then and there what was wrong. Ashe was sure enough dying!

Quickly, the cell door was unlocked and thrown open with a loud metallic clang. Holding a loaded and cocked revolver in one hand, the deputy cautiously approached the dying prisoner, who appeared to be gasping his last breaths. Not sure what to do next or how he was going to help Ashe, the deputy gently kicked him in the side. "What's the matter with ye, Ashe? Huh?"

There was no response, other than the continued deathly gasps and coughs of a soul seemingly not long for this earth. Deciding that he must go and fetch a doctor, the deputy kicked at Jack Ashe one more time, just to see if there was a different reaction. There was!

Before the surprised deputy knew what was happening, Ashe's hands flashed toward him. Turns out, the perverted prisoner had been putting on the whole time! Grabbing hold and jerking the old man's booted leg with all his might, Ashe pulled the deputy off balance and down onto the hard floor.

*Bang!* The loud report of the pistol firing erringly toward the timber ceiling echoed through the dank basement, yet the deafening sound had no effect on the sleeping drunk in the adjoining cell. In sudden powerful movements, Ashe knocked the pistol out of the deputy's hand, rolled over on top of him, and began bashing the old man's head against the rock floor. He cracked the head as if it were a walnut, and in mere seconds the life of the elderly deputy spilled out over the stones in a bloody mess.

Jack Ashe then hurriedly limped up the stairs and out of the jailhouse into the darkness and rain. Gimping along the boardwalks and muddy streets on his stunted foot, only one thought ran through his mind. It was an overwhelming desire that inspired him and kept him moving. Molly—it was the thought of Molly! He had to find Molly and get her back. So with that intoxicating motive, he hopped and dragged his bandaged foot out of Waynesville, as the sound of a barking dog faded in the distance.

After fetching Henrik Stenson and Jee Man Sing at the train station, August and Molly carried them up the river through a pouring rain. Stopping the covered buggy where a long drive turned off the muddy river road and led to a looming frame house, August let the boss take a gander at his and Molly's new home.

It sat imposingly on a rise, just at the foot of a steep mountain rising behind it. The rainy weather had so far prevented painting the exterior. Nevertheless, it was impressive to look at from the distance, at least August thought so.

"We decided we wanted two porches," August explained, referring to the long pillared decks running the length of the first and second stories. The house's silver-colored metal roof extended out to cover the upper deck.

"Yes, I see that. How wonderful!" Henrik replied, albeit it seemed pretty plain to him. But he was not about to reveal such a notion.

"Look at them two big chimneys, sir. All eight rooms have got a fireplace. We shouldn't get cold, I don't expect. Should we, Molly?"

"Nope—hope not! My favorite thing is the shiny roof," she chirped enthusiastically. "I think it's so purty when the sunlight reflects off it." August nodded proudly, and Stenson thought Molly was absolutely correct.

"Yes, Molly, I'll bet it is." Henrik was trying to sound interested. "Where did you get your tin, August?"

"That engineer from Chattanooga—the one in charge of installing our new mill—he knew of a lot I could get hold of right cheap. So we sent off for it. It's a real thick gauge, and I reckon it'll last a good long time."

"Don't expect we'll have any leaks, either," Molly joked.

"Ha—I bet you're right there, Molly. Well, are you going to take me over to see it or not, August?" The ride up from Pigeon River had been a long one and they were all soaked. Henrik figured it was about time to get out of the rain.

"Yes sir. Let's go take a look-see."

To his surprise, Henrik found that the interior of the house was completed and already furnished. The bead board ceiling and all the trim work were painted, pretty blue wallpaper decorated the walls, and Harriet and Beth's hand-sewn curtains draped every window in the house. Not only that, they even found a hot fire burning in the kitchen's wood stove where a pot of coffee was boiling. And that was not all they found in the kitchen.

Harriet was in there fussing about, getting ready to pull a skillet of fresh-baked cornbread out of the oven. "Just in time, you folks are! Hello, Henrik—you too, Jee." Both men bowed toward Harriet, looking very surprised.

"Mrs. Hargrove, so good to see you again," Henrik replied, as he removed his silk top hat. "I declare, what is this you've prepared for our arrival? Well, pardon me—I presume you've made this for us?"

"Yes, yes, Henrik. Thought you might want some cornbread and molasses with your hot coffee. Molly and I will fix some supper later."

"I wanted to offer you our house to stay in while you're here, Mr. Stenson. It's ready, and we ought to get it broke in good before Molly and I move in—course after we're married. We'll move into it two weeks from now, when we get married. Hope you'll still be here and can come see us get married, sir." August stumbled a little with these invitations, from nervousness surely.

"Well, Mrs. Hargrove, how nice of you! I'd love to have some of your famous cornbread and fresh-brewed coffee." Then turning to August, "Yes, certainly! If you will have me and Jee here in this beautiful new house, how could we turn you down? About the wedding, we hadn't planned to stay more than a week, but we'll see. Maybe we can stay. We'll have to wait and see how things look up at the new mill."

"Course, we'd love to have you stay here, sir. That's what me and Molly want. While you're here, we—Molly and me—we plan on staying here too—not together. I mean we'll be sleeping in separate rooms and all, so she can cook for us. She wants to, don't you, Molly?"

As all heads turned toward the young girl, her gorgeous, angelic face lit up with a big smile. "Mrs. Hargrove said she would help me. I'd love to cook and make your stay here as comfortable as can be, Mr. Stenson! There's plenty of room!"

Impatient to tell his boss, August awkwardly broke in, "Mr. Stenson, I've got a big surprise waiting for you up at Ugly. All this rain has slowed progress on the new mill, but we have something else that ought to be pretty exciting for you."

"You do, do you? Well, I can't wait to see what all this excitement is about."

"Well then, sir, we'll ride up tomorrow, and I'll show you. Now, what do you say we get us a bite of Ma's cornbread and molasses?"

The next day, August and Henrik Stenson got up early and rode in the rain up the East Fork River to Ugly Camp. It had rained on and off for more than a week now, and the river was flowing much higher than normal. After a brief and gloomy meeting with Everett Clinard, looking over the books, August and Henrik toured the new sawmill facilities, with George Abbott guiding the bosses. In one towering building, two huge boilers and high stacks were installed. Swarming around this equipment, busy men were in the process of fitting steam and water pipes and erecting huge pulleys and other mechanical drive equipment.

In an adjacent structure, the sawmill was basically erected, and Henrik watched as the engineer and millwrights adjusted the many different-sized pulleys, power transmission belts, and other pieces of equipment. George explained how the two huge circular saws, stacked one on top of the other, would allow his men to saw logs up to six feet in diameter. Henrik was duly fascinated, and he encouraged George to get the mill up and running as soon as possible so they could get on with supplying that new customer in

Lenoir. Left unsaid, but uppermost in Stenson's mind, was the fact that the company absolutely required the additional revenue to pay for this enormous capital investment they were looking at.

Then the three men walked over to the mess hall, where Claude was waiting. August's tough bull-of-the-woods looked unusually nervous for some reason, as they sat down to talk at one of the crude dining tables.

"How's it been going, Claude? August tells me you've been working on something quite different up the river, and you're going to show me—if it ever quits raining."

"Yes sir, Mr. Stenson. It's quite different all right. You're going to be real surprised, I suspect." Looking toward August, he wondered how much of the secret had been revealed or how much he should talk about. Claude was still terribly worried that the splash dam was not going to hold up long enough for them to blow the gate. They had waited an extra two days so that Stenson could witness the operation, and with all the rain of late, the spillways were not able to handle the increased flow. The splash dam had been overtopped with water cascading across the crest of the entire dam. "What about it, August? Okay to tell him everything?"

"Yea, sure Claude! Don't guess we ought to wait any longer. We've whipped up Mr. Stenson's curiosity real good by now. Go ahead."

After more than an hour of explaining and discussing, the whole splash dam matter was laid bare before Henrik Stenson. August and Claude then waited in anticipation of a tacit approval of their initiative and ingenuity—or his wrath over such an ill-advised scheme. Neither of them had mentioned there was a certain level of risk involved in the operation. They could not see a need to bother the boss with the little details or nuances of the plan, as long he understood the overarching concept and strategy.

"Well, I'll say! That's quite the plan, men. When are you going to wash the logs down here?" To their relief, Henrik seemed to have bought into the scheme.

"Well, sir, from the looks of it outside, the rain has stopped, and the sun is shining—at last! I'd say we might as well go ahead and turn the water loose now. Don't you think, August?" Claude wanted to race up there as fast as he could and set off the dynamite charges.

"If you feel up to it, Mr. Stenson, let's ride up with Claude so you can see the dam. Then we can find us a high perch, off a ways, and watch him blow the gate. Reckon you're not too tired?"

"Not too tired to make history like this. It ought to be a sight to see!"

George Abbott's men at Ugly Camp were ordered to higher ground, while a select team scurried up both sides of the river all the way to Shining Creek. They were to warn the loggers to stay out of the path of the pending flood for the rest of the day. Henrik, Claude, and August rode at the briskest pace possible—but not so brisk that Henrik might become suspicious or alarmed. Now that the rain had stopped and the sun was shining, both August and Claude had far more confidence that everything was going to be just fine with the splash dam. It would surely hold up for another few hours, if not days.

On the hard ride up, August could not help running the plan through his head time and time again. Soon, Claude could light the fuses, explode the dynamite, blow away the gate's prop poles, and loose the power of thousands of tons of water upon the East Fork River. It would be a deluge for the ages in Haywood County. If it worked like planned, then the same strategy might as well be used next year and the next and on and on, until there were no more trees to cut or logs to float on the upper East Fork.

On the approach to the dam, a suitable spot was found where they could ride out into the middle of the stream and get a good look at the structure. The water was brawling swift and strong, causing the horses to move slowly and carefully pick their path between the huge slippery rocks. At last, the three men were positioned far enough out in the river, so that they could see upstream between the trees.

All at once, there it was! They could easily see it. Looming dead ahead of them and about a hundred yards further up the river, was the monstrous splash dam! Henrik could not believe his eyes.

"Holy God!" he said aloud, loud enough to be heard above the roar of the water. "I never dreamed it would be so big!"

They could not see the dam's high log structure. It was hidden behind the continuous curtain of glistening and frothing water that streamed over the top, from one end to the other.

"No wonder Clinard's books were so dismal. The expense..." Henrik stopped in mid-sentence when he heard a sudden and ominous loud-cracking sound, like the noises of an entire forest of huge trees snapping and popping and falling to the ground. At first the three men watched in awe, before a feeling of terror quickly overcame them upon the realization of what was taking place before their very eyes. They saw the linear shape of the water flowing over the dam instantly contort and convulse into a chaotic storm of waves and torrents. Then, before they fully comprehended their dangerous situation, the confused mass became a huge thundering wall of water, rushing and crashing headlong directly at them.

August and Claude knew instantly what had happened—their damned splash dam had failed! And literally playing out in front of them were their worst fears—no, it was beyond their worst fears, because now they found themselves directly in the path of a great torrential flood of their own creation. Both of them rushed to grab Henrik's horse and get him the hell out of danger. But they could not move fast enough! Before they knew it, the wall of water was upon them, sweeping all three men and their horses away like grains of sand before a crashing ocean wave.

Near about this same time, Molly was puttering away in her new house, not knowing whether August and Mr. Stenson would be coming back down to Forks of Pigeon that evening. August had nervously confided the splash dam plans to her the evening before. When he left that morning, he had mentioned that they might not return until the morrow. Nevertheless, she was preparing some fixings to eat, just in case they showed up late that night.

The new spring house out back was a ways off from the house, perched beside the creek that ran through the property. In this little outbuilding, their milk and butter and various other perishable foods were stored in a cool pool of running water diverted from the creek. All afternoon, Molly was running back and forth either to the spring house or to the new outhouse located even further away, near a patch of woods and out of sight. These crucial little structures were so new that the paths to them were not even beaten yet—but Molly was doing her best to wear them down.

Unbeknownst to her, each time she made one of these forays for water or food, or to take care of necessary business, a pair of greedy eyes leered and followed her every move. Hidden in a dense thicket behind the new house was none other than her father, Jack Ashe, who had been on the loose for more than two days now. Inexplicably, word of his escape had not reached the Hargroves—or Molly, so she was completely unaware of the danger that lurked so close by.

Jack Ashe was in a bad way, though. The bare stunted foot that he had dragged around for miles and miles, through the woods and brambles, was now a bloody raw mess. Only one thing kept him going and allowed him to endure the intense pain. It was the thought of having Molly. Every minute of every hour of every day was consumed with an incessant lust to hold her and to have her again. He wanted to feel her once more in that same way he had before. Maybe she missed him and wanted him too. That possibility, as well as his lascivious yearning for her, kept him alive and going. Now that he had found her again, he meant to have what was his.

Ashe had followed that young stout son-of-a-bitch, the one that nearly killed him, to Molly. He was surprised and envious of Molly's fine new house, or at least he thought it was her situation. Ever since that son-of-a-bitch—the one he had knifed—left earlier that morning with the older, fancy-pants man, Ashe had been lying in wait, watching and plotting. As far as he could tell, only Molly was inside the house now, but surely those two men would be coming back before dark. *Don't have long to get her and have her*, he mulled, trying to decide if the time was right to call on her. After he had had her real good, if she was not of a mind to escape with him somewhere out of the reach of the law—like his deep forest hideaways—well then, he reckoned he would have to put her out of her misery, just as he had done for her mother. And then he could take care of that young son-of-a-bitch—and maybe even fancy-pants.

In the dim twilight, Molly walked the new path to the outhouse one last time before dark. It was on the way back into the house, just after she passed through the back door, that Ashe crashed in behind her as fast as his gimpy foot would allow. Realizing he could not catch Molly if she got away, he caught her by the hair and fiercely yanked her into his dirty clutches.

"Ahhh!" Molly's loud scream was cut short when Ashe muffled her mouth with his hand.

"Now, now, dear, let's don't scream. Ain't ye glad to see me, Molly? It's been such a real long time."

Sweet Molly was terrified of this monster. *He's supposed to be in jail*, she thought. Ignoring Ashe, she struggled and scratched and clawed in an effort to free herself.

Ashe yanked her hair tighter still and forced his other hand against her mouth and nose so hard that giant tears streamed down her face, as she tried to screech out in pain. Of course, the sound was squelched, and Ashe snugged Molly ever closer and tighter against his body.

"Simmer down, Molly. Don't make me hurt ye now. Can't let ye go till I know ye ain't going to run from me. You goin' hush up that screaming? Say! You goin' be quiet now?"

Her huge frightened eyes were full of tears, as she tried to move her head to show she would not scream. Ashe was pulling her hair so hard she could barely move her head.

"Now then, that's better, girl. That's my little girl. Good Molly."

Although Molly was trembling and sobbing, she was as mad as a hornet and filled with hatred for her father. When Ashe moved his hand from her mouth, he found an even more convenient place to rest it. Pulling Molly's hair back with another quick painful yank, his free hand slid down her dress to find the mounds of her breasts. These he caressed and squeezed to feel their sensational roundness and softness.

"Oh, Molly. My, how ye've grown."

"Stop! Stop it!"

Molly tried to brush his hand away, but she was no match for his brutal strength. He just kept rubbing and fondling her, harder and harder.

"You sure feel good, Molly! It's been so long, I pert near forgot how good ye feel."

Jerking, wiggling, and contorting her body to escape Ashe's brutish hold on her, she hollered out at the top of her lungs, "Ahh! Please let me go! Let me loose! Ahh!"

Ashe was not a man possessed with a well-controlled temperament, however. He was growing more than a little aggravated at Molly's defensive measures. It was almost as if she did not want what he wanted.

"Can't let you loose, Molly! Leastwise, ye'll run off. I believe it's so. Now why don't ye let me feel ye real good down here?" Certainly, he did not wait for an answer before forcing his hand even lower and trying to grope her private parts through the thin cotton dress.

"Stop!" she screamed, "Stop!" Then she began stomping and viciously trying to assault her lewd attacker. "Stop—please!"

One of those hard stomps fortunately landed directly on Ashe's bare stunt foot, and as soon as it did, his own screaming drowned out Molly's cries for help. The kitchen briefly became a riot of noise and intense action, as they both howled mightily and wrestled. Jack Ashe desperately clung to the hair on Molly's head, as she used every ounce of power and grit in her to try and break loose. But it was to no avail. She was never going to escape Ashe's grip as long as he had a breath in him. Suffering horrible pain in his maimed foot, he managed to jerk Molly into his clutches again, and immediately flung her hard onto the floor. Before she knew it, he was sitting on top of her and pinning her against the floor boards with his heavy body, while leaning forward to get a big kiss.

It was wishful thinking on Ashe's part. Molly shook her head violently in resistance, and as a last futile measure spat in his face. Taken aback by his daughter's defiance, Ashe hauled one arm back and then slapped her in the face as hard as he could. When that failed to squash her struggling, he let her have it again. It took three of these awful whops to calm her down, and then he started trying to have his way with her.

As he ripped back the top of Molly's dress to reveal her bare breasts, a cold-blooded thought crossed his mind. *She's never goin' to go with me willingly. Goin' have to do away with her too—soon's I've finished having her!* It was not something he dwelled on, mind you. It was only a flashing notion that went away as soon as he buried his face against one of Molly's bare breasts. But before

Jack Ashe could relish the erotic feel and taste that he so hungrily craved, a strange sensation of horrific hurt and then blankness overcame him. He could not taste or smell or feel Molly anymore. He could not taste or smell or feel anything!

# Chapter 24

## East Fork Treasure

Over and over August rolled under the water, fighting for some sense of orientation and trying to gain the water's surface to breathe. For the first ten seconds or more, he and his horse tumbled together, until he crashed into an unforgiving river boulder. A second's pause and probably a broken rib or two he owed to the behemoth rock that had been fretted by the river's water for eons. But the interruption served him well, as he was now separated from the horse, but again hurtling head over heels along with the raging current. In less than a minute, he miraculously popped up to the surface and into broad daylight, where everything was spinning so fast he could not get his bearings. But he gulped the delicious, life-saving fresh air while he had the chance. When the broadside of a rushing log smashed into him, nearly taking off his head, he grabbed hold for dear life.

August knew he would not be able to hold on for long. The log was too big for his arms to clutch around, and the current was too strong and turbulent. Any little variation in the powerful forces that were sweeping him and the buoyant log forward would undoubtedly tear them apart, and in no time at all he would be underwater again. Although it was difficult to think clearly, as he dodged and tore through one low-hanging tree after another, an intuitive thought came to him—what he had to do. When he saw the next tree speeding toward him, he reached out and tried to hang on, but the branch broke!

*Damn!* August cussed to himself while anticipating the next one he could grab. When he saw another one coming, he seized hold of the limb, a thicker one this time, and desperately hung on. The swift-flowing water slapped and swept his dangling body nearly prone with the surface, while he clung for dear life. His position was untenable though. There was no way he could hang on like this for another minute. Hand over hand, he worked his way toward the bank until he was able to latch hold of another higher branch and pull himself completely out of the water. Finally, he was able to catch his breath, while poised precariously across the limb running under his belly. His side hurt terribly. *It's got to be a broke rib*, he told himself while assessing his situation. The limb he was wrapped around looked like it was about to break, and he knew he had to move quickly. *Damn, it's not going to hold!*

Kicking himself in the ass mentally, he got a move on. Sidling over the limb on his belly, he slowly wormed himself toward the bank as far as he could go. When he could advance no further, he looked around for a stronger limb to hitch himself to. There were no more! He was stuck—stuck out on a slender broken limb, with the roaring torrent a mere two feet beneath him. *Damn it to hell, I'm stuck!*

With no other options, August had to simply hang to the limb like a big ol' possum for as long as it would bear him up. While dangling and waiting for fate's next cruel turn, his mind whirled between feelings of guilt for this fiasco he had created—and the sensations of that last kiss he had with Molly. And there was one other thing that kept popping into his head. *If this limb breaks, I'm a goner for sure.*

When Jack Ashe fell limply to the side, Molly looked up and could hardly believe her eyes. Standing there with a smile growing from ear to ear was Jee Man Sing. He was holding the cast iron skillet that he had used so effectively to knock out the treacherous man who had dared to assault her. Without uttering a word, the valet found the largest knife in the kitchen, rolled the unconscious Jack Ashe off of Molly, knelt down, and then surgically plunged the carving knife straight into Ashe's still beating heart. Jee left the knife be, gave Molly a slight bow and head nod, and then went back upstairs to his room, where he quietly resumed his wait for Mr. Stenson's return.

Molly was beyond horrified. She was a wreck! Without even changing her torn dress, she wrapped a shawl around herself and immediately raced in the dark down to the Hargroves' place, seeking their assistance and comfort. Within five or six hours, Hack and Molly met the sheriff and a deputy up at the new house and gave them the full details of what had transpired. It turned out to be an unusually short investigation, and one that did not even include an interrogation of the Chinese valet. The lawmen were impressed, and rightly so, with Molly's fortitude and strength to resist the will of a man like Jack Ashe. Very few men could kill another man with a knife, like Molly had done. And to be so accurate and precise with the thrust—the sheriff and his deputy were simply incredulous.

Side by side, Hack and Molly stood on the front porch in silence and watched the lawmen ride away, leading a pack horse behind them with Ashe's body draped across it. As they rode off and disappeared into the darkness, Hack turned to Molly and she looked at him and then they wrapped each other in a big affectionate hug.

"You done good, Molly—real good!"


The next day, up on the East Fork River, the loggers and furious farmers throughout the valley were taking stock of the terrible destruction along the path of the great splash dam flood. All of the logs that were cut and lying along the river above the sawmill had been easily flushed downstream by the raging waters. But the great chain above the Ugly Camp dam had not held, and even the Ugly Camp dam itself was washed away by the tremendous wall of water. The bucked saw logs simply kept on going, riding the crest of the torrent right past Ugly Camp and all the way down to the fertile valley land of the lower East Fork.

There, more than a thousand huge poplar and hickory logs were left high and dry in the farmers' recently cultivated fields. Not only were most of the sprouting corn crops washed away, but literally tons of rich alluvial soil were eroded and sluiced to other spots further downstream. Also, many cabins, barns, and outbuildings below Ugly Camp were either destroyed or suffered irreparable damage. Yet the disastrous results were not limited to just this.

When the wall of water overtopped the Ugly Camp dam, causing that dam to fail, the entire sawmill site was inundated. The loggers' shacks, mess hall, church, shops, flume, portable sawmill, and even the brand new mill were either washed away entirely or significantly damaged. And still there was even worse news.

Sadly, Henrik Stenson's body was discovered under a pile of poplar logs down about Rufus Edmunston's Crab Orchard farm. Poor Claude Johnson was found lifeless and hanging from a hemlock tree not far below Ugly Camp, and all three horses washed up near Charlie Hardin's cabin. It was only by the grace of God that there were no other fatalities associated with the splash dam flood.

George Abbott's search party discovered August around midnight—the night of the flood—still clinging to his broken tree limb and alive but badly battered. At least August was not dead, and when he later learned of Henrik's and Claude's fate, he broke down in tears. Never could he have imagined that this grandiose splash dam scheme could go so terribly wrong. No amount of rationalizing or reasoning could place the blame for this catastrophe with anyone but him.

It was his fault, he figured, and he would never be convinced otherwise. Two of August's best friends in the world were now dead because of him. And this would undoubtedly be another black mark scribed next to his name by Whoever was keeping the tally—wherever. For the rest of his life, he would bear the guilt for the tragic deaths of these two fine men, as well as that bushwhacker Posey feller he had killed over in Cherokee County, almost four years ago.

A couple of days after August was carried down to his new house, he and Molly sat on their front porch. The morning sun breaking over the near mountains was beginning to peek through a low mist hanging over the river. Now mind you, August was not actually sitting. With two broken ribs and bruises covering his entire body, not to mention the nearly healed knife wound, he was actually propped up in a little daybed that Hack had thoughtfully brought up for the purpose. Just inside the house, in the new front parlor lined with pretty blue wallpaper, another man lie in stiff repose. The tortured body of Henrik Stenson, barely recognizable when found, was contained in a closed walnut casket.

Molly sat at August's side, diligently transcribing the words he muttered barely loud enough for her to hear.

*June 10, 1887*
*Dear Mrs. Stenson and Hanna,*

*I deeply regret to tell you Mr. Stenson has been taken from us. He was swept away in a flood and drowned two days ago. We plan to give him a Christian burial as soon as possible if that suits you. Please let me know if you have other desires.*

*August*

August took a quick look at the note and thought it ought to do. "Okay, Molly—looks good I reckon. Now please take it down before Pa heads to the station. I reckon he can get a telegram sent out this morning."

If he had known to whom and where to send a note to Claude Johnson's family, he would have done that too. However, George Abbott was accompanying his nephew's body back to West Virginia for interment in their family's cemetery. All costs, of course, were being borne by the East Fork Lumber Company. August had made out a generous check from his own bank account to Claude's mother, since he was not married. Surely, this would not compensate for the man's life, but it would perhaps relieve Mrs. Johnson of financial burdens for a while. At least that was August's intention. And he told George Abbott to hurry back as soon as he could. August would need him to sort through the mill's wreckage and help decide what must be done with the company.

On the hot Sunday afternoon of June 12th, a good-sized crowd gathered at the little cemetery behind Piney Grove Church. Family and friends of the Hargrove family, such as the Edmunston clan, had come from all over Haywood to be there—from the settlements of Pigeon River, Waynesville, Forks of Pigeon, and the remote reaches of the east and west prongs of the Pigeon. Of course the faithful Chinese valet, Jee Man Sing, was there as well, standing next to Molly and looking sadder than anyone had ever seen him. All of these mourning souls were at the graveyard to say their goodbyes and bury a man who most had hardly known.

August stood next to Molly too, floppy hat in hand and wearing a black cotton shirt bought special for the occasion. One denim pants leg was stuffed into the top of his boot and the other hung free. It was all he could do to stand up, his ribs hurt so bad. As he watched Henrik Stenson's coffin box descend into the hole in the ground, another bout of heaving sobs overcame him. Hack, Rufus, and a couple of their old war buddies—Francis Christopher and Garland Henson—played out the hemp ropes until the box hit the earthen bottom with a soft thud, whereupon the four tag ends were simply tossed into the hole. As these men backed away from the grave, the Good Reverend Shook stepped forward to offer up a few choice words to God and all the mourners who were gathered around the grave.

"It's a sad thing to do what we are gathered here to do, ladies and gentlemen. But we all know these things don't happen by a schedule, like the railroads run on or the celestial bodies conform to. No, they happen when we least expect them sometimes—and for reasons that we mortal humans cannot fathom.

"Henrik Stenson was a successful and distinguished gentleman by all measures. August speaks very highly of the man. He related to me how the two of them built the successful gold mining operation in California—Skidaddle, I believe it was called. And then when August came back here, the two of them invested heavily in the East Fork Lumber Company. Henrik was apparently a man of great wisdom and compassion and chose for a business partner one of our very own. A wise choice we all know." Then, after pausing briefly, Reverend Shook unexpectedly asked, "August, would you care to say something at this time?"

*What—what the hell?* August had not meant to give a speech and could not believe his ears. No way was he prepared to say anything in front of all these people. Besides, he had not wanted the preacher to talk about all those things—all of his business dealings with Mr. Stenson, especially the East Fork Lumber Company. That venture certainly didn't turn out too good, thanks to his own bad decision to build the damned splash dam. *What should I say?*

August looked around nervously, then lowered his head and stared into the grave. "Uhh—I—I just want everybody to know that Mr. Stenson was—he was a good man and sure was right good to me. I'll never know, don't reckon, what he ever saw in me that night on that big Mississippi riverboat. I was all down and out—that's a whole 'nother story, and I reckon I won't get into it here—and I was lonely, real lonely. All of a sudden, Mr. Stenson came over and started talking to me for some reason or other—just walked over and talked to me. He saw something in me that I couldn't even see in myself. Anyway, after that we got to be right close—me and him and Mrs. Stenson and Hanna—and we did real good out at Skidaddle."

Another thought popped into his head then, but he was unsure if he should mention it. *What the hell*, he figured he ought to get it out for everybody to hear. "Don't reckon I should ever have built that splash dam. I'm sorry, Mr. Stenson."

Then he stopped talking, looked over at the preacher, and gave him a nod that he was through. The good reverend picked it up from there. "Thank you, August. We all know how dearly you loved Henrik Stenson. And we all believe that it was fortunate for him that he got to know you and your family."

August was not so sure, as he squeezed Molly's hand and cut a glance toward Hack and Harriet. His parents managed a weak grin of reassurance, before slowly turning their attentions back to the preacher. In just a few short minutes, Reverend Shook was beseeching the Almighty to let Henrik Stenson rest easy and take him into His everlasting world.

"And now, Father of the Lord Jesus, we give You this upstanding gentleman, Henrik Stenson, and ask that You forgive him of his worldly sins. Open Your doors for him and lead him into the Kingdom of the Lord. Please comfort him and let him look down on this earth so he can follow his loved ones. Let him see and know that all those he has left behind will forever remember and love him. We ask this in Thy name, O Lord God. Amen."

At the conclusion of this abbreviated service, August stepped over to the grave, reached down and grabbed a handful of earth, and then chunked it on top of the casket. Afterward, a throng of folks mobbed around him and Molly to offer their condolences. But the commotion was short-lived. It was so hot and humid, everyone was anxious to get back to their homes, where they might enjoy the rest of the Sunday afternoon. However, Rufus and his two Rebel comrades lagged behind, assuring August and Hack that they would stay and cover the coffin box.

"Ain't nary way we're goin' leave this feller without covering him up proper like," Francis Christopher allowed, as he took up a shovel and he, Rufus, and Garland got to work.

With the wedding only a few days away, August and Molly stayed as busy as the honeybees in the forests and fields. Molly's nights were spent down at the Hargroves, but during the daylight hours, she nursed August's body and spirits, while the painters white-washed their house's lap siding and carefully applied a willow green tint to the shutters and trim. Frequent visitors to the new house were the norm during this period.

Harriet and Beth were up almost every day, fitting and finishing Molly's lovely wedding dress. Everett Clinard came by almost daily to work with August, going over the books, tallying the losses, and writing checks to the East Fork farmers—those who had presented claims, so far. And would you believe that these two unlikely friends had reason to celebrate one afternoon when Hack showed up with a telegram? The missive was from Henrik Stenson's lawyer in Pittsburgh, and he wrote to inform August that Stenson had had the good sense to take out a substantial insurance policy to protect the company from the risk of fire and other disasters, not including floods. However, since the splash dam flood was actually a man-made disaster, he thought the company stood a reasonable chance of reclaiming most of their losses. The lawyer allowed that he would endeavor to file a claim to recoup a substantial award. Upon learning this, the two of them began whooping and hollering so loudly that Molly had to run outside to see what was the matter!

And on this same day, more unexpected visitors graced their threshold.

"Joseph, Eugenia—I can't believe it! You made it!"

"Hello, August! How are you?" That was all Joseph Edmunston could say before he and August greeted each other with huge bear hugs.

"Ohhh! Ahhh! I'm sorry, Joseph. I've got a couple of broke ribs. They hurt a sight."

"Sorry! Pa told me all about everything. Real sorry, August."

"Hello, Eugenia! Believe I'd rather give you a big hug."

"Hi, August! It's good to see you!" and then they proceeded to embrace, but not nearly so strongly.

"And look at little Basil! Hello, little man! Look how big you are!" August took the little blond boy in his arms and held him out to look at.

"He's going on three years old now, August. Looks just like his father, doesn't he?" Eugenia offered with a chuckle.

Then they all turned toward the open doorway, as Molly walked out to see what all the racket was about.

"Molly, here they are! This is Joseph and Eugenia, and this handsome little boy is Basil!"

"Oh, how good to meet you! We weren't sure if you could come or not. August has told me so much about you. Please, please come in."

"We've heard a lot about you too, Molly," replied Eugenia, and then they all followed Molly inside her beautiful new house.

It turned out to be a very pleasant visit, just what August needed to distract him from the woeful sawmill business. He was surprised, though, to learn that Joseph and Eugenia were thinking of moving back to the mountains. Come to find out, Eugenia's father, Will Rhinehart, the man who had been so kind to the two alleged criminals, was looking for another business opportunity. His wooding business had dried up substantially. Not only was the wood getting harder to find and log around Memphis, but more and more coal was being substituted for wood to fuel the boilers of the river steamboats and the ever-growing number of railroad locomotives.

While listening to this incredible turn-of-events, a random thought crossed August's mind, and he decided to explore it. "Say, Joseph, it just occurred to me that you and Mr. Rhinehart might want to go into business with me here—that is, if I decide to rebuild our sawmill."

"What? You're thinking about starting over?"

"Not sure, but I might. 'Spect Mr. Stenson would want me to. The insurance money should cover most of the lawsuits and replace our mill. That's what the lawyer and our accountant tell me. We still own the timber rights to more than twenty thousand acres up above the Crab Orchard. And I believe we can still get the furniture factory business down east again. Why don't you think about it?"

"That right?" Joseph looked over at Eugenia, who seemed more than interested, and then at little Basil, who was sitting on Molly's lap talking to her. "Sounds interesting! I'll run it by Mr. Rhinehart and see what he allows. Okay?"

"Yea—sounds good! Before you and Eugenia head back, we'll have to go up on the high East Fork, if I'm fit, and I'll show you our entire operation—or at least what's left of it."

On the warm summer evening of the solar equinox, the little country Piney Grove Church once again served as the venue for a community gathering. Farmers and farmers' wives, who had worked all day in the fields, kitchens, and barns, now packed the rough-hewn pews. Every last Edmunston was there for sure, as was the elderly Bee Woman. Just outside, under a reddish earthen mound and wilting flowers, another body lie still and quiet, waiting for the big event. Henrik Stenson would not miss August's wedding for anything in this world, nor would his wife and daughter for that matter. Pernilla and Hanna had seats near the front of the sanctuary, and these beautiful and elegant blonde women had caused more than a few tongues to tattle and wag.

Suddenly, a hush came over the crowd, as a small organ filled the room with glorious sound. Moments later, Molly walked deliberately through the open doorway with Hack close at her side. He looked prouder than a peacock spreading its plume. And no wonder—the bride-to-be was absolutely enchanting, evoking audible gasps from more than a few of the stunned onlookers, including the two lovely Stenson ladies. Molly's white, silk satin dress spilled onto the floor in a pile with its short train in pursuit, as she slowly made her way to the front where August, Joseph, and the preacher awaited.

This beautiful sweet creature who August had rescued from the wildest and most depraving of circumstances was about to become his bride. *Who'd thunk it*, he mused, staring in amazement at her. She was the treasure he had always longed for. Nothing in those Skidaddle mine holes could compare with her. He had dug her out of the East Fork wilds, and now he was going to take her for his wife. August meant to love Molly Hargrove with all his heart, and make her a good husband. That was what he aimed to do.

# Chapter 25

## Lost Burro

(In the year 2005)

At the Fort Smith, Arkansas, truck stop, Clint finally got through with his important business—inspecting the facilities. Not one to dawdle, he was hurrying back when he was surprised to see some sort of altercation in progress. It appeared to be a man manhandling a woman, of all things! *Unbelievable!* he thought, while failing to recognize the female victim. However, after glancing toward his empty Chevy, he immediately surmised what was going on and who the woman could be. *It's Claire!* Without another thought, he broke into a sprint and launched himself at both the abductor and Claire. Reminiscent of his linebacker days with the Wolfpack, he bowled them both over onto the hard concrete pavement.

Claire hit hard against the unforgiving surface and was addled, but Clint was on his feet in panther-like quickness. He grabbed the man by the throat and roughly pulled him up off the concrete. The sleazy truck driver struggled to get free while grinning real big, showing the very few yellow teeth left in his head.

"Bet she's good, ain't she now, feller?" Reaching behind him, the man instantly pulled a snub-nosed thirty-eight from a holster and proceeded to level it at Clint's head. But Clint would have none of that. A wild maddening craze erupted within him, and he was royally pissed! Before that truck driver could cock the pistol and take proper aim, Clint hauled back and punched him hard in the face, knocking the man back onto the ground.

*Bam!* The gun fired aimlessly, missing Clint. In the blink of an eye, he was on top of the damned man. Knocking the pistol out of his hand, Clint relentlessly launched one punch after another at the truck driver's face.

Claire was crying out as loud as she could, "Stop, Clint! Stop! You're going to kill him!"

Finally, a bystander jumped in and tried to pull him off the man. Clint shook the do-gooder off but stood up and backed away on his own. All out of breath and concerned for Claire's wellbeing, he reached down to help her up. But Claire ignored the compassionate gesture, looking anxiously over his shoulder. "The truck's on fire!" she cried out.

Clint turned to see both the gas pump and the red Chevy in flames. "No!" Impulsively and foolishly, he ran over to the truck, but there was nothing he could do. The cab was entirely ablaze.

"Get back, Clint! It'll blow up! Get back!"

*Damn it all,* he fumed, before spotting their suitcases in the bed of the truck. *I can get those!* In mere seconds, Clint had grabbed his and Claire's bags and was running back toward her.

*Boom!* The percussion of the exploding gas pump knocked Clint to the ground. Fortunately, he was out of reach of most of the scorching tongues of fire. Claire ran over and threw herself on top of him, snuffing out the smoldering flames on his back.

"Oh, Clint! Are you okay?"

He strained to twist his head around in order to see his beautiful Claire. When their eyes locked, expressions of pure sympathy and concern for the other were unmistakable.

"I'm okay—are you?"


Clint and Claire spent all afternoon making painstaking statements to the police, in order that the entire story and every detail of the truck driver incident was told and recorded. It was not a great surprise for them to learn that the horrid man had served time for past sexual transgressions. With barely controllable contempt, they watched as he was cuffed and hauled off to jail.

The police and firemen determined that the errant gunshot had undoubtedly set the gas pump ablaze. In scant seconds, the fire must have jumped to the truck, they rationalized. Hours were spent working with the insurance company to report the circumstances of the truck fire and to obtain a rental truck. Clint was heartbroken at the loss of his old red Chevy, and the replacement vehicle that was brought over did not help his feelings one bit. It was a black 2005 Ford truck with four-wheel drive. Although he was not a Ford enthusiast, he allowed that given everything else that had transpired that day, the truck swap could have been worse. At least the four-wheel drive might come in handy.

However, the wrap to this awful day had a silver lining, believe it or not, and would actually mark a turning point in the couple's relationship. Standing side by side at the counter of the Holiday Inn, they looked expectantly at each other when the young clerk asked, "Two single beds or a double?"

Nodding in knowing approval, they both turned to the clerk and replied in unison, "Double!"

Of course, the first thing they did that evening was bathe away the filth of the truck driver and the grime and soot from the fire. After that, they soon found themselves in each other's arms embracing passionately. Clint and Claire had fought for and saved each other's lives that day. For these difficult trials, they now felt a much closer attachment, and it no longer seemed necessary to hide their true feelings from one another. Why should they, for heaven's sake? They were adults after all, each one divorced and alone in this world, with no one to share life's pleasures and burdens. Both felt a deep inner respect and affection for the other, and tonight these feelings morphed into more than that. Clint and Claire discovered and celebrated their newfound love.

They were able to shed all pretensions and inhibitions and do what they had wanted to do for a long time. Although both of them were extremely tired and sore from the day's exertions, they expressed their love in a way that would leave no doubts of their innermost affections. And if one might still wonder how these expressions of love might have played out, let us imagine that Clint did indeed become Claire's cowboy on this special night in a Fort Smith, Arkansas, motel room.

There was time to make up, and Clint kept a heavy foot on the pedal the next day, as he and Claire trucked along I-40 through Oklahoma. Truth be known, both of them were still basking in the afterglow of the sensational night they had spent together. Claire sat tight against him, her hand on his leg, and occasionally she leaned over to plant a kiss on the side of his face. Every now and then, out of the corner of his eye, he would catch her staring at him.

"What?" he finally asked, after she sneaked one of those peeks.

"Oh, nothing. Don't mind me looking at my cowboy, do you?"

"Don't reckon so. Not much to look at," came the embarrassed reply.

"Well I beg to differ with you there, sir. It's a right pleasurable sight, I do believe."

After a quiet interlude of a minute or so, Clint brought the conversation around to their current mission. "Claire, I sure hope that old Southern Jackass mining claim is located on private property. Won't be able to do anything but look if it's on government land. I know for a fact that Skidaddle is in the national park. And we'll be able to drive all the way up to it, I believe, with this four-wheel drive truck. Ha! It's a Ford, though—we'll have to see about that."

"But I thought you had finally been able to talk to the landowner. Didn't you?"

"Turned out, the man who owns the property bordering the park—it includes the Lost Burros Canyon—is a wealthy absentee owner. He lives in Los Angeles and, believe it or not, returned my call. The property's been in his family for years, he said. But he doesn't know the property very well, and it's been years since he was in the Lost Burros Canyon. But he gave me the name and number of one of the tenants who looks after the property."

"Well, that's certainly fortunate, isn't it? Were you able to talk with him?"

"Had a good chat with the man, as a matter of fact. Juan Lopez is his name, and he says he'll show us the way up Lost Burros to where the government land starts. Let's see, what's today, Claire—Tuesday or Wednesday? I can't keep track."

"It's Wednesday, silly. Why? Do you have a train to catch?"

"It's just that I told Mr. Lopez we'd try to make it to his place by Friday. We're going have to push it to get there, though."

"We'll drive through the night if we have to. I'm sure we can make it!"

"Thanks, Claire!" Clint was obviously appreciative. "I need your steadiness—and confidence. Uh—which reminds me, I've been meaning to talk to you about something else."

"Fire away, cowboy!" With a tight squeeze of Clint's leg, she meant to show him that he could talk about anything with her.

"Well—it's about my problem. Hmm—I'm not sure how much you know, but the reason I had to leave the school was—well, it's like this, Claire—I had a drinking problem." He looked at her quickly and then turned back to the road. There was no telling what her reaction might be, so he waited nervously for her response.

"I know, Clint. Whether you've noticed it or not these past couple of years, I've been paying quite a bit of attention to you. I know about your problem, and I've been worried sick, too."

"You have—well, I'm really sorry if I've worried you. I guess everybody must know by now. I'm going to beat it though, Claire! I know I can—with you to help me. I can do it! I'm not going to drink anymore, because I don't want to hurt you. And damn it to hell, I don't want to hurt myself either! I promise you, Claire, I'll beat it. If it hadn't been for you last night, I'd drunk myself to sleep after that terrible day we had."

"It's not going to be easy, Clint. Let me know when you're struggling with it, and I'll try to help, any way that I possibly can. Together, we'll beat it though!"

There was another thoughtful pause about then, before Claire decided to get things back on track. "Ready for me to drive this Ford truck, cowboy?"

The final legs of the journey to California took Clint and Claire through Oklahoma City, Albuquerque, Las Vegas, and finally across Death Valley. Thank goodness the rest of the trip was uneventful, other than the ever-changing grandeur and beauty of the American countryside. Clint had rented a room at the Wildrose Inn in Panamint Springs, finding it to be the nearest civilized boarding facility in the desolate region. From there, a twenty-mile jump north through the desert on a two-lane paved road would take them to another lesser improved road. By back-tracking south on it for fifteen more miles, they could reach the jeep road leading into Lost Burros Canyon. Clint's topo map showed that this dirt path snaked up through the canyon, all the way to the Skidaddle ruins.

At noon on Friday morning, after getting lost down an endless road, they finally found Mr. Lopez's ranch. In his sixties and clearly of Mexican descent, Lopez greeted them as if they were family. "Good to meet you, Clint—Claire. We've been expecting you. This is my wife, Maria. We're both very happy to have you at our home.

"Hello—could I get you some drink—water, wine, or cerveza? And I make tacos. We would be happy for you to take almuerzo with us." Maria was insistent to share their lunch, so the four of them sat outside on the terrace under a vine-covered arbor. Here in this pleasant setting they got to know each other better, as well as quench all hints of thirst and hunger.

Juan and Maria's three grown children and their families lived in other ranch houses spread across the immense piece of property. Together, they worked as caretakers of the land, chasing off drug dealers, squatters, gold diggers, campers, and other encroachers on the property. It was all extremely arid land and not much good for farming, but there was enough water, brushes, and grasses to support small beef and goat herds. For years now, the Lopez's had lived in constant dread that the absentee property owner would finally relent and sell his land to the government. Most of the surrounding property had already been gobbled up, and they figured it was just a matter of time before theirs would be parkland too.

"Yes, yes—I know this place—this Hargrove Spring. I don't know the name Hargrove Spring, but I know the spring. I can take you there—yes?" Juan Lopez left no doubt he could find it.

As they all looked at the old map, Clint pointed to it. "Yes—we'd like that very much! Is this spring—maybe it is Hargrove Spring—is it on your property?"

"Yes, yes—it is on my property, Clint. I will show you!"

Claire felt her excitement building. "What about the mine, Mr. Lopez? Do you remember seeing a mine here?" she asked while touching the "X" on the map. "It was called the Southern Jackass and must be about a quarter of a mile north of the spring. Do you know it?"

"No, Claire, I can't remember a mine—this Jackass mine. But I don't ever explore that place very much. It is steep and—how you say—treacherous."

"Think we can drive up the canyon road, Mr. Lopez? I've got a four-wheel drive."

"My sons use mostly four-wheelers to go up and down that road. But I believe you can drive your truck, Clint. It will be difficult though. Do you want me to go with you?"

"By all means! We can drive to the Skidaddle ruins, and on the way up you can point out the spring. Then tomorrow, if you have no objection, Claire and I can go back and look for the Southern Jackass. That sound okay with you?"

"Good—good! Yes—it is okay! We go then!"


It had obviously been an old wagon road at one time, undoubtedly used to haul ore out of the Skidaddle mine and supplies in. The Ford truck was nearly as wide as the path it was following, and sometimes wider where the erosion was especially bad. Surprisingly, a strong creek paralleled the rugged path—in places crossing it—and willows and cottonwoods sprouted from the bordering rocky terrain. Growing mostly along the creek and up the lower slopes were lush green plants of many varieties. Scrub bush, desert holly, and grasses abounded in the lower reaches, and in the higher places pinion and juniper thrived. Even colorful wild flowers hugged the rocky creek banks and the sloping sides of the canyon walls.

Slowly and surely, Clint guided the truck between the rocky abutments and over the watery crossings up Lost Burros Canyon, eventually gaining almost four thousand feet in elevation. About four miles into the canyon, Mr. Lopez asked Clint to stop the truck. Whereupon, the three of them got out and Lopez led them into a yawning side gulch where the water was streaming out of the canyon floor. "Here is the spring! You see there is not water above here. But this spring is strong. I believe it is your Hargrove Spring, Clint."

Clint's and Claire's hearts beat quicker, as they gazed appreciatively at the place where the water was literally spewing out of the ground. Clint studied the remains of old rock foundations and walls that appeared to have contained the water at one time. Then his eyes started searching the surrounding terrain, trying to understand where the Southern Jackass might have been. On the opposite side of the stream and road, in a rare level area, the crumbled ruins of an old rock house could be seen—exactly as indicated on the old map. Then he looked to the north, in the direction where the Southern Jackass mine was thought to be.

"Yes, it sure might be our spring, Mr. Lopez! Then the mine, if there was one, would have to be up that way—up that steep gulch." Clint pointed up a dark ravine to emphasize his hopeful pronouncement. "Don't you think, Claire? The house is over there," and he looked back in that direction.

"Yea, you're right! Sure seems so, Clint. But it's so steep up that—that gulch. Do you think we can climb up it?"

"Yea, I think we can. We only have to go a quarter of a mile," he said with a reserved confidence. "Mr. Lopez, have you ever been up through there?"

Lopez's head began shaking back and forth. "No—nobody goes up there—only goats and rattlesnakes—and wild burros."

Clint and Claire looked at each other, their eyes opening wider, brows rising slightly, and an uneasy feeling coming over them.

"Well, Claire, I guess you and me will have to give them critters some company tomorrow, huh?"

"I'm up to it if you are, Mr. Cowboy."

They spent the rest of the afternoon exploring the ruins of the old mining town, which stretched across an expansive plateau located about a half-mile above the spring. Signage identified the site as that of the once-thriving Skidaddle, which was destroyed by fire in 1897. It was definitely located inside the Death Valley National Park, and visitors were directed not to deface or remove remains and relics—or disturb the diamondback rattlesnakes.

Clint and Claire saw remnants of rock foundations, the crumbling walls of the stamp mill, a towering brick chimney, myriad artifacts, large and small pieces of metal, sections of piping, and deep pocks that disappeared into the mountainsides—their openings covered with rusting steel bars. Both of them were duly impressed with the remains of the old mill town and its obvious historical significance.

On the way back down the canyon, Clint at last confided to Mr. Lopez the story of Dick Rosehl and how he was buried by a landslide in the Southern Jackass mine. Then, infused with gumption after spending the entire afternoon in Lost Burros Canyon and feeling a renewed confidence in his and Claire's mission, he resolved to ask a favor of the old gentleman. "Sir, I was thinking that if you were of a mind to loan Claire and me a pick and shovel, we might do some poking around tomorrow when we come back. I believe we can work our way up that gulch above the spring and search for evidence of the Southern Jackass."

Lopez proved to be very understanding and accommodating. "Is not a problem, Clint, if you and Claire want to come back and poke round some more. I would not advise it. You saw how rough it was, and you must be careful of snakes. But I don't think you will find a mine named Jackass. The only jackass to be found in Lost Burros Canyon, are the wild burros. You will find many mountain goats and wild burros around here."

*We'll see*, Clint thought, as he looked to Claire for a sign of faith in their crazy undertaking. The Southern Jackass was the only lost burro he wanted to find, and he had a good idea where it was.

# Chapter 26

## A Dark Family Secret!

The Wildrose Inn was an old family-owned motel that seldom got mentioned in postcards or emails home, unless of course the AC malfunctioned. Clint and Claire had no complaints there—it was plenty cool enough in their room. But the walls were paper thin, and their neighbors' activities on both sides and overhead were plainly obvious and disturbing. The walls rattled, the ceiling thumped, and the moaning and screaming was incessant. So Clint and Claire were inclined to talk in low whispers, and slept—and whatnot—with upmost discretion.

As the two of them were snuggling on the bedsheet, Clint just blurted right out and asked, "Are you proud of me, Claire?"

"Of course I'm proud of you—anything I should be particularly proud of?"

"Haven't craved a drink all day today. Been so busy, I guess. Can't believe what all we were able to see. Skidaddle and that Lost Burros Canyon were incredible! Don't you think?"

"Funny how such an extreme terrain can be so beautiful! The creek and waterfalls and greenery—how can it be so green with all those trees and plants?"

"Has to do with all that water, I'm sure. The spring we saw must be Hargrove Spring. And the remains of the old house were there, just where it shows on the map. It's got to be Hargrove Spring. Ha—my great-grandfather's spring!"

Claire gently rubbed her hand back and forth across his chest and craned to look into Clint's eyes. "I'm excited too, Clint. We're going to find evidence of that old land slide. If anyone can see it, you will—the famous geologist!" she finished with a giggle.

"We'll give it a try, that's for sure!" Seems there was something else he was sure of just then. He wrapped his arm around Claire, pulled her in closer, and they locked in a passionate embrace. After that, their thoughts turned away from the Southern Jackass and toward an exploration of another sort.

"You know something, Claire. This Ford truck isn't so bad after all. We could never have made it up this trail without the four-wheel drive—no way!"

"Amazing how it just keeps going through the deep holes in the creek and crawls right over those big rocks. We're almost there, aren't we?"

"Yea, it's not too much further. Boy, sure is hot out and not a cloud in the sky." Clint had already stripped off his shirt.

"I expect we're going to burn up today—even in that shady gulch we're about to explore. Won't be any breezes in there for sure. Wish I could take my shirt off," she jested, making Clint smile.

The Lost Burros Canyon was hotter than a blast furnace that next morning when they finally reached the springhead. Heat literally radiated from the rocky escarpments, and the two treasure hunters could definitely feel it. Both wore shorts and hiking shoes picked up in Las Vegas, where they also had purchased backpacks and water bottles—Clint had not saved everything from the Chevy truck. After donning their new packs, he gave Claire fair warning before they took off and tried to break through the thick scrub bushes.

"Now, Claire, let me take the lead. I've got the pick and shovel. Keep your eyes peeled and your nose radar tuned for rattlers. They'll hit me first, I guess."

"Nose radar! What do you mean 'radar?'" Claire chuckled in bewilderment.

"Snakes stink! Sometimes you can smell them before you see 'em! Don't you worry too much, though. I won't let 'em get you!"

"Well, that's a relief! Sure you don't want me to carry the shovel?"

"I've got it. You ready?"

"Never more so! Giddy-up!"

Excited beyond anything he had experienced since his football days, Clint busted through the thick brush blocking the entrance into the deep chasm, and Claire followed close behind him. They worked their way up a steep incline, and the further they went the wider the ravine became, it seemed.

After only a few minutes of strenuous hiking and climbing, Clint suddenly halted to see how Claire was fairing. "You doing okay?"

"Whew! Yea, it's not too bad. This brush is unforgiving though." She was already sweating profusely and was more than happy to take a breather.

"Sure is! Looks like it's opening up somewhat."

*Eeyore, eeyore, eyore!* All at once, they were both scared witless by a series of loud, lusty bellows echoing throughout this little gulch they were in. Out of nowhere, a wild burro sprung out of the dense bushes in front of them and fled up the ravine, braying in terror.

"Ohh!" Claire reacted. It was not a scream, but she could not contain herself. "Oh my! What was that?"

"We're okay, Claire! It was just a burro—one of those wild burros Lopez said to be on the lookout for. I believe it was more scared than us."

"Oh my, it scared me to death!"

"It's okay. Every burro within five miles of us is on the run now. I'm sure we won't jump any more of them. You ready to go on?"

Claire gathered her wits about her, nodded her head, and within moments they were hacking their way through more stiff green vines and brush. When they had climbed two hundred yards or so, Clint stopped and started surveying the ravine. It was far more expansive and, interestingly, the slope was much gentler for the next little ways.

"Look over here, Claire! I believe it's an old path or trail!"

"Where? Oh...hmm...hard for me to make out that it's a trail."

"Yea, but someone or something's used it. Not sure if it's a goat path or an old Indian trail or what. Look over here where it's been smoothed—and here—see this notch. And look—here's another little pocket above it—see!

These are foot holds—that what's they are! They've been deliberately cut into the face of the rock to ease the climb up this little cliff. Sure enough, that's what they are! Who knows, Claire? Maybe Dick Rosehl and my great-grandfather hacked out this little path. I'll bet they used it hundreds of times to get to the Southern Jackass. That is, if it's up there."

"Hmm—I think you're right! I can see it. It's grown over pretty bad, but let's try and follow it up a ways."

"Okay, let's go!"

Using the footholds and a couple more sculpted steps that were uncovered, they climbed up the low cliff and worked their way further up the mysterious path. In several places, where it disappeared into scrub brush or shrubs, they just blindly waded in and desperately hoped they were not going to tread on top of a rattler. After pursuing the old pathway for another hundred yards, they came upon a feature in the ravine wall that caught Clint's attention.

"Hey, hold up here, Claire! What's this?" He was puzzled and the question, although put to Claire, was really one meant to focus his mind.

"What is what? Why are you studying that pile of rocks so hard?"

"Hmm...well, if you look up here, just over my head, there's an opening of some sort—a crevice." Clint jumped up on a rock and stuck his hand in the hole to see how deep it went. "Up here at the top, it's been cut out with a hand drill and explosives, I do believe. I'm certain it has! And all these rocks weren't moved here by gully washers or erosion—or by accident—no way! Look at them! They've been placed here to block this opening for some reason. See how they've been purposely laid up. They're fitted together with the heaviest stones at the bottom. Hmm—very interesting!"

"Wonder who—or why they went to so much trouble to block the opening?"

"Well, I'm sure of one thing. The Indians or old Spanish miners are not responsible. They didn't use explosives. I'd say there's a good chance this was one of Dick Rosehl's claims—his and Great-Grandfather Hargrove's, maybe."

"Really! You think this might be the Southern Jackass claim?"

Clint did not reflect long before responding, "Well—let's think about it, Claire. Remember that letter from Dick Rosehl's daughter to August Hargrove? She said he was covered up—or 'interred'—by a slide at the Southern Jackass. Well, this is definitely not a landslide. And we've not gone a quarter of a mile from the spring yet—not quite."

"So, we're going to keep on going?"

"Guess we might as well. We've come this far. But—but on the way back, if you're game, I'd like to explore this old mine if we have time. Won't ever have another opportunity like this again. Would you let me do that?"

"Be mighty hard for you to slip through that tiny hole." There was no way she could say that without a grin.

"Real funny, girl! No—in an hour—no more than an hour—I can take out enough of those rocks at the top, for us to pass through. What do you say?"

"Us! You want me to go in there with you?"

"If you're of a mind to."

"Well, we'll see. I might try it."

Then they began working their way up the ravine again, following the old trail. In less than five minutes, Clint suddenly stopped in his tracks and began gazing up and down.

"What is it, Clint?"

"There it is, Claire! It's the slide! Over there—right where those two cottonwoods have sprouted! Wow, it's huge!"

"I see! Why, the slide's almost filled the entire ravine."

"Yea—almost! There's no way anybody could have dug Rosehl out using hand tools."

"Poor soul!"

"Yep—he was unlucky for sure."

They stood there in the shadows of the deep ravine for the next several minutes, gazing at Rosehl's likely rocky grave. Clint thought about the horrible death the man must have suffered, if he was not killed instantly. Claire reflected on the daughter and tried to imagine her pain. She may have stood in this exact spot looking at that massive slide.

"Where do you think we should put it?" she asked, breaking the quiet.

"What?"

"The monument marking Dick Rosehl's final resting spot."

"Oh, yea—guess we could put it almost anywhere around here, where it could be seen. But do you know what? A small ground monument will eventually get covered over by the scrub brush. Maybe we can bring someone up here to carve his name in the face of that rock over there—big enough and high enough where everyone can see it good." Clint walked over and reached his hand up on the wall of the ravine, so Claire would not misunderstand where he meant for the memorial carving to be done.

"Why, I think that's a grand idea! Maybe we can find someone around here who'll do it at a reasonable price for us."

"Right! We'd better get it done pretty soon, while this is still private property. If the government ever gets hold of the land, it'll be illegal to deface this wilderness setting. When we get back to the motel tonight, let's break out the laptop and start looking for somebody."

"Sounds like a plan! It's going to be so nice—" Claire was actually getting teary-eyed thinking about the man who had lost his life there more than a hundred years ago.

"Okay, Claire—what do you say we go do us some spelunking?"

"Can't wait! Let's go! Rest in peace, Dick Rosehl."

It took very little time for them to hike back down to the other old mine site—at least that's what Clint had surmised it was. His labor estimate to clear away the pile of rocks over the entrance was a little light though. During the hottest part of the day, with the sun bearing down on them, he and Claire slaved away for two hours to make an opening large enough to crawl through. Even at that high altitude in the Lost Burros Canyon, the temperature was hovering near one hundred degrees Fahrenheit. Sweat poured from their dirt-covered, drenched bodies as they pried, lugged, and heaved heavy rocks.

"Now I know what it must feel like to work on a chain gang," Claire joked, while leaning on the shovel and taking a breather.

Clint stopped to admire her and rest a minute too. "Mighty pretty prisoner, if you ask me! Can't see you chained to a bunch of men in striped clothes, though." He was about to make a witty reference to the sex offender they had the run-in with, but thought better of it. "I didn't think it was going to be so hard to get in there, Claire. I'm sorry. We've 'bout got it though."

Thirty minutes later they had cleared a good-sized tunnel that one person at a time could wiggle through.

"Okay—I'll sneak through there first. Got your flashlight, Claire?"

"Got it! Be careful! Think there are any snakes?"

"Probably—I'll shoo them away for you, how's that?" Although the banter was intended to reassure his girl, Clint was scared to death that his entrance into the dark mine would be welcomed by the horrible singing sound of a den of rattlesnakes. "Here goes, Claire," and with that curt announcement, his head disappeared into the tight opening. Claire watched him slither in headfirst, with his legs and feet kicking and wiggling and finally disappearing into the mine. And then, shortly, she heard him holler, "I'm in, Claire!"

"Do you see anything?"

Clint switched on his little flashlight and watched the beam hurry across the floor and around the jagged rock walls of the mine. "Looks like a mine to me. Can't see all the way in though. It's pretty deep! You coming in?"

She had resolved to follow her man. "Okay—coming in!" And with a good deal of effort and struggle, Claire finally joined Clint, who caught her as she slid into the darkness and his arms. Feeling his hands and arms grabbing and holding her strongly, she could not restrain herself. "Thanks! That's a mighty good grip you've got on me, cowboy!"

"Ah, I couldn't help it Claire! It was dark!"

Then they both stood up as high as they could and shined their light beams all around the mine, trying to see into the darkness and learn more about these confines they had slithered into. Claire, being taller than Clint, had to stoop slightly in order to move around. "See these hand drill marks here? Rosehl—if this is his mine—drilled this rock trying to follow a quartz vein. Wonder if he found anything?"

"Yes—I can see them. How far in does it go?"

"Don't know. Let's see—careful of snakes now!"

The floor of the mine sloped downward as they moved slowly and carefully into the deeper reaches. Clint studied the walls and ceiling carefully, looking for evidence of the ore the miners might have been after. "I see a lot of quartz left behind, Claire. Can't tell much about it though. My light's too weak."

"This must be the end!" Claire had moved ahead of him and was shining her more powerful beam at a rock pile. The roof of the mine sloped steeply downward toward the floor at that point, where it met the top of the pile. Clint moved beside her and stared at the illuminated rocks.

"You're right! Guess it's where the claim petered out."

Claire perceived the disappointment in his voice. "Sorry, Clint. I know you were hoping to discover something interesting."

"No—this is great! This is what I wanted to see! I got to see where my great-grandfather might have done some hard rock mining. Let me have your light so I can take a good look—see if there's anything in there."

Having to almost squat, he moved on ahead, shining the larger torch around the walls and looking for anything interesting.

"Everything okay?"

"Okay, Claire! Almost to the end now—so far, no snakes!"

"Careful!"

When Clint had gone as far as he could and reached the rock fall, he was squatting like a baseball hind catcher. Casting the light over the rocks spilled across the floor, he looked for anything out of the ordinary—a mining artifact or loose piece of ore. He wanted to find something to take home and show Aunt Nannie. Then, suddenly, something caught his eye! *What's that?* It was a glint—or a reflection! "Hold on, Claire! I think I see something!" He played his light over the rocks, and then he saw it again! "Come on up here, Claire! I may have found something!"

When she caught up with him, he was filled with excitement. "There's something behind one of those rocks. Hold this light for me, so I can move a few of them."

Claire sensed the thrill in his voice and became excited herself. "Sure! You don't smell a rattler, do you? Be careful now!"

"No—don't smell a thing except this dry rock dust. Saw something glinting back at me when the light hit it. I believe it could be something interesting!" Then he began taking away the rocks one by one, until he called for the light. "Here—shine it right in here so I can see better!"

Claire obediently moved closer and directed the beam into the little hole Clint had made.

"There it is!" Reaching between a crevice in the rocks, Clint felt the object with his fingers and then carefully pulled it out for inspection.

"It's a gold badge!" Claire immediately exclaimed upon seeing the star-shaped thing.

Clint rubbed it against the coarse material of his shorts, polishing the grime away. He wanted to see if there might be some kind of inscription on it. Claire was squatted right next to him, looking on anxiously.

"There's something on it. Let's see, it says 'Sheriff' and under that is— 'Cherokee County.'"

They looked at each other with befuddled expressions.

"You're right, Claire! It's a sheriff's badge all right!"

Claire confused him even further. "Is there a Cherokee County out here?"

"Damned if I know! There's one in North Carolina though!" Clint strained his brain to make some sense out of this unusual find, but came up blank. "Let's see if there's anything else under those rocks!"

While she held the light, he dug into the pile, quickly pitching the rocks to the side, one after another. All at once, he backed away in pure shock, almost falling backward. "Whoa! What the—?"

"What's wrong, Clint?"

"You're not going to believe this!"

"What? What is it?"

"I think there's a body under all those rocks!"

Claire's eyes opened to saucer size, and the light from the torch made them appear even bigger. "No! You've got to be kidding!"

"There's a body in there. I'm sure of it!"

"We'd better get out of here then! We'll have to call the police—or the sheriff, I guess."

"Now hold on a minute, Claire. I want to be sure of what we've got here. We need to uncover more of the body, just to make sure. Let me see what we've got."

So as she held the light, he moved the rocks away until the entire gruesome corpse was uncovered. Their dancing lights revealed a fully-clothed skeleton. Likely, the dry conditions in the mine aided in the preservation of the clothes, which consisted of dried-out leather boots, denim britches and shirt, and a buttoned-up wool coat. There was no hat, but strands of dark hair could be seen next to the bony skull, which had been staring straight up with those big hollow eyes for who knows how long.

"Well that's it, I guess. Do you think this might be Rosehl? Maybe we got it all wrong." Clint was befuddled with so many thoughts running through his head.

"Maybe. Was he a sheriff? You want to check the pockets to see if there's any identification?"

"Well—I guess we could. Don't expect the local sheriff would appreciate it though. Let's see now—" Checking one coat pocket, he felt something right off! "Found something!" It appeared to be an old piece of newspaper folded into a little square. As he opened it very gingerly, Claire held the light so they could both see real good.

"It's an old photo, Claire!" They studied the faded and creased picture closely, and were actually able to read the caption. After several seconds, a puzzled Clint turned toward Claire in disbelief, "August Hipps? It sure looks like my great-grandfather though!

"Do you—this dead man couldn't be your great-grandfather, could it, Clint?"

"No—he's buried at Piney Grove Cemetery, over in Bethel. It can't be him!"

"Well—I wonder who it is. Who's that August Hipps then? Did you check the other pocket?" she asked anxiously.

"Okay—easy, Claire. Just a minute—let me take a look." His hand shot into the other pocket and immediately he yelled, "Got something else!" Fishing out another folded and tattered piece of paper, he hurriedly opened it. Then, with their heads bumping together, Clint and Claire read the yellowed document with extreme interest.

> # WANTED
>
> **$100 REWARD!**
> $100 in hard coin for information leading to arrest of AUGUST HARGROVE.
>
> Hargrove is an escaped MURDERER from Cherokee County jail. He is a short man of stout build with reddish-blond hair and is 17 years old. Thought to be travelling with a lanky man by the name of Edmunston. Contact Sheriff Buford Posey in Murphy, N.C. if you have any information.

Directly, Clint's hand with the "Reward" poster slowly dropped, along with his mouth. Incredulous at the words he had just read, he could only stammer, "I don't believe it!"

"It says your Great-Grandfather Hargrove was a 'murderer!' Surely not!"

Clint was deeply confounded, "A reward! They offered a reward for him, and he was wanted! Can you believe it?"

"No, I can't believe it! I'm so sorry, Clint!"

"Oh, Claire—this is really a dark family secret! What am I going to tell poor Aunt Nannie?"

# Conclusion

### (In the years gone by)

Over the coming years, August and Molly Hargrove raised a fine family on their little farm in the Pigeon Valley. They became upstanding citizens in the community and worked alongside of their neighbors to make Forks of Pigeon one of the most prosperous farming settlements in Haywood County. But unlike most, August shied away from the farming business. Leastwise, he did not consider himself to be much of a farmer. His attentions were directed elsewhere.

The splash dam disaster haunted him until his dying days. Nevertheless, August found in the depths of his soul enough courage and determination to resurrect the sawmill business. He worked tirelessly to recompense the East Fork Valley farmers and to build another sawmill village at Ugly Camp. Importantly, Pernilla Stenson had brought some good news with her, when she travelled across the entire continent to pay final respects to her husband and attend August's and Molly's wedding. Provisions in Henrik Stenson's will called for August to inherit the East Fork Lumber Company—lock, stock, and barrel—along with the small amount of capital and significant debt associated with the enterprise.

By working with the insurance company, lawyers, and the Chattanooga company building the replacement sawmill, August got things rolling again. George Abbott returned to salvage what he could of the wrecked mill and coordinate the new construction work. And, of all things, best friend Joseph Edmunston decided to return to Haywood, along with Will Rhinehart. In time, these men became August's full partners in the East Fork Lumber Company.

The company's prospects improved tremendously when Rufus Edmunston and his aging father, Basil—known to be stingy with his timber—were enticed to contribute resources to the lumber enterprise. These old friends of the Hargroves granted timber rights for vast acreages of Edmunston land along the lower reaches of the East Fork River. This acquisition, along with the existing timber rights, extended the East Fork Lumber Company's operation for decades to come, ensuring a long-lived, thriving, and prosperous lumber industry for August and his new partners.

Obviously, August worked hard to recover from the greatest mistake of his life—so far. He forever condemned himself for the ill-advised decision to go along with the splash dam scheme. However, that singular failure drove him to work harder in order to make things right again, in his professional career as well as his personal life. He did indeed become a good husband for Molly, and upon the dawn of the twentieth century, things were looking up for the young Hargrove couple.

**(In recent years)**

Clint and Claire returned safely from the California adventure, their relationship having been ratcheted up several notches. Before coming back, however, they were able to find a stone carver in Las Vegas who agreed to inscribe the memorial to R.A. (Dick) Rosehl on the ravine wall—adjacent to the Southern Jackass mine. And it was none too soon either! The wealthy landowner who employed Juan Lopez and his family finally decided to sell out to the government. Five years later, the entire Lost Burros Canyon, including the Southern Jackass and the mine where the mysterious corpse was discovered, was swallowed up by Death Valley National Park.

Within a year after their successful mission, Clint and Claire were married and settled comfortably in an old, revitalized Craftsman home in West Asheville. Both of them remained at the Asheville School for Boys for the rest of their teaching careers, with Clint eventually working his way up to assume the headmaster's responsibilities. And it should be noted that he managed to sit a precarious seat on the infamous wagon and never fall off it again—with Claire riding shotgun next to her cowboy, of course.

As for the corpse they discovered in the old Lost Burros Canyon mine, the Inyo County Sheriff and his crack investigators eventually identified it. The documents found on the body and the gold sheriff's badge led them to the furthermost western county in North Carolina. A thorough research of the Cherokee County archives brought to light the strange case of August Hargrove and the mysterious disappearance of Sheriff Buford Posey. A comparison of the DNA extracted from a strand of hair from the corpse with the DNA of present-day Posey descendants was conclusive beyond all doubt. The body was that of Sheriff Buford Posey.

In the years to come, after his Aunt Nannie passed on, Clint took up the family-history standard and became the unofficial keeper of the dark Hargrove secrets. The darkest one, of course, being August Hargrove's doings out west and especially the business of the reward poster found on Sheriff Posey's body. Due diligence; research of old family letters, newspapers, and the Cherokee County archives; and a fortuitous link-up with Hanna Stenson's great-granddaughter in California allowed Clint to unravel most of the mystery. But neither he nor the Inyo County Sheriff's Department ever learned how Sheriff Buford Posey met his demise or came to be entombed in that old mine in Lost Burros Canyon. And that was just how Dick Rosehl and August Hargrove would have wanted it.

The Stenson connection provided much information about August Hipps' heroics on the doomed riverboat *City of Cairo* and the Central Pacific train that got buried by a snow avalanche. There was also plenty of surviving evidence to bring to light August's notable role in the Skidaddle mining operation and his association with the town sheriff, Dick Rosehl. Admittedly, it took Clint a while to understand the rationale for the use of the alias Hipps. But after uncovering the letters home to worried Hargroves and Edmunstons, he eventually worked it out.

Hargrove tales from the West, Molly's rescue from an abusive father, the historic splash dam disaster, and the birth and resurrection of the East Fork Lumber Company provided fodder aplenty for Clint Hargrove to chaw into. In fact, August Hargrove's legacy turned out to be rich beyond all expectations. With unbounded zeal and dogged determination, Clint eventually laid bare the crux of his Hargrove family lore. Indeed, he found that August Hargrove had fled to the Wild West with a reward on his head and gold in his mind. But, as Clint learned, it was only after his Great-Grandfather August returned to the North Carolina mountains that he discovered a proper treasure. Deep in the wilds of the East Fork River Valley, August found his precious Molly.

# The End

# About the Author

Carroll C. Jones was born and raised in the mountains of Haywood County, North Carolina, in the small paper-mill town of Canton. He is a direct descendant of the Hargrove, Cathey, and Moore families who pioneered the Forks of Pigeon region of Haywood County (present-day Bethel, NC), the setting for *August's Treasure* and the first two books making up his *East Fork Trilogy*. After attending the University of South Carolina in Columbia, where he played football for the USC Gamecocks and earned a degree in civil engineering, he began an extended career in the paper industry lasting more than three decades. Carroll's professional work led him out of the Carolina highlands to Brazil, South America and then back to the U.S. where he eventually settled down in Pensacola, Florida. Now retired and living in Morristown, Tennessee, he juggles weekend retreats to the NC mountains and fly fishing, with his love for writing. To his credit Carroll now has five award-winning books: *The 25th North Carolina Troops in the Civil War*, *Rooted Deep in the Pigeon Valley*, *Captain Lenoir's Diary*, *Master of the East Fork*, and *Rebel Rousers*—winner of the prestigious 2016 President's Award from the North Carolina Society of Historians.

You can find out more about Carroll and his books on his website at carrolljones.weebly.com.

CPSIA information can be obtained
at www.ICGtesting.com
Printed in the USA
LVOW11s0109030617
536731LV00002B/2/P

9 781945 619250